THE
GUARDIAN OF THE
MYSTICAL ROSARY

ADESOJI ADEREMI

THE GUARDIAN OF THE MYSTICAL ROSARY

iUniverse books may be ordered through booksellers or by contacting:

iUniverse
1663 Liberty Drive
Bloomington, IN 47403
www.iuniverse.com
1-800-Authors (1-800-288-4677)

ISBN: 978-1-5320-7594-0 (sc)
ISBN: 978-1-5320-7604-6 (e)

Print information available on the last page.

iUniverse rev. date: 07/19/2019

ACKNOWLEDGEMENTS

A good piece of art work is not always the entire work of only one person. Contributions must have come from several sources, directly but especially indirectly in areas which concern the source of inspirations. I should greatly appreciate the encouragements and contributions of the following personalities in the way of constructive criticism, their candid opinions so honestly given:

Engineer Adelani Aderemi, Mrs. Oluseun Dada Aderemi, Air Commodore Ibidapo Shomade retired and MS Bolaji.

I should not forget the patience and endurance of my family members, especially my wife, Oluseun and children, Adesegun and Adebolu, which proved much needed during the period of working on this project.

DEDICATION

This work is dedicated to my parents, late Chief Albert Folorunsho Aderemi Ogungbe and my mother, Mrs. Emilia Wuraola Adewola Ogungbe and all the good people who have identified themselves with the Forces that fight EVIL.

PROLOGUE

"Good Material"

Adam is rugged, fearless, a hell of a fighter. Karl is craggy, never knew fear, fights like hell. One is GOOD the other is BAD. Both are noble and honorable, each albeit in his own way; both are qualified 'Good Material'.

Adam serves nobody. Karl obeys no one, respects nobody. Totally independent, they are on their own.

Irrefutably, nevertheless, in the order of nature, no good material lies fallow. Consciously or otherwise, a good material would be used by one or the other of the two seemingly opposing forces in nature.

And PASSION!? Could Humans be enslaved by anything else stronger than passion? Rugged Adam and craggy Karl will not work with talk less for anybody but both were soon delivered by the captivating hands of their own passions into the itching waiting hands of the respective forces that have chosen at the present period in time, two particular organizations for their ultimate expression.

These two organizations, each powerful in its own fashion, were soon to find themselves in a protracted conflict and battles, that centered around the possession of a certain legendary mystical ROSARY.

Adams suspects there is more to this façade of holiness in the organization that is trying to enlist his services and he is set, for that reason alone, curiosity, to go along, if only for a while, and see the bottom of it.

Once Karl finds himself indebted he never forgets, for he owes nobody, and when he willingly gives his loyalty and support he gives nothing but his best, and Karl's best is the best in HELL.

The sudden death of Adams ushered in a strange enigmatic man in black, always in mask, and just then as if to balance the sides, in one of nature's equalization games, came in a certain Fadi Zokalaus, like a perfect replacement for Karl whose identity for then must be hidden for reasons very soon to be made obvious. This story distinguishes between the maskman and any other masked men or men in mask.

Sooner face-to-face, hands to throats, these two toughies soon find themselves in a fierce struggle for a spoilt millionaire's leggy daughter – a ransom, who was soon going to become a sacrifice to Bwallangwu, a legendary monster deity, Lucifer's personal foreman on earth at that particular period.

Several other events which will bring these two Roccos together will reveal still a lot about their strange fate.........And for the mysterious rosary, it proves soon to be the most comprehensive archive of the expressions of natural laws ever compiled, so compact and yet so complete and all embracing and most of all, SELF PROTECTING.

Here we witness the GOOD and the BAD at it again and this time in a 'somme nulle', the winner takes it all. The human race might just be saved if the GOOD triumphs, otherwise it is certain doom for human race....and for the GOOD to triumph it must beat the BAD to the mythical Rosary, and Bwallangwu, the Agbaamole, the monster must be destroyed in the ways of the Tripple Rs(RRR), otherwise it would be doom for humanity.

ORISHA, the god himself started it and by GOD he must finish it.

CHAPTER 1

THE GOOD MATERIAL

"Time for prayers! Wake up! Time for God!" "Time for prayers! Wake up son of man! Time for God!" It was 0500hrs on this blessed day of 7 July 77. Bible in his right hand, silver bell in the left, dressed in his aging white ankle length caftan, evangelist Raphael Alabo was at it again. "Wake up! Son of man, wake up and pray to your Creator. Pray for forgiveness of your sins. The kingdom of God is at hand!"

The young man had been waiting, rather impatiently. He had opened his door as soon as he heard the clergy man's monotone early morning shouts. He had gotten out of the house, crept after him, whip in hand. The clergy man did not know at first what had happened to him. Complicating the issue for him was his long robe, but simple matter, reflex action, he threw away the bell and with the same move reached down to pull the robe up to waist level just as he deployed reserved energy into a race that would have been meant for Olympic competition.

Chief Barl Enlaye watched the scene on the street from the window of his towering house with utmost satisfaction borne of intense pleasure and seeming gratitude. Wonderful! Very good!" He exclaimed followed by a typical kind of indescribable epileptic-like laughter that drained the saline juices out of his tear ducts.

Obviously Chief Enilaye had not been the only person concerned about the disturbance of his early morning sleep. That sweet half- sleep-half waking state that has become a special blessing from the gods to the rich elders. There was one young man who had just moved in into a room in one of those apartments called 'face- me- I- face- you" and at times, 'face-me-I-slap-you' for the fun of it. Karl was particularly irritated. He couldn't even tell whether it was the activities of the clergy man or the sight of the man himself. Right from his first night in that neighborhood, he had been so disgusted and promised to do something about it. He had gone out in the afternoon of the second day to secure a horse whip. Just when chief Enlaye was thinking in frustration what to do about the matter he suddenly saw the young man issuing some well measured whiplashes on the back of the clergy man. The scene had been very pleasant for him and most satisfying.

Chief Enlaye did not feel like sleeping again. He just paced up and down his long room until the young man returned from his chase. He took a long satisfying look at him and nodded in a whisper, "good material". Smiling briefly, he picked up the bedside phone, dialed and issued some instructions into the mouth piece. "Jobilah! Come and see me immediately!"

<hr />

Millions of people are in this world each with his own whims and caprices. Addicts and sadists alike, some can bring their dreams and intents to reality by themselves alone to some reasonable extent. Some are not able to as much as lift a finger on their own. This latter kind of people need people and would always need people to help them, and in several cases, to use….as tools. These categories might just be the most dangerous. Chief Barl Enlaye needs tools. He has many tools, of course, but in this present moment he needs a special tool. Ruthless is not enough, the tool must have brains and know how and when to use it. A GISFA. The tool must be a GISFA. GIFA is a well known acronym in the camp and which obviously a very handful of people possesses. Guts Intelligence, Smart, Fast and Anticipating. Making it harder to obtain is that such a person must be a man to be trusted. Very odd combination. A last virtue that has complicated all. A very rare gem such a tool must be. A very special tool.

So many had been recommended. So many had been brought forward, tested so many had failed. Chief Enlaye performs the final test called TOT, the Test of Trust. Up till that particular moment all but one had been "washouts". The last one that just could be managed, for want of any better tool, has just blown it. To begin with, Ojo had been allowed to see a little in the chief's security arrangement, all which must be kept secret. Afterwards he was sent to deliver a bag containing One million Naira to some people in a location described to him. He had proceeded with 3 men as escorts. Josh Ojo had surprised his escorts, knocked them cold and had taken off to his village where he buried the money. He was later picked up by some guys in a bar where he was having a beer ; he put up a fight but was eventually overpowered. They took him to a place where they tortured him into revealing some facts about Chief Enlaye's security set up in the organization. He had failed woefully. Only if he had known that everything had been set up, including the money that is fake. He was brought back to the chief who shot into his mouth with a Dane gun, saying as usual, "a mouth full of hot pellets is too busy chewing to tell tales." Quite many had been thus wasted.

This might be the best day in the chief's life as his chief commander, Jobilah strongly opined that the special material he had been looking for is sure to be that young man who had just moved into a room among the block of rooms close to the chief's compound. 'Haah! My chief, *ohun ti a nwa lo Sokoto, apo sokoto yin l'o wa.*[1]" He had declared enthusiastically in Yoruba witty saying.

Unknown to chief, Jobilah had been watching Karl for quite a long time, even well before now when his boss was seeing the tough young man for the first time. Jobilah had watched with admiration and a tingle of jealousy, this young boy, tough, craggy, in the free- for- all fight at the recent *Gbomoja*[2] bazaar. Gomoja bazaar seems, for all intents and

---

[1] What we want to go and obtain in Sokoto happens to be right here in our pocket. (Sokoto is a town about 1000km away. Apo sokoto is trousers pocket)

[2] Omoja means puppy. Gbomoja hence literarily means Carry the puppy.

purposes, to have been organized for the sake of those kind of people who itch to beat people or to get beaten up. People rarely go there with any serious intention of purchasing anything; of course there are as well few item on display, none of which for sure is breakable for obvious reasons; anything can spark off a fight and within the twinkle of an eye the whole bazaar venue has turned into an arena where blows are traded for blows. Apart from that, the Local Government chairman is always kind to provide a puppy purportedly to raise money for laudable development of the Local Government Area. The puppy, of fine breed, goes to the highest bidder. It soon turns out that virtually everybody wants the puppy but rarely anybody wants to part with money. Hence a stampede is another opportunity to steal the puppy. In most cases the poor thing gets eventually torn into several pieces marking the end of it. The police only hang around to amuse themselves. Also present would be managers and handlers who make their annual visits to Gbomoja to fish for talents. A man like Karl couldn't have failed to be noticed by a man like Jobilah.

Jobilah had been watching and tailing the boy. Shortly before the man named Obembe was reported to have committed suicide Jobilah had watched with his binoculars how it actually happened. Mr. Obembe had stooped over the Ishasha River to wash his face that fateful morning. A young man had appeared from behind and, in what seems like out of mere but malicious curiosity, had tapped the old man's balls from behind. Jobilah had watched with unflinching amusement how Obembe had made something like a good forward roll into the river. Curiously He had also watched the young man left without taking Obembe's watch nor his fat purse.

Gbomoja and several other events had shown how good a fighter Karl is. And come to think of it a yet unparalleled boxer if only he could keep to the rules. Jobilah knows exactly how and why he was banned from boxing. Banned for life from the rings. Karl's fights never ever ended in the rings. He does not recognize towels, he just keeps punching and he takes the fight all the way as far as the opponent's home. The meanest of his fight on record was his fight with Lakula the 'boy thunder'. The events that led to Karl's disqualification were remarkable, of course. He just refused to stop pounding the poor champion even at the sound of the bell signal. Karl still found his way to the hospital where Lakula was admitted to go and issue some more blows, in the process manhandling some nurses, ward maids and one doctor and he got away before the police arrived only to proceed to his victim's house to go and dish out to the wife and children their own little fair shares. He got off the hook on medical grounds. Temporary insanity bordering heavily on paranoia schizophrenia that makes him to run amok with a tendency to continue like a robot whatever he might be engaged in at the very moment. So much for the medicals. Karl of course has no money to give anybody. No savings, no steady jobs. He lives off the ground. He lives on the impulse. He takes what he needs wherever he could get it. That is Karl.

"I want to know everything about this young tiger!" Chief Enlaye had exploded on Jobilah that fateful morning. "Karl or what do you say his name is?"

"Well, my Chief," Jobilah opened his file and commenced, "Karl's presence was first noticed in the free-for-all at Gbomoja. He immediately caught the attention of greedy boxing managers who did not know on time that the boy is never one to make money for anybody. He fights only because he wants to fight and he does not stop until he is satisfied, referee or no referee. And his fight does not end in the ring, he …."

"Background! Family, etc!" The chief interjected impatiently.

"Hmm, Chief, no traceable background. No family, chief."

"What do you mean!? Did he drop from the sky?"

"My chief, I have investigated this boy for quite a while now, thoroughly, you know me chief. If he had any family, I, Jobilah Okworikwo would have found out."

"I want to test this boy. Make arrangements!"

"Hmmm, not an easy issue, chief. This boy is an unusual problem."

"Solve it! Or what do we do with problems!? How can anybody even be a problem to you, Jobilah?"

"My lord, this boy does not submit himself to anybody. Not for money or any other reason whatsoever. Evidenced in his case with the boxing merchants, he is nothing but like an animal, totally uncontrollable. He will not work for anybody. He makes no deals, chief, he won't deal. He doesn't listen, so how do you get to test him?"

Chief Enlaye turned red, red hort. And Jobilah, out of experienced knew what to do. He moved back as his chief exploded like a musket. "Jobilaaah! For GGGooood's sake Jobilaaahhh! Why do I pay you!? Is it for you to cccome and and nn and be asking me questions which I employed you to provide answers to!? Jobilaaahhh!"

"Easy, easy, my lord. I, Jobilah can find a solution. Jobilah will surely find a solution but chief, I have to think deeply, reach deep down inside of me to find solution to this uncommon situation."

"Then think! What are you waiting for? Think! Think! Start thinking!"

"Yes my lord and Jobilah has started the process of deep meditation, but...." cunning Jobilah, "hmmmn, a trouble free mind is tantamount to correct productive clear thinking and deep meditation."

"What is causing obstructions?'

"If I can secure my chief's promise as concerns Agola's properties, my chief, nothing would constitute a better stimulant to deep concentration and meditation the type that could call to the deep where the solutions to this type of problems reside."

"Hmmn. You just solve this problem and Agola's properties are yours."

With Agola's properties assured, Jobilah's journey to the deep and back to surface didn't take much time and he came back with something quite practicable and easily translated into a workable strategy by his now trouble-free mind.

"Chief, my lord. Knowledge is power. This young toughie might not deal but one thing is known for sure about him. He does not forget a favor, however small....and once he become loyal he remains loyal."

"You are just preaching. Give him whatever he wants. I will provide..."

"No, not like that, my lord. Karl's loyalty is not for sale. We must earn it. The first task is to get him to accept a favor form us. He avoids being indebted which is surely why he does not accept favors. My chief, I have just conceived a good idea."

"Talk, Jobilah."

"We are going to do this young man a great favor. A favor he will never forget, then he becomes ours!"

"Mine!"

"Oh yes, yes, yours! My chief."

New Weyos is full to the brim. New Weyos is the newly commissioned archers' club situated along Ife road in Gbongan. Friar Maria marveled at the ease with which Adams was getting bull's eyes. Every single shot was bull's eye. He fixed an arrow and as he took aim, asked, "young man, how long have you been shooting?"

"As long as I could recognize a bow, old man."

"You are very good, exceptional." He pulled, aiming carefully. Just before he released a man staggered by, oozing alcohol, and sniggered, "hey, pastor, are you as good a shot with bows as you are with women?"

The ex-clergy missed even the board in what could be recorded as the worst shot of the season. The two then had some more rounds, in silence, before they retired to the bar to have some drinks. They both settled for the local stuff, *sekete*[3], sweet and very dazing, care not taken. Friar Maria was just wondering the best way to broche the conversation when Adams said, somehow curiously, with a smile, "Father Maria, you make me curious."

'In what ways, my son?"

"Many ways. Firstly, Maria is a woman's name. How come you…. bear…."

Smiling with a sign of relief the old man replied, "long story, son.."

"You can summarize, father."

"I don't know any of my parents, having grown up in an orphanage. My mother was said to have come from Bembe with me as an infant. I

---

[3] Local drink brewed with ripe plantain.

think I heard that my father deserted us for a reason nobody could tell. Well, not to be long winding, my mother died when I was two years and some months. The orphanage, not knowing much detail about me except my mother's name, Maria, put it down as my only name on record. You know, they put a tag, 'Omo Maria' tied to my wrist for recognition.".....and looking hard into the eyes of the young man, "and I am not ready to change that name for anything in the world, boy."

"Well," Adams shrugged, "a name is as good as any other if it serves the purpose of identification."

"She was the only parent I ever knew.....wouldn't change it for all the gold in this world."

"Anyway, holy man, what did you say I can do for you?"

"Hmmmmn," the clergy man appeared to be weighing his words and making a final assessment of this young man. In retrospection, early that morning Friar Maria had nodded with satisfaction as he watched young Adams walked briskly cross the street, bent down and set free a fowl that got itself entangled in a rope. He had watched the previous fortnight with a mixture of awe and respect as this boy nearly got himself beaten to pulps fighting for charity. He remembered the scars all over his lithe body were sustained when he plunged himself into a burning fire to rescue a co-tenant's wife. All efforts to trace his parental background, place and date or birth have so far proved fruitless. He appeared to have just started, suddenly to exist. Could have dropped down with the rains from only God knows where – Jupiter. But one sure thing, parent or no parents, records or no records, here is a perfect prototype of a philanthropist. The fast that the young man is an exceptional archer, an acrobat with the agility of a cat, fearless and a hell of a fighter makes the typical combination the clergyman had been looking for. It took him well over 270 days to convince himself beyond reasonable doubt that this is just the boy; there had been no other person like him. He was very pleased.....his hunch is positive. Come to think of it, reflecting, 'the beauty of his neighbor's wife might have been impetuous, but what about the helpless chicken? And surely this lad does not look like one to first set free a trapped fowl before setting about stealing it. He is just good to humanity and animals.

Good to nature. A man of nature. He had waited for the cue of traffic to flow past, murmuring to himself, "good material," as he crossed over to meet him. "Good intention," he had commented, "noble ideals, young man. I wonder who pays you for all this."

"Nobody has to pay."

"I am Biodun Maria."

"Yes I know you. The one removed from office at Akiriboto."

"Yes…hmmn..you are right...with ignominy."

"Em, well?"

"I have a job for you."

"Who said I am looking for a job?"

"As a matter of fact I ought to have demanded of you a favor."

"What favor?" eyes glowing bright. It could be true we are all sadist or addicts in our own individual ways. Adams really couldn't resist obliging to help.

"With a warm fatherly smile the older man had said, "Can you come to New Weyos? We might even have a game or two of archery……. Then we discuss….huh?"

At the archery club Father Maria actually saw and felt what he had not seen or felt about Adams until he was that close. There was something utterly sincere and relaxed about him and yet there is that feeling of immense potential power.

"What did you say I can do for you, clergy?" Adams asked again.

Then Friar Maria spoke in a very solemn voice and the most cautious of manners, "Aaadams, he said," for a quite a long time now we have been searching for a man, brave, courageous and daring enough to agree to help us and…hmmmn….trustworthy enough at the same time to confide in and entrust the mission..'

"Mission?"

"Em..Task."

"Task?"

"Risky."

"What risk."

"Telling you this much alone is the beginning of the risk."

"What risk? Mission, Task, Risk. What da hell!?"

"Relax, son"

"I'm relaxed, clergy, but you are the tensed one."

"Haah, you got me there."

"So what is all this mission, task and risk about?"

"We cannot afford to make mistakes…nevertheless, the enormous screening we have given you so far is extremely encouraging …enough to convince us to go this far. More and more would be divulged to you in necessary bits as we flow along."

"Screening me? What for? What are you talking about?"

"At last we can be rest assured that in the worst scenario whatever we tell you you would never divulge to another soul."

"I don't understand."

"Promise, to start with."

"Clergyman is what I know of you…Is there something else in the dark?"

"You promise before anything else, son?"

"And why would you trust me?"

"So far son, you are the best we can trust. We are convinced of your integrity."

"Ok clergy, if you already know me then go ahead and spill. I am no story teller."

"I take that as a promise….?"

"I have given you my word."

The older man bent forward, looking sinuously all about him, and spoke in a low voice, "to recover a very important item from the valley of the crocodiles."

"An item in the valley…"

"An artifact."

"Valley of…."

"And to deliver it to a destination to be described later."

"What da hell!? So much secrecy..and what…Valley of crocodiles! …" Adams just burst out laughing.

"No jokes, son,"

"I am laughing; you are the one cracking the joke, clergy."

"It is not a joke, son."

Adams laughed again as he looked the older man over. "Then that item must be very, very important. What took it there? A crocodile?" laughing again while the older man managed a chuckle this time around, but didn't say a word for an answer.

"What is this item of..em...artifact?" He asked.

"The blessed Rosary." The man replied looking anxiously in anticipation of the young man's reaction.

"What did you just say? A rosary!?"

"Yes, my son. The most blessed rosary. The blessed most holy rosary. That is what it is."

"You want me to go down the valley of crocs just to pick a rosary!? A mere rosary!"

"No, no, son, not mere but the most blessed..."

"You don't give me any of your holy, holy bullshits. I don't share your fate. I hope you already know that! Otherwise your research on me is not complete."

"No, no, son, take it easy!"

"We are talking of my life! I don't even know what to think of you now. More than being a clergy, hmm, clergy.....In fact I said you make me curious."

"In what way again, son?"

"So many ways. Queer."

"Now you are insulting."

"Tell me, reverend, pastor, evangelist, or whatever the holy, holy titles, tell me, were you able to screw the woman? I mean ball her that day before they caught you?" Adams asked sniggering poignantly as he swung his legs down the stood, getting ready to leave. But contrary to his expectations the old man said calmly, undisturbed and genuinely fatherly, "I never knew you could be any vulgar, son. Anyway I have never cared about what people think or say about that funny matter and I never would, son.....but for you, you are so important....you deserve to know because what you feel about me has become extremely important. So I will tell you exactly what happened."

"How you were caught?"

"No, son, How I was framed."

"Some women could be tempting. Elizabeth is strangely beautiful."

"I have no use for her."

"So what happened?......God's own truth," Adams demanded as the old man called the bartender for a refill of their mug of sekete.

"Mrs. Elizabeth Alomaja Funwontan came to me after the Sunday service 14 July, exactly 4 years ago yesterday," clearing his throat, "she confided in me the problems between her husband and her and I duly offered advice after we had prayed together. Son, that sort of problems....em...Look, son, I did what I considered the best. I prayed for her."

"Hmmmn...the usual."

"A week later, the 21st, on my birthday, that terrible woman came back to my office smiling heartily to tell me her problem was solved. She said she came to thank me and I was joyous for her, thanking God. She came forward and em...son, God the almighty in heaven knows it was a fatherly hug but at that instant someone threw open the door and shouted that we were ....Oh Jesus! I have never been so embarrassed in my life!"

Adams started laughing, gulping his drink. The sekete has suddenly developed better taste.

"You know, young man, we humans are all too prepared to believe and propagate certain types of stories. Certain categories of stories appeal to us naturally. Before you could call JJ the whole community had heard about it. Worst still it continuously acquire new dimensions. Every mouth retelling it adds its own according to its mood and imagination, most especially our women folks. My dear, what was a simple hug in an unlocked office finally metamorphosed into a rape story. Just tell me, son, could you believe that?"

"Rape, I know you wouldn't attempt that in your office but the rest of the story, I wish I was endowed with the third eyes so I could know what to believe. Sorry, old man, just being frank."

"Then I must convince you because it's so important that you have a reasonable measure of confidence in me, otherwise how could I ever convince you to undertake our assignment if you doubt me?"

"Convince me...With what?" More laughter.

"But if you eventually believe, regardless of what the rest of the world says, would you undertake our assignment?

'How? With what? Some holy lawyers…..more holy rosaries… c'mon oldie."

"But what if I give you a proof that gets you convinced beyond doubt?"

"Then I might really give genuine considerations to your mission. If you could just get me convinced. But remember, old man, I am not a toddler and I am not stupid.

"Then Come with me, briefly." Taking him by the hand he led the young man into the conveniences and about 3 minutes later they re-emerged at the bar, the clergyman satisfied and smiling sadly, Adams fuming with rage. A long silence ensued with occasional glances thrown in each other's direction while they quietly sipped their sekete which taste now in Adams mouth he could not define. He just drank.

The clergyman broke the silence. "I grew up to know. Nobody could tell me how it came about and the reason why for that matter. I was never to know who did it and the reason why. But the fact remains now that a castrated man has no sexual use for a woman."

"But why didn't you explain this to…"

"Explanations make sense only to interested ears. My son, what I just showed you has been known to some people in this town, yet some of those people are still among those who prosecuted me. Heeeh, if you want to hang a dog you first give it a bad name. Who would even listen?"

"I still don't get it, old man. Is it that bad that justice cannot be obtained with this fool-proof evidence?"

"Then the matter becomes worse to the extent of losing my life."

"Then it is that bad and sure you know the reason."

"I constituted a cog in their wheel, but don't let's over flog an issue of such less importance. We all have what we live for, son, don't we?"

"Hmmm….yeah."

"Mine for now is the Blessed most holy Rosary," he said with a solemn sign of the cross.

Adams looked at him thoughtfully, still not sure what to make of this old man who has started making impact on him. "You confuse me, making me curious more and more. I wouldn't say you are crazy but why in gods' name would a sane man be talking of this idea of going to the valley of crocodiles in the first place, only for the reason of recovering a Rosary?"

"You already mentioned it. In God's name."

"Let's be serious. Which god would insist on the very one rosary in the valley of crocodiles?"

"It's the most blessed."

"Make another one and bless it!"

"Not that easy even if possible."

"Than to go face crocodiles? Hallucinations or simply fanatical or....is it..."

"I have a great capacity for sekete, young one."

"All fanatics hallucinate."

"Hun hun..."

"But can't you just for god's sake go to the market and get a special rosary for your God to give special blessing? Or at best have a special one customized for you and give it a very special blessing."

"If that were possible it would have been done. There can be no duplication. No other one as long as the world and heaven remain. No other one can serve the purpose for which this special one has been made."

Adams put his mug down looking hard at the old man and said, "then, Father Maria, there is something about this rosary of yours that you have not told me."

"Oh the blessed, most holy Rosary. Most radiant of all, ranking even more than diamond. Shining so gloriously bright down there in the valley of crocodiles. Curious people have been going up the hills to see the shining object down the valley, including treasure hunters, but very, very few know it as a Rosary...the most blessed."

"And you want it recovered by all means?"

"Oh yes. It is what I live for now."

"Then organize a mass attack on the crocs first. Award a big contract and you would be surprised the number of suicide companies that would tender applications. Kamikazes!"

"It's got to be kept secret."

"Meaning the legendary object ever shining in the valley would suddenly disappear…...."

"Even the spot where it has been removed has to be kept shining. So a replica for its replacement has been made."

"Beautiful! Hnnn.. I say there is a lot underneath the clear water!"

"You can say that again, my dear, but as I said earlier on, a lot would be divulged as time goes on…gradually."

Giving him that mind probing look, "you don't really like me, though it's hard to call you an hypocrite."

"Why did you say that? Why do you think so?" Meeting his gaze squarely, but surprised.

"How many have attempted this mission so far?"

"Six already."

"What was their fate?"

"Adams, I will always tell you the truth, however bitter. They were eaten by crocodiles….but"

"Haa, were they all orphans?

"Why….?"

"Clever. Nobody would look for orphans!"

"Now before you get a wrong notion…."

"So I would be the 7th sacrifice save for only one problem….I am not stupid."

"Listen…"

"No! You listen, old man," growing furious, "if you people are looking for a regular sacrifice for your god of crocodiles then you've got to capture them. I would not be easily fooled into walking there by myself…"

"Adaaaams!" the clergyman's tone was unusual, bringing the young man to attention, making him the more curious. "Listen, Adams, my son. Those people were not pure. Not pure at heart. Some went with a greedy self serving purpose, not sure of coming back to us n they lay their hands on the rosary, make money with it one way or the other or jeopardize it. We believe they were eliminated by their own bad fate. The most holy Rosary is intrinsically protected. No unworthy hands can take it. Adams," placing his hand on the young man's shoulder, "we don't worship any god of crocodiles, we are not a cult and we don't make such human sacrifices."

"If you like me why send me?" shaking the old man's hand off his shoulder. "Why not your son…..hah, sorry you have none…"

"You are the most qualified. Nobody yet has your qualities. After the 6th person we were worried and we have become more careful. We have watched you, tested you in our own ways. You are so pure at heart. You can get the rosary. You have all the requisites, all it takes and if it has to be taken you can get it. You are chosen, son, by nobody else but God himself."

"Which God? The same that chose the first 6 unfortunate ones?"

"God didn't choose them. They volunteered. Yes at first we thought we could trust them, so we told them and they jump on it. We did warn them, of course, that the Holy Rosary can never allow itself to fall in the hands of the unworthy and any person with evil intention on it would never return alive. Well, they never returned and we are sorry about it but we warned them….they never returned..and the Most blessed Rosary shines on ever in its glorious incandescence." Finishing his statement with a sign of the cross.

"And you wouldn't know how it got there?"

"Perhaps for its self protection…but with time you would know more."

"Why is it so important to you people and what are you going to do with it when you get it?"

"The two questions are alike and carry the same answer which we cannot divulge now. I can only assure you that it is for the benefit of the entire humanity. It can never be used for a selfish purpose."

"Bullshit! I have heard that before.'"

"I don't bullshit! Not in God's name. Not at my age and not by my condition."

"How can you convince me this time around?"

"If I am able to?"

"I sure would go for your Rosary."

"In that case we can't possibly hide our nakedness from you forever. We would have to let you in into our little circle."

"Now, now, now. The little puzzle is beginning to fall in place. I know all along it's got to be some sort of organization."

"Don't be alarmed. Not the sort you think. We care for humanity."

"And how far have you succeeded?"

"Well, to a reasonable allowable measure. We can't change God's plans but we assist. Adams we know you wouldn't belong to any group or organization. You remain as free as air. So really you don't have to belong to ours and it's not our intention to make you. Just do this thing for us as a favor. And whatever the case might be we want to be sure you would keep our secret secret."

"Until then...the convincement."

"Could you come to church on Sunday?"

"You know I don't go to church"

"I know that. But could you?"

"Which church?"

"The Holy Rosary Church of Gbongan."

"It's all about Rosary and....holy.."

<hr/>

CHAPTER 2

The Honda CD175 jerked, coughed and packed up about 5 kilometers out of town. "What da hell!?" exclaimed the rider. When he finally discovered the problem he shouted again, "what da bloody fuck! This thing was at half tank yester night. I have done only 5 kilos and the bloody tank is empty! Impossible! Damn it!." He cursed and cursed as he inspected the tank for possible leakage, which he didn't find.

He had alternatives: Push the machine back to Gbongan 5 kilometers away; push it ahead to Wakajaiye about 6 and a half kilometers; or leave the machine by the road side, take a lift either way to get some fuel. He decided to stick with the machine because of thieves. So he started to push, and typical of Karl, in the direction of Wakajaye his original direction. He figured he was going to save time that way.

Karl is a very strong young man. Sure he could manage without difficulty but what about the low dark cloud overhead, threatening to add insult upon his injury. He had pushed the not too light machine just about a kilometer when he perceived a typical noise from behind.; a mini Suzuki motorcycle knick named 'Ladygay' within the community because of its size and because it is ridden mostly by women. Of course a young woman was on top of this particular one. She rode past, then about 50 meters away she stopped, hesitated a bit, seemed to make up her mind, and then she turned and rode back and stopped close to the young man. Big beautiful eyes wide open in fear, she alighted gingerly, eyes opening wider, hands cupping her provocative breasts, she volunteered,

"Mama warned me never to stop for strangers especially in an isolated place such as this.., but, but I shouldn't leave you like this just in case there is something I can do to help you."

"Just the hell do ya think you can do?" Karl snarled in an arrogant voice, "you wanna push my bike while I ride your toy? And why would mummy warn ya not to stop for men in isolated places? Rape heh?"

The girl just smiled, "well, I might lack the power to push the big thing but at least I can ride while you push it to start. You know, I put it in second gear, hold the clutch, power on and when it gathers speed I let the clutch in. I've handled one of these before," eyes opening wider adding more radiance to her beautiful face.

"Tough little chick. She used to ride big machines. But what da hell gave you the fucking idea that I have problems with my kick starter?"

"Oh please, don't be angry…I guess I should have asked you before what the problem is."

"So you can fix it. Tough little chick who has handled big machines." Karl spat looking at her disdainfully.

"Well I'm sorry if I have hurt your pride but there's no need to waste time, the rain might start any time. I could at least ride fast to Wakajaye to pick a mechanic for you!"

"Who the fuck told you I need a gaademn mechanic?"

"But at least you are going to need something."

Now Karl looked at this girl who still was gentle and willing to help despite his ways of treating her. "I don't have a gaddemn mechanical problem. You wanna help then ride as fast as your toy can take ya ass and get me some gaademn fuel!" he spat again, "but I bet ya rolling burst you gonna get your big ass bloody soaking wet. Cos it's gonna rain pretty soon!"

"Now wait a minute! I know you can manage even if it rains, you'd rather push the bike in the rain than to accept help from a lady. But I don't have to be treated like shit just because I offered to help! If you don't want my help no big deal, you only have to say so and I would go my way." Lovely eyes rolling and seeming more beautiful in anger, "and I don't even have to go all the way to Wakajaye or Gbongan to get the fuel anyway…"

"Oh, piss in my tank or tap it off the palm tree? Wonder girl.. Bionic woman." He snorted, looking up a palm tree. The girl just laughed. Karl, one way or the other, became physically relaxed. He disliked women and naturally all women feared and shy away from him. This one somehow is different.

"You forgot, superman that I didn't push my toy, as you call it, to this place. I rode it and thanks to designers it rides on the same fuel as does yours."

"So?"

"So I just give you a little." She replied, opening her tank, "I have full tank and all we need is a hose to draw it and we are in business!"

Karl looked at the girl in amazement, beginning to like her maybe, but said, "Oh no, no, no gaademn hose," and feeling macho, "but I can carry up the little thing and pour some fuel into ma tank."

The girl laughed, touched his muscular arm slightly. "Oh no, I don't want you to turn my little darling upside down," with a mock cry, and both laughed, "but there is a way out…"

Karl could do nothing now but watched this clever little girl, in wonder, who seems to have solutions where he the man does not think to find it, as she opened his tool cover. This girl, he thinks as a drop of water dropped on his hand from the sky, who seems to have no limits in her resources and capacity to help. God himself must have sent her at this particular period to help him. Well he had heard talks about God several times. Maybe He truly exists.

The little hose connecting the tank to the carburetor was obviously too short but that of the big Honda was long enough for the job at hand. In no time the girl removed it and connected it to the fuel switch of "Ladygay", switch opened to allow fuel to collect in the tool cover of the Honda. A few trips forth and back and there was something comfortable enough in the big bike. "This I believe should take you up to the nearest petrol station at Wakajaye."

"Yeah. I will fill up both tanks of ours at Wakajaye."

"Yours may take a little more time before it picks," the girl said as she mounted Ladygay and before Karl could say any other thing she was off.

"What da hell is wrong with ya? Come back here!" just then his own picked. "Tough little dummy! Trying me heh? I will catch you up in no time at all." But he didn't have to ride too fast, for just a little distance away he saw the girl with Ladygay parked by the road side, and coming in a stylish way by her side, he bragged triumphantly, "so you've decided to stop of your own accord, tough girl. Clever, because you know I'd've caught you up in no time at all."

"I've got a flat tyre!"

Karl alighted and inspected, taking his own time now to play the helper. Hands akimbo, he said, "yeah, we need a vulcanizer. He'll fix it in no time at all."

"All we do now, superman," the girl said with a confident smile, "is just take me on your big bike to Wakajaye. The vulcanizer there is a family friend. He will come and recover the bike."

The ride to Wakajaye, though a short distance, was phenomenal. The girl held on to Karl like she had never even seen a motorcycle before. What sort of fate would bring a girl this close to Karl? …hmmmm… body to body. He never got this close or is it that they never got this close to him. Not really that he hates them but he just enjoys frightening them, or embarrassing the ones that dare him, with things they wouldn't want to hear, such as, "for what you have just done I will fuck you." Karl might see a well dressed girl and asked her politely, "please ma, do you shit?" or something like, "when were you balled last?" This habits of his drive women away from him to avoid embarrassment. Now in this situation, he was typically out of the waters. Oh God! This soft body, in contrast to those of the boys who dared to wrestle with him. Then there was cause to apply the brakes. What the hell! Sweet Jesus! The feel of those breasts on his back, nipples sending ripples up his spines! Never! Well, who feels really knows it. And amplifying this experience is the soft sweet scent of body spray on this girl. He never knew this side of the opposite sides before. Experience is the best teacher. Nature, as usual, is now at work.

Nature is the alchemist using Karl's body at this present moment as the crucible to alter Karl's mind, even if only slightly, with the girl's body, performing a three-fold job of agent reactant, the catalyst and the fuel! How he feels and what he is experiencing set up emotions which constitute the fire, that essential element used by Venus to effect the psycho physicochemical alterations. Karl's mind would alter a bit. Karl would continue to frighten girls but this one…no. And if the treatment persists long enough, who knows, the advanced, matured compound, love, might be the end product. And Venus would have completed her devine assignment.

As he approached the fuel station, with a somehow feeling of reluctance, he applied the brakes, this time a little too hard, and the girl's reaction a little too exaggerated, Jesus Christ!

Karl wondered what was happening to him. The alchemist at work, maybe. He found himself waiting till Ladygay was brought in a pickup van that had been sent down immediately they arrived at Wakajaye. He stood over the vulcanizer and virtually supervised a work he had never done before until the tyre was fixed. Definitely the air must have somehow leaked through the valve as there was no puncture discovered. Anyway the girl confessed that she had been riding on low pressure for quite a while. "Lazy, careless me." She chided herself.

Curious enough, Karl didn't mind getting late to his destination that day. He seems to have now an emergency. Whatever his appointment, well, maybe nothing so pressing that could not be delayed a bit for this 'very humanitarian service', or at worst, rescheduled. What da hell. But really maybe nothing so urgent but the fact is he never compromised like this ever before in his rugged life. Not for a girl's problem that has been virtually solved. But what is happening to him? He even found himself chatting. Karl chat with a girl!. Of course they talked. He was even a little excited. Getting even as far as obtaining her address. She is a worker, a nurse and she stays alone at N0 1005 Olurin Crescent, Owoope, Gbongan.

Life, gradually at first, but definitely so, has taken a new turn for Karl. Having found a viable alternative outlet for his over-abundant energy and libido, and mortido ceding again more to increase libido, he experiences a certain piece of mind and relative harmony. He has become slightly solemn. Whatever was it that had been missing in his life, the result of which was restlessness, uncoordinated outputs into society and misplaced aggression, he wondered. Surely everyone has a culmination of forces or pressure yearning for discharge or expression of sort. Accumulated pressures yearning for discharge like coiled spring yearning for release. The right avenue, choice of target and action are determined by the condition or state of the mind. Positively or negatively polarized. How and where discharged follows as well one way or the other the law of cause and effect, and that of polarities not precluded. The force itself not discharged renders the host restless and reckless in a bid to find balance out of seeming eccentricism, and in a bid to find suitable receiver or vice versa. Once in a while a being finds himself in the manipulating hands of the alchemist. The alchemist is never relenting. The alchemist is itself a program embedded in a law, and sometimes a law embedded in a program. Once the elements are complete and the situation is right work is automatically in progress. The alchemist has worked and the eventual result for now is what would soon be confirmed as love for Miss Abimbola as far as concerns Karl. Venus had moved in to coordinate the direction and object of discharge of Karl's energy. Love has regulated the opening of the pressure valve. Bimbo's apartment has become a second home for Karl. He doesn't see her as the same as all the other girls. No! Definitely not the same, Bimbi, as he calls her, is different from them all. "The rest are dirty and lousy. Bimbi is clean." He has come to discover what Bimbo is – the compliment of one pole of a magnet, just as the south is to north, which makes it to exist unique a s a magnet. Otherwise no magnet. To hell with any other thing. It is food, shelter and Bimbo.

Though Karl sleeps in her house virtually every time she has declined his proposal for them to live together. "All is yours but not now, my love. Sooner or later I assure you it's gonna be." When they stay together they never really talk much. They just make love, untiringly.

Just like flying to pilots, each experience is never the same as the previous. Each round is a remarkable scene. For the third time in the week the bed had been repaired. Might soon be condemned B.E.R, care not taken. Each round a testimony, a sorry case for the bed. Each a bad time for the building itself. The young man is so full of energy. The young girl so good and equal to the task. Software-hardware, Bimbo knows where to touch in his mind and body to set him off again and again like a raving machine that he is, making each round a phenomenon. The whole area vibrates. Not really like an earth quake, with Bimbo's expert hands on his balls, a pneumatic drill might not be too bad a word. Gone are those days when the neighbors used to rush in seemingly to rescue when she shouts. Now they know better. Now they know she couldn't hide it when she comes. Once, an old night guard exclaimed about 200m away, "stupid, jobless, useless youngsters!" It must have made him remember his active youth days. May those days rest in perfect peace. And Karl discharged the juice of life into her. The cleanest, perfect fluid, the living concoction of nature, and experienced peace.

"I don't even know your parents, Bimbi." He loves to call her Bimbi.

"I am an orphan."

"Really? How come?"

"My parents died in a motor accident when I was four. They had kept me with a nanny and set off on a second honey moon."

"Sorry about that."

"Oh c'mon, man, you are always sorry for my case, my Karl. What about yours?"

"Well, at least you know that your parents are dead. I don't even know mine. I never knew mine. One thing sure is that to be born a man needs a father and a mother. So I must have gotten them. No doubt."

"It's a pity, oh my love." She said as she rubbed the hair on his chest. "Really a coincidence of fate that we share." snuggling closer and deeper as if to get herself swallowed by his body. "I know you were not brought up in the orphanage."

"Yeah, baby, I ran away at 3. I found it better to live off the ground

than to abide by shit regulations, shit food, shit people in the shithole...
orphanage you call it."

"At three years! How did you survive?"

"As a matter of fact I always got what I needed. Simple as ABC."

"From where?"

"Any bloody fucking gaaddem where it is available, baby."

"And they allowed you?"

"C'mon. I stole whatever I needed. I broke into houses to eat food.
I never at times even felt the need to escape. I just eat to my fill and
leave."

"And they never caught you?"

"Several time I was caught but as I said, I had no plan to escape...
No need..."

"So when they caught you what happened? What do they do
to you?"

"Most times nothing. They just left me."

"Whaooo! I guess because you were a toddler...?"

"Not really that, well of course that helped. But even when I grew
up I never attempted to escape. And when they caught me I used to tell
them where they kept their monies, jewelries, treasures and valuables!
That if I wanted to rob them I would have done just that. Made away
with their stuffs. But that it's just food and necessary survival stuffs
that I entered their house for. Things which meant nothing to them
anyway. Because Karl never broke into a poor man's house."

"Whaaaooh!" A kiss in the right ear lobe, "go on, tell me more."

"It is a fact and they believe me. They let me go. Some laughed.
Some pitied, hmm those ones who pitied, that is their business. Karl
needs no pity from no gaddemn body." He lit a cigarette before he
continued, "The Awolusis even asked me to live with them."

"Whaaoh!, Well...?"

"I left that very same week."

"What a chance, Karl, but darling, why?"

"Heck! Nobody pushes Karl around! Nobody tells Karl what to do!
That's why. To hell with their good food and all the shit stuff the rich

wants to boast about! Imagine they even wanted to send me to school! School! Me!"

"Why not!"

"Teachers! Tell you what to do! Shit! I don't like teachers. Shit!"

"So you had to do all these terrible things to survive, my love." A kiss on the hairy chest.

"Yeah, yeah I had to survive and I just took what I needed. Nothing much. The soul doesn't need much for maintenance. And all is not bread alone...well something like that I heard from a church one of those rare times. Heck! Karl will survive anyway, any manner huh..?"

"And as you grow big.... no calling the police on you?"

"Some big boys proved tough before and I beat them silly. I left but as I did not take their properties what da hell? But then as soon as I realized I could make money by beating people I quitted breaking into peoples' houses."

"That is interesting! You beat people and make money!? How possible?"

"Haaah, street fighting, baby. There's a lot of betting in there. They give me my share which is always enough. They dare not."

"But Karl, you could have become a professional boxer."

"Shit! Shit rules. Shit regulations. Referees...shit! Nobody tells Karl when to stop. It ain't there fucking business once we start. Just between me and my opponents. If he is tired he should jump out of the ring."

"Karl," in a very solemn voice and low tone.

"What baby?"

"Something you need to know, Karl. I find it difficult to hide anything from you now. I don't know why," both balls in her hands now, "Karl, you must know that I had a man before I met you. It's you I love but the man has been good to me."

Wriggling under her touches, he said, "baby, your mind is in conflict. But never mind, I will solve the problem. I will solve the problem for you. I know exactly what to do."

"Oh, what would you do, darling?" Caressing the balls passionately and a kiss on one. "Cut his balls off?" she suggested teasingly, "castrate him?"

"Exactly. And we shall see how good he can continue to be to you."

"Is it because of these that you need me?" squeezing the balls which made Karl jump in reflex action, almost falling off the bed,

"Huuh! That hurts. Baby, you've gotta be gentle with these things. No spares in the market. Not even in the famous Alaba Market in Lagos."

She heeded the warning. She actually became more careful, gentle and more passionate. Soon they vibrated in unison. Two sex machines made for each other. What commenced slowly soon climaxed to the Pneumatic drilling operation, drilling to climax, ending in a devastating explosion that woke up the neighbors. As usual. Even the night watchman guarding Popoula Guest house a little less than 200 meters away got the message and rained abuses and curses. As usual.

It was 0430 hrs one Saturday morning about a week afterwards that Karl received a phone call from the General hospital. It was a female voice, a nurse perhaps who had demanded to speak with Bimbo. Surprised, Karl had demanded in reply, "Is she not over there, on night duty. She is on night duty, isn't it?"

"Oh yes she is but she took permission to go somewhere about two hours ago and now we have an emergency!"

"Have you tried her apartment?"

"Yes, but the phone is all the time engaged."

"Ok, don't worry; I will get her for you in no time at all."

"Thanks. Very kind of you. Please tell her to hurry up."

"Never mind. I will bring her myself."

"Oh, that is most kind. Bye."

Within seconds Karl had slipped into a pair of jeans, snickers and shirt and zoomed off to Owoope. The sound that welcomed him at Bimbo's apartment was such that he had heard several times before. The unmistakable sound of moaning with pleasure, "oh Ajala that is nice…" and he went berserk. Totally berserk, the only thing in his mind being the name, Ajala, now a beacon for the homing missile that he had become. He virtually walked through the door, the pieces falling all over the place. He went, as if programmed and practiced and from behind just reached for Ajala's dangling busy balls and cut them off.

A hard punch knocked the poor man cold saving him from further struggles.

"Bimbo shouted, "Karl please don't!"

Quite unusual, the police were there on the spot, record time. It took six able bodied men and a shot in the left shoulder, Karl's strong hand, to subdue him before they took him away hand cuffed. Bimbo, wrapper around her body, was weeping vigorously. Tears, surprisingly and for the first time in his miserable rugged life, came out of Karl's eyes.

"Bitch!" He said, as he looked back at her, "I will come out and come back and fix you."

⬦⬦✳✦⬦

CHAPTER 3

Adam had attended several churches and a lot of the occasions he had enjoyed the services and had even been inspired once. The last one he attended bored him stiff. He just couldn't bring himself to perform, like the rest of the people, a lot of obligations. What broke the camel's back was when he was demanded along with others to stand up and say all the dirty things he'd ever done in life; how they fornicated, stole, committed adultery etc. Not that he was not aware that he was clean of majority of these 'dirty things', in fact he could be counted the cleanest of them all, but he just didn't buy such idea. He watched them as they got up in turn and did it. To him he thought they were all under duress. He thought a confession made when a man did not feel inwardly like confessing is a waste of time. When it got to his turn and was called, he stood up walked to the front as expected and made just a statement, "I don't confess to men, but to God," and walked out amidst murmurs. That was about 3 years ago and the last time he went to church.

This time around in his clean dress, as he approached the gate of the Holy Rosary Church, he said quietly to himself, "I hope this is not the same an I hope I would not be asked for tithe. I don't have a dime."

As he entered, he looked around for familiar faces. A woman smiled at him affectionately and he smiled back. He could find no trace of the Friar Maria.. Soon service commenced. To him it was a parade of repeated drills of standing, sitting, kneeling down and singing. Reasons for these he couldn't comprehend. They even spoke and sang in some languages very solemn. He wondered who taught them. Anyway all he wanted then was Friar Maria. He had to be smart though in following through the drills. As nobody told him that he needn't close his eyes at prayers in this church, Adams looked odd standing with eyes firmly closed, palms together held out in front of face, his strange attitude exaggerated by the way he dressed.

Though this one was quite different in many aspects, the matured attitude still could not keep him from dosing off into a sleep. He had dreamt right away where he saw himself being baptized and anointed. He woke up as others were trooping out at the end of the service, and he exclaimed half aloud, "what the hell!"

"Shhhh! don't swear in the house of God, young man, "said a voice behind him. It was Father Maria.

"Where the hell have you been all this while?"

"I've been around young man," replied the man, "get up and follow me."

The $2^{1/}_{2}$ kilometer tunnel that led from the cloak room of the church terminated in a big cave. It was cool and cozy in there; the wonders of God will never end. Three men including Father Maria took Adams through the tunnel. At interval of 10 meters exist a burning torch which might not illuminate the entire tunnel but more or less constitute navigational light ; a sort of beacon..

Something persisted in the cave that was strong but gently nerve soothing. Breadth so fresh and natural, the gentle flow of the little stream that ran through plays its tremendous part in this aspect of adding splendor to nature. But of course mature is inherently beautiful. Its man though, due his inability to recognize natural intrinsic beauty, that tries to rearrange nature to meet appreciation of his deceased imagination, thereby defacing it. Nature is intrinsically beautiful without the artificialities of human modifications.

Adams noted there were eleven people seated in a semicircle folded in the ways of the yogis, with a space for one left and in the centre was a bald headed old man with very white long beards and moustache. The old man smiled concernedly as they took Adams close to him. Adams noticed they exchanged greetings in a very unusual manner. He only bowed but the rest he did not understand. Then he saw his Friar Biodun Maria went and occupied the empty space.

The old man's smile widened as Adams was introduced to him by father Maria.

"Peace be onto you the pure at heart, the chosen one, the savior of his helpless children," he said. Adams must have said in his mind, "what the hell is this old man talking about?" To which the old man seemed to have replied, "you may not believe, young one, you may find all very strange, unrealistic, even funny, but it takes God himself to convince the adamant. Was it not God himself who convinced Jonah when he refused to carry His holy message to the people in Nineveh? Was it not the almighty Himself who convinced Saul who later became Paul, and stopped the persecution of his people? You're no doubt Gods anointed and you shall be convinced beyond doubt."

"We shall see," said Adams half aloud, then aloud, "we should not waste much time on preambles, old man," and added rather impatiently, "I don't belong to you or your organization or whatever you may choose to call it. But the fact is that I'm ready to do things for the promotion of humanity. And I find the entire talk about this Rosary ridiculously funny, to tell the truth. But if you insist on the Rosary, you've got to convince me how its recovery will serve as a savior of humanity. This is why I am here and we should just skip the Jonah and Saul of Paul part of it and get it over with snappy."

"Oh yes, yes, I've better begin, chosen one. I am Father Gbashero."

"My name is Adams!"

The old man ignored with the same smile and continued. "We shall begin by telling you a little bit about the Rosary but first you will have to take an oath."

"A what?"

A bible was trusted into his hand before he could object. "'Raise your right hand chosen one."

"I am Adams, Father Gbashero," raising his right hand anyway. The next few sentences like incantations heard from the old man's mouth had a definite effect on the whole cave and occupants. Adam's skin prickled with goose pimples all over his body, body hairs standing on edge erect. Finally the administration of the oath ended with the following words repeated after him by Adams.

"…….i swear by the almighty, most holy God,
that what has been disclosed to me so far
and what would further be revealed,
I will keep secret…."

"You may now sit down, chosen one." For the third time Adams reaction was to remind him his name, but he had not yet fully recovered. He seemed to have been dazzled. For the next 5 minutes nobody talked, finally Adams brightened and broke the silence.

"So what about the Rosary?"

"Hmmm," the old man began, "the most holy of holy Rosary lies at this present moment in the valley of crocodiles…… oh God.."

"And what is the special thing about this particular Rosary?"

"Oh son, one side of the holy Rosary shines with the brilliance of diamond, while the other side is opaque, black in color. On the side that shines of each bead is written certain codes and formulas which constitute solutions or antidote to the problems that are engraved in codes as well on the opaque side of the beads …"

"Whaat?" Adams was on his feet. "You mean you are running some form of organization in here and this is your headquarters… Jesus Christ…C'mon old papa, what is this? Is it Mafia?"

"Not at all son. Far from it, chosen one."

"I am still Adams! And I think I'm getting interested, very interested."

"Listen. You see, it has always been the unavoidable order of things; black against white, darkness against light, negative against positive, bad against good. Well this duality of things hold true within this lower sphere of the upper world. These qualities are just complements of one another, and of course the words 'good and bad' are relative terms, aren't they? It is just that one has to find himself on one side of these polarities. And whatever name you might want to call us, we know where we stand and it is for the good of humanity."

"What then is your aim?"

"Our aim is to continuously prevent the evil ones from carrying out their intentions."

"What intentions?"

"To incapacitate the good side so as to be able to perpetrate their evils undisturbed and finally enslave the whole of mankind!"

"With what?"

"With the Rosary if they are able to lay their hands on it."

"Sounds interesting but who made this Rosary, and how did it get to the valley?"

"All we can tell you, young man, is that the Holy Rosary is not made to harm. Just as with all creations. Nothing is ever created bad in itself. It is but the application of it by man. The powder, bombs, missiles, all dangerous arsenals are but misapplication of most natural laws, by people of the world. The Rosary, chosen one, is an archive that contains yet the most advanced laws and formulas in the universe and the hope of humanity lies on its recovery, and I believe God has now brought the hour nearer. You of course are the chosen one. I know it, I feel it, I….."

For a long while, Adams was left alone in retrospection. When he raised up his head, he asked genuinely, "why then must God do things the hard way for man? If he has to redeem his people, why must there be a struggle, a fight, why must there be opposition? Why must his people be enslaved to start with? Why must we suffer? Is HE not the Almighty? I asked not to despise God, but can you explain, old man?"

"Son, that is about how we mundane can realize what he has done. We are low in understanding of the totality and implications of his divine laws. So we rarely appreciate them. He gave us the free will which we wanted and we abused it and as a result we have sunk ourselves deep in sins that we are hardly any longer sensitive to God and his laws. We have become so thick headed that it's only things that come the hard way that can make any spiritual impact on us. We accumulated a lot of debt which we have to settle. With understanding of the laws things are easier but we have refused to understand. That is the reason and genesis of our suffering. Just imagine, the difference between forty days and night and forty years! The way God delivered the Israelites was the best for them otherwise deliverances would have served no purpose. It is one of God's own laws revealed but unfortunately very few appreciate it. Human beings push themselves into bondage and slavery through indiscipline of all definitions. Evolved minds can never be in bondage. Here comes again the law of Cause and Effect. Man has lost recognition of who he is. However, through suffering, if he is sincere, he learns to know who he is and his true position in the scheme of God. He eventually could define and maintain his relationship with his creator. He knows what he is, what he is not, what he should not be and what he should become and should not become. At such a point in his evolution he is ready to give all it takes to effect the necessary changes, and this, young man is the point where we can say that man is truly ready for God's deliverance. Man, then should be allowed to realize his own very self. Know his own values and then makes his own choice. The key point is the word choice. He has to make the choice as a result of an informed judgment. Otherwise deliverance is of no spiritual value. Just as a golden necklace is of no value to a fowl. God in his infinite wisdom will always choose the right time, based on this aspect of man's readiness, to deliver his people."

"When you say man, does it include even those unfortunate souls who find themselves born into certain woes, miseries or other without being responsible for them?"

"Where we are coming from is much farther than what we can realize. The more we know the closer we realize the truth. The absolute truth is that God is neither partial nor arbitrary and would always ensure that nobody who plants cassava would harvest potatoes. It is what you sow that you reap. Where, when and how we sowed these things we might not easily remember...After all can you remember everything you did yesterday? Talk less of the life in a past incarnation."

"Well, some spiritual philosophy which we shall conclude later. The hot question now is how the hell did your rosary find its way deep down the valley of crocodiles? I thought the bank vault could be more practical and efficient, huh."

"Well as it is, it has been an effective save place since. One of God's way of doing things."

"Look, please, I need more than all this."

"The old man looked around, obviously in silence consultation with the rest 12 occupants of the cave, who gave him their positive sign. Then he took a deep breath and with the exhalation of the breadth, said, "then I'd better commence from the very beginning, but please, Friar Maria, could you fill my jug of water please?"

Father Maria took the jug to the stream and soon came back with it filled with about the most natural water in the universe. That done the old man took a glass and commenced.

"Orisha, the ancient deity had 2 sons, Orishagbemi and Orishadami. They were twins and he was very fond of them. All problems, all, were known to being solved by Orisha. Orisha was vast in the law of nature and their applications and how the entire things work. Provided Orisha was made aware of any problem he definitely produced solutions to them. Well, he brought his sons up the mystical way but it was quite obvious that they could not know everything that their father knew. And as he advanced in age and apprehensive of the ultimate call that could come any time, and for the benefit of human race he made a compilation of the laws and formulas that operate in the evolvement of problems and the corresponding formulas of the solutions. These he engraved minutely on a special Rosary. The former on the opaque side while the later on the bright side. He handed the Rosary over to his children who quickly got acquainted with its usage. Thus in the event of evolvement of any problem of any definition, could be troubles, disturbances of any kind, outbreak of epidemic diseases, etcetera, they checked the opaque side to find the law under which the problem evolved, then they checked the incandescent side to find the formulas with which they derive the solutions and remedies to such problems. So, no doubt as you can see, Orisha made the Rosary in good faith and before he ascended to heaven his 2 sons had become adepts in the usage of the holy Rosary in solving problems for humanity." The old man stopped briefly to drink water.

"When Orisha eventually ascended to heaven the people missed him dearly but they soon got used to Orishagbemi and Orishadami who used their expertise in the use of the Rosary to solve problems for them. They became very famous and relied upon by the people who regarded them as *olugbala*, meaning 'savior'. Needless to say that they had become very powerful. They could do and undo." A pause to take water.

"Hmmmmn, my people, power is a delicate issue and could be dangerous. Just like our famous sekete wine, very sweet and very intoxicating. If you are not careful it would get you drunk. Well, Orishagbemi maintained a balanced head. He must have followed their father's advice not to concentrate too much on the power in possession otherwise it is tantamount to drinking it and the more you drink and enjoy it the more the tendency to get drunk. Unfortunately, Orishadami, his twin brother, could not go along with his brother on the principle of 'use only when there is the need.' No, Orishadami grew increasingly impatient and would not wait for the need to arise. That made life dull for him. His own idea, which he tried to inculcate in Orishagbemi is to create the need since they had the power to do so. Cause the problem, using the laws and formulas in reverse and solve the problems therefrom, which serves better his own idea. For his own idea was for people to worship them and pay for their services. He was no more satisfied with the usual voluntary token of appreciation from the redeemed. But he failed to carry along his brother, Orishagbemi, who would not involve himself in such an act he regarded as despicable. He tried in turn but in vain to convince his brother that such way is negative and an abuse of power and responsibility. He reinstated the fact that the problem formulas are meant to serve as an index to the solution formulas but not to be used in reverse to create problems for humanity that they are meant to protect. He would not be a party to such practices and as long as he lived he would make sure it would not be practiced. Well it is said 2 captains cannot stir a ship. Two captains can handle a ship provided they help each other to maintain the same heading. Once they differ that's when the problem begins. These twins disagree vehemently. They maintain a council of priests which as a result of these differences became divided into 2 equal parts and subsequently the whole community became divided but now into unequal parts. The fact that the majority fell into the side of the much elegant and eloquent Orishadami serves as a pointer to the fact that human beings, most of the times, do not know what is good for them and would always give their support to what would eventually destroy them, most especially so in a predominantly negative period as ours." The old man coughed and water was given to him.

"Hmmm, chosen one, this event developed and led to the greatest struggle between twins brother. The venue where the 2 brothers fought and struggle for the Blessed Rosary on that little elevation by the valley of crocodiles, grass has refused to grow till date. It was in the course of this struggle that the Most blessed Rosary dropped down the valley of crocodiles. Well, son, Rosary gone, twin brothers beat themselves to death, the fight continues among the followers. On the long run, Orishagbemi's family, kins and followers had to take to their heels owing to their numerical inferiority, to save dear skin. Here they settled in Gbongan and found rest, shelter, water, secrecy and peace of mind in this cave. So far this secrecy and security has not been beaten. The only entrance through the tunnel is at Oluwada, a village 5 km away. At first there was no problem of detection as the whole of this area was a thick forest but when habitation got extended to this place we decided to build our church right on top of the entrance of the cave. So, chosen one, you have now been let into a secret which you have taken an oath to keep. Our utmost mission now is to recover the Rosary. If we are able to do that then our brothers would have a chance to repent. But if we fail the chances are narrower. The worst comes if they are able to get the Rosary, in which case we would be finished. The whole of humanity and all what Christ came for, God forbid, might go down the drain."

"Well, old papa, your Rosary case is both emphatic and interesting. But if all is true about it what makes you think that Orishadami's people have not succeeded in recovering it?"

"That we know for sure because we have our envoy there who

continues to report the presence of the Most Blessed Holy Rosary, shining in its glorious incandescence." He made a sign of the cross and the rest followed suit except Adams.

"And you don't think they stand a better chance than you? They don't hide but you do."

"Of course, but we have committed the matter into God's hands and He is on our side. We have an edge there, son. No man who is not pure at heart can ever recover the Rosary from among the crocodiles. And a pure at heart can never be found among Orishadami's people."

Adams shrugged. "All a matter of opinion and all would soon be proven. And all this pure at heart garbage….? That's why I say about God doing it the hard way for his people. Is there no other way? Tell me, holy ones, is this all he can offer to help? Mind you, this fight is as much as his also, the way I can reason and figure it. It is to save his people. Isn't it?"

"My son, Saint Paul said spiritual things can only be discerned spiritually. Your inquiries certainly reveal the heart of a seeker. God's own reply to your curiosities will definitely make your heart purer than crystal and as usual, he would chose the right moment and means to speak to you."

"Then tell him to book appointment. I'm a busy man!" Adams could not hide his irritation and impatience. He lost his temper. The cave dwellers made serious signs of the cross of the most solemn kind. They were bewildered. A deep silence pervaded for some time quite long which Adams eventually broke.

"Well, Father Gbashero, let me just confess that I am curious about your rosary, for a lot of circumstances seems to be surrounding it but I am ready to bet my black nigger ass that someone is fooling some people somehow. I will go for your mission but don't you make a mistake about it. It is this curiosity that is making me to go. Nothing else! Not for any of these bull shit holy, holy stuff you are trying to feed me. I'm curious. Men, I'm game! And, holy roses, I will get to the bottom of it all for all of us to see."

The bewildered cave men gave a sign of relief, and looking around the cave interior and shifting his gaze at the occupants, he continued, his voice a little louder, "If you still want to leave in a cave in the 19th century, good for you. It's your choice. But for me I'll lead my own live and take my chances in the cities. So don't give me that crab about the chosen one. I don't belong to you, so you look for your chosen one among yourselves in the cave. I am not a caveman. But as I said, I am curious. You have arouse my curiosity to the marrows and I will go get your rosary for you and by so doing I might just bust what some clever dudes have so long been covering, old papas."

CHAPTER 4

Provocation, it could have been correctly argued, pushed Karl to have acted on impulse. But when a man castrates another such case could be complicated. To worsen the case, bad luck, the poor man bled to death. Karl's charge was for murder. No defense for him. Not in Gbongan at that particular period anyway. Besides, Karl is not a first offender. He is notorious. Then good riddance to bad egg.

He sat down reflecting, head in hands, in his little cell. Just yesterday he was a free man but today......? He ran a mental picture of how it had all happened. From the Gaademn day the gaadem bike ran out of gaademn fuel. A bloody fucking bitch came along on her gademn toy to offer a bloody fucking help. Hmmmn, for the very first time in his gaademn live he fell in gaaddemned fucking love...and bloody possessive. Deep, uncontrollable emotion and anger made him to cut the balls off the stupid ass of a mother fucking bastard. An act which has now ended him in a gademn cell. And only a gaademn miracle can prevent his transfer from cell to hell.

The noise of the turning of the keys to his cell door woke him up from his reveries.

"Hey you Karl the castrator! Out!"

"I promise you I will remove 2 more balls before I die. Idiot!" he snarled as he walked in front of the warder.

"If you knew what I know you wouldn't be talking to me like

that," the warder beamed gloomily at him. Then he knew his days were numbered.

It turned out that Karl had a visitor and a female at that. Karl just stared at her as both stood either side of the iron rods which seems to offer her the adequate protection required from him. Though not enough to prevent a spittle that landed right on her nose.

"Karl, please. I promise I will make it up to you when you are out."

Karl spat on her face again and she wiped it off with her handkerchief.

"Bitch! You bitch, you went and testified, huh?"

"Karl, I had to. What else could I have done? Please."

"I'm gonna die because of you, bitch!"

"Karl, please listen. I've got a message for you."

"What bloody message do you have? Bitch! Medicine after death! Message to deliver to somebody's gaademn father in heaven or hell, the heck?"

"Just listen, Karl. Please." She looked around to make sure nobody could overhear what she was about to say. "Words got around that they are gonna hang you along with four others on Friday. That's 2 days to come." Karl's eyes were wide open but she continued, "But my uncle said to tell you to prepare. He is going to set you free."

He looked at her, not knowing what to believe. "To hell with your uncle. He is god, isn't it?"

"No Karl. Believe me, he is more than a god. Listen, this is what he said you will have to do."

<hr />

Karl lost the last grain of hope when on Friday the notorious inspector, accompanied by 2 other hefty armed policemen came to open his cell and with a sarcastic cynical smile, greeted him and called him 'almighty' before they led him out. He watched as they kind of threw other four prisoners into the 'Black Maria' and at that instance he felt a pang that he had missed something important in his life. What it is he could not explain. "Well," was the only word he could utter as he shrugged and entered the ominous vehicle. Deeply in thought, he never expected the end could be so early and sudden, and for that matter, on a stake.

Two dispatch riders took the lead with siren blaring. Even when there was nothing so important siren blaring was usual in that place. An open land rover jeep containing 8 ferociously looking policemen with rifles extended followed, then the 'Black Maria" with the prisoners well handcuffed and locked up behind in its safe cabin with the driver in front with 2 armed guards. A second land rover jeep similar to the one in front, with the same compliments of armed policemen took its cue behind the 'Black Maria'. The procession was headed for Osogbo where the prisoners were going to be executed.

"Bimbi bitch and her gaademn uncle."

Karl had prepared and had rehearsed several times what she said he had to do. At first in disbelief but gradually as it happen to be the only semblance of hope left, a miracle if it is, he prepared with certain quantity of faith. But they didn't show up! What must have happened? Did they make any attempt and were caught? Or was it that he deserved a last horrible joke from Bimbi who rated her uncle as more than a god. "Shit! Bloody fucking godamned, mother fucking, father ass licking shit!" went on and on in his mind when he was catapulted against other occupants by the sudden slam on the brakes by the driver. Karl and the others could not see what had happened. It was a trailer vehicle that had packed up on the road really at a bad place and so narrow was the access that there was hardly any room for other vehicles to pass. But fortunately it happened at that particular junction where exists an untarred road that cuts back the highway one kilometer ahead. And when Karl saw the diversion sign and all was normal again a terrible sadness overcast his mind. He was depleted of what resembled hope.

The second sudden braking that sent the prisoners tumbling on top of each other was accompanied by a rather rowdy report. The 2 dispatch riders had run into a thin wire pulled across the road which flung them mercilessly onto the rocky ground. What followed thereafter was a lot of explosions and gun fire exchanges. All happened within two and a half minutes. Then there was a chilling silence later interrupted by a gentle breeze seemingly sent there to clear the smokes so as to reveal some unexpected sights. Amid the clearing smoke was the Black Maria, standing alone and genuinely lonely. The land rover jeep that was keeping her wake was now upside down, in flames. The one making the lead could be found now by the side of the road, functioning now as a crematorium the best way it could and seeming to be excelling in the newly assigned function. No soul moved. Chilling, unending silence. Suddenly a masked man came out off the bush, walked directly, deliberately to the 'Black Maria', opened the front door and pushed out the dead driver and guards. He took the wheel, started the vehicle and drove away.

The big van was immediately driven to a bush path, then driven for about 15 km and arrived at a clearing where 4 similarly attired men were standing by. Quickly they blew the door open and four coughing condemned men stormed out of the big van. Karl walked quietly to the door after them, looked around and jumped down, "surely some are godlike," he chuckled, looked around again and nodded with a smile. No doubt in his mind that the mission was for him. He waited curiously what would follow next. He noticed a black G-wagon Mercedes Benz and a range rover, all glass tainted. He was immediately led to the G-Wagon and the left rear door was opened for him. It was then he noticed a man, covered in topcoat, hat on head, was seated inside. As he took his seat quietly the man offered his hand as he said, "compliment of Bwallangwu. I am Jobilah. You are welcome back from the gate of hell."

Karl took the hand, shook it but just looked at him.

"How about the 4 prisoners?" he heard the voice of a masked man, to which the man who introduced himself as Jobilah responded, "Were they not being taken for execution?"

"Yes sir, by hanging."

"Then at least give some of what belongs to Caesar to Caesar. Well you can still do them a favor though, last favors. Ask them if they still prefer hanging, if not, shoot them and let's get out of here."

Karl turned and looked at this man again as the Benz was driving away, the range rover taking the lead.

Karl was taken to the dwelling of chief Enlaye who heartily welcomed him. Karl had regained himself and decided to cut preambles right away. He made it known that the only person he wanted to see is this Bwallangwu.

"But of course, young tiger, you will definitely see Bwallangwu but only when the time is ripe."

"What time? Banana time?"

The chief laughed and Jobilah followed suit and stopped a fraction of a second his boss stopped.

"I have realized that this is an organization and there's bound to be chains of command," Karl spoke again. "Okay, I'm grateful but I think the less time we waste at each chain link the better for all of us."

"Perhaps I would have introduced myself if you had relaxed and had not taken over the scene, young one. Don't be in a hurry. *Howu, eni a n gbe'yawo bo wa ba kii tun maa n ga'run.*[4] We are together now. Son, I am chief Enlaye."

"Good to meet you, chief em.. Enlaye. But I personally would like to thank Bwallangwu. I am grateful, of course I owe him one, yeah, Karl owes him one. You don't wanna tell me I only have to go through you ......"

"Listen!" chief now getting irritated.

"I think the young man would require some explanations," Jobilah quickly interjected to calm down the chief. Then turning to Karl, "Bwallangwu is not a thing you can see ...em...at least not right now anyway but..."

"I am the representative of Bwallangwu worldwide. I coordinate all his activities," the chief broke in and Jobilah locked his jaws. "A lot exists that could be revealed to you about us, depending....hmmmn,... But for now be sure that we are the most powerful, unstoppable, fate determining organization in the universe. We shall unfold a lot to you with time but we shall not put the cart before the horse. To know us, first you have to be part of us. Join us, declare your loyalty. And when you thus become part of Bwallangwu and Bwallangwu becomes part

---

[4] The husband to whom a wife is being brought does not have to peep again.

of you then the benefits, uncountable benefits of Bwallangwu become all yours to share."

Karl lost himself in thought as the 2 men looked on in expectation. Then he spoke, "Chief, I am grateful for all the pains it took to get me out. I am indebted, yeah, I know that but I am not compelled to be enslaved by anybody or organization..."

"No, no, no, young man, you are getting it wrong and too hard for that matter. We only ask you to join us as fellows, as equal, but not as underdog."

"I prefer to be on my own and wait for the opportune time to return the favor to err...Bwallangwu."

"Wrong again. Son, Bwallangwu only wants to take care of you. Not to indebt you or trap you to use you. He has not even asked you to return any favor. This little thing is no favor to Him. *Oke aimoye*[5]."

"This is what you are saying. You would not even allow me to see him so I could know his mind."

"I told you He is no ordinarily seen like that."

"Sorry sirs," said the adamant young lad. "I'd rather be alone."

"Ok, young lad, if you so wish. This is a chance millions are crying to get. Think well!"

"That is it. I am gonna be on my own."

"I will like to remind you, young man, that you are about the hottest commodity in the market now. Dead or alive, you are worth a fortune. At least a quarter of a million dead, one and a half alive. Does that make any impression? Even your own father could sell you to lay his hands on such dough at this hard time. Only Bwallangwu can offer you the protection you need. Otherwise you are a gold fish."

"Thanks sirs, I will take my chances."

"Ok then, lad, the door is still open anytime you find it necessary to come and hide under Bwallangwu."

"Ok. Fair enough."

"There is just one more thing, Karl."

"What?"

---

[5] Thousands uncountable

"We would like to make sure that you do not expose us. If you are caught you could be made to talk. Hmmmn…think about that and see you very soon.."

Karl was ushered out with no less dignity accorded, wondering at the executive allure of the entire arrangement, of the business of getting him out and the style of this people, but mind made up.

"Jobilah," chief Enlaye called after Karl had disappeared.

""Yes, my lord, what do…."

"Jobilah! I like his guts. I like the vibrations I get from that young lad. But what has to be done must be done. Keep him in sight at all times. You understand me?"

"Yes, my chief."

"I know they will really hunt him, oh my my. Even his friends will join up in the hunt for the money. And if he is caught, Jobilah?"

"He could talk."

"And we don't want that to happen, do we?"

"No, my lord. Bwallangwu would not like it."

"Then keep him in sight. At the instance he is caught you do what you have to do."

"Understood sir. What a waste that might be."

"Yes, Jobilah. Such a promising young tiger. I hope it wouldn't come to that on the long run."

"Fingers crossed, my lord."

"Keep those fingers on the trigger."

———◆◆✕◆◆———

THE MAN HUNTERS

Karl had immediately deserted town. Karl never remains in one same place for long. According to Chinua Achebe in his 'Things Fall Apart', *Eneke the bird says that since men have learned to shoot without missing, he has learned to fly without perching.*[6]

After an initial attempt to trace Bimbi, who seemed to have

---

[6] Chinua Achebe in 'Things Fall Apart'.

suddenly vanished, he had postponed her matter till some opportune time. The time now is for himself, to survive. From village to village he pitched his tent about. And by hell he would survive. With the new moustache and full beard, with the dark shades and with the alert mind tuned to maximum sensitivity, Karl might survive. Survival, a game he was born to play. Playing ingeniously and patiently. Playing for time to erode some memories. By which time many other crimes and possibly worse ones would have been committed, Much dust would have settled on his posters to make them become gradually unrecognizable and insignificant. Much rain would have fallen to wash them to the point of obliteration. Even hunters would have lost interest out of fatigue. Surely, other crimes, events and issues would definitely overtake his own. But it will take a long time and Karl is one hell of a resilient person. He could out-wait a vulture.

He sat at the bank of Osun River with his fishing line in water, thinking. He is now not much confused but certainly very curious. He thought of Bimbi. He was not sure if he really wants to see her now. He wanted that before for only one reason. To kill her. Now that this uncle of hers has saved him has altered that situation. He couldn't predict himself on what he might do on seeing her. So he wouldn't want to see her yet. And who is this uncle of hers? Who makes things happen? Bigger than a god. Is he this Bwallangwu they wouldn't allow him to see....until he belongs to them? Bimbi said that he is more than a god. Who could be more than a god? Is it why he could not see him? Who really are this Chief Enlaye and the much subservient Jobilah? Surely they are in positions to be reckoned with in the outfit. They seem to have a lot of experts in so many trades and walks of life. It really must be a very powerful organization of some sort and right at the head must be this Bwallangwu of theirs. And could this Bwallangwu, more than god, be Bimbi's uncle? Yes it has to be so, otherwise why would they come to rescue him out of such a precarious situation if she had not asked them to do so? But Karl does not belong to anybody, group or organization even if it were much more efficient. Surely he could count this one as efficient. Under the gentle breeze he dosed off, his back against a tree.

He woke up with a start; a sun beaten hot barrel against his ear confirmed his premonitions of danger.

"Get up, Karl," said the rough voice, "I have been trailing you for the past 2 weeks."

Karl slowly got up. "Who are you?"

"Never mind. I'm just the poor mechanic you're gonna make rich within the next few hours."

"Don't you think to get rich as a mechanic it's spanners and pliers and some grease stained overall you need...not a gun."

"Shut up! Move over there! Lie down on your face! Your hands on your head!"

Karl did as was told and the man briskly ran his hands over his body and retrieve his hunting knife.

"Now get up and move!"

"Where to?"

"Back to town, my friend, where I'm going to collect my reward. Oh thank you God. I've always known that I am not going to die a wretched man."

"Way back to Gbongan is more than 22 kilos, man."

"That is what makes a long walk, but boy, for a million I could walk from here to Sokoto. Now move! And no clever ideas, otherwise 250000 Naira is still some good dough, if you know what I mean. Any funny stuff you get it!"

Karl just stood still.

"I say move!...you hear me? You move or I kill you."

"You probably realize the difference between a quarter and a million? I'm worth more alive than dead."

"Dead or alive you are worth something. If you don't move I'll kill you!"

"I heard dead men weigh a lot heavier, especially some of us with large bone structure. Are you gonna carry me over 22 kilometers...?"

"Shut up! Carry or drag I would if I have to. Now, move!" the man push Karl annoyingly with the muzzle of the gun. Exactly what Karl had been hoping he would make the mistake of doing. Shifting aside slightly in a way of moving, he was able to put himself in a perfect position for his next move, making utmost use of their shadows. Swift and stealth. In one lightening move his hands were grabbing the barrel, he was bending forward and his heel made a connection on the man's groins in a ball-crushing impact. A shot was released that went over his head. The mechanic turned man-hunter was on the ground instantly, hands on groins, wheeling and reeling about. Karl recognized him immediately; his old time motorcycle mechanic and friend. "You!?" he exclaimed. The man, in a desperate last bid to save himself, attempted to throw the knife but not fast enough. Karl shot him in the face. "Hmm, these people said it. Even your father would sell you...and your friends would join the hunt."

The gun must have been loaded with the B shells. It made a wreck of the face.

So what next? As usual, he stated on the move. He is shifting base.

It did not take him much time to realize that there is scarcely any place that is safe for him. Even the posters of him pasted in public places were drawn with his full beards, moustache and sun glasses. How come? How the hell did they know all this? Even in villages! Have they been able to come that close? If so, why haven't they caught him yet? Even at Fatte village the curious look the villagers gave him was worrisome. As he checked into the Lafatte Inn the comments of the receptionist unnerved him. "Hey, you kind of look familiar," he had said as he handed over the key to his room and Karl had given him a direct hard look and replied, "yeah, fella, you look familiar too. I lodged here a couple of years ago."

"Well I was employed here only 3 months ago."

"Then we could have met somewhere else, couldn't we?"

"Small world. I hope the room suits you sir. If you need anything just ring the bell." The receptionist said and went back down stairs. That meant trouble thought Karl as he checked over the room. He felt the familiar uneasy feeling. The usual premonitions; the functioning of the circumstantially developed sixth sense. He looked around in vain for any handy good weapon, but he had a second thought. Staying there and fight would not favor him. It would only make things worse. He removed a rope from his rucksack, tied one end to the sack and lowered the sack gently down the storey building to the ground through the window which he closed afterwards. He then opened the door, stepped out into the passage and locked the door behind him before he went downstairs to the reception. He noticed the receptionist talking to someone on the phone. He moved close, his movement seemed to have made the receptionist to drop the phone. "Well, my friend," he said to him, "I've gotta go buy some bananas. Could you order a bottle of champagne for me and have it ready before I come back. I'll collect it on my return," and with a wink, "we might even have a drink together if you have nothing against champagne."

"Anything against champagne!? You must be joking!. Ain't no fanatic, man. I would break my fast anytime for champagne. Tell you man, I even have something to celebrate."

"And what could that be?"

"A jackpot, man, I won a jackpot!"

"Well then you better make it 2 bottles." Karl said as he walked out with a corky smile on his face.

Barely 3 minutes afterwards 3 hefty men came in, one of who talked with the receptionist.

"He just got out now to get himself some bananas."

"Yeah, I told you he is an ape. Sure he has not gone away?"

"No. His sac is still in the room upstairs. The only thing I would regret is not honoring his invitation for champagne before you guys take him."

"No problems. You could still accompany him to our cell for your drink. Champagne and bananas, huh."

"No, man, that is very kind of you. But I could buy a lot more champagne with my rewards later on. But you trust me, without bananas." That produced some laughter while the police men sat themselves at a table, ordered a round of drinks which the receptionist gladly paid for and they waited rather impatiently for their man to come back with his bananas.

Karl watched the hotel with a pair of binoculars from the top of the little hill about 800 meters away. He took particular note of the disposition of the police. They had virtually surrounded the hotel.

"Very good," he muttered, "very, very good." He let the binoculars hang back on his neck, ate some bread and retracted his steps back into the bush. Some minutes later he found himself killing a snake. Surely that snake would have killed him, he reflected. For a snake bite on the head leaves no allowances for first aids, such as tying up at a junction to stop the flow of poison. Where would they tie in such a case, the only junction being the neck. Worse than hanging. He remembered what he had heard several times that you never relax until the neck is cut off a snake. He did that and packed the long reptile into his sac.

Usually he camps near water if available. So he didn't stop until he got to a little stream. He made fire and relaxed while his snake was roasting and saying to himself, "snake barbecue, taste like a mixture of fish and chicken. Who knows, it might even be the best."

By his wrist watch it was getting to 1700 hours. Well, he thought, he might even park up here for the night. But then, holy shit! That all too familiar feeling again. A feeling that has saved his life number of times uncountable. A divine help from a well developed function of the pineal gland. A feeling he dares not ignore. Instantly he climbed a tree, and binoculars in place, just a look in the right direction sent him jumping down the rough stem; no time for a decent climb down. Holy roses! Were they waging a war against him? Close to 200 men with all sorts of weapons and to worsen the case, is a squad of bloodhounds! With robot-like precision and practiced speed he stuffed his things into the sac, not forgetting his dinner. In one giant leap he crossed the stream in a bid to give his assailants as much gap as possible. Now and then the words of chief Enlaye reechoed in his ears, "you are the hottest commodity now in the market. Even your own father would sell you out......Only Bwallangwu can offer you the protection you require......"

"Bloody bloodhounds!" he cursed. Karl knows the terrain like the back of his palm. He knew he could make a play thing of even a battalion of soldiers in that jungle. They wouldn't be able to route him out unless they set the whole place on fire. But for these goddamned mother fucking father cheating bloodhounds locking on his tail like homing missiles. That advanced functioning of the olfactory specially endowed them as their own inheritance from the creator. Whatever the case he had to take care of the situation, however it might be. "It's a game, remember," he chided himself with a sardonic smile, reminiscent of a fatal game of life and death. "Yeah it's a game and the winner never stops. He never gives up."

In his sac were wraps of salt, dry grounded pepper, some cubes of magi condiments (monosodium glutamate), cigarette lighter, box of matches and sugar. No weapons, saved his knife which is of little use against hundreds of men armed with guns. And bow and arrow? Yes, he uses his fishing rod as a walking stick in the villages, feigning bad leg or old man, but same could be bent into a bow in emergency situations and it has prooved very effective. Now he has to get to the double barrel which he had hidden in the bamboo grooves, about one kilometer from his present position. He wasn't making good progress. The men and dogs were gaining on him. They were fresh, he was fagged out. Really tired.

Knowledge is power, so it's said, but it has to be manipulated to produce power and used effectively. Otherwise it is useless. It might even prove dangerous. There existed a deep gully which he knew around that area. It is almost 15 feet deep and 30 feet wide and runs in length almost half a kilometer. He also knew a certain portion of it which is not more than 12 ft wide which is covered by weed to the point that it is invisible. He changed direction right away to that part of the gully and as he approached he increased his steps in preparation for a long jump, giving room for mistakes. He jumped, not very accurate, and landed at the edge on the other side, one leg sliding inside. He practically, survival instinct, uprooted several shrubs, grass and weed in a frantic effort to keep himself from sliding into the gully. He managed to pull himself up and he made a good effort afterwards to cover the area to avoid recognition.

The grunts of the dogs grew uncomfortably louder as he balanced himself f about 25 meters away on the other side of the gully, with his makeshift bow, powerful and ready. As the pursuers got within 3 meters of the edge on the other side he pulled and released an arrow. A dog started howling painfully on the ground. A little commotion followed. "There he is! Go get him now!" All rushed forward and five dogs were released. In about 2 great leaps 4 dogs took their last jump on the surface. They were down the deep pit together with the most desperate men who probably wanted to be first to lay their hands on the most expensive bounty of the century. The others seem to have applied shoe brakes and were able to crawl to an eventual stop amid shouts amazement and curses. "Bastard!" And in another second the whole forest was a vibration of assorted guns, rifles, pistols, Dane guns and all what is available. Karl was instantly behind a rock, and the rock shading his movement he got to the opposite side of it. Every attention and gun fires concentrated on his previous position. He shook his head as pulled and took aim. Instantly another dog was down, howling and struggling for survival. More gun shots reported at his new position, but shielded by the rock, and now bent double, he proceeded hurriedly to put as much distance between himself and the bounty hunters, amidst this confusion, for he knew for sure that it won't be too long before they would figure out what to do to get back on his trail.

"Six dogs down, one more to go. Bloody bloodhounds."

He got to the bamboo grove and finally recovered the double barrel inherited from his mechanic turned assailant. He checked it and found only 2 shells. He thought for a while. He is no more in doubt about what he has to do. He knows where he has to go and what he must do before he gets there. He climbed a tree and discovered that the hunters had reduced in number. About 25 now with a dog. They were about 600 meters away. He climbed down gently, not to tear his trousers, now that he was going to town. He wasn't really in a hurry anyway. He was glad the night was closing in. "Very good," he had said. He moved another 200 meters until he got a good cover behind which he waited. The question now is how would they come in the right direction? "Heck, I don't have to worry," he assured himself, "their bloody fucking dog will lead them to me."

At a range of 60 yards he squeezed the trigger of the double barrel and what followed immediately was the howling of the dog and the yelling of the men whose legs had blocked the paths of the pellets. They must have learnt now to take cover. "He has a gun1 He has a gun!"

They shouted. Some took off in the opposite direction while some glued themselves to the ground. The old experienced hands threw themselves behind available covers and were shooting frantically in his general direction, as Karl made away out of gun's range, muttering along, "They would sure get to town but with no mother fucking hound to lead them to where I'm heading."

"Danger, danger, danger. In the forest, in the village, in town, you're never out of it, wherever you are until you are free." Karl had been telling himself at every encounter, most of which nearly claimed his skin. And really he was never out of it especially here in town, for he had to put 5 men out of action and 2 dead for sure before he could enter the building. He made it at last to chief Enlaye's study who he found smiling gracefully, admiringly but more of gallantly, as he bid him welcome.

"Welcome, son, I have been waiting for you."

Karl did not take his offered hand and the chief did not take offence. "You have to destroy 7 of my best guards to get to me who as a matter of fact wants to see you. What an irony. Did you really have to?"

"Not when the first two I tried to talk to tried to kill me."

"Kill you?"

"Did you send them to rusher me in with clubs and knives?"

"And what about the other five?"

"If I had been taking chances I wouldn't have survived this far, talk less of talking to you now."

"I understand. By the way, I must really congratulate you, Karl. Nobody! I mean nobody in history had ever penetrated my kingdom, as far as to my own very study."

"A dent in your claimed effectiveness, isn't it"

"No, no, no, no. Rather a plus on your impeccable record. All the more reason why I want you. Everything that I have witnessed so far concerning you confirms and strengthens my desire and resolve."

"I wouldn't want to belong to a lousy organization."

"We are rather a family."

"Whatever you wish to call it, whatever I want to belong to must be perfectly efficient."

"It took some efficiency to plan and execute your rescue mission, young lad."

"Agreed, but how come I got here now? I could have killed you."

"You are not here to kill me and you know that. But listen. If you are able to get here it is not so much because we are lousy but much more because you are that good. You have no equal; the very reason why we want you. And when you join us we become greater."

"You know perhaps I could have been captured and there lies the risk of exposing you, but you allowed me to go away that easy…"

The chief moved closer, putting his hand on his shoulder, "Son, you wouldn't have been able to exposed us. You wouldn't have talked to nobody. That we are sure of."

"Hey, you counted on 100 percent loyalty even before I declare. Efficiency huh?" Karl said in rather loud voice and moved in a way that dropped the chief's hand off his shoulder.

"You were never out of our sight, son," the chief said with a smile. "When I said you wouldn't have been able to expose us just take it as gospel truth."

"You go tell that to the monkeys, chief."

Chief Enlaye looked at him and smiled again. "We could do with some respect here, and don't be naïve. You really perforated old Sammy's face. Didn't you, boy? Boy, you could outkick a horse. And always the balls," he laughed in a fit. "and sorry, rather unfortunate you couldn't take your fish. It was a tilapia but a double barrel is a better catch any day for such occasion. Given the chance I would sure choose the same."

"Very impressive, chief, but how did you know?"

Moving closer again, and taking his hand in a fatherly way, "you hid the dbarrel in the bamboo trees where you had to recover it later to take care of the last dog. And that was thoughtful of you, son. We really appreciate that. Not really for you but for us. They could have trailed you here."

Karl could not hide his surprise any longer, "How the heck did you get to know all this, chief? An accurate step by step record of my escapade!"

"I told you, son, we would have made sure you couldn't expose us.

If you had been caught, well most unfortunate, we would have had to do what we have to do. Fair enough? And tell me, young tiger, how was the snake barbecue?"

"Hmmn, excellent, chief. The best the situation could afford. The taste is a combination of fish and chicken. I still have some left..." making for his sac.

"No, no, thank you. Very kind of you, Karl. Some barbecues are better eaten in the bush, not in town."

"And what protection would you people have for me? What can you offer me?" Karl demanded abruptly as a matter of business, his face very serious, matching his tone."

"The best ever."

"I counted more than 200 man-hunters in pursuit. Apart from hiding and feeding me, ...Em....You should know now Karl is not one for a harem way of life."

The best protection, son. Unbeatable."

"Details?"

"Karl, you have demonstrated much to yourself that full beards, moustache and sunshades are not effective enough. Hide and seek and running around would not help for eternity."

"So what do you offer?" Karl demanded rather impatiently"

"A new identity, Karl. Simple." The chief made his common gesture of simplicity. "We will give you a new face, a new name, a new identity. Our surgeon is rated the best in Africa. A new life, Karl is what we are offering you."

Karl smiled and took the offered hand.

"Welcome back once again from hell to safety."

————◆◆❯❮◆●————

CHAPTER 5

The original plan was scanty. Rather simplistic and typical. Fria Maria and Adams would proceed to Ile-Ife by the end of the week. They would lodge in Hotel Diganka. Adams would select the period at night when they would go to the valley where he would take the Rosary and replace it with the replica provided.

"You see, very simple," Father Gbashero had said with a glitter in his eyes. "You go at night. A night when there is no moon, so nobody would be able to see you. The replica must remain inside this black little sac otherwise it would shine in the dark and attract attention. You descend the valley, remove and replace the Rosary. Remember again, the Holy Rosary must be put as well inside the black sac. Then come out and up the valley. Hmmmn, once you take the Rosary and replace it don't waste time oooo, you hear? Just come out quickly. Then you and Fria Maria go back to the hotel and as soon as day breaks you come back to Gbongan....Any question, son?"

Adam clapped his hands, "very good and detailed plan. Elaborate and well thought out!"

"Yes my son," and all the members threw each other a glance of admiration.

"Who worked out this careful plan?"

"We all sat down and carefully worked it out," replied the old man with a proud smile on his face.

"Very clever but is that all?"

"Yes, that is all, chosen one. Is there anything you wish to add? But you can…"

"So easy, just like that!?" Adams snapped his fingers in demonstration."

"Of course. All you need is God's blessing," said the old man," and one of them quickly added, "and which you already have!"

Adams looked at them the exact way you would look at monkeys. Anger mixed with surprise prevented him from laughing. "It is getting clearer now."

"What is that, son?"

"I know why you people have not recovered your rosary all these years. Simple, I'm sorry to say is a word that has deeper meaning."

"Hmmmn. I did enough English. What do you mean?" One of them asked, hiding his irritation.

"You mean to tell me I should just walk among crocodiles at night and just take your rosary, and come out neat!? A night without moon, as you instructed. If it's that easy why haven't any of you cavemen gone by yourself all these years to recover your goddamn Rosary?"

The people made faces and sign of the cross in opposition to the young man's seeming blasphemy. Then the old man replied concernedly, "chosen one, the pureness of your heart will keep all dangers aloof. Just as Daniel was thrown into the lion's den and no harm befell him," and the rest chorused, "oh gracious Lord!"

"You are the chosen one, son. All you need is what you already have. God's hands on you. God's protection."

"I see." Adam said still looking at them in amazement."

A member whisper into the ears of the old man something important he seemed to have forgotten.

"Oh yes, and we have this gown for you as an additional measure. It is iron. See. Try it on."

Adams looked at the garment and shook his head. "I see," he said again. Then just out of curiosity and sheer fun he decided to try it on. He was bruised and he sweated profusely trying to walk in it. He attempted to bend down the iron ground maliciously into his waist.

Then he mimicked the motion of picking up the Rosary and that was a drama.

"This is ingenious! I am sure one of you is the engineer who designed this and of course another one of you is the blacksmith who manufactured it to specifications. Very, very ingenious!"

"So you see, all you need is…

"Oh no thank you, I know what I need now! Please before you say any other word just help me outa this thing. That's all I need now."

As the people looked at him, confused, he snapped, "Get me outa this metal cupboard fitted with arms!" and as they helped him out he added, "the ancient knights' armors certainly would be a better idea. Did any of you try this on?"

"Sorry, son, we just thought we could….."

"I know and that really is very ingenious."

"Well, son, as the chosen one, all you need is God's own…"

"The hell I'll tell you all I need!" exploded Adams." When you were making your wonderful plan and designs I expect you to have called me in. Maybe we would have made a more comfortable knight's armor instead of your metal cupboard fitted with arms. Again you made your suicide plans and you want me to go feed some crocodiles. No sirs! I have already made my own plans and that's what I'm gonna follow, provided I'm still the one to recover your miserable rosary."

"Now that is blasphemy!" A member counter-exploded! "You shouldn't blaspheme. It is the Most Holy Rosary! Not miserable!"

Adams ignored him and said as a matter of take-it-or-leave-it, "I want the following, cavemen: (1) A light portable gas mask, (2) A can of nerve gas. Fluothan or neothyl would do. (3) A headlamp and finally (4) A helicopter service."

"What!?"

"I don't know how I can explain for you to understand, but one thing should be crystal clear right now. We're gonna do it my way or you wear your goddamn iron masquerade and go recover your…err… holy Rosary yourself."

Amid the rowdiness that ensued, the old papa, always serene, said, "okay, okay, my son. Explain what you need these for. Why the nerve gas?"

"To disable the crocs and other inhabitants of the cave during the time I'm gonna be busy doing my things in their valley."

"And such things exist and really work?"

"You just provide whatever I ask and I would do my own part of the job."

"Ok, but what about the gas mask?"

Adam shook his head and just asked genuinely, "Can you get a crocodile specific nerve gas? I mean a nerve gas specifically designed for crocodiles."

As none of them answered him he said, "cavemen, the gas mask is to prevent the gas from incapacitating me so that I can carry out my assignment down there. So the gas is meant only for the reptiles, not for me. I am going to wear the mask. You people should understand that. Simple enough…abi?"

"Ok, ok. We understand you now. But what about the helicopter?"

"Don't tell me sirs that you don't understand that as well."

"Em…emmm…"

"You want me to descend the valley on foot. Right?"

"It will cost a fortune!"

"I thought your rosary is worth more than the fortune of a generation. What is it that you are worried about? The necessity or the expenses?"

"But that thing makes noise. And we want to do this thing quietly."

"Have you consider how long it would take to descend the 3.5 kilos dangerously rough valley ground? The heli would get in in a fast operation and before the people realize what might be going on I'm in and out of the valley and we are outa there. They would get there later and find the rosary still shining and all their worries would be forgotten."

After much consultation with the members Father Gbashero said, "ok. If it is necessary we would provide it."

"Good." Adams began to explain, "The helicopter would hover above the valley while I get lowered down by a winch. I would spray the nerve gas to put our friends there out of action before I remove and replace the Rosary. The headlamp, of course lights up my way while affording me the opportunity to use both hands. Any clouds?"

"The only question is how do we get to acquire all these requirements? And still maintain secrecy?"

"I will make all necessary arrangements," replied Adams. "All you need to do is just provide the fund."

"I know a firm that can accept the helicopter aspect of the job," butted in a member called Fria Jillas and who was speaking for the first time since the commencement of the meeting, "they are close to me and in fact, they owe me a favor."

"Really Fria Jillas. That is wonderful then, oh gracious God?" Fria Maria replied surprisingly.

"And they would keep secrets. Guaranteed." Concluded Fria Jillas.

"Well, then," said Adams, "I guess we are now in business. Aren't we?"

<hr/>

The name Bwallangwu remains only a word, a dreaded one as that in some people's imagination. Very few know of its existence and extremely few had moved close, and certainly, none has ever seen him. This particular day, as usual, on Fridays, chief Enlaye was present in its very front, 2 meters away in front of the black curtain behind which the creature was talking to him.

"I have brought the most important information to you my lord, the mightiest of the mighties," trembled the chief in front of the black curtain. Then came the terrible voice that accompanied a somehow overlabored breadth which blew hard against the curtain.

"Enlaaayeeeeh!!!"

"My lord." Trembled the chief.

"You know very well that you should not bother me with trivialitiesssss."

"No, my Lord. It's certainly not a trifle. It is about the R R Ros Rosary."

"I am sure you are still aware of our situation concerning the Rosaryyy."

"Yes, my lord. We cannot by ourselves recover the legendary rosary from the valley of crocodiles because of the gimmicks of our enemies. So we have been waiting for their so-called holies to get it."

"Yes, Enlaaayeeeh, and our plan is simple uuuu."

"Yes, my lord. When they succeed we move in and snatch it from them."

"And if it becomes impossible for us to use it again…?

"We destroy it, my Lord, to make sure our enemies don't use it."

"Good, gooood, Enlaaayeeeh."

"I am honored, my lord."

"All their past attempts failed and for the last decade they have not made another."

"That is right, my lord."

"So why are you here to bother meeee?"

"Words came in this evening, my lord, that our enemies have scheduled another attempt for this week."

"Very gooood. This is news, Enlaaaayeeeeh."

"Thank you my lord."

"You know what to doooooh. Have your men available at all access to the valley to get the rosary from the holy bastard that goes in if he comes out alive with it. Don't forget the safe distance for you. As a result of this innate vibration phenomenon it is not safe for us to get closer than 20 meters radius of the valley. But the pure dog who goes in has to come out if he succeeeed. Is is not? Or would he sleep there for ever?"

"No my lord, Yes my lord he has to come out."

"Then get it from him. You know that is the only wayyyy or do I have to bring you back here for tutorial?"

"No, my lord. But this time the enemy is making his attempts from above."

"From where?"

"From above, my lord."

"From heaven?"

"No, no, my lord, he wants to use the helicopter."

Heli what? What is that?"

"Helicopter, my lord. Those flying machines that can hover, my lord."

"Hmmmn, is that what it is called?"

"Yes, my lord. They call it helicopter."

"I remember Leonardo Da Vinci made a sketch of something like that some decades ago and we laughed when he could not find material to make one yet. Has man finally found a way to make it?"

"Yes, my lord."

"And it works?"

"Yes, my lord. They have perfected it."

"And it will be used to take rosary from valley?"

"Yes my lord."

"Hmmmn, and do you have any problem with that?"

"Hmmn, my lord…emm,"

"It makes the job easier for you, Eeenlaayeeeh. Think, thinnnk, Ennlaaayeeeh."

Chief's Enlaye's 'my lord' response was drowned by the terrible deep breathy voice that threatened to tear the black tarpaulin curtain.

"You will not bother me with trivialitieees."

"No, my lord. I will not."

"All I want to hear next is the good news. That you have brought rosaryyyy."

"Yes my lord."

"Now, go, Eennnlaaayeeeeh I want to rest."

The first thing the chief did on getting home was to send for Jobilah.

⸺◆◆⸻◆⸺

CHAPTER 6

The replica they had made of their Rosary was missing and they had searched for it in vain. After another 2 hours of frantic search they had decided to call off the operation and re-schedule it for this particular day, giving the 14 days allowance for making another one. Every other arrangement was re-scheduled, especially the helicopter service that the influential Fra Jillas was able to convince without hassles.

This time around the prayer was rather short, well; at least, compared to the former one and Adams had kept his eyes open. Many of the others open their eyes quite often, occasionally and would quickly close them if they met the gaze of others. This is because the very first replica disappeared during the first benediction prayer, held for the successful recovery of the Rosary. As far as Adams was concerned this particular prayer session was perfunctory and not so necessary. Left to him alone they could have just referred to the last series of prayers which he believed had covered the whole mission. The last phrase had hardly been finished when all had opened their eyes which no doubt went straight in the direction of their Rosary in front of Father Gbashero who lead the prayer. And the later, even as he prayed had his left hand on the thing and when he had to raise his left hand the right hand went automatically on duty. These 'cavemen' according to Adams, had witnessed a lot of miracles but this last one concerning the disappearance of the replica right in their presence during prayers baffled and shook them.. It's like invisible forces had been operating in connection with their mission even before it started! All released a deep sign of relief by the time this second replica was eventually handed over to Adams. As if a heavy responsibility had been lifted off their shoulders and now over to Adams and they looked at him in sympathy as they waved him from the safety of their cave and wished him good luck. He departed with Friar Maria, first on foot, later by bus to the garage where they boarded a vehicle to Ile-Ife. They passed the day at Hotel Diganka as planned and by 2130hrs a Peugeot 403 arrived to pick them to the hangar.

Adams, seated at the back of the helicopter, looked out into the night and thought as he consulted his wrist watch, "these guys certainly are not in a hurry, but no qualms, the deeper the night the better." It was 0030 hours when the pilots were suddenly called back into the hangar for a 'very important message'. Time now being 0100 hours as they reappeared, he wondered that they were suddenly so eager this time around that they had even put on their helmets right from the hangar. The pilot mumbled some barely audible words of apology as they climbed up into their seat and one offered him a can of soda. They strapped themselves in and started the engine preparatory for takeoff. Thirty minutes later they were hovering above the valley.

"Yes, yes, go on down, down, down buddy," Adam encouraged the younger man doing the flying enthusiastically. Finally the giant iron bird was 3 meters above the flat ground but somewhere about 13 meters from the bottom of the valley where lay the Rosary, shining in its glorious iridescence, like the bright stars it forms, in the manner of the milky way..

Adams had put on his gas mask, strapped on his head lamp and got into the loop of the haphazard winch.

"Ready to go, boy?" asked the co-pilot who had assumed control of the winch. An aged man from the look.

"Yes I'm ready sir. Remember, please, a single tug on this control rope means stop; two tugs means lower while three hard consecutive tugs means pull up and please do not hesitate."

"Nothing to worry, boy. I have your back and good luck."

"My regards to the crocs, buddy," said the young captain enthusiastically.

Adam pulled once as he was lowered to about one and half meters to the bottom of the valley and he was stopped right there. He could notice the movement of the reptiles and he said to himself, "I wonder when they fed last." He opened the can and said one of the sayings he had not forgotten from the bible as he delivered their gift, "gold and silver I have not, but what I have I give onto you. In the name of the alchemists, sleep!" He sprayed and sprayed and waited until the last sluggish movement of the reptiles had stopped, and moving his head about to shine light on the surrounding he could see all reptiles lying flat on their bellies in soulless slumber. Gingerly he gave the rope 2 tugs and he was immediately lowered to the bottom, nursing the thought on the way down, "just suppose one or 2 of the crocs had acquired a gas mask?"

He quickly did what he had to do and had finished in a minute. He had put one shining Rosary in the little black sac and had spread out another in form of the Milky Way, the way he had found it. Let the devil be deceived, who gives a damn. Though the cheapest gas was eventually bought but equally effective and the effect was supposed to last about 3 minutes but, "what the hell!?" He had only spent a minute 25 seconds when he noticed one giant crocodile slowly raising its tail. "Holy Rosary!" he shouted as he yanked 3 times at the control rope. "Take me up! Damn it!" And of course the guys up there were not sleeping. They got the message and complied; only the journey up was a bit slower as gravity took its toll. He desperately pulled clear his legs as a big one came for them. No wonder, his premonitions, but thank God, he is safe, and the winch cable is strong enough. Shouldn't cut today of all day. No! God forbid.

Just a meter to the helicopter the winch suddenly stopped. He looked up into a powerful torchlight that was a good match for his headlamp, "What's the matter with the winch, brothers?"

"Nothing is wrong, boy. Winch is perfect except that we've gotta talk with you."

"What!? You wanna talk to me then pull me up, guys."

"No buddy, we talk like this," said the co-pilot.

"Yeah, perfect position to talk," added the captain.

"Some funny jokes!? Shit! It's late now for shit jokes, men. Pull me up and let's get the heck outa here!"

"You are the one wasting time, boy. Keep quiet and listen!"

"Shit, men, what the hell is it?"

"First put off your head lamp as the only light we wanna be seeing is ours."

"Jesus Christ! You guys going nuts?" He complied anyway.

"You see, fella, we have to have the rosary before we pull you up," declared the co-pilot.

"Why sir? Am I not coming up all the same?"

"We have our orders, boy. Might seem the boss doesn't trust you. You might not release it when you get to safety. So he wants us to have it before then."

"That's crazy, guys. C'mon!"

"Sorry, buddy, we are just carrying out our orders."

"And after you have the Rosary?"

"We pull you…..to safety!"

"I can't believe these cavemen can….."

"Look man, you hand over the rosary otherwise we don't pull you up. And for your info, our endurance is running out."

"Crazy. I don't like it when people don't trust me!" Adam said as he removed the little sac from his pocket and the co-pilot extended a hooked rod. "Take your miserable rosary!" he said angrily as he hooked the little sac onto the rod. "Now take me up! This is not the most comfortable of all positions at mid night."

"Ah boy, to safety. The boss said to put you to safety."

"And what are you waiting for?"

"Our boss, buddy, not yours."

"So?"

"Safety for you is not up here with us, but down there with your colleagues. Oh sorry, buddy, I used the wrong word, pull. It should have been push."

"You mad?"

"Sincere apology and since you are holy, you should have no

problems with your fellas down there. Safe journey buddy and say me well to them. I guess they are waiting for you. Bye, no hard feelings."

The winch was cut and, "Arrrrrrhaaaarrrh" Adams fell down the valley about 11 and a half meters away.

The giant machine pulled up and gained height as it flew away into the moonless darkness.

"Not too bad," the pilot said.

"Not too bad at all," replied the co-pilot, "and Bwallangwu will be pleased."

"It's nice doing business with you sir."

"My pleasure."

"And what's the name sir...em...for my invoice?"

"Jobilah."

———◆◈◆———

Fadi Zokalaus, pronounced, Zokalos sat at the bar of Simpas hotel, sipping his ogogoro gin as he waited for a call girl of his choice.

"You're new here I s'ppose," said an old man, with a pronounced emphasis on 's', across the table, dressing nearer and smiling in a kind of manner that repulsed the young man.

"Oh, you are right. I am new here, very new and I hate fagots."

The old man gulped his remaining drink and got out of sight. "Gaademn bloody ass licker," spat the young man. Moments later he caught sight of a girl and beckoned her, smiling.

"Hey, pretty, why don't you, for a change come and sit your little ass here by me and get treated to some drinks?"

"Not a bad idea, handsome," she replied, wasting no time, and moving close. "I enjoy seks[7] with 2 shots of ogogs.[8]"

"Barman!" Fadi called out, patting her buttocks, "a glass of sekete with 2 shots of ogogoro."

"Hmmm, handsome," sipping her drinks and snuggling closer, "you must be pretty new in this environment."

---

[7] Slang for Sekete.
[8] Local ging named ogogoro

"My second time of hearing that this evening."

"Problem with small towns. We all know each other sort of."

"Anyway, I came to town just 3 weeks ago"

"Really!?"

"Yeah, but why so surprised?"

'Hmmmn, to think that anybody could be in town for even a week without me knowing the person."

"I see. Small town really. But I didn't start coming here until 3 days ago." Fadi replied cautiously, giving her a thorough look.

"Then what the hell have you been doing wasting the hell out of sweet rosy life, handsome?"

Fadi felt the stiffened nipples against his shoulder, then the bulge in his trousers, smiled and put his hand around her shoulder, "No doubt, baby, all the days I've missed would be recovered tonight, huh."

She felt snuggled with him and pulling her very close, smelling her cheap perfume, he asked in a low tone, "you got any guy as handsome as this disturbing you tonight?"

"Honey, with you around, nobody dares move near me now." She replied, leaning on him and putting her hands around his neck. He gave her a peck and said as a matter of fact, "I'm gonna stay the night with you."

"That is cool, baby and I'm not expensive..." looking at him expectantly. "Baby, I'm gonna give you the wonders of your life. I take a hundred."

"C'mon baby, little ass," tapping her buttocks, "am I sure you are ready to work for a hundred bucks this night ...despite all you've gone through today?"

"What do you mean...c'mon man...you know I'll give you a nice time. You know I'm the best there is in town...em...you will find out," looking expectantly, rubbing his chest.

"Shall we put it this way? If you satisfy me, baby, I'll give you a hundred and fifty bucks in the morning."

"Whaooo! You bet your life I would!..Hmmm...why don't you give me a hundred now and fifty in the morning...sweetheart?"

Zokalaus smiled and counted money, "fifty now and some more tomorrow."

"No, handsome," snatching the money simultaneously, "bring some more. C'mon, what will I do with this?...I won't go...I won't do it."

Zokalaus opened his palm, "then give me back my money and I go find someone else while you go find yourself some dull oldies to cock your little bottle tonight." And pulling her up he added, "never mind the drink. My pleasure."

She sat down, drew close and pleaded, "please, can't you add something...little more...even twenty....?"

They finished their drinks and went upstairs into her room.

It was 2300 hours and they had already undressed when Zokalaus said, "you know something, baby?"

"What? Sweetheart?"

"I always drink some wine at the bedside before I sleep. Some old habit that has become character."

"Oh I like your style," excited, "I guessed right when I saw you! You are not like the rest....those cheap...very cheap dudes. Well, red, white...em which one shall I tell them to bring?"

"You like red?"

"I like all of them, and since you prefer red wine, then we make it red. You see,..but wait let me get the wine first." She put on something and dashed downstairs. He muttered, "her name is Patience, now she is being very impatient."

She soon came back with a bottle of red wine and 2 glass cups which she hurriedly filled up and, smiling, the man picked one and said, "you're breaking all the rules tonight."

"Rules? What rules?"

"First, these glasses are not for wines. These are more or less mugs. Secondly, and more important, baby, the man is supposed to serve the lady."

"Oh, fuck the rules. Who made them anyway?" They both laughed but he said by way of a replied, "I don't know for the white man, but since you are already breaking the rules, why don't you go get me a cup of water from the tap in the toilet."

"Water and wine together?"

"Obey first and then observe."

"Strange man." She got up and kind of dashed in and out of the toilet in seconds with a glass of water, but not fast enough to notice all the activities of Fadi Zokalaus. They drank the red wine and the man put the water on the bedside table, saying, "this is for midnight when I might get thirsty."

"I wondered," she had replied.

They made love afterwards and as soon as they finished, the girl fell into a very deep sleep. "Sleep well, baby, you need it." He got up and slipped into some dark wears which he took out of his hand bag. He opened the fake bottom of the bag to reveal an arrangement of concealable weapons. He took a knife, a pistol and a small bundle of rope, then closed the bag. He opened the window and smiled as he looked out into the dark quiet night. Then he tied the end of the rope to a leg of the bed, check the firmness before he lowered himself down onto the side walk below. Minutes later he had found his way into chief Agola's house, a couple of meters down the street. It was not all so uneventful. He had to break the neck of 2 guards and stabbed one to death. He moved silently and acted like lightening. He entered the chief's bedroom and found him snoring. He woke him up and covered his mouth and found it easy to persuade him not to make a sound and to open his safe. Of course the difference is clear between the man with the butt of a pistol and the one who has the muzzle on his neck. Agola acted obediently.

"No alarms, chief. I won't forgive."

Fadi got hold of the papers, briefly inspected them and nodded in satisfaction and no sooner than that he heard the siren of police. "I said no alarms!" He punched the chief who fell down unconscious. In a flash he had stooped down and cut off his balls. He got out through the back door as the police arrived.

The girl was as he left her, with something looking like a little smile of satisfaction in the corner of her mouth. He pulled off the black wears and mask which he stuffed together back into his bag and locked it.

He looked himself over, hesitated, and went into the water closet and moments later, he came out and slipped back into bed beside the girl.

Six o' clock in the morning he woke her up. She yawned lazily and a feeling of guilt and self disappointment already appearing on her face, gradually becoming sad. "Oh my gosh!.....I....I…"

"Never mind, baby. I know it's not your fault. Believe me. It must have been the rigors of the day."

"I must have slept off! ….and you didn't….baby, you should have woken me up…"

"I also slept off. It must have been the combination of ogogs and the red wine."

"Oh my God!"

"Never mind," as he counted one hundred naira, "take this for my likeness for you."

"Whaoooo! You are the best. I know it was my lucky day. Thank you so much. Oh, I am really sorry.."

"No, I say don't worry, but keep it to yourself, otherwise you know what the other girls are…"

"Ok, ok, ok all other times you come it's me. It's gonna be me always. Only me. Even when you are broke, I will understand."

Bending down to give her a peck and tapping her buttocks, he picked his bag and left.

<hr />

Chief Enlaye sat in his spacious office and smiled as he read the headlines and the front page of the Daily Sketch over and over. Jobilah entered.

"You called me, my lord."

"Oh, come right in, my Commander. Sit down." He was so hearty this morning and Jobilah was relaxed and happy for that. He laughed and Jobilah followed suit.

"Have you seen this? Ha, ha, ha, ha." Both laughed but Jobilah was on his toes, always ready to stop with precision.

"Coffee?"

"Yes sir, Thank you sir." Jobilah poured himself a mug of the black strong coffee.

"My young tiger is not doing badly at all....just..just look at this... ha..ha, ha, ha," both laughed, Jobilah being careful not to spill the coffee.

"He is really wonderful, my lord."

"And I must confess, I am particularly happy the way you handled the Rosary matter...ha, ha, ha, ha," Another laughing session, and of course a sort of parade for Jobilah to be performed with accuracy.

"I have the honor, sir, to have pleased Bwallangwu."

"And now, Jobilah, you know I always fulfill my promise. Agola's properties are now yours. Here are the papers."

Jobilah thanked, and smiled pleasantly as he went through the documents, an action he had to postpone as soon as his chief went into an unusual fit of laughter which he is totally unable to control and which could last sometimes for upwards of 5 minutes. This particular one was a four and a half minutes fit and when it subsided he said, "Jobilah, look at the headline. Read it, Jobilah, read it!" But then he was reading as well, and both were reading,

"KARL THE CASTRATOR STRUCK AGAIN! WANTED DEAD OR ALIFE! 500,000 NAIRA!"

Then he brought out another, the Daily Times. "Look at this one, Jobilah." Jobilah looked and both read together,

KARL THE BALL CUTTER AGAIN! AT LARGE AND WILD! SHOOT ON SIGHT! DANGEROUS! HALF A MILLION, DEAD OR ALIFE!

"Jobilah, let the police continue to look for their Karl, and we shall continue to look after our Fadi Zokaulaus, ha, ha, ha, ha, ha ha hu chu huchu hn, hi, hi, hi. pshi, pship, shi, sshi...." Here we go again and too bad for Jobilah. It seems this one would last up to 6 or more or even 10 minutes to come out of it.

Fadi Zokalaus lay on his back by the side of Lake Olubula Entertainment Resort, smoking and getting used to the fat cigar.

"This gaademn thing makes you open ya mouth too wide and gaademn flies are too indiscipline around here."

This way of speaking he also has to work on. "Heck! Too many regulations!" He caught the reflection of 2 girls as they walked along beside the clear blue water of the beautiful lake and one of them reminded him of Bimbi. He felt an urge he couldn't explain. An odd admixture of pain, anger and pleasure, blended together so perfectly that he couldn't differentiate them any longer. To him Bimbi has been the only girl equal to the task and who has the right tools at that. For all apparent reasons he had never set his eyes on her since the meeting at the prison yard or has she been kept away from him? Right now he couldn't even sincerely answer the question as to whether he would kill her or kiss her when and if he sees her again. The only unmistakable thing is that there lies in his heart a great yearning to get hold of her. Nevertheless, there has not been too much regret in his new life. Dull and uneventful at first, but the fact that he could stay and discuss among people hunting for his own very hide, hearing all their plans and schemes and be so free, as free as air, and could sometimes contribute in such discussions has become extremely interesting to him. It is such a fun he wouldn't want to miss for anything. The reality now is that all things being equal, he has become invincible. He is now virtually the invisible man. Certainly doctor Payida, the so much celebrated African laureate is truly a magician. To him, the doctor is the best plastic surgeon in the whole wide world. Dr Seyi Payida of the Bwallangwus. The Bwallangwu whose members only hear about and none that he knows has ever seen. Sure this Bwallangwu must be great, the only organization that could, "offer him the adequate protection." And that is a fact. They gave him a new face, a new look, a new outlook, a gap between the front teeth that has altered his way of pronunciations with an unusual emphasis on sss. They had even tampered with his vocal cord so that when Zokalaus speaks knees knock in fear. His left shoes are a centimeter higher than the right which has had an effect on the way he walks. To cap it all they gave him a new mind. The mind therapy thing or mind reprogramming to be explicit. The program instructions are still vividly audible in his mind. "....from now onwards you are not Karl. You might have heard of Karl but he is not you and you are not Karl. You will not respond to any mention of Karl, it does not concern you! Because you Fadi, you are not Karl. Fadi is not Karl! Fadi is Fadi and Fadi is better. You are Fadi Zokalaus, aged 28, born in Modakeke in 1957 of Mr Augustus Zokalaus a palm wine tapper and Mrs Rebecca Ojuolape Zokalaus, a bush meat trader. Both parents are dead. They died in the Modakeke and Ife fight. All the habits of Karl are forgotten and forbidden. From now onwards you breathe, eat, sleep, walk and think like Zokalaus. Unlike Karl who is fond of eating coconuts and guguru (roasted corn) with booli(roasted plantain),you Zokalaus prefers instead boiled yam and red oil. Unlike Karl who when in toilet is fond of standing instead of sitting on the commode, you Zokalaus will from now on do the right thing. You Zokalaus has made a habit to never eat in between meals, and you will prefer pounded yam to apu. You will drink wine and liquor and no more burukutu."

As a matter of fact, Zokalaus is different from Karl. Everything has changed from that of Karl. Even the way he does his things, well some drillings but certainly no more earth quakes. The greatest surprise about the reality and authenticity of this Man Zokalaus came when he went to vote with his voters' card and everything just went neat.

CHAPTER 7

It was 0200 hours, raining cats and dogs. Terrible wind and thunderstorm. A frightful night it really was. Friar Maria lay unusually closer to the woman who in turn, more out of fear than any desire to be cuddled, held on very tight. They had both ended the recitation of psalm 93 when they were aware of a rush of wind and waterlets into the sitting room.

"Oh gracious God! We must have forgotten to close some of the louvers!" Getting up hurriedly, the clergy man said, "I'll be right back, my dear." She let go of him as he slid out of bed and she held tight the pillow in place. Friar Maria went towards the wind direction, located the opened louvers and closed them tight. He turned to hurry back into the comfort of the woman's bosom when a strong hand held him from the back and covered his mouth and a muffled voice spoke. "Don't make a sound, Father Maria. Just cooperate. I'm not here to harm you."

The clergyman shrunk in fear and surprise and when the pressure of his mouth was released he managed to whisper, "who are you? What do you want?"

"Tell your friend in that room to wait, that you have to go into the toilet."

"She is my wife!"

"You are wasting time!"

"Dorcas!," he called out above the sound of the rain, "hold a second darling, I have to ease myself. I'll soon be by your side. Don't be afraid."

"Who the hell s afraid? Dummy!" she yelled indignantly. "come back at day break for all I care!"

"Something I learnt over the years. You hurt her pride she would do all you want her to do unwittingly." Friar Maria volunteered submissively.

"Move over to the toilet." The man relaxed hold on him completely. The Friar was still not sure of his own state of mind suggested by the numerous times he kept looking back over his shoulders at this figure who seemed somehow familiar. He opened the door to the toilet and as he flicked on the light switch he jumped, hands held up in front in a kind of defense at the sight of a masked man who slowly walked behind and closed the door behind them.

"Relax," the man told the clergyman who seemed to be drilling his back into the wall at the corner of the toilet.

"Who are you?" He managed to ask."

"Never mind, you would know later. First, I want you to tell me what happened to Adams."

"We were told the nerve gas did not last in effect for thirty seconds.…That before he could perform at all any aspect of the mission the crocodiles recovered and…and…oh my God…ate…him.."

"That is a good story, and a credible one for that matter. Now," moving towards him, "tell me your own part!"

"My what!?" Trying furtively to disappear through the wall. "And he was the one that made provision for that gas himself…"

"Tell me your own role!"

"My role…err…was to escort him as far as the valley but for the terrible diarrhea that prevented me…only to hear afterwards the saddest news of my life. I was sick instantly and for 3 good weeks. Not the diarrhea but I just broke down and disillusioned. I couldn't bear it…the thought that I brought such a good boy into this…that I killed him. Disillusioned… …he is pure…not supposed to die. So confused now about my faith. I don't even know what to believe any longer. May

God forgive me…I didn't mean to hurt him….Such a nice boy…..such a good heart…such…"

"Save all that for later and thanks for the sympathy. Incidentally I believe you. I know you were actually sick. You were admitted at Graceland hospital. I saw you there and I read your sick report. You suffered from high blood pressure. You were discharged at 0900 hours Tuesday morning but you had to wait till the end of environmental sanitation before you came home."

"Haaah! You know all these?…How do you know….exactly!…. everything to details!"

"Let's just say I wouldn't be able to answer that now because I'm not sure who I am yet.. One thing I can assure you about your disillusionment is that your faith is true and genuine. So don't lose it. But listen, you good, innocent but ignorant ex-clergy. You have been used. By who exactly I assure you I'm gonna find out. There is a traitor in your cave. A dangerous reptile among you cavemen. Nevertheless I still choose to trust you partly because of your hospitalization but mainly because of my inner convictions. I could be wrong but I would find out, won't I Friar?"

"My God! I could never harm that boy…but the gas…the nerve gas…was…"

"Bought and tested before he was given."

"Oh God! But what must have happened?"

"The only thing we know that happened is that he did not return plus some cock and bull stories behind it. But we shall find out the whole truth in due course."

"Oh Jesus of Nazareth! …But who are you?" And as the man was just looking at him, not replying, he added, "and you look…."

"Like the boy?"

"Exactly…Not exactly but certain…."

"You can regard me as his guardian angel, a ghost perhaps or you might even suspect that the boy had a twin brother who has come to avenge his brother's death or simply a maskman who cannot afford to reveal his identity for now for very important reasons."

"Well," said the Friar resignedly, "I may not understand your motives, whoever you are, but if you are truly on the side of the good then the God of the good would protect you in each step you take. For I thought what started had come to an abrupt end with the death of that good boy but it might just be…em..”

“That the drama has just commenced old man. What has happened so far are just preambles and preparations. Let nobody make no mistake about it. The game has just begun!”

“And God the omnipotent shall be with you.” He said with a ray of hope reemerging in his face. “Was He not the one who protected Jonah in the belly of a fish for 3 days…3 days!,” showing 3 fingers in demonstration, “Was He not…”

“Yeah Daniel and lions. Save all that, old cargo. If that god were all you claim him to be then why the hell does he allow all these problems to occur in the first place before deploying valuable resources to resolve them? Afterthought, huh?”

“Well, my son, whoever you are,” Friar Maria replied solemnly, “Even if I had the insight to provide answers to your spiritual questions I might not possess the wisdom and the right words to convey such to your mind and thus be able to convince your curious searching, permit my use of naïve, mind, but what I know for sure is that the Almighty himself will reveal himself in some ways to his worthy soul and at his own time. You see, son, the whole thing is a riddle, much like a code encompassing several laws including and especially karmic, both individual and collective societal. And the Lord is both mathematical and sequential in action, just and impartial. He surely will make Himself revealed to his people as they deserve and we shall see how we are part of the causes of what happen…”

“Save this preaching for the church, old clergy,” changing countenance, “Who are those helicopter pilots? And how do I get them?”

“I don’t know them…I didn’t see them….you know…my diarrhea…toilets…”

“Who was that holy man in your cave who recommended the firm?”

“That day in the cave?”

"Whichever the hell the day! Someone recommended the firm! Isn't it"

"Oh yes! That was Friar Cardinal Jillas Mansuri. He is the one that knows connections of such nature. A man of reputation."

"Never mind, he may soon have to defend that."

"You might still require helicopter service?...Errr...another attempt.....errr", expectantly looking at the masked face. The rain had stopped and consulting his watch and noting that it was getting to dawn, the young man said as if in response, "I have to go but before I depart oldl man, I am sure you want to live older, if at least to see the end of this thing."

"By God's grace! If He wishes."

"Then this should be between us. Remember that if the traitors can hurt me they would hurt you as well. You have to keep very secret this sudden night call of mine and any matter concerning this discussion tonight and many more that might follow later. I wouldn't want to hurt any soul, including you, clergy. So don't bring about the ugly situation."

"But what are you going to do now?" He held him by the arm as if he was suddenly going to disappear like a ghost, "all is lost now, isn't it?"

"It will depend on a lot of things but I don't really think all is lost yet. But what has happened has convinced me that your Rosary is genuine and some if not all the myth about it. The cave men are not the only ones interested in it. It includes the modern town dwellers."

"*Yeepa! Awon iran Orishadami!*[9] All is lost…"

"Not really yet. But first I must find out the traitor, investigate these sons of Orishadami and possibly, bring back the Rosary. And for these to be done with minimum obstacle, clergy, I have to remain a secret. So keep me a secret."

"I promise you in the name of God."

"You can't even afford to breathe it out to anyone. Don't discuss it even in your dream. Those people are everywhere. By the way your sudden attack of diarrhea was planed. To show you how ubiquitous they are." The strange man emphasized to make the man understand

---

[9] The generations of Orishadami

the seriousness of the situation. And before he disappeared, the old man asked, "How do I contact you? …just in case I hear or discover something useful…"

"It's like you would be more useful than I thought."

"Body and soul. Anything you need."

"You are still the bell man, aren't you?"

"Yes, for the past 6 years now since I was pushed out of office. Why?"

"And as far as I know, the pattern of your ringing, especially for the early Morning Prayer has been very consistent."

"By His mighty grace."

"So do not suddenly change that pattern except when you have something for me."

<hr>

Chief Enlaye woke up this morning a trifle too hearty. The previous day he had been given permission to go ahead with his much coveted life ambition by Bwallangwu. An ambition he had kept so secret even almost from himself. Except from Bwallangwu. He had immediately sent for Jobilah.

Making Jobilah sit in his front and he himself sipping brandy, the chief had suddenly become normal, "I want operation PAKUFINRIN executed in 6 weeks.."

"What! But sir, is it not too early? Considering election is still about 6 months away."

"I know but I have my reasons, hmmn, best known to me. But, Jobilah, I will let you know later. Besides, I suspect there are more in number than we accounted for and if we make all our moves almost within the same period it's definitely going to be too obvious and, of course prone to greater risk. So it makes sense to allow enough time in between attacks to cool things down….to avoid suspicion…"

"Yes, my lord, I see your point. Only I was under the impression that you were not going to do it in this manner."

"And I want Aborungun first."

"Aborungun!? Sir Aboripe Aborungun!?." Jobilah exclaimed in surprise and hoping the chief would smile and tell him it was a joke.

"Oh yes, yes Jobilah. Why are you surprised?"

"But he is not on the list!"

"I have just included it! He is on it now and so are some others."

"Why sir, if I may ask?"

"Did you just ask me that…er…I beg your pardon."

"No sir. I only just…err…in fact I don't know what I said sir."

"I am in a very good mood today, so Jobilah, don't spoil it."

"No sir. Not at all, my lord."

"I'm sure you remember my birthday?"

"But sir, if we have to hit Sir Aboripe Aborungun it has to be the last."

"Why so?"

"An attack on chief Aborungun could definitely mean a war!"

"A war! So let it be. Who is afraid of war? Aboripe's war? Who is afraid of Aboripe Aborungun's war? You, Jobilah, maybe…."

"*Emi ke?*[10] No chief, no sir, far from it. It's not fear, but caution. We are not prepared."

"What do you mean? Not prepared?"

"I mean…er…we haven't got the means."

"And what do you mean by that?"

"Weapons! You know, my lord, the chief rarely moves and when he does, it's a convoy of arsenals. And we haven't got the means to outfight him if it comes to that."

Now looking at him intently straight in the face, as if down into his very being, the kind of gaze that has always sent Jobilah's knees knocking against each other, the chief outputted, "Jobilaaah it seems your belief is at variance with mine….hmmmn…what a pity. But let me tell you what I believe first. Maybe that would help you in your own interpretations and orientation. Jobilah,"

"My lord,"

"To me the word 'means' refers to you.. Once I have you, Jobilah I

---

[10] Myself?

have 'means'. Simple! Once Jobilah is around and alive and still willing to serve Bwallangwu, I lack nothing. Aaaah, but for Jobilah now to turn around to tell me that we don't have 'means' is a pity....unfortunate...," now raising his voice, "and if Jobilah does not initiate the process of reconciling his own belief with mine immediately it could become something more unfortunate! Jobilaaaaaah!!!!" Like a dragon, the chief could have spat fire.

"Well...er...my lord, ...oh yes, my lord, after all, man's greatest means is his mind. In fact, it would only take some concentration, hmmmn, some deep thinking concentration and meditation to evolve solutions to any kind of problem, however urgent and complicated."

"So what are you waiting for? Think, start thinking, Jobilah. Meditate and concentrate!"

"Of course, my own chief....if not just this little thing that has been disturbing my faculties, creating a lot of diversions and blocking the deep profound meditation that is required to bring right from the depth a solution for this sort of..."

"Hmmmn, Jobilah, have I not given you Agola's properties?"

"Chief, yes and I thank you so much but with the estate in my possession and a beautiful girl such as Toun as my mistress I would think and be lost in meditation from Gbongan to Mecca and Jerusalem."

"You are becoming a pain in the ass, Jobilah. *Howu. Alaseju alejo, a fun un l'onje tan, oko re tun nle!*"[11]

"Sorry, chief. Pain ke? In the ass...of my chief? Oti o. God forbid I become a pain in my own chief's honorable ass! *Rara o Oloun ma je!*[12] Only it's just the thing that has been haunting my desire so to say and from past and present experiences such desires not fulfilled constitute a formidable barrier in the way if creative thinking and profound meditations....and who else apart from you my chief can I run to for help?" and shrugging in resignation, "but if the chief does not see it that way then I would have no other choice than to withdraw my request and try my utmost best to meditate....I wouldn't...,"

---

[11] Yoruba witty saying. 'Expectations unbecoming of a visitor; after satisfying him with food his prick is rising.'
[12] God forbid!

"Jobilah!"

"Yes, my lord,"

"You handle Operation PAKUFINRIN successfully then you can rest assure of a successful retirement in the estate with the queen of your desire."

Jobilah prostrated full length. "Oh my honorable lord, chief Jeremiah Ogiripua Enlaye. You are next to Bwallangwu. Once you have me, Jobilah Okworikwo, you have 'means'. Consider Operation PAKUFINRIN successfully executed. I will handle it like magic."

"Yeees, yes, magic. That's what I want. Exactly."

"Heeeh, chief. Work has started. I have started thinking., In fact, chief, I will soon be lost in the deepest meditation that to bring me back to surface will require...require one Imam, *babalawo to gbona*[13] and a pastor of the C and S who might have first mistake me for somebody who has died for forty days and forty night..."

"Jobilaaah!" As a matter of fact it was his chief's shout that brought him back to surface. He was already lost in the deep. "You will not clown with me!"

"Never!" Now more sober, "I should be able to brief you on a sketch plan by tomorrow evening sir. There are some things I like to sleep over. Do not worry sir. Your belief has been right all along. Once you have me you lack nothing. You have 'means'. You have everything you need and I will never disappoint you."

Of course, Jobilah dared not disappoint. He dared not break his promise. The second day he was with his chief in the evening, with the sketch plan.

"This is a rough sketch of Sir Aboripe Aborungun's convoy party," he said, using a diagram. "This, this and this leading armored vehicles are armed with 9mm machine guns and bazookas. This and this following them are missile launchers; this is the radar, em ...the launcher is a radar controlled missile launcher and this one is the control vehicle, a C4V for that matter."

"C4V?"

---

[13] A witch doctor that is very sound.

"Oh yes sir, Command, Control, Communications and Computers Vehicle," Never missing the opportunity to show off, Jobilah continues with ostentations, "It's the Command Post and is commanded by a retired colonel. The vehicle is an American Dodge Ram and is completely bullet proof. These ones keeping the wake are armored cars like the ones in the front but this one among them is a tank buster and these two are communications land rovers. He is armed to the teeth and has built in enough redundancies. The chief is either found in his car positioned here and of course, bullet proof or in the Command Post, the C4V. He takes no chances. In fact 6 of his men have their only job of pressing buttons to alert police in emergencies and to bring in his own reinforcements. He keeps these men widely separated in the convoy and they don't know each other."

"Impressive," commented Chief Enlaye silently. "He really prepares for war."

"These, nevertheless does not mean that he is not vulnerable, my chief. Even the armored reptile alias crocodile has a soft underbelly. All we need is weapons, men and the right time to use them, of course with a good strategy and tactics. *Howu, a kii saa gbon bi eni tin tan ni*[14]. Toto, o se bi owe o." Jobilah paused and coughed before he drops his demands. "My chief, all we need is weapons...arsenal, and this is a list of our basic minimum requirements. Roughly estimated at $15m"

"Whaat!? Fifteen Million American Dollars!? Just to get a man!?

"Sir it is Sir Aboripe Aborungun. He is not just a man. He is more than a battalion!"

"We don't really need all this," going over the list for the fourth time. "We don't have to match him weapon to weapon before we can get him. Remember, Yorubas say 'ogbon ju agbara lo! Wisdom surpasses power. What matters is not only what you have but how you use it."

"Honestly, chief, I have been ransacking my grey matter since yesterday and I am still thinking, my lord."

"Think more!"

"In which case we can play for more time till I ...."

---

[14] A man deceiving us is always one step ahead.

"Six weeks!"

"Anyway, chief, if we must fight now, at least we must have this, these, this and these," showing him on the list, "certainly adding up to 8 million dollars."

"We can only spend five."

"Then we must get the rest 3 million from somewhere and chief I already worked out a plan to that effect.....subject, of course to my chief's approval anyway."

"That's why I like you. Let me hear it," the chief brightens up.

"We will collect it from chief Bobade."

"Bobby Nero? Are you alright!?" looking at Jobilah from head to toes and at the level of the brandy in his cup. *Bobby ko se awo wa*."[15]

"Yes chief. We will collect it from Bobby Nero. He will give us chief."

"And how do you convince him to do just that?"

Jobilah now showing off, "I just discovered that he loves his daughter more than his own stupid light complexioned ass."

"Haaah, ah aah! I think I am beginning to believe there is a lot more in your head than I accounted for. Go on, keep talking." But before Jobilah could say another word the chief had entered a session of that laughter, "hahahaha! Hithithithit tchutchuctchuchu!" and jobilah tagged on.

"Oh hoh hoh, my chief thought I stole his brandy before, hahaha hauhauhau" And he stopped no more than half a second after his chief stopped. Practiced accuracy.

"Go ahead and talk to me, my Jobilah. Refill our glasses first and talk. Put ice and lemon for me." He hurriedly gulped what remains and Jobilah collected the cup. Jobilah never liked better this rare mood of his chief. He can get anything he wants from him on such occasions and pouring himself a greed fill, he continued.

"So my chief, we can even ask him to borrow us 5 million and I strongly believe he would oblige us just for the simple favor we are going to do for him....the return of his daughter..."

---

[15] Bobby is not in our secret.

"Borrow…yes, yes…borrow! That's the right word!." At this point he went into a frenzy, shaking and vibrating with uncontrolled or rather a controlling laughter which would leave him with tears in the eyes, tired and helpless in the next 5 or 6 minutes. Jobilah seized the opportunity to do justice to the brandy.

———◆◆◇◆◆———

Chief Johnson Bobade, popular among his friends as Bobby, sat with his wife, Susan in the big living room. A more than averagely happy family, to say the least. The chief is not too happy about the prospect of their daughter, Angela, going to stay on her own. But after much persuasion, especially from his wife whose thinking is that, with her daughter out of the way, her husband might have some more affection for her, he resigned to the turn of events.

"After all, Angy is 21," she pleaded, "she is a big girl. She can take care of herself, and when a kid is growing up, my dear, we have to give her a free hand."

"Hmmmmn. All those useless boys going about in tattered jeans," the chief now voicing out where it pains him."

"But that is vogue. Don't be old fashioned, darling."

"They dd don't even wear pants."

"Oh Johnny, don't be ridiculous…remember she has invited us to dinner tomorrow. Our Angel does not keep bad company. You know that already, don't you? Besides, we have even brought her up well."

Yes. I know that my Angy is a good girl," self consoling, "and what time are we expecting her today?"

"I have told you 3 times already today, Johnny. She would be here one thirty. Just about 2 more hours."

"Okay." He reached for the phone and after a reply, said, "yes, this is me. I want you to cancel my appointment and reschedule it for 7:30 in the evening.

For Chief Bobade, Angela, his dearest daughter, is ever on top of his priority list. He seems to be existing for her.

Ten minutes to two, the black Mercedes 500S rolled in noiselessly and stopped gracefully in front of the big estate mansion. The chauffeur quickly came around to open the door for the sensational master's daughter. The poor man swallowed so hard he almost swallowed his Adams apple as he caught sight of her ankles which she stretched out gracefully to come out of the car. Gathering her gown, she quickly ran inside and the next few minutes witnessed her being hugged and kissed in turn by loving father and relieved mother. Pretty soon, the trio were well seated at table enjoying her favorite dish - amala and ewedu.

"Thank you, papa. My flat is looking wonderful," she said excitedly.

"Don't talk while eating, Angy. You might..."

"But it was you who was even laughing so terribly at table yesterday.." getting back at her mother.

"Naughty girl."

"You too will not start again. You will let me enjoy this amala...huh?"

"You better talk to your daughter."

"By the way, I am yet to have the bill."

"Oh, papa, it's just three hundred and fifty thousand naira but I have to pay in cash for the aquarium as it's not included."

"And how much is the aquarium, love?" Susan asked.

"The best among the lot is twenty five thousand naira with the golden fish. But there are cheaper ones....."

"No! You will have the best."

"Oh! Thank you, my dearest papa," with a hug and a peck on the cheek, "I will never separate from you. Never!"

"You would pour ewedu on his laps ooo," cautioned Susan with a tinge of jealousy.

"But of course, you are already leaving me, having decided to go and stay away alone."

"No, papa, but I will always come home."

"And you are always welcome, my love. Any time." Holding her close.

"And papa,"

"Yes sweetie," swallowing the ball of amala in his mouth smoothly as the ewedu made it so frictionless.

"I...I ...met a boy who..."

"I know! I know!" The particular ball of amala in his mouth made a free fall and landed roughly at the bottom of the stomach. "All these useless, brainless, jobless boys who want you for yyyy your beauty and mmmmm money!"

"Johnny!" his wife called out. "C'mon, John!"

The chief stammers a lot when he is excited. He couldn't eat his food any longer and the much feared thing eventually happened. He poured ewedu on his laps. "If ff I s ss s see en en anybodddy m messing arrround with my my m my y you I w wil kkk kill him. I swear! An an and hhe wwill die."

"Of course, if you kill him he will die," Susan, said as she led him away to wash off and change. By the evening all had quietened down and Angela was ready to leave. Another episode of hugging and kissing, these ones more passionate as of departure rather than that of arrival. This time around a black Cadillac took her away.

The drive to her flat was not supposed to be more than fifteen minutes but they spent much time on the way buying a lot of things especially those that mama told her to stop eating. Eventually they arrived at the luxurious flat.

"Would you carry these upstairs please?" She demanded of the driver.

"Yes, of course, Miss Bobade." Responded the driver. His arteries nearly bust open as they stood in the rather too small cabin of the lift. She had to open the front door for the driver whose hands were occupied with the stuffs he carried for her, and entering after him she had flung her hat over the settee and had loosened her hair in her usual carefree attitude once she is out of her mother's site.

"Please put the stuffs in the kitchen for me, would you?"

"Yes miss B.." The rest never came out as a strong hand rammed his head on the walls. He went limp immediately, bleeding from the nose. Almost immediately another hand had grabbed Angela from behind, covering her mouth and nose with a handkerchief soaked in chloramphenicol. Emerging from the kitchen the tough looking man opened the window, looked down and signal to some men coming out of a parked bus with a mattress which they quickly held at the corners firmly to received a parcel coming down the 2 storey building. As he picked up the limp girl effortlessly he told his burly second to, "get the hell outa here!" And as the latter went out through the door he threw the girl down. She was caught expertly by the men down below. They put her in the bus and all entered, including Fadi Zokalaus who had jumped down through the same window.

◆━◆◆◆◆━◆

Chief Bobade was uncontrollable. Practically berserk. Susan had fainted repeatedly. The police couldn't get much information from the driver whose only input was nothing more than that a strong hand had grabbed him from the back so he couldn't see his face. For the fifth time he was interrogated at the hospital and he was able to add a little more piece of information; that the person was very fast. All the while the chief was bouncing, twisting and wriggling like a snake thrown into fire, Mrs. Sue Bobade had been brought to the same hospital after her several fainting sessions and had now recovered.

"Mmmmmy d ddd daughter! T T this ttown is no mmore safe ffor dd decent pp people!" Chief Bobade continued to stammere.

"We assure you sir," said the police, "we will do our best. We will bring your daughter back home to you."

"H hh hurry up with yyy your b b b best. This is ttthe second dd day I c can't sseee anything yy yet."

The third day the chief had a call.

"Is that your honor, chief Bobade? "Demanded the grater-rough voice of the caller, the note of mockery slightly discernible.

"Y yes. Who is calling?"

"The newspapers carry very interesting news headlines and beautiful pictures nowadays. Especially the Daily Tribune of yesterday. Her picture is so beautiful and I wonder why they didn't put her on page three."

"W who the hell is this?"

"Pity she was not dressed for it but despite that she still looks sensational."

"Look here you funny m man." Anger now mixed with frustration and expectation. "Who the hhhell are you!?"

"We also watched the television, you know. And the beauty is ever more captivating."

"Look h here you…" Anger now taking the upper hand.

"No, no, don't hang up, Just relax,.,for your own good, Chief Bobby, relax."

"What the…"

"Chief, you would have to keep those newspapers for her pictures. I mean you will need the pictures but we wouldn't because we have her life with us."

"What! Who is this!? Hello, hello! Who the hell is there?" The line was dead. The chief dropped the receiver and sank into a settee, thinking millions.

Through the window of a room in a nearby hotel a man watched the chief with a pair of binoculars. "How is he doing, buddy?" asked his partner.

"He is sweating," replied the man.

"Good for his health; he is getting fat. Give him a minute and give him another call."

The chief got up nervously, paced up and down, seemed not to know what to do except turning around in the same spot. He almost hates his wife by now but first thing first. Suddenly the phone rang again and it was remarkable the speed at which he picked up the ear piece.

"Hello! Who is it?"

"You damn well know who it is!" It was the very rough voice that shouted down the line.

"What…w whoo are you?"

"Oh Bobby…thinking of your daughter? I am sure you want her back."

"Yes! What do you want? Please…"

"Simple thing, Bobby. Just five million."

"Five million naira, I will give you now. Just tell me…"

"Dollars! Bobby! You want your daughter?"

"Yes! Yes!"

"You get 5 million dollars ready and wait along Ife-Ibadan express way at exactly 0900 hours in the morning tomorrow. Got it?"

"Yes but where and how would I know you?"

"Just get the dough ready and wait for further instructions."

"Ok."

The next call was 0600 hours on Tuesday. He answered immediately.

"You will see a blue Peugeot 505 LA2404HF some 5 kilos from Ikire. Raise your cap 3 times as a sign. We will be there with your daughter. And you listen! No police. Get it?"

"Yes…yy..but, hello, hello..Oh shit!" The line was dead again.

At exactly 0845 the big Cadillac was by the Ife-Ibadan express way, about 5 km from Ikire, as they said. Not given the exact place to meet the kidnappers, apart from that inaccurate description of the location, he had chosen a place he thought was secret enough which is close to an uncompleted building at Wasimi. A few meters away and hidden from view are the police, 6 of them well armed. The chief had been working with the police and they had set a trap for the 'bastards' as he described them.

"And since they want you to raise your cap as a signal then we might as well use that as our own signal to gear into action." The chubby police boss had said, smiling at his own cleverness. "And you don't worry, chief, we will nail the bastards and get your daughter for you."

"W what d do you mean you get m my daughter for me?" The chief looked hard on him. "D don't go and do anything c contrary to what we have planned to do. You will wait till I get my daughter safely before you show yy your police ff face!"

"Chief, don't worry. It will work out fine?

"Just don't do anything to endanger my daughter's life. Follow our plans."

"Chief, the plan is well rehearsed and we know our job. All will go just perfect. Hmmm, simple job. Don't worry."

"W When they kidnap your own d daughter you can relax and

don't worry and call it ss s simple. I I will not relax until I get my daughter back."

Left to the chief alone, kidnappers are not supposed to be arrested alive and not having enough confidence in the police he had arranged his own team, quite unknown to the police. He had given them a final order before departing Gbongan that morning.

"You make sure that my daughter is with me before you start shooting. If you people injure my daughter I will kill you. And if you kill any policeman I don't know you. You hear? Especially you, Sunny, that closes your eyes when shooting."

"No sir."

"We don't know from which direction the bastards will come but I have arranged for 2 bulldozers to block the road in front and at the rear when we see them come out of the bush. They will just come out of the bush path onto the road when we give them the signal. So y you with the walkie talkie d d don't fail and that is why I have given you 12 walkie talkies. All of them cannot fail at the same time and if you fall asleep jj just continue like that because if you wake up I w will kk kill you!"

Chief Bobade had never sweated in the dry season scotching sun like he did on this day in his life, not even as a road worker in his suffering days before he made his money. He had never in his life been so frustrated and disappointed. He had to yield at last to the pressure of the police, who had become so tired and bored to death, to go back home after waiting for six hours and thirty minutes. His sleep that night was all sorts of nightmares. His wife, Susan had recovered and had been so sad and restless, more so from chief blaming her for the kidnap of his daughter. As a matter of fact one wouldn't be too wrong to think that poor Susan might have delayed her own recovery. The chief had opened 2 of his mails and had spent more than 15 minutes on each trying to understand the contents. He opened the third, this time a very small parcel and, while his eyes bulged out on seeing the content, the phone rang and the voice was familiar, only rougher and meaner.

"Chief Bobade! Do you recognize what you are seeing in the parcel?"

"Well..a finger nail…"

"Of course, you can recognize your daughter's nail."

"But bbbbbb…"

"I said no police and I meant no police. That finger nail is to give you a benefit of doubt. Next time you try nonsense you will be receiving the finger itself."

"But bb the police…" the phone was dead. Very soon it rang again. "Hello, are you there?"

"It seems you don't know how serious the situation is. This time it is six million dollars! Understood? If you want her alive!"

"Yes yes! I will give you…you just don't hurt her."

"No police!" and the phone was dead.

"Hello, hello!" Oh mm my God!"

Susan was yet to make up her mind whether to ask him what has transpired between him and the kidnappers or to just keep quiet, and when she finally mustered courage and asked, the chief yelled, "they want me to thank you for making it possible the kidnapping of mm my daughter."

CHAPTER 8

The ringing of the big bell had been noticeable different this morning. Some people might have wondered what got hold of the retired clergy man turned bell man, but anyway it was dead on time. So what the hell?

Though the full moon makes clandestine movement in the night rather difficult, it also makes shadows. The masked man stole into Friar Maria's house without difficulty and he found the latter waiting for him.

"How is your wife?"

"Sleeping like a baby that she is. I gave her some sleeping tablets... hmmmn...necessity. God forgive me."

"Everybody does what is necessary, so what a hassle?"

They had talked for a long time. The clergy man had discovered some evidence that points out Cardinal Jillars Mansuri as the double dealer in the cave, but the people he deals with are still unknown to him. "I'll keep on looking."

"Yeah. You keep looking, old man. You might even find something not really connected but that would prove highly useful."

"Serendipity."

"Look, Friar, for a long time I've become certain that your adversaries are not just some other primitive group at the opposite end struggling for some Rosary. There is more to it. They are big, real big. They penetrate everywhere. Imagine the helicopter issue and your diarrhea. They are even right there in your very cave which I may regard as your headquarters."

"Oh my Jesus!" Making many signs.

"And when you are up against such people you've got to get more active, otherwise, a sitting duck, they catch you up and wipe you out. I am sure they are waiting for the right time to do just that."

"But the Lord almighty has not allowed that to happened and would not. Never! He will always protect us."

"You seem so certain."

"Because we are existing for a purpose."

"So you just sit and fold your hands"

"All we need is faith and prayers."

"If that is the case why do you need me? You do not understand. Even the lord's people have always been very good warriors. Your holy book is full of such testimonies. Prayers help but David still had to come out and threw the stone, hmmmn… some catapult…"

"Are you suggesting that we degenerate to the extent of fighting against our brothers?"

"Yes if necessary. It is called self defense. A God-given right."

"God is defending his people."

"The angels of God, under the able leadership of Archangel Michael had to fight against Satan's forces when it was found necessary. Don't you understand? That is the problem I found with you people! This group of yours!"

"But when we are attacked we can fight back."

"How can you fight effectively if you don't know how to fight? You think such fight is traditional wrestling?"

"So what are suggesting?"

"You train and prepare."

"Are you trying to change our nature or what else are you suggesting?"

"Adaptation or evolution."

"I have grown used to you as a young man exactly like Adams, full of divine spirit and who would never hurt a fly."

"You are wrong, I still kill mosquitoes and I would not hesitate to blow the neck off an armed robber. What would you do in your own case? Kneel down in front of him and start praying for him as he cuts off your neck? Ooold man, the God who has given you this precious life would not blame you for exercising your right to defend it. Acting otherwise would be the apex of folly and ignorance, provided you like and appreciate the life anyway."

"The Lord Jesus still prayed for them who were killing him."

"I am not comparing myself to Jesus and I don't think you should either. But it's up to you. Look, Jesus had a mission and he was well aware of it and without his will, oldie, I don't think anybody would have been able to harm him. I think my own mission is different. I am no messiah and if I am I have not been told by God. I can't even perform any other miracle apart from putting something in my mouth to relief hunger and I don't think you and your other cave members are any different, if you are not deceiving yourself. Look man, if you allow your enemy to kill you now you die for nothing. Worse still, God should punish you for allowing a bad man to decimate the number of those on the good side. It doesn't make sense! Yours can never be like that of Jesus, so stop pretending it is!"

"You're confusing me but somehow seem to make some sense, though childish but what do we do? Raise an army? Ridicul..."

"Exactly. Bravo, you just hit the point!"

"What point? No, no, no, I was just...."

"You need a fighting force."

"Childish!"

"Action! What the hell!?"

"Nonsense!"

"You need money!"

"The root of all evil! Ridiculous!"

"I see. Look, you need people, strong men. You need backing!"

"How does all this fit in?"

"The whole lot of your proceeds from thanksgiving, etc, etc, cannot buy even one riffle!"

"A what?'

"Guns! Ammo, cave man. I'm talking of munitions."

"Rifles and guns! Oh my God! What for?"

"What for!? To fight! To defend yourself! For your information bows and arrows, swords and spears are no more in vogue. Or you still wanna use clubs, cavemen?"

"Oh my Jesus! What am I hearing this midnight, *Kini mo nf'eti gbo yii laaro kutukutu, iwo Oluwa mi?*"[16]

"Good news it is. *Iroying ayo ni*[17]. Gospel truth itself, clergyman."

"We are talking at parities. My father's house of worship to be turned to an armory of arsenals?"

"To clean the den of thieves!"

"*O wa d'oju e bayi ooo. Yeepah!*"[18]

"Even then, do you know where to source munitions?"

"What for!?"

"Here we go again. Now you have a choice, Friar. You just give up and forget about fighting your enemy. Or take your chance and give him a fight! And if as you said God is behind you, you might just win."

"But a fight if necessary does not have to be taken to such a ridiculous extent? It would mean death!"

"So be it. It has come to that! They are planning to kill you anyway. So what choice do you have?"

"*Oluwa ko fe'ku elese bikose ironupiwada.*[19] What the Lord wants is the repent of sinners!"

"Does He want sinners to kill you first? Good memories, Friar but I suppose that verse was not inserted in the bible just of recent."

"What do you mean?"

"I mean the holy crusaders knew about it as well and so are the Israelites, still fighting like hell in Palestine."

"Oh my God! You know the bible but you are reasoning like... like..."

"Go ahead, old man. Finish up."

---

[16] What am I hearing in this early morning, oh my Lord?

[17] Good News it is.

[18] Now the matter has reached the serious point.

[19] God does not want the death of sinners but his repentance.

"Okay, son, technically you have defeated me but we don't have to take life unnecessarily"

Whaoooh! That's the key word, old man." Holding the man's hand jubilantly. The key word is what you just mentioned. "Unnecessarily." You see, the original meaning of the 5th of the 10 Commandments, way I think, is not just 'Though shall not kill,' but, I suppose, 'Though shall not kill unnecessarily.' Cheers, old man we are finally meeting at a junction."

"I would never be able to persuade the church to accept this as a solution talk less of using their offerings to procure weapons of destruction."

"I know you are all confused. Don't even tell them anything as this would jeopardize everything. This thing is supposed to be kept secret, remember? If anybody knows about me now you would have another dead pure-at-heart in your hand."

"I gave you my promise, didn't I" said the old man eagerly and with a lot of relief. "But how are we going to go about it? Em the men, the money, the backings, all those things you mentioned?"

"Now my turn to tell you that God would provide. I came here just to carry you along."

"Hmmmnnn...."

"By the way, how do you feel about what's happening in this town nowadays, especially the kidnapping of chief Bobade's daughter?"

The old man made a face. "Disgusting! For 5 million dollars said the papers. Oh my God, where is he going to get that amount of dollars?"

"Foreign exchange; banks, bureau de changes and black market."

"What a shame! The rich too are not safe." Then looking at the masked man who was pensively concentrating on something, he asked, "but why did you ask?"

"Oh, nothing really," he shrugged, "just to change topic. Some other things to talk about before I go."

"I see, but why don't we talk about religion and God for a while. It's just about one thirty now. I mean the love, the glory, and the wonders of our God the almighty father towards us..."

"Yeah, yeah, that is fine but not now, Friar. Truly speaking, I've got some other places in which to make appearance before dawn…kind of urgent. So, clergy, some other time."

"Don't even bother to utter a word of apology. I already know your answer before I asked."

Chief Bobade woke up with a start, still unable to differentiate between the dream state and reality as he felt the cold edge of a knife against his throat, and a strong hand covering his mouth. The voice, in contrast, was gentle, almost soothing but with an unmistakable suggestion of force.

"Don't utter a word, chief. Just rise up and come with me quietly."

The chief seemed at first to hesitate but eventually complied.

"We need to talk privately," the voice said when they got to the sitting room. Then the chief lead him to his study.

"Lock us in, and chief, please chief, no alarms. I mean no harm."

The hand relaxing hold on the chief's mouth and the latter started furiously, "Www what do you want from me? Is it mm money? Yy you people jj just want to kill mm me this yy year!"

"I only want to talk with you but it's very important that you don't attract attention, hence the knife and the rough gesture. Sorry, chief, I apologize."

"Who are you?" Curious now.

"If you wouldn't mind drawing your black curtain and then put on the light."

The light revealed a man dressed and masked in black and this frightened the chief.

"Is it money?"

"No chief. It is about your daughter."

There was an immediate change in chief's countenance, "Are y you the kidnapper? Are you the one who h ha has been phoning me?" Safe the knife, he would have held him.

"If I was I wouldn't have come here. Would i?"

"Then who are you? What do you want? Why are you dressed like an armed robber?"

"Have I robbed you? I said I want to talk to you...about your daughter. Look, chief, time is going. I have to dress like this for some very important reasons. I might make myself known to you when the time comes and it's my guess we would become friends. But now there's no time to lavish."

"So what about my daughter?"

"Tell me, chief, what is the latest on her?"

"What are you? Police?"

"Don't let us waste precious time. I'm not police'

"You are not police, you're not armed robber, you're not kidnapper... then..."

"Relax, chief. If in about 1 minute I can't get a positive answer from you I will go away."

They looked at each other for about 45 seconds then the chief shrugged, "Ok kay, there is nothing new yet"

"What attempt have you made so far?"

"None."

"And what do you have in mind?"

"Nothing, nothing."

"Chief Bobade, you've got to tell me the truth."

"I am helpless. What else can I do? You know it all. It's in the papers. They asked for 5 million dollars!"

"Are you going to give them?"

"D Don't worry about that. The police are handling the matter now. I'll do what they advise me to do."

"Chief, you must realize that I'm trying to risk my neck for you and I think you've got to cooperate with me."

The chief looked at him thoroughly, seizing him up, sort of, and looking into his mask squarely, he asked, "What concerns you in my affairs that you have to risk your neck for me? Talk!"

"Let's just put it that I'm a philanthropist."

"I don't believe you."

"Well, you are right but I assure you I have a good reason to stick out my neck. Now do you believe that?"

"I have told you all I know."

"Ok, if that is all you have to say. It is often said that it is possible to force a horse to the river but not so easy to force it to drink water. Is it?" And he made his move to depart, he added, "no doubt the police would try their best the way they are trained but if you joke with those mean bastards they will kill your daughter. As a matter of fact, the chances of getting her alive are slim even if you pay the ransom."

The man backtracked and the chief grabbed his hand, saying, "ww wait a ss second! Ww what do you m mean by that!? ...that the ch chances are slim, even if I give them their mm money?"

"Well, chief, you are a man. You've got to start facing reality now. There are 2 things very important to kidnappers. First the money or whatever it is they are after, being prime motive in this particular case and their identities. If they have allowed your daughter to see their faces it is very unfortunate. Or do you think they would turn loose anybody that can identify them?"

"You m mean I will never ss see my daughter again?"

"Not really. That is about what I'm here to discuss with you."

"Ok let's discuss."

"Don't shout."

"I'm not shouting."

"Now tell me all what has transpired between you and them."

"They want money. 5 million. It is all in the papers."

"And what are you going to do?"

"What do you think I should do? In my place what would you do? My little daughter! Five million is small compared to my daughter's life. Of course I will give them and get my daughter back!"

"Hmmmn. You really think that is what you should do?"

"Look man! Don't tell me you're h here dressed like this to preach to me about the law. The last time I told the police and we set a trap for them they did not fall in it. Instead let me show you what they sent to me." He hurriedly opened his drawer and brought out a little envelope. "This is ww what they sent to me. See, see. Do you know what this is.?"

"Yeah a beautiful finger nail of the little finger." Sarcastic.

"My daughter's finger nail! And the bastards said if I tried it again they would send the finger instead. And for my punishment they added one million!. So they are asking for 6 millions now!"

"I see your point and I sincerely sympathize with you. But the question still remains. When you pay would they return your daughter?"

"If I d don't pay they will kill my daughter!"

"You stand to lose both if you don't apply wisdom."

"What do you mean?" Chief either finding the fact hard to grind or not wanting to grind it at all. "They c can't do that!"

"I know your records, chief. I know you as a man who could face facts, no matter how hard it hits you, otherwise, I wouldn't be here wasting my time."

"Then what do you expect me to do? Fold my hands and do nothing while those bastards do what they like with my daughter?"

Hmmmn, chief, I have explained the situation and the possibilities. The earlier you put emotions where it belongs the better you would be able to concentrate for an empirical analysis of the matter at hand. Let me reemphasize. You are faced with 3 possibilities: Number one, you could lose your daughter and nothing else. Second, you could lose both daughter and 6 million hard currency on top. Third, you could get your daughter back without paying a dime of ransom."

"How is that possible?"

Seeing the sudden interest and tiny ray of hope, the masked man spoke more slowly but deliberately, "Turn against them, no compromises, and join in the fight against the devil."

"And my daughter?"

"Fight for your daughter! Rescue her! Fight the devils! Fight the bastards and snatch her from them! That is the third option which I think if you were not directly involved, I mean were you to be advising somebody instead, I am sure it would be your first and only option. But as it seems, emotions is the more dangerous robber, kidnapper, depriving us of our rationality when needed and that is what these bastards play on. Think about it…And by the way when next do they want you to bring the money and how?"

"They warned me not to tell anybody otherwise they will cut her finger and send to me…imagine, by mail! My own daughter's finger!"

"How would they know? I'm no police. Besides, chief, if you're eventually going to fight for the life of your daughter it's high time you started developing your own strategies. It's not enough to think all the time what they're going to do to you. Think about what you're going to do to them!"

"We are talking about my daughter here. I don't want them to maim her. I don't want to take chances."

"Exactly what a man should consider. Men take chances based on the options before them."

"And what if something happen to her?"

"Do you think it is that easy for kidnappers to release their captives?"

"No stupid chances…"

"Exactly. The chances would be weighed. The risk would be minutely calculated. The key word here is surprise."

"They should not know this."

"Nobody would know if you don't tell them you told me."

"Do you think I'm mad?"

"Okay, chief, what were your last instructions?"

"They want the money Thursday evening at the children's park."

"Here in Gbongan. Good."

"My man is to sit on the bench behind the hibiscus flowers with the money in a black suitcase. Their man will come and tell him what to do."

"Good and what are you planning to do?"

"All I want is my daughter."

"You could play for time. You could tell your man to tell them that the money is not complete as you have to be careful how you gather the dollars so as not to arouse the suspicion of the police. It is a good story and very credible, chief. We are talking about six million dollars. Otherwise would they accept some in Naira? They would buy that story. It's a good one."

"Ok, oK, b but don't go tell them I talked to you,…otherwise they would cut my dd daughter's finger!"

"My turn now, chief, to ask you if you think I'm mad?"

"somebody in mask, how do I know?"

"He is the only one you have now if you mean to rescue your daughter."

"And where are you going to now?"

"Where I came from, chief," the man answered, backtracking to the door, and added, "remember your options, chief. Think of your daughter and think of all the possibilities. Think about your options and think about your pride. Bear in mind that such lowly castes are never trustworthy. Lay emotions aside, think for a while; if you are able to rescue your daughter, gallantly, chief… Bobby…Bobby Nero..No Nonsense! Think of your options, chief…"

He opened the door and in a flash he seemed to have just faded away.

———◆►◄◆►◄◆———

Jobilah with Zokalaus and a third man, smallish and nervous, called Denne, stood by the window of a room on the third floor of a storey building where they had a fantastic view of the Olufi Memorial Children's Park.

"Fantastic weather, isn't it?" commented Jobilah.

"Excellent for my aim," replied Zokalaus as he unpacked from his briefcase the dismantled rifle parts with telescopic sight and silencer.

"Five minutes to go," said the smallish man, "I hope they show up."

"*O di dandan*,"[20] said Jobilah, "they will surely show up…in fact, here we are, look, that must be his man taking his seat."

"Any suspicious movement around?" asked the baritone voice of Zokalaus who as yet concentrated setting up his weapon. He had just rammed in the magazine and about to screw in the silencer.

"None that I can see yet," replied Jobilah, still looking.

---

[20] Compulsorily

"And do we really have to use that thing...if ..." demanded the smallish man now, becoming nervous.

"Relax boy, it might not be necessary. Just for precautions. Most especially for your protection. If they make trouble with you or there's trouble from anywhere Fadi would shoot and in the commotion you can get away. Again, once the man is dead he couldn't tell a soul whatever you might have discussed. Could he? Then all you would have to say, just in case, is that you wanted to ask him some questions and all of a sudden he just collapsed. What offence would anybody have committed by that? It happens every day. You are not carrying any weapon, are you?" Jobilah doing his best to calm the man.

"I only pray that all will pass without any incidence."

"The rifle is only just in case. Look, boy, this is your only chance to restore the chief's lost confidence in you. If I were you I'd make good use of this opportunity and I'd stop shivering."

"Ok ok ok I will go now..Now I go!"

Zokalaus shifted his gaze once to look at the man. It was not really possible to know from his reaction how he felt about him.

"Remember what to do, reinstructed Jobilah, "you sit down quietly and exchange bag. Then tell him where to go pick the girl."

"And how about the girl? I mean..."

"Shut up! Just go there and do and say what I ask you to say and go away with the bag towards the road. The car will be ready and waiting to pick you up."

Zokalaus fixed the telescopic sight and trailed the weapon on the figure dressed in suit, cap in hand, on the bench behind the hibiscus flowers in the park. He had a bag in between his legs similar to the one Denne is carrying. A few minutes later Denne himself appeared in view. Zokalaus shifted aim onto him as he walked unsteadily towards the park 200 meters away.

"You mind telling me what Denne has done to warrant his being sacrificed?" he asked Jobilah.

"Naaah. He is a green fool. He fucked up in several occasions and he is becoming a risk to the organization."

"No details?"

"Maybe later."

"Hmmn, I am not surprised."

"What do you mean!?"

"I mean he really must be a fool. Only a fool would swallow the shit story without suspecting the bullet is meant for him."

"Hmmn, Fadi, I've got to get within earshot so that I can pick whatever they say. I don't trust that jittery thing. *To si ngbon tetete bi ewe oju omi!*"[21] with a cruel laugh, "well I expect a good job from you."

"You know you've got nothing to worry about."

Moments later Denne was seated beside a man in black suit, white handkerchief in breast pocket, cap in hand and a similar suitcase to the one he himself carried in between his legs. "Sure the man," he told himself. He fidgeted terribly, heart threatening to come out of his chest. It took him about 3 minutes before he could ask, "Do you happen to know a man called Bobby?"

"Oh yes, yes of course, and he has sent me a message"

"Oh really? Where is the message?

"Why do you ask? Do you know him too?"

"Yes. Yes. What is, w where is the message?"

"What is your own message?"

"Look, we just quietly exchange bags."

"No, no, no, man you tell me so I know for sure."

"Look, you don't wanna fuck!" Denne felt it's time to act brave.

"Okay, where is the girl?"

"The money is in that bag?"

"You tell me where the girl is."

"You are wasting our time and you are taking risk! You don't wanna fuck! Do you?"

"Ok the money is not complete yet."

"Why!? You don't wanna fuck!"

Reason being the chief don't wanna attract police attention by withdrawing such large money from the bank. You said he should do all his possible to keep the police out of it. Didn't you? Well he is doing just that."

---

[21] Imagine him shaking like a leaf on top of water.

"So how much have you brought and when are you bringing the rest?" eyeing the bag.

"Nothing"

"Nothing!"

"Until complete."

"Then what the hell did you bring that bag for?"

"You said bring bag and I bring bag. We are just following your instructions."

"Ok I will go tell my people," getting up and coming back after taking a few steps forward, "wait! When will it be complete?"

"The chief said by next Thursday. That's a week today. He can only withdraw in unsuspicious bits. Then he has to change into dollars again."

"Ok, a week, Thursday. And tell him not to fuck! Ok?" Feeling relieved and genuinely tough now.

"OK!"

Denne finally left, somehow proud of himself. Behind the flowers where Jobilah concealed himself he looked at him and muttered to himself, "very stupid!"

From an hotel room adjacent the park another pair of binoculars watched the 2 figures as they sat and conversed. He smiled and he was about to lower the viewing object when he caught sight of a movement behind the flowers and he brought himself to attention. He thought he had seen that figure somewhere before. He focused the powerful instrument very well on the man but he couldn't find a clue. Then as the figure moved hurriedly away it clicked. The height, the slightly bent posture and the style of walking all added up to reveal it all.

The telephone rang again and again chief Bobade picked, still tensed but a little better. He has been apprehensive of the next reaction of the kidnappers. But a lot of the calls that day had been from friends and sympathizers.

"Who the hell is it this time?"

"Chief, I must confess, I am impressed."

"Who is this?"

"That was good of you keeping the police out of it. Wise and thoughtful, though we expected you to have done better. Thursday is far but all the same we give you the long rope. Thursday you say, no hanky panky! Since you want to keep your daughter with us for another week, it is ok by us. But come Thursday if the money is not ready …well, your guess is as good as ours."

"Y you sure my daughter is ok?"

"Yes, of course. Are you already afraid something might have happened to her? It's your fault! But relax. She's ok. You will see for yourself. We will make the exchange right there."

"I want to talk with her."

"Not now! I told you she is ok but if you mess up she will not be ok at all."

"I want to be sure she ok now."

"She is not here with me! What do you expect? To carry her about all over the country? You just mess up on Thursday then you can blow her a farewell kiss."

"Where?"

"Same place. Children's park. 1930hrs. Your man must dress as usual, black suit, white handkerchief in breast pocket, same bag and no police!" the phone cut immediately. Suzan had been listening to the conversation and equally lip-reading her husband but she has not dared asked a question.

The police were all over the place and were not happy as the chief seems not to be cooperating fully with them. The district police boss, Inspector Gbadamosi had talked to him several times. "Chief your full cooperation is vital to enable us catch these loonies. We need information of your conversations from you but you have not been cooperative."

"What do you mean that I am not cooperating?"

"Wee, you are not going to tell us that you have so far not been talking with them, are you?"

"If they tell me anything I will tell you. Didn't I tell you the last time?"

"But nothing since then, chief. Think of your daughter."

"The hell I think of my daughter. I will give you all the assistance you need. You know I'll give because I want you to catch them. Didn't we set trap for them together the other time? Any time they give me any other instruction I will t tell you so that w ww we can set another trap to catch them."

Back there at the police headquarters Detective Sergeant Sam Ilori talks with his boss

"Sir if the chief had given us his full cooperation this job wouldn't have been so difficult to deal with. It is similar to the case of the Ososos which we cracked within 72 hours."

"Yeah, I remember. And that is a good job you boys are doing presently with his phone. He is going to pay up exactly 1930 hours on Thursday at the Children's Park, Isn't it. I want you to move in with your boys at the right moment and meanwhile keep listening."

"You can rest assured sir, this time around they've had it. I promise we will catch them like baby birds."

"And make sure the mother does not fly away!"

"No chance sir. I promise."

<hr>

Chief Bobade read his mails on Wednesday, as usual the head line first. As he opened the Daily Sketch he saw a letter a sealed envelope with the following written on it: EXCLUSIVELY FOR BOBBY. The chief hurriedly opened the envelope with anticipating hands. Inside he saw an inner envelope and he opened it, almost tearing it by mistake. He read the content.

"You will find your way to the beach of river Ishasha where we will be waiting for you at exactly 1930hrs. You will come alone with the money and there we will make the exchange. As per the previous arrangement, let your man still go to the children's park. He will be dressed as instructed and will carry the same bag. Same time, same procedure. Remember! No police must intrude into this our own little arrangement. You want your daughter? You comply. It is up to you. Now haven read this instruction, TEAR the paper immediately."

The chief read the paper over and over again, seemed to be thinking on what to do when the phone rang and he picked it up. "I said tear the note!" A voice he recognized commanded. So rough and mean! The chief's hands worked more effectively than the shredding machine. A couple of meters away a pair of binoculars watched through a window of a hotel.

"Very good. He is tearing."

"What a pity," said Jobilah.

"What pity? Six million dollars is chicken change to him."

"No, Fadi, that's not the matter."

"Then what is?"

"His daughter. His lovely daughter."

"He pays we give her back to him. Isn't it?"

"She has all the qualities."

"Don't get it."

"Bwallangwu wants her."

"Shit! What for?"

"Beautiful, succulent, hmmmn, chief Enlaye will take her first, that I know for sure...hmmmn," seemed to be thinking aloud, "I think I would have her next...yes I should have my share this time around. You can have her too before Bwallangwu makes a mess of her."

"A mess!?" Asked Zokalaus, "Kind of strange. Isn't it? This Bwallangwu who nobody sees. I wonder what he does with the girls."

"You don't wanna hear it, kid."

"Well, if you don't wanna say it that is ok." Always resenting the word 'kid'.

"Horrible!" insisted Jobilah who wants to talk brave, "Kid, it's horrible, I mean it!" emphasizing the word and staring dramatically at the young man who asked casually, "what is it?"

"You have one dick. Isn't it?"

"What do you expect?"

Sometimes Jobilah can bear this disrespect, especially when he thinks he has something to impress the boy with, so as to gradually inculcate the respect into him. "I mean genital. You have only one, kid."

"Do you have two?"

"Listen, kid. Bwallangwu, I heard, has 16. One main organ and 15 auxiliaries. The main organ goes into the victim's cunt and introduce some solvent into her in a way of ejaculation after a terrible orgasm. This solvent or his sperm, so to say, kind of juices her up and the ancillary organs with sharp snouts cuts openings into all parts of her body and suck her dry, leaving just bones and skin. I'm.."

"Enough!" was the rough voice of Zokalaus.

"What's wrong with you, kid? Getting yellow?" demanded the older man with pride and satisfaction.

"If that is what it means to be yellow, then yellow I am," admitted the man coolly.

"You can have her before she becomes carcass, anyway. But that will be after me."

"Thanks, but that is not how I like women. I don't like them to that extent."

"What's the matter with you? Lost your balls in detention?"

"I like them only when they are willing. I don't fuck enslaved girls."

"No wonder."

"No wonder what? All these days I've been asking about Bimbi. At least you could have told me something about her where about."

"That you have to ask the chief yourself."

"Of course I would one day."

"Bet the hell you would. Right now let's get the hell out of here. I sure need a good rest before I get to Alabe village.…..hmmn…succulent girl."

Up in the ceiling, a figure had crawled back carefully to the position of his own room. Lowering himself gently down into his room, he immediately led himself into the bathroom to wash off the dirt and cobwebs. He then changed into a flowing gown with an cap to match. He folded the dirty overall and put it in his bag. He had a good look at himself in the mirror and was surprised at who he was looking at.

With the false goatee and moustache, even his own mother would've had a hard time recognizing him. It was just an hour service he wanted from the hotel. Ever since he caught sight of Jobilah at the Children's Park he had been tailing him. He had followed him to several places where it was possible for him. As they entered the hotel 'De Whit' this afternoon he had come too and had requested for a room to rest for an hour or two. On a long journey from Kano he said he was and would be proceeding to Badagry. And he needed to rest a while before he continued. On getting a room he had climbed up the ceiling and much to his fortune he was able to see Jobilah and his companion through the hole in the ceiling and much more to his fortune he could hear all what they were saying very audibly.

Taking a final look around the room and satisfying himself that he had not left anything behind he stepped out into the passage and came down to the reception, looking really like an Alhaji; Alhaji Meturare, which he called himself. As he settled his bill the receptionist and some two girls hailed him, "*ranka deeh deeh,*" and he tipped them handsomely.

CHAPTER 9

Angela, gagged, feet and hands tied, has been hidden away in a farm house in a village called Alabe about 7 km away from Gbongan. She was being guarded by two armed men.

"Hey, Joe, Joe!"

"Yap, Sammy. What is it?"

"About that radio message! The chief will be coming here tomorrow....to this place!"

"So what? ...We just do our job."

"You don't know what, heh?"

"What?"

"I think he is coming to have a nice time. That girl is beautiful and juicy. Isn't it?"

"Yeah. So she is."

"Heh, look, you don't dig?"

"Dig what? Talk straight!"

"Well...after the chief's departure..err..why don't we...errr.. Joe, you dig?"

No reply from Joe who seemed to be considering and making some decisions. Sammy persisted, "You can have her before me, I don't mind."

"Yeah, but I'm going in now and you keep on the look out!"

"What!"

"You said I can have her before you and I have decided to do it now."

"Suicide!"

"No shut up. Chief won't be coming until 9 pm after their meeting and now it is only 6:30. There is time enough. He won't notice anything."

"What if anybody else just come?"

"Oooh, shut up!"

"Alright...but I think it's better we just wait till after the chief must have come and departed....and we would have the whole night to ourselves."

"And suppose they just come and take her away, you dummy?" he said stopping in his track, "where do you stick your goddamn rod? Into a hole in the wall?"

"Well, be gentle. You know...if.."

"Never mind. I know how to make them willing. I have the magic touch. You remember?"

The girl was at the corner of the room dimly lit by a *fitila* (mud ware lamp). She shrank back as Joe entered and shrank further as he approached, terror in her eyes as he kneeled in front of her to speak to her.

"Heh, sweet, I've come to help you but you've got to cooperate first."

Tearful eyes opened and lifted up to look at him as he dropped a hand over her left breast, fondling the nipple. The girl shrank back but he moved closer.

"You should realize the fact that I'm really, really sticking out my neck." He put the second hand on the right breast, sizing and fondling. The girl heaved, shook her head and her whole body.

"I must be frank to you. If I didn't like you I wouldn't be doing this. I mean trying to put my entire life in trouble over you. You know what I mean and the least I expect is for you to cooperate."

Now the girl seems to be getting wild only she couldn't shout. Neither could she put in much of a struggle with her limbs tied.

"Look, I don't have to do this. I don't have to put myself through all this but if I am not satisfied with you I'm not going to be sacrificing myself to save you."

He untied her leg and he made to remove her pant, to which she struggled and kicked wildly.

"Hey, use you brains! You are old enough." He applied some force now and she really grew wild. "Look here. You are in danger. I could take you far away from here in less than an hour and deliver you safe into your father's hands. All you have to do is cooperate."

He pulled her pant and it became a fierce struggle as she twisted her legs and he tried to separate them. Eventually he was able to separate them and he didn't even mind the pant again he just pulled out his member. He forced the legs apart and he was probably trying to find his way inside when he felt a cold uncomfortable object against his exposed balls, with a voice to match, "if you move or even attempt to breathe too hard I will blow off your horrible wall nuts."

His organ went limp and shrank but even a man about to have an orgasm couldn't have trembled that violently.

"Now get up!" Weapon instantly transferred to the back of his neck. "Button up and get ready for the role of the good Samaritan which you promised her. Now untie her hands….good….remove the gag…excellent. You are big and strong, very well, now pick her up and don't turn around if you want to live. Put her on your neck…no, no, not like that..across….yeah..exactly, like that…yes… I say don't turn! Yeah…now walk backward, yes, c'mon, c'mon, c'mon, come."

They were soon out of the farm house. Sammy was spread eagle outside on the ground.

"Now follow that path and no funny moves. I will kill you even if I have to kill the girl. Do you understand? Now move! You say you wanna have her? Now is your chance. You have her now. Move!"

Very soon they got to Alabe River where a canoe with an outboard engine was tie to a tree by the river side. The girl was lowered into the back on the man's command. "Good, now get in, start the engine…very good." He cut the rope as the over-powered canoe launched forward into the accommodating river. They were gone for almost one hour when the maskman retrieved Joe's walkie talkie and told him to jump into the river. Joe had no choice."

Happening almost simultaneously about 7 km away was the greatest hide and seek game chief Bobade had ever played in his life, not even as a kid. He had put on a pair of jeans and snickers, dark blue T-shirt and a long peak cap with some funny mean eye glasses. He looked much different from chief Bobade. Before then he had given the order not to be disturbed and had locked himself inside his study. The police were parading outside his house. Chief Bobade had later climbed out through the window and had jumped down into the flower beds where he had initially lowered his baggage. He had had to remain there for almost 5 minutes until a guard, who had chosen that particular area to smoke his cigarette, finished and moved away. Maneuvering his own guards and the policemen and climbing his own wall was quite unusual to him but he made it out of necessity. Quickly he had taken to the bush path where a trusted guard had kept a Piagio tricycle. As soon as they put in the slightly heavy load of cash they had ridden for about 45 minutes to Ishasha River where they transferred into a boat that took them to the beach. They made it there by about 1932 hours.

The chief came out and walked the white sand of the beautiful shore while the guard pushed the boat ashore. He looked around and he turned abruptly at the sound of the corking of a pistol. A man appeared from behind a tree, masked and dressed in black.

"I said you must come alone!"

"I couldn't carry the bag of money alone! He is my personal guard, he means no harm."

"Where is the money?"

"In the boat. Where is my girl?"

"Your daughter is safe. I will tell you where to go pick her once we have the money."

"You said we were going to make the exchange right here! Why haven't you brought my daughter?"

"Sorry, chief, it's our insurance against your traps, chief. You are a very resourceful man and we don't take chances, chief Bobade. If I don't take this money away from here safely your daughter would die."

"Treachery!"

"Chief, you don't get it. You are in no position to argue and the earlier we get this over with the better for your girl. She shouldn't be in this terrible harmattan cold for too long. She could catch pneumonia."

"You bastard! We make the exchange right here! Go get my girl!"

At the sign from the masked man 2 other masked men emerged seemingly out of nowhere. "Chief, you and I will stay here while these two will go get the money. By the way there are more than a dozen rifles trailed on you. So no funny moves."

The money was brought and checked and then transferred into a bigger boat brought by the masked men. One of the masked men recovered a walkie talkie from the chief's boat along with his guard's pistol. "Now go to the abandoned catholic church at Tabu. There you will find your lovely daughter. If I were you I'd hurry down there because this cold is unbearable especially for a young tender girl like you have. Adios amigo."

"I IIIf she catches pneumonia you will see what I will ddd do to yy you." And turning to his guard he said, "let's hurry and gg go get my girl"

<hr />

The meeting of the chiefs of Bwallangwu was still on when the news was brought in to the chairman in person of Chief Enlaye. His countenance changed and added more enthusiasm, and one could say that the news became a good catalyst in bringing a somewhat long argument to a logical conclusion. Likewise it produced an excellent effect on all what can be referred to as appetite, for no sooner than the meeting had ended that he had proceeded with his small entourage to Alabe village where he was going to have a personal but private interview with a young succulent girl before turning her over to Bwallangwu. He had eaten first and taken 3 shots instead of his usual one of *opaeyin*, a local gin in which is drenched assorted herbs meant to produce a boosting effect on his libido. The Bwallangwu high chief is set to give himself the treat of the year. This young tiger is wonderful. Six instead of 5 million dollars....and they were looking for eight! Wonderful! Worth all celebrations.

It was first a surprise at first finding Sammy sprawled on the ground outside the farmhouse, then confusion. The chief went berserk, Jobilah haywire and Fadi dangerously calm. They dashed inside the farmhouse and just as was apprehensively expected they found the lonely fitila throwing its dim light on the gag rag and the cut ropes that were used to tie up the girl. Zokalaus picked the rag in his left hand and the ropes in his right and uttered just one statement, "bull shit!" His voice deep, rough, menacing and sending shivers.

An artistic combination of pouring of cold water and slaps brought Sammy back from the abyss. He grumbled, confused and touched the back of his neck and the swollen head. Zokalaus shook him violently, "What the hell happened to you and where is the girl?"

"I received a terrible blow from the back and that is the last I can remember."

"Where is your partner!?"

"Errr...rrrr"

Zokaluas slapped him again. "Speak and save time. Damn it!"

"Eeer...Joe was going to eeer. Joe, Joe, he went into the farmhouse t tt to the girl...and the... the blow on mm.."

"Then, gentlemen," busted chief Enlaye dramatically, *"eni to gba'di lo ja'leke*[22]. Find Joe and you find the girl! Jobilaaah!"

"My lord, my lord!"

"I am sad, Jobilah! My heart is broken."

"He wouldn't have gone far, my lord. We will catch him."

"Yes you must catch him! Tonight!"

"Yes, my lord."

"Alive!"

"Of course, my lord."

Jobilah wheeled about and rattled orders. Zokalaus obeyed and got into action. He immediately took the radio and issued out a series of instructions.

"Bwallangwu Operations Center for Mobile Headquarters!"

"M HQ, Go!"

---

[22] Lit: The person who tapped the buttocks is the one that cut the waist beads.

'I want you to send 100 men fully armed including Sunny Alaja and his hounds down here at Alabe right now! Time is 2105hrs and timing!"

The chief just held Jobilah and he shook in the attempt to shake the latter. "Haaah! Joobilaaah! Jobilaaah! You have broken my heart!"

"Easy, easy, my lord. I'll get them back. I'll get her for you. As soon as they arrive Sunny's hounds will smell them out even from a crab hole. I assure you, my lord, we will get them."

"Alive!"

"Yes sir! Alive."

One could only imagine a lot and the combination of things that was happening to chief Enlaye, ranging from the need of Bwallangwu and that performance enhancing stuff named 'opaeyin'.

CHAPTER 10

The maskman found chief Bobade awake when he stole into his bed room. It was 0200hrs. As soon as he made his presence known the chief just grabbed him.

"I have been waiting for you! W Where have you been!? Let's go get my dd daughter! I'll give you anything! Anything!"

The man had to first break his strangling hold. "Chief, you are choking me….and please be quiet! You're gonna wake people."

"Let's go now and get m my daughter before she catches pneumonia!"

"I thought you've given them their money."

"Y yes and the bastards told me to go and pick her at the old catholic church at Tabu!"

"Then go. Do you need me for that?"

"I went! She was not there! Oh mm my daughter!"

"Sure you gave them exactly what they demanded?"

"Six m million! I gave them!"

"I told you, didn't I?" And he added absentmindedly, "If I were faster I could have stopped you."

"What d did you say? Stopped me? How could you have even known? I had no choice but to follow their instructions to detail for the sake of my d daughter!"

"I analyzed and explained the various possibilities and your options."

"I'm ready!"

"To fight!?"

"Fight!?"

"For your daughter!"

"Yes! B B But…"

"Now the only option remaining is to rescue your girl…and for that you've got to fight. You might just be able to rescue her otherwise you lose both."

"I will fight! I will kkk kill them. I I ww. *O ya, o ya, o ya.*"

"You are still strangling me… and quiet!"

And suddenly the strong chief seemed to grow weak and as he held the maskman, he pleaded, "please help me before it is too late."

The man felt pity and sympathy penetrating his soul. "that's why I'm here," he replied, soothingly. "It is not going be an easy fight."

"I am ready. Even if it is the last thing I do in what remains in my life."

"We're gonna need some hardwares, arsenals, chief, and some good men to use them."

"Yes! We will buy!"

"Weapons are not cheap, chief."

"I am not cheap either."

"Hard currency!"

"I I have money! Look I gave those bbastards 6 millon dollars. I am still worth more than that. I c can sell everything to recover my dd daughter."

"Very well, then, we have to hurry."

"Where do we start and …"

"I need to make some contacts, err… a couple of phone calls.."

"Come, come here. Use my phone. You can even make international calls to anywhere all over the world."

"Then we would be finished before we even have a chance to start."

"What do you mean?"

"Reporting ourselves to the police. Chief, your phone is tapped."

"Tapped…my phone?"

"Yeah for sure by the police and maybe by some others. They always do that. Don't you know?"

"I seeeee."

"I'm going to use the coin box around the corner. I will be back in 10 minutes."

Joe's only aim now is to get as far away as possible from Gbongan. Otherwise he is dead. He would even prefer to die to being caught by Bwallangwists. The swim ashore was very long and tiring but he dared not stop. As he hurried along he made some survival itineraries. He would make it on foot to Wakajaiye where he would take the midnight train to Orileowu where he has an uncle who would arrange for his immediate travel out of country. He moved along, breathing like a buffalo, hunger and fatigue competing against the wish to save dear skin but not having the upper hand yet, but gradually. Eventually, after a while, believing that at least he had put a reasonable distance between himself and Alabe, he succumbed to the promised benefit of a little rest, just a little, if only to gain some renewed energy that would enable him move faster, run even as necessary, he slumped against a tree, then sat down.

Joe was woken up abruptly by the sound of dogs and footsteps. "Jeesus Christ! I am finished!" He sprang up and broke into a run for life. It was a matter of minutes later when he was caught.

"Where is the girl!?" was the first question Zokalaus asked him."

"I don't know! He has taken her!"

"Who!"

"I was just going to carry out our usual periodic check on the girl when suddenly this guy appeared from nowhere and disarmed me!"

"One guy? Which guy!" Asked Jobilah.

"No, two of them. They were two and very strong."

Zokalaus slapped him. "Where is the girl!?" Even Jobilah felt the effect of that terrible voice.

"He has gone with her...in a canoe."

"Jobilaah!" chief Enlaye's voice was heard on the manpack troop radio.

"Yes myymy lord!" Jobilah stammered.

"Updates!"

"We have caught Joe, my lord. We caught him alive…as you ordered."

"I'm talking about the girl!"

"Errr…em…we will get her as well.…we will soon get her sir!"

"Jobilaaah!"

"I promise you sir. Now that we have the stupid guard, we wee wee…"

As soon as the troops arrived Zokalaus had told Jobilah to leave the matter to him. That he would handle it and feed him continually with the progress by radio but Jobilah had insisted on going along and taking active part in the hunting and recovery. Jobilah in turn had persuaded Chief Enlaye to leave the matter to him, that he would return and deliver the girl and the fugitive in just a matter of little time but the chief was not going to do that. He started out with them but after close to an hour and he was getting tired, he had yielded to their persuasion to stay back, even if only to rest the night in the farmhouse. Of course, in his comfortable room and he would be kept abreast of their minute to minute developments by the troop radio.

This development was unbearable. The implication is great. A precious gift to Bwallangwu!

"She must be found, alive!"

Operation Catch My Baby.

Money, weapon and the men to use them translate to certain power. Power itself, an enigma, to be used and managed well, otherwise it becomes trouble. Chief Bobade supplied the funds and pretty soon an army of sort was raised under the command of a masked man. For now the main concern of the power is to rescue Angela, the daughter of chief Bobade in Operation Catch My Baby.

The men assembled consisted of the Nigerian civil war veterans, veterans of the Ife-Modakeke conflict and a lot of trainable raw hands. The training ground is Tonkere. Here the men were assembled with their weapons, looking tough, mean and ready, genuinely or make believe, especially those ones that were seeing action for the first time.

The masked man smiled in retrospection. Of course knowledge is power but the efficiency of power comes from its prudent management, especially of the information that help in begetting it. Meaning?

He wondered if he had told the chief that he already had his daughter would he still have been so committed to the point of raising of an army of this magnitude? Of course the mind to punish the 'bastards' would be impetuous but to what extent and by what timing? Would he have agreed to join in a war against Bwallangwu? Satan's advocate himself on planet earth. For this matter is not just the gathering of volunteers and freelancers for the rescue of some adored kidnapped daughter but a full scale war against a formidable force. The war mongers themselves. It is total war against the devil. A war, once started must be finished to avoid annihilation by the enemy.

That night he had taken the girl to his hiding place and he could remember, with agony, the surprise and disappointment in her eyes when he tied her up again and shoved a gag into her mouth. "You are still a prisoner." He had said ironically, half to her half to himself. The girl just went limp as the light of hope, being rekindled and shining brighter with every step they took away from her captor, gradually dimmed to extinction. As the first roundish drops of warm tears from her eyes landed at the back of his hand he had bent down and kissed her on the forehead, saying, "Not for too long now, angel. Besides, you never really experience freedom until you had been a prisoner." And locking her up he had left. And he had her all along the time he was planning her rescue operation with chief Bobade, her father. He was sorry to have had to do that, but the question still remains. Would the chief have still provided enough money for the weapons and the training and remuneration of the army?

"Now if you are ready we go get your baby." He had said as the chief strap on his bullet proof vest. He had tries his level best to persuade him to stay behind and let the boys handle the rest but the latter was very adamant.

"Now, chief, you have done your own. The rest is ours. Leave it to us and watch what we can do within the next few hours."

"I I I if I stay back how do I watch what you can do within the next ff few hours?"

"I must remind you that you are our back bone in this outfit and it would be unwise to expose you to danger unnecessarily. A lot of us can be replaced but you are indispensable."

"I ccc cannot just be killed like that! I'm not a cockroach! I can take care of myself."

Even after the argument had subsided they still found the chief grumbling to himself. "Me, me stay away from this action? They must be joking. I am in it now, from my toe nails to the tip of the hair of my head."

Had the man agreed to wait for them in the camp it would have been for the maskman a simple job of just going to his hideout to pick the girl. Now with him around he had to work out a make belief; a credible demonstration. Then they had moved: the maskman, the chief and 2 others, after giving the next in command some instructions. The presence of the chief still bothers him but he would know what to do next when the time comes, he assured himself. And if it comes down to the fact that he has to tell him the truth, "the chief would just have to understand. "I had to raise an army and that is it."

"What did you say," asked the chief.

"Oh nothing..err…just reciting some psalm."

"So you are a Christian. I'm a Christian too but I don't know any psalm. What psalm was that?"

"Err, psalm 23."

"And how does it go?"

"Some other time, chief. Sorry, we must maintain absolute silence."

"Ok, hmmm," the chief whispered and put a finger on his own lips as they moved along.

As they approached to within 200 meters from the building the maskman froze suddenly in his track and the others halted just as sudden.

"What's the matter!?" the chief asked in a hushed voice. "You see something?"

"No, some feelings I got."

"Feelings..? What feeling?"

Within seconds the man was half way up a tree, watched by the bemused companions, especially the chief, as he surveyed the surroundings with a pair of binoculars. "JeesusChrist!" they heard him exclaimed as he jumped down.

"What is it," asked the chief, crocking a sub machine gun.

"Armed men advancing in great number…and bloody dogs!"

"My enemies!" exclaimed the chief, cocking again the sub machine gun thereby ejecting a live round.

The mask man seized the walkie talkie and shouted orders. "Heaven for Michael, heaven for Michael!" for his call sign is Michael in the camp which itself is heaven.

"Archangel, this is Heaven, go ahead!"

"Advance holy support in full force. I repeat advance in full force. Over."

"Copy that."

"Michael out!"

The troop arrived within a couple of minutes and the maskman briefly explained the situation to the serge major, a dedicated civil war veteran, who he has put in direct control of the soldiers, and his instructions is, "I like you to make sure nobody moves near the building. Keep the enemies' heads down with your fire while I go in…"

"In a flank," supplied the serge major.

"Yeah, while I go in a flank. Tell your men to shoot straight at the enemy so they don't kill me. Anybody who so much as move near the building 10 meters shoot to maim!"

"Yes sir!" replied the veteran who always wondered at this maskman they never see his face or even know the reasons why he wears the mask, looking so young but active always. Lakunle Oshoroga, the serge major, could recount so many young and naïve leaders they had had during the war. He remembered those he admired before death separated them and, especially those few he himself had shot to death to take over effective command of some few lucky remnant of men after a major attack. Lakunle looked at this particular one, masked, and realized inwardly that he could never raise a finger on this one. He would rather protect him with his own life. The reason why he felt so he could not yet explain.

"Extended line formation. Go!" cracked the rough accustomed voice of the battle tested sergeant major, as they got within 100 meter of the house.

"Lying position, Take!" and the men were all flat on their belly with their rifles in ready position. The serge major looked through his binoculars and issued another hot one, "Range 200!" which made each of the rifle men to adjust immediately the rear sight gadget of their rifles.

"Now they are within 120 meters and get ready." Supplied the maskman.

"Range 100!" cracked the veteran and his men followed suit.

"Get the dogs at 100 and start firing to keep their heads down. I will move when I see the dogs down," he said as he looked through the binoculars. "And remember; don't kill unless a man moves that close to the door."

"Cpl Tunde, get dog on the left! Cpl Alagbe, you get the right one on my command."

"Yes sir! Yes sir!" responded the two sharp shooters to their serge major.

"The rest of you commence shooting immediately you hear their shots!"

The first 2 shots came seconds later and so accurate, sending the dogs down and what followed next was the breaking loose of hell itself in an exchange of fire between two opposing sides 100 meters from each other.

Amid the commotion of the gun fires the maskman made progress in a flank and in a couple of minutes had reached the rear door. He had to shoot the lock but the gun shots drowned his pistol shot. He got inside and found the girl. He quickly withdrew his knife from its sheath and cut her loose, her eyes widening in horror at the sight of the knife, initially not knowing his intention. Next, he removed the rag in her mouth, saying, "now is time for real freedom, baby. Father is waiting for ya."

As he was about to pull or pick her up the girl shouted with eyes wider opened. The mask man wheeled about instinctively and there crashing into the room through the front door was Fadi Zokalaus. Fadi's pistol cracked instantaneously …but…empty! The masked man aimed, hesitated, then holstered his own pistol. Then the 2 men rushed at each other. It was a savage, brawny, free styled unarmed combat between 2 men, equally strong, equally endowed aiming apparently at the demise of each other. When all attempt to subdue each other failed Fadi brought out his knife. The mask man followed suit, and the fight continued while the girl was just shouting. At a time Fadi stabbed the mask man on the shoulder which made the latter to drop his knife. Hands on each other's throat, Fadi raised his knife to finish the job but the man caught the knife hand in mid air. They grappled and struggle. Fadi managed to free his hand and raised it again. The maskman caught it again and as they held each other both looked into each other's eyes and momentarily seemed to be transfixed.

The police siren introduced another dimension into the whole battle ground. Both sides stopped firing and took to their heels. The two combatants in the house suddenly released each other, looked around for the girl who was nowhere to be found. The police had come. The mask man escaped by the rear door while Zokalaus escaped the way he had come.

All became curious in the camp as to what might have happened to their commander, the maskman, but then in about 18 minutes later when he made appearance they were relaxed and joyous.

"I could have finished all your sentries. You guys have to be more alert!"

"Yes sir, but we were alert sir!"

"More alert, I said."

"Yes sir." Stuttered the guard commander, but the mask man himself did not wait. He just went straight to his tent.

"I don't think we are the problems," the guards grumbled among themselves after he had gone, "he moves like *aljanunnu*."[23]

"Yes. He can penetrate anywhere unnoticed."

"I think there is something unusual about him. Are we sure he is human? He behaves like a ghost."

"Maybe he is."

Chief Bobade came in excitedly while the medicals tended the maskman's wound.

"I I am grateful, very grateful," he said excitedly, "How's the wound?"

"Very deep cut in the shoulder. He has lost a lot of blood but he is young and very strong…"

"Grateful for what?" the maskman had asked the chief, half expecting his reply but feeling rather sad for the disappearance of the girl.

"For my daughter, of course. I have my baby now. She ran out of the building and I was there to get her….errr…catch my baby!"

"Yeah..catch your baby! But, chief everyone here had contributed, most especially you."

"No, no, no. this is the happiest day of my life that was beginning to be miserable. For some time I thought I 'd lost her."

The mask man smiled pleasantly.

"And this, this thing," continued the chief, touching the bullet proof vest on his body, "this thing worked! I don't even know the bullets on which side hitting my chest as I rushed to pick my daughter. Some in the front and a couple in the back. I was so confused and turned around several times on the same spot. I thought I was dead!"

Everybody in the tent laughed. "Now you are alive to appreciate your daughter more."

"But how did you get the wound?" asked the chief.

"Stabbed by a man I wouldn't mind meeting again."

---

[23] Spirit.

"Oh yes, yes, you will meet again and that time around you will kill him."

The mask man had wondered what the chief would do now that he got his daughter back. Obviously he would not be blamed if his support leaned out. However noticing the fighting spirit still in the chief he ventured to find out

"I was thinking you would like to relax now that you have your daughter. You don't have to get involved any longer, but perhaps occasionally you might like to render some help we might demand of you."

"Whhat!? R rr relax for what? Nobody maltreats Bobby Nero and his family without getting punished. They have bought it dd d dozen prize. C c can you imagine my own d daughter, Angela, c cannot even recognize me again? Mmm my own Angela struggled with me...Angela struggled with mm me. Look at my face...scratches....finger nails!"

"Struggled! What do you mean!?"

"She f fought to escape! She c cannot recognize me again! My own baby Angela!"

"Where is she?"

'In there in my tent. I'm arranging to take her to the hospital."

The maskman immediately postponed his recommended bed rest and followed the chief to his tent where they found the girl, docile but rather looking confused and starring at the blank space. But as she caught sight of the maskman she got wild. It took strong men and not just one to subdue her.

"Sorry chief, she had gone through a lot within these few terrible days." The maskman said sympathetically. "Her mind had been put through more than its fair share of horrible experiences. You're right we're gonna need the services of pros on this. But we thank God first for having her back, and then we can get the required medical treatment money can procure."

"I will get the best for her. Trust m me on that....I..will...."

He stopped himself short as the maskman staggered and they rushed to his side.

"Yeah, I guess I'm overdue for that rest now." He finished and they helped him back to his tent.

He had a refreshing sleep but he woke up with only one memory and dominant thought prevailing on his mind. Who could be that man who could match him strength for strength and guile for guile? What is in that man that affected his soul to so much extent? He had a chance to at least shoot him even if he was not going to kill him. Why didn't he shoot? Yet he was sure it was not due solely to his innate dislike of killing. It is something more than that. It is an occurrence at a level of soul itself; words are simply not adequate to describe it. It was as if he was about to hurt his own very self; terminate his own very life. Why is it that even every blow and kicks he managed to land on the man he himself could feel how it must have affected the man? Or was it his own mind playing some tricks on him? Perhaps some of the tricks of these grand children of Orishadami....the Bwallangwists. And he, could he possibly have become such an easy subject of hypnotic suggestions? The more he ruminate this the more he gets himself bewildered. Should the forces that be present him with what has become his heart most wanted desire now- the opportunity to meet that man again, no matter how precarious the situation, and again with an advantage, he would still not be able to kill the man. This is very strange and something that had never happened to him before in his life. A soul recognition at a vibration higher than the objective mind is yet able to comprehend, talk less of interpreting.

———◆❖◆———

CHAPTER 11

THE ORDAINMENT

Fadi Zokalaus lay down on his stomach as he was being oiled and massaged buy tender hands. Despite the seemingly bad news the ceremony would not be stopped. It must be conducted on schedule. This ceremony, or rather, ritual is conducted once in 5 years and only when Bwallangwu wishes. Bwallangwu has seen the qualities he likes in Zokalaus and the young man is going to be made a priest.

As he lay there, while nimble, experienced hands of beautiful girls worked on his tough sinewy, muscularly defined body in preparation for the great occasion, he thought how well it would have been if on this very day of his ordainment as a Bwallangwu priest he had brought the ransom girl back to Bwallangwu. He was not very happy but then it was not his fault at all. The ugly situation should have been prevented in the first place. She shouldn't have been taken away from them at all from the farmhouse. For this he himself would like to blame Jobilah, his immediate commander for being old fashioned in the conduct of the affairs. But the most predominant subject of his thought and preying ravenously on his mind was that of that strange mask man that he encountered that day. Nobody as far as he could remember had ever grappled with him like that, man to man, in his life. He never feels the strength of any man but he felt this one. Though he couldn't see his face there was something he noticed ; something that got him momentarily motionless when they had looked into each other deep into the soul, so to say. Who the hell is he? Where did he come from? Why did he mask himself? He remembered when he ran out of rounds the man had a chance t kill him but strange enough he chose to fight with him hand to hand...he holstered his own, against him Zokalaus! How many among men would not seize such advantage when they come face to face with the Tiger of Bwallangwu? And why in his own turn was he hesitating to kill this man? Why, strange enough, did he himself feel that sharp pain when he stabbed the man, as if it was the man that stabbed him? What was that unexplainable sensation he had when they had looked into each other's eyes? He wished he had seen his face but again why the hell did he cover his face with that mask? This unending questions had ranged on and precipitated into one solid wish; he wished he could meet this man once again and this time around he would wreck into pieces that mask, first to see his face and then to answer some question before finally killing him...kill him...hmmmn. That last piece of intent lingered unconcluded. It was the appearance of chief Enlaye in the room that broke his train of thought.

"Well, Tiger, how are you doing in preparation?"

"Not so bad, chief."

"This should be the happiest day of your life, son. Now you have a chance of rising to be closest to Bwallangwu, only next to me! He personally chose you to be a priest. You know, son, several people had been recommended for his approval but he had rejected. Even Jobilah, your field commander has been rejected 3 good times!"

"Was it not you sir that recommended me?"

"No, not me. I wouldn't recommend you until after 3 years of trustful service. Not me at all."

"And I have not even served 5 month. Who then could have recommended me?"

"Agbaamole himself chose you as his priest."

"Bwallangwu!?" Exclaimed Zokalaus in surprise, making move to stand up, and the chief stopped him.

"No, no, no continue."

"How does he know me?" looking more surprised.

"Agbaamole knows everybody that serves him well and truthfully without ulterior motives. He is aware of exceptional participations in every mission. A sort of automatic records exists for him. He knows the qualities he wants and I must confess I was not surprised too much when your name came up on the list, breaking his own regulations. Believe you me, son, Agbaamole goes through our minds like files."

"Hmmmn. Interesting," Fadi replied.

"Now herald the beginning of a new phase of your life. You will be above mortals and would be able to decide their fate to some extent. They will be but puppets with their control strings in your hands. Soon you will enjoy the opportunities I've enjoyed for years. A lot just know that Bwallangwu exists but you will be empowered to go close. You will not see him, nobody does, but you will be able to take instructions direct from him whenever he so wishes, otherwise all other times you follow the chain of command. Hmmmn, young man, putting a hand on his shoulder, "you have a very bright future. I can see you growing to be the next CBS (Chief of Bwallangwu Staff) without rival. All you have to do is remain obedient and steadfast...... You seem not too happy, son.... what else could be on your mind on this great day of yours?....."

"Yeah, chief, the thought of that girl getting away and the implications of that. I mean the trouble that might ensue when she starts jabbering."

The chief smiled confidently. "That's part of what I have been telling you. There is nothing to worry about."

"What do you mean, chief? That girl must not talk!"

"She will not be able to sing to anybody and if she ever does, nobody will understand her.'

"Now, chief, what do you mean sir?"

"Why do you suppose, over there at Alabe, I insisted in partaking in the hunt? Certainly you wouldn't think to partake in the thoroughfare. No, son, I'm too old for that."

"Now I am beginning to understand, but just beginning. I still don't get it" replied Zokalaus in his deep voice, looking straight ahead, not at the chief, but ahead.

"Hmmmn, son, there is a lot yet to be understood, and more and more. It is one of the powers that would be bestowed on you gradually, one by one, once you are ordained, step by step, and at certain times as Agbaamole dims fit and it depends much on the kind and nature of assignment he might be sending you."

"Powers...what powers?"

"You would be able to deprogram a subject on sight, the effect of which depends on how strong the subject is, not physically but psychically, and of course, how advanced you are yourself. Now, reprogramming is a higher attainment."

"On sight...But the girl was not in sight that evening."

"Good! I told you, you have potentials so endearing to Agbaamole. No, she wasn't in sight but there are other ways. If a high initiate like me is able to step on a total of 21 footsteps of hers in the direction of the hunt I've got her. Unfortunately, that night I couldn't find any apart from two footsteps of males."

"And that is why you agreed to return to the farmhouse I suppose, sir?"

"Exactly! So it remained one last option which if not available it would have been a source of worry."

"A third option..."

"Yes, son, but not my favorite, as it is very strenuous."

"And what would that be sir?"

"Now you want to know why I collected the ropes and the gag from you in that place. You remember I did?"

"Yes sir, but I never attached any meaning to it."

"Hmmm, *aye toto fun un*,[24]" the chief said in some of his witty Yoruba sayings. "Vibroturgy! ...hmmmn...psychometry.... son, a high initiate can remotely connect with a subject if in possession of certain items the subject recently held on his or her body. That is what I returned to the farmhouse to perform. I hope you would no more be surprised when you hear that some thieves do not come for money but clothes, especially under wears, pants. I could not get that girl's pant

---

[24] A saying to venerate the potentials of earthlings

but the gag rag worked equally well. They both cover orifices and," making a face, "albeit the one down there is slightly better. But that of the mouth worked equally well." The chief finished in deep tone.

"Hmmmmn"

"As I said to you before, mortals would be but mere puppets in your hands. Under your own very control! They would be chess pieces and you the player."

"Including the offsprings of Orishagbemi? The one you once talked to me about."

"Well, they are our greatest obstacles but their days are numbered. We will wipe them out and eliminate them. Of course you will lead the operation. That's Agbaamole's most coveted wish. It will please him so much. OPERATION PATAPATA."

"I only wonder why that has not been done all these years."

"Haaah, they are the only ones who could recover the Rosary. That is why Bwallangwu has kept them alive. Hmmmn, to use them, ha ha ha ha. *Omo buruku l'ojo tie loto*[25]."

"But what else are we waiting for? The Rosary is with us now."

"I seriously want to present the issue to him again. Then he would give the go ahead. It is all in plan."

"Chief, do you really believe all this shit story that surrounds this Rosary?"

"Why not? The Rosary is real and if the Rosary is real then the stories are real."

A little silence ensued after then and after a while the chief suddenly and rather concernedly said, "son, yesterday it was brought to my notice the report of a man who is said to be as strong, as fast and as versatile as you…"

"The report is correct. He is good but I'm stronger.!"

"Who was he?"

"I don't know...yet sir."

"His strategies are remarkable and his tactics ad methods are adequate. He took the girl and nearly fooled us into making us believe

---

[25] A bad child has his own special day of coming in handy.

it was Joe who made away with the girl. If not for the hounds that helped in locating Joe fast enough."

"Something that could have been prevented in the first case." Fadi retorted.

The chief looked at Fadi silently as he was making up his mind on something. Then Zokalaus broke the silence. "I admit sir. He is good."

"And it takes a great man to admit the qualities of his rival. Such seldom makes mistakes. It means you're greater, son." And another period of silence during which chief Enlaye intensified his gaze on Zokalaus, this time rather imploringly. He said, "you will do it as a special job for Bwallangwu, and Agbaamole will be pleased. Find him."

"The hell I will sir."

"The thought of such a man being on the side of my enemies makes me extremely uncomfortable. Find him for me...find him for Bwallangwu."

True, Chief Enlaye has a good reason to find the maskman but Fadi Zokalaus has a more compelling reason to find the man. "Yeah, sure, the hell I will find him," he assured not really directly at the chief but more to himself.

"Some other thing bothering you, son?"

"Just wondering, chief..."

"About what?"

"D you think he might be one of chief Bobade's goons...in fact what are the BWALLINT findings on this matter?"

"Yes, Bwallangwu Intelligence has been assigned but has not come up with enough useful Intel. The notion so far is that he is one of the freelancers arbitrarily gathered by Bobby in his desperate bid to save his daughter."

"And he has succeeded, of course, in his contract."

"Yes, son, you can say that again. Because no ordinary man could recover a victim from Bwallangwu."

"Hmmmmn," Zokalaus, muttered soberly.

"Must be one of those Ife-Modakeke war cracks. But Bobby is a poor judge of character and assets. I bet you he would not know his real worth."

"Why then the mask if he really works for him?"

'Obviously to hide his face even from Bobby. Could be a relation of his or a known person, or what if he has a terribly battered face... from the war?. But what the hell! What is biting you?"

"Two things."

"Mention them."

"First, he doesn't look like anybody's goon to me. I know the type when I see them."

"Anybody can be made to obey in one way or the other...after all Bobby also gave us some good money," he quickly added not to irritate Zokalaus. "And the second thing?"

"How come he never delivered the girl immediately....I mean between Thursday evening 7:30 and Saturday afternoon is more than enough time, even if the distance is from here to Lungi in Sierra Leone."

"Hmmm. Might just be trying to be clever. Squeeze some more juice from desperate Bobby. Doesn't that make sense? It also means he has his weaknesses and I am glad to discover that! He would sure belong to us and it is sweet to imagine what a formidable tag team the two of you would be! Or the ability to perform 2 miracles at the same time; You on one side, the maskman on the other. He can continue to wear his mask if he chooses, for all I care, ha ha ha ha, tchi tchi tchi. Please find him. I can never allow him to fight against me. He has to be on my side or he dies. Find him and for sure Bwallangwu will appreciate."

"I said I would sir." Zokalaus replied between his teeth.

The chief went out and the girls came back inside to continue with the nerve soothing massage in preparation for the ordainment of a priest to be, who must be conditioned body and mind to receive the vibrations of Bwallangwu in a ritual that takes place 5 years interval."

⸻◆▸◆◂◆⸻

The rhythm was fantastically hilarious, energetic and hallucinating. The wild waist twisting dance was spectacular, infectious and energy sapping. The atmosphere provoked by certain fragrance of incense was in many ways compelling. Occasionally and continually the whirl dance would stop abruptly and chants and incantations are recited in deep solemn nerve-soothing tone. For the third time Fadi Zokalaus, his glistening body lying on a wooden table, went into a trance. The ritual went on for seven hours on the altar in front of the abode of Bwallangwu. Again and again Zokalaus was led to the inner shrine which has been visited on several occasion by chief Enlaye and past alike. There he answered questions and took oath and made promises in front of Bwallangwu himself, with only a black curtain obscuring his view of the devil himself. The initiation was to prepare the young priest's body and soul, to empower him to be able to stand in the presence of Agbaamole whose aura is de-enervating, de-energizing and shocking to electrocution, so to say. The voice penetrates your whole essence and many an initiates in the past had simply collapsed in his presence, even after the ritual.

"The wish of Luuuucifeeeer," said the agbaamole, "is to take over the world…..completely….and I am here in this world to perpetrate that wish. I am here to carry out the wish of Luciferrrr!!! My enemies are all those who try to prevent the perpetration. What do you do to my enemies?"

"I, Fadi Zokalaus, destroy them!"

"Gooood! Have you given yourself completely to Lucifer?"

"Yes."

"Goood! From now on your soul is accepted by Lucifer and is now in custody of me, Bwallangwu the Agbaamole. You have given willingly your body and soul?"

'Yes."

"Your body is now the bread, your blood our wine and your soul would join that of Lucifer to make him strongerrrr!"

"Yes."

"You will serve me whole heartedly. My wishes take priority in your life. You will sacrifice anything for the supreme messenger of Lucifer. Everything that is yours now belongs to Bwallangwu. There will be no turning back! The day you turn against me you will die!"

"If I ever have a reason to turn back and I turn back, then I die!"

The overlabored breathy words of the unseen deity behind the black screen stopped and the young man was made to kneel down while he was given a calabash of some concoction to drink and he took the final oath.

> "I Fadimefa Zokalaus, on this day pledge complete body, mind and soul in front of Bwallangwu, the agbalagba irunmole. I will have no separate wishes thereon except those of Lucifers. I will keep secret all I have known and yet still to know, including my instructions and the identities of Bwallangwists. I swear to destroy the enemies of Lucifer and I will not stop until their roots remnants are destroyed. I will sacrifice everything for Bwallangwu and the day I turn against Bwallangwu I will die. So help me Lucifer."

A gentle but very warm breeze blew from behind the thick black curtain. As the youngest priest was led out of the innermost chamber to be welcomed by the priests that gathered in the outer chamber who, by initiation have not been able to gain access to the deepest, clapped perfunctorily, some obviously saddened by the implication of this very inaugural initiation.

The big drum was beaten 3 times, signifying the end of the ritual, trumpet sounded and whirl music and invigorating dances recommenced and this time around as Priest Fadimefa Zokalaus, now in his priestly long robe, put on him on emerging from the outermost chamber, finally emerged into the open, the beat changed. The tempo was raised and four young, succulent virgins in skirts made of grass threw themselves at his feet. Then the music stopped and chief Enlaye said, as he put his hand on his shoulder, "I am proud of you, son. I must confess, you are the strongest. I could remember when I took that concoction when I was being ordained years ago, I staggered and the chief priest, may he rest in peace in the bosom of Lucifer, had to hold me."

"That was terrible. What was it, sir?"

"Hmmmn, son, my priest, Tiger, what you took in there was the blood of Bwallangwu, the Agbalagbaamole himself. Your entire body constitution has been retuned to the essence of Bwallangwu and is now in the process of gradual upgrading. You know something in our enemies book that says something about avoiding taking blood in any form?....hmm.. This is where we are above them. You are now above mortals. Gradually you will feel the changes. And you will have the rare opportunity of knowing the several names of Bwallangwu according to the level of the add-ons to the initiation. Such names you could use to perform some feats in time of need. You are now a priest." Then pointing down encouragingly at the girls, he said, "well, make yourself treated to the gift of Bwallangwu. They are virgins." Then he moved away to join the elders, who have been waiting for him for instructions on arrangements of further activiries.

Priest Zokalaus looked down at the girls, at their juicy body and young, succulent, thrusting naked breasts and contrary to expectations, especially of those jealous eyes, his face narrowed as if focusing into what seems like adjusting a welding oxyacetylene flame, piercing the crowd. He looked around minutely, painstakingly, then shrugging, he allowed the effect of the contagious music to infect his soul and he joined in the whirl dance which became wilder with the increasing raise of its tempo. This time Jobilah went to his side and spoke furiously, "you have refused the offer of Bwallangwu!?"

"I have not refused any offer from Bwallangwu."

"You ought to have selected one or even two from those succulent virgins and she is yours for the night! And ever after if you wish!"

"What is your concern? Where is Bimbi!"

"Ho, ho, ho, now that you are a priest you would soon know." Temper rising.

"So tell me. Tell the priest." Matching his temper.

"I don't know. How would I know? Don't forget I'm not a priest."

With this last statement Jobilah walked away from the dance arena only to go and fulfill his appointment with wine.

The black range rover headed toward Iwo road that fateful morning, the tainted glass obscuring the occupants from the view of outsiders At the wheel was Jobilah and Zokalaus by his side. Sitting behind were Joe, Sammy and Denne. "We're going to collect some stuffs for the chief from some people at Fatte," Jobilah had said aloud to the hearing of everyone.

They just reached Owode when Zokalaus turned and poured the content of his silenced sub machine gun into the amazed occupants of the rear seat. They stopped and pushed them out.

"Heeerrrr, what a mess!" exclaimed Jobilah, "next time allow me to tell them to get out before you do this job...priest."

"The aim has being achieved! With minimum risk to say the least. The boys will clean up the mess. What a hassle!"

On the way back Zokalaus had demanded, "so where is Bimbi now? You could tell me."

"I told you to find out for yourself. What the hell? What are you going to do with her anyway? Look if I were you I'd just leave the matter as it is. I wouldn't worry about revenge any longer. You are a priest to the benefit of it. So what are you worrying about?"

"What da heck are you talking about!? Who the hell is talking about revenge?"

"Then why are you looking for her?" Jobilah asked as he lit a cigarette.

"She is my woman!"

"Your what!" coughing, "you must be joking!"

"What da bloody fuck do you mean by that?"

"Look I'm no priest. I don't know a damn thing except what I'm told. So you go ask chief if you want to know the where about of your errr.. woman. Jesus Christ, ha ha ha," he laughed. "By the way, you were given some juicy succulent things, young virgins! Never been touched, oh my god, you refused. Now you are asking me about..errr....go ask the chief."

Zokalaus went straight to chief Enlaye who welcomed him with allegations and reported cases outright. "In addition to the few I have witnessed myself; reports coming to me from here and there are unbecoming of a priest! A high priest and possibly a chief to come! You should bear it in mind that your life changed the day you were ordained. You should become fatherly now, think of and think for others. You are no more the always solo Zokalaus who does things his own way and who does not give a damn what happen to his people. A priest is not supposed to snub his people, talk less of maltreating them."

"They misbehaved sir and discipline is the backbone of any strong organization."

"I may have to agree with you but to an extent based on all these report before me.....and what the hell happened between you and Thomas that you had to throw him down a 2 storey building? The boy is a priest's brother, don't you know?"

"If I tell you sir, you would kill him yourself."

"He still could have died from that fall. So what happened?"

"I heard him telling some of his rotten friends that I'm a pansy."

"Pansy. What does that mean?"

"A fagot. He called me a homo. Being a priest's brother is the more reason why he has to know what to say about a priest!"

"You boys of today watch a lot of cinemas and gather a lot of funny slangs. What a gain is faggot for Lucifer's sake?"

"Homosexual."

"Haah! Anyway take it easy. And by the way, what went wrong with you on the night of your ordainment? Many able bodied men would have rushed for such girls without the need for much enticement. They were virgins, you know, carefully selected. Bwallangwu's special gift to his newly ordained priest. Refusing such lovely things could attract all sorts of remarks from various sources. What is wrong?"

"Incidentally, that is what has brought me here now, sir."

"No, you are here because I sent for you."

"I didn't see anybody sir."

"Same story yesterday. What is happening, Fadimefa?"

"Is it possible for my chief priest to send for me, and I Fadi, would refuse to come?"

"I wonder."

"I tell you what sir, when you send those boys they don't deliver.

They turn back on the way and come and give false report for reasons best known to them."

"If that is the case it would be sorted out. Now what?"

"Well, chief it's about half a year now I've kept my balls hanging miserably in between my thighs. Where is my woman?"

"First this manner of talking of yours amuses me for a chief, but more seriously, when have I become your woman's keeper?"

"I was told to ask you as nobody seems or pretend not, to have a clue."

"Who is your woman, son?"

"Bimbi."

"The chief instinctively threw down his fountain pen and said, "son, I shouldn't worry about her any longer."

"What!? Why?"

"Are you asking?"

"Yes sir!"

The chief looked at Zokalaus. A look that would melt the spine of many a tough men. Such a look that would have crippled Jobilah. This young priest just returned his gaze.

"I am beginning to hope that a saying that goes that, 'no matter how good you are to a monkey it would end up tearing your dress,' would not one day apply."

"I beg your pardon, chief."

"I expect you to know how to behave and heed warnings, especially a priest that you are!" The chief lost his temper and exploded, "Once you are told to forget an issue, you forget it! Is that clear, priest Zokalaus?"

"She is the only woman I know. The only woman I can recognize! She is part of my life and you want me to forget her! Just like that!? Is it possible to forget one's own life!?"

"Zokalaus! I wish this is not happening. I wish this has never happened! Never!!!!"

"I want my woman!" He shouted back to the amazement of the chief. This really had never happened before.

"Alright, if you have to be told, after all you are a priest. She is in the service of Bwallangwu."

"And so am I, chief!"

"Oh my god! You have failed to understand a very basic fact! And it's a shame!"

"To ask for my woman!?"

"She belongs exclusively to Bwallangwu! You got acquainted in her line of work! That is all, if you want it the hard way. She finished her assignment and its over!"

"We are talking about Bimbi!"

"You were just an assignment. A mission!"

"She's my woman!"

"Don't forget your pledge, young man! You swore to serve Bwallangwu with everything you have!"

"My woman is not included! My woman is not part of the pledge! Bimbi is not part of my pledge! She is my woman!"

"Zokalaus! I made you! Is this how you are going to repay me? Hahaaa."

"I know what I owe Bwallangwu and that is what I pledged. Operationally and other aspects, have I ever shirked away from my responsibilities? Have I ever refused even the meanest and most dangerous assignments? At the risk of my neck I will perform for Bwallangwu. I will carry out his duties and that is my understanding of what I pledged. I never pledged to be deprived of the only woman that means something in my life."

"All this my woman, my woman, do you think she has the same feelings for you?"

"That is why I want to see her face to face so she can tell me that and that is what I expect from you to arrange Sir!"

"You see, when an elder tells you something, the best you can do for yourself is to listen and obey. What you are asking for is impossible, son."

"Unless you are telling me she is dead!"

"She is not your woman. She was just carrying out an assignment for Bwallangwu. So forget about her."

"She is the only one that can tell me that."

"What my young priest is telling me now is that he can struggle for the same woman with Bwallangwu..."

"Oh no, no, no, chief. I am talking about Bimbi! Why are we carrying this thing to such a riddicu…." He stopped himself.

"Oh yes, don't stop. Ridiculous extent! Zokalaus!!!," the chief burned and roared. "To God who made me, if you were not a priest I would have had you thrown physically out and straight under arrest! This is what we were saying about this ordainment! Too young in the system but that is the way Bwallangwu wants it! Consider yourself lucky, otherwise…"

"Look, chief, where is Bimbi!?"

"I say forget it!"

"No!"

"*E ma gba mi ke.*[26] Are we not in trouble? I have never seen this before in the history of this organization!"

"Tell me now sir. Where is Bimbi?"

"Alright, alright, she is presently carrying out an assignment for Bwallangwu somewhere in Tanzania and don't ask me what the errand is. You don't have the need to know of everything in the organization. More so that you have exhibited this sort of behavior."

"When is she coming back?"

"In a couple of months she should be back and you will find out for yourself who she really belongs to and much as I like you this is the last time you will exhibit such a behavior in my presence and even for her own sake!"

"Yes, chief."

Zokalaus was at least relieved. At least she isn't dead. When there is life there is hope. Chief Enlaye pampers Zokalaus and everybody knows. He wouldn't like to discipline him right now because he needs him for a mission. An operation which if successful would constitute the beginning of the realization of his much coveted dream. He thinks he has to take it easy with him for now. Not that he still wouldn't perform under any condition but he knows Zokalaus operates better and is more resourceful when he willingly cooperates and he, Enlaye, is not one to allow sentiments to come in the way of success of the

---

[26] To my rescue.

operation. He would discipline him later. But then, still very furious, he called Jobilah, as he usually does when he has some problems to solve.

"Jobilah! This young man is getting out of hand. What do you think…?"

"But sir you know the matter is beyond me. It's beyond my powers, chief. He is a priest and issues among priests are handled among priests. But you made him priests, chief….small boys..hmmmm."

"I didn't make him priest! Bwallangwu did! Moreover I didn't call you to come and criticize but to give me your opinion. Your suggestion!"

"Oh, my chief. I think you ought to take it easy with him for now. Later I think Bwallangwu will find a solution to his problem."

"Y yes yes yes, Jobilah, you are right. That is it. I will take your advice and take it easy. I will personally take his case to Bwallangwu after Operation PAKUFINRIN. Anyway, how are you preparing your men?"

"We are in top condition now and we have rehearsed several times. Everybody knows what to do. We are ready. But chief, I still do not understand why it is so necessary to eliminate chief Aborungun. I can't reason it out."

"Don't reason out anything! The decision has been taken! Why do you want to reason out again!?" the chief shouted, "Yours is to transform the decisions into reality! All the reasoning have already been done!"

"Yes, my lord."

"Now do you have any other useful advice or suggestion?"

"That is all, my lord."

"Now just go back to your men and rehearse!"

"Yes my lord."

Qqqqqqqqqqqqqqqqqqqqqqqqqqqqqqqqqqqqqqqqqqqqqqqqqqqqqqqqqqqq qqqqqqqqqqqqqqqqqqqqqqqqqqqqqq

CHAPTER 12

"Don't shout!" A man whispered into his ears. "Don't move, just listen. If you have to attend the meeting of the Council of King makers, do not go by road. You might be ambushed and the ambushed party won't be interested in taking you alive."

The voice was very quiet, the hold was very strong. How could one have moved anyway? Who was this strange man and how could he have entered his house talk less of his very bedroom in spite of his acclaimed unbeatable security? And just the manner he had appeared he seemed to have suddenly disappeared because all had been quiet again! Or was he still there?

Chief Jimmy Aboripe Aborungun finally took the risk of opening his eyes.....or was it a dream? A nightmare?...Nobody! Neither was there any sign of anybody haven entered. Or was he hallucinating? But if it was somebody who the hell was he? Who could have beaten so easily his security, the pride of all securities! Was it a ghost then? Quite possibly. But the message hammered persistently in his head. Sure there was going to be a meeting of the *Afobajes*[27] and he intended to go by road.... Ambush!

"Who the hell would be interested in ambushing me? For what?

---

[27] Kingmakers

Who might want to commit suicide? But….I think I'm overworking…I need a rest…a vacation….a holiday."

"Ooh, what's that again, Jimmy?" Mrs. Titilayo Aborungun grumbled in her sleep as she turned and cuddled her husband, "talking in your sleep?"

"Then it must have been a nightmare as nobody else has seen anybody. Otherwise, trust Titi, she would have shouted like she did the day she ate pepper."

"Ooh, stop it Jimmy"

The chief put his strong arm on his wife who moved closer to put her head on the deep hairy chest of one of the most powerful men in Yorubaland.

<hr />

A pair of binoculars searched for men and equipment of the ambush party from the opposite side of the road that cut through a high land.

"Most important are the bazookas and the rocket launchers. Small arms can't do much damage to the chief's bulletproof car."

"Yes. I've got 2 good boys whose main task is to take care of them."

"Why not 4?" asked the maskman as the sergeant major looked down the road about 8 meters down. "Since they have the initiatives; we can't locate them yet until they fire."

They had brought the troop and garrisoned them some 50 meters back and both had crawled back to edge of this highland where they had succeeded in pinpointing the equipment and the layout of the ambush party. Later they had had the men join them.

Time passed slowly but surely and after an hour the masked man relaxed, smiled and said, "Well he should have passed by now if he is going to attend the meeting."

"The meeting deh start for 1030, no be so? The serge major asked in his Pidgin English.

"Yeah, the meeting starts in about 10 minutes and he is yet more than 6 kilometers away and if I knew anything about the chief at all, he certainly would never be late."

Two minutes later he consulted his wrist watch again as he looked down the road and he smiled in relief, "very, very good. He is not going to attend. Wise man.....What!? Oooh! Foolish! I warned him!" He had sighted the chief's convoy.

"Send the message!" He told the radio man.

The convoy was approaching. It draws nearer gradually with each circumferential rotation of the wheels reducing the distance between them and a certain hell. It seemed as if nothing was going to happen but the man was quite sure that the Bwallangwu men were around. But where? He could see a grader coming harmlessly from the opposite direction of the road to that of the convoy. Perhaps nothing was going to happen.

All of a sudden the grader slowed down and turned its blade sideways, thereby blocking the road. And just like termites coming out of the ground men dressed in wrapper and shirts trooped out with Dane guns, spears, bow and arrows and cutlasses while the unmistakable sound of machine guns reported from some concealed locations. A man rushed forward to throw a grenade at the chief's Mercedes Benz but was brought down by the chief's defense boys. Then it became a real battle. War! The maskman sighted the bazooka as it blasted one armored vehicle and his men concentrated fire at it and within seconds later the bazooka and the carrier were blown sky high. More attempts to get the Mercedes Benz were frustrated as the toll of fallen men increased. The Bwallangwu men were desperate at getting the chief but the chief's fighters picked them easily and the battle goes on and where the hell are the police? By the time the smoke had cleared the armored vehicles had all being got. The Command post was on its back.

"Shit! Where the hell are the police!? Bloody 10 minutes now after the message!"

He had decided to call the police at the onset of the attack. In fact he had gotten the message sent to them immediately he had sighted the chief's convoy approaching. Just as he heard the faint sound of a siren a rocket was launched which virtually picked the black Benz up sky high and smashed it on the road. Sighting the position of the launcher the men opened fire, "Gaademn too late!" the maskman shouted. Every party started disappearing as the police siren grew louder.

"Withdraw your men!" he told the sergeant major. From his concealed position he notice curiously the Bwallangwu men, who were carrying the dead and the wounded, concentrated more on those dressed in wrapper and shirts. Then it clicked in his mind.

"Give me two men," he told the serge major before the latter withdrew with the rest and under his directives, the two started shooting at the men in those Eastern traditional attire including the men trying to carry them. "Cripple them mostly!"

The news all over the media throughout the country was that there had been an ambush in which Chief Jimmy Aboripe Aborungun's convoy had been attacked and his people mercilessly massacred by a group of people believed to be Easterners. More to the expectation of those who believed dogmatically that the chief is a demi-god, chief Aborungun was said to have vanished into thin air. He was said to have been teleported by 'Egbe', a Yoruba magical power of teleportation. The news went on to say that some men had been arrested through the timely intervention of the police and those would be helping them in their investigations. Twenty men were reported dead and 42 on danger list. More news to be released.

The maskman was in chief Aborungun's house that night.

"I know you would come," the chief said as he locked the door of his study behind them. "You move like a ghost. I thought it was a nightmare yester night. Are you sure you are not a ghost?"

"You have just touched me, chief."

"Hmmn, the sense of distance, touch, smell, in fact, all objective senses can be simulated, my young eeerr... ghost."

"Your people believe you were teleported by Egbe. Wonderful! How does it work?"

"Sorry, I employed the services of the much slower Egbe's sister," replied the chief.

"And what is that?"

"I left earlier on by helicopter to attend the meeting."

"But now your people and even your enemies believe you're really invincible."

The chief laughed heartily and then stopped abruptly to ask, "Who wants me dead so bad?"

"Must be your enemy. Don't you think so?" Being sarcastic.

"Now I remember all you told me but who are you and why do you wear that mask? Or do I say thank you first, and with what? Just name it."

"Unfortunately, I'm just who you already called me. So you don't have to bother to thank me. We ghosts don't take compensations either."

"Then to what do I owe this special divine service? After all to those much has been given much is expected."

"Suppose I say that you and I, man and ghost, are puppets in the hands of the almighty pulling the strings...well his work is better when we are willing."

"Ghost language. I'm getting lost."

"By our actions we just might be able to prevent a national disaster, chief."

"A what!?"

"An imminent civil war."

"I don't get it."

"This time around between the West and the East."

"Kidding me or do ghosts hallucinate?"

"Chief, I witness the ambush live and even did some shooting against your attackers. A sizeable proportion of those men were dressed in Eastern attires, wielding Dane guns, machetes and all sorts of local weapons.. The Yorubas would not take it kindly if one of the most respected chieftains in their kingdom is killed."

"I am still baffled. But what would cause a big rift between the two powerful nationalities? Unthinkable!"

"You don't catch the joke yet?"

"Still seems incomprehensible...disjointed. Ghosts are faster, I guess."

"Chief, someone or some people want a war between the two major peoples. Some people set the stage like that. Even the media already carried it that it was the Easterners that ambushed your convoy and massacred your men."

"Not so ridiculous yet."

"I know those men were not Easterners."

"How?"

"I stayed behind to find out. Someone or some people want a major disaster for some reason I cannot yet fathom. We have to prevent this war by all means."

The chief let his head hang loose as he paced about in contemplation in the big study, then he came back to face his enigmatic night visitor.

"You surprise me all the more. I still like to know why you go about in mask. Hiding from your enemies I can understand but I am your friend."

"I am hiding also from my friends"

"Why?"

"That's what ghosts do."

"How did you know about the ambush in good time to warn me? Do I suppose you sold them out?"

"Like for 10 shekels or something like that?"

"Well…"

"Strange enough I do not belong to anybody"

"Then such an operation of that magnitude and seriousness, you agree, is a top secret and would take a lot to scoop, even for a ghost."

"Do you underrate the ubiquity and capabilities of ghosts?"

"C'mon, man."

"I bugged their chief's office the night they had a kind of ceremony."

"You bugged?"

"Modern gadgets could be handy to modern ghosts."

"Who are they? Political?"

"A powerful cult."

"I guess as much."

"They call themselves Bwallangwists."

"Whaat!?" The chief was physically startled at the mention of this name.

"Bwallangwists, chief, don't shout."

"Are you sure!?"

"What da heck!?"

Now the chief hung his head in thought for a longer time. The ghost, looking at him and waiting, seemed to have all the time. Then the chief asked again seriously, "Look! Who are you and please not this ghost crab!"

"You might know later. What's important now is to prevent the looming disaster and any further attempt on your life by ...err Bwallangwu.."

"If it is really Bwallangwu....hmmmmn....It takes a hell lot to go against Bwallangwu," the chief said slowly, somehow sad. "I never thought it would come to this so soon."

"He is already on your neck. What other choice do you have?" It has to be done!"

"By who!?"

"You, me, others. We have already started!"

"Like seriously!?" sadly laughing. "It would be war!"

"So? It is already war! And what does it take to fight a war? We have an army...well still growing.,..you have the power and the influence we could use and all the required important connections, local and international. You are the king maker, so to say?"

"Oh yeah. Just like mosquitoes, tsetse flies and termites organizing forces, attempting to bite an elephant to death!"

"Not the exact situation. More like bees and wasps against some smaller animals, even man. A good number of wasps or bee can sting a man to death. Again those small ants have been known to make a snake bite itself to death. A king becomes a slave if he refuses to fight when invaded. An army is defeated if it continues to think all the time that its enemy is invincible."

"Some remarkable ghost proverbs. Good ones...but tell me who and who are the backbones in your arrangement...err ...army."

"Later maybe, with time."

"Hmmmn," the chief smiled, "beautiful...and the only member

I might know wears a mask…so I can't even describe him nor even connect them to anything."

"It means your identity is secured if you give us your support. I'd rather fight my enemy anyway before he comes and catches me like a sitting duck."

"I am no sitting duck!"

"Sorry, chief, I forgot about Egbe."

The chief looked at him or rather his mask and got into some silent thought briefly,

"What is the worth of your army? Your strength? Just how much weapons do you have?"

"Not much yet. For now something like 100 men and like 50 million Naira worth of arsenal and potential to get more."

"Not bad…not too bad but you will certainly need more than that…more than weapons" he added pensively.

"We shall get whatever we need, actual and improvised."

"I like your spirit. The spirit of a real fighter."

"Talking about spirit…talking about ghost…spirit abounds with ghosts."

"Funny….and you still won't pull your mask so that at least I know the person I am dealing with in this precarious situation and perhaps the most important phase of my life?"

"No, thank you. I appreciate."

"Aren't you underrating me a bit?"

"No chief, I am not."

"Then maybe you are just being careless?"

"Not in the least."

"What if I call my guards to come and pull off your mask?"

"You mean the ones that ushered me into your bedroom at night?"

"All the same, the power of numbers is still to reckon with."

"Then that might mean," replied the man, picking his words deliberately, "that you are interested in starting the war right here in your house."

Shaking his head and giving him a look over, he said, "no. I don't think you are the man I want a war with. At least, not now. And if you

THE GUARDIAN OF THE MYSTICAL ROSARY

are that good as to penetrate my security every time you like, just like that, as if you designed it for me, then, I am not a fool. I'd rather have you on my side. Maybe we could combine forces. But there is a slight problem if we have to operate jointly."

"What could that be, chief?"

"You operate at night, *Ijakumo funra ara re,*[28] I operate in day time, *eeyan ni emi*[29]. So how does it work?"

"That shouldn't be a problem."

"Then meet me by dawn tomorrow at the bank of river Akinjole. Then we go some place in my yacht…hmmn….a pleasure cruise around the coast of Gbongan and we discuss, at full length, in privacy."

"You got it, chief, I would be there."

The masked man turned to go, the chief rushed him from behind. Just a few seconds later the man lowered the bulky chief gently on a seat and vanished from the house.

———◆◆◆◆———

Chief Enlaye could not contain himself. He paced up and down the big room, dancing, so to say, shouting occasionally with every shout making Jobilah jump where he stood.

"What happened Jobilaaah!"

"It's all what I have explained, my lord."

"Tell me what happened again, Jobilaah!"

"My lord, despite the outside interference, we were able to crush his car."

"And he was teleported by Egbe! Jobilaaaah!"

And Jobilah jumped again. That was his third time of explaining to the chief the report of the ambush on chief Aborungun's convoy in ops PAKUFINRIN. There was once an occasion when he had to report a certain matter all over for a dozen times. He wondered with horror how many times he would have to this time around.

"This is double disaster, Jobilah! A complete wreck! *Iya wa di'ya*

---

[28] The jackal himself. (Ijakumo is a nocturnal animal)

[29] I am a human being

s'ada si'kun, ikun lo tan, ada sonu.[30]The mission failed, Aborungun is still alive, and some of my men were captured including a priest! A priest! Are you not supposed to be watching out for each other?"

"He got shot on both legs, my lord and if I had dragged him any further I would have been captured as well and that, my lord would have been a worse disaster for Bwallangwu."

"And this outside interference!?"

"My lord, it is the maskman. He has an army!"

"And what do we have, Jobilah?"

"An army sir. He took us by surprise."

"And who is supposed to take anybody by surprise?"

"We took our target by surprise, my chief, but this maskman…"

"This maskman. Who is he?…Ooh, this man is a pain in my ass!"

"Sorry sir!" Why Jobilah has to apologize for anything concerning his chief's ass is yet to be explained.

"I want him! Jobilah…I want him!"

"I promise to get him for you my lord. I will kill him!"

"Alive!"

"Yes sir! I will kill him alive!"

"Are you confused!? I want him alive! Recruit him! He is going to be an asset, isn't it?"

"Yes sir, He he is an asset." Obviously not liking that aspect. He is not too comfortable with people who might end up outshining him in his own aspect in the organization. He already has Fadi as one case to deal with.

"Whatever it takes….anything he wants….Jesus, I never new or believe there are men like that outside Bwallangwu organization, So we bring him in."

"You are correct sir. I will bring him in. Now about these people in police custody?"

"They must not talk!"

"I understand perfectly, my lord."

"I am sure you know what to do. I don't want a problem!"

---

[30] Like double jeopardy for a hunter who threw his cutlass at ikun (a small animal like squirrel) and missed. The animal got away and the cutlass, missing.

"We have 2 options sir. We bust them loose or we eliminate them right there in that custody."

"Eliminate them as soon as possible! And make a plan to get my priest out quick!"

"That won't be a difficult problem, my lord. I have some faithfuls with the police. I will give you an update before noon. But there is one problem sir."

"What is that?"

"Fadi is in hospital. Shouldn't we allow his wounds to heal before we bust him out? After all what does it cost us. He is a priest and he will not be able to talk till he is brought back here to regain his mind from Bwallangwu"

"Alright, I will think about that but get those others eliminated quick!"

⸻◆◆◆◆◆⸻

The maskman was not taking chances. Chief Aborungun's moves the other night has shown that the latter is full of surprises. If not for necessity of the situation and how important the chief is in his scheme, he should have avoided him at least until he is ready to reveal himself.

He had left camp with a section and had advanced towards river Akinjole, maintaining contact with the camp all the way. He secured a good cover behind a rock and surveyed the surrounding all the rest of the way to the river. The meeting was scheduled for dawn, about 0500hrs, but he had decided to be there by 0300hrs. At 0400 he could notice, through his night viewing glasses, some men, armed lightly, rowed in in a canoe. They got aground and quickly deployed, taking positions behind covers. He took his walkie talkie and called camp

"Section B, Standby,"

Section B standing by. Confirm speaking?"

"This is Michael," he responded on hearing the voice of his sergeant major, "advance within 75 meters of target, left flank and hold. All ears out. Copied?

"Roger that."

"Archangel out!" Then he gave his boys the silent signals and just like him his boys moved like ghosts. One by one they took care of the men that had arrived in the canoe, leaving only the leader.

The humming noise of the yacht, accompanied by waves and splashes of water, announced the arrival of the yacht by 5 minutes to 5 am. The beautiful yacht, steaming in her majestic splendor came in and finally made a full stop at the bank.

The masked man broke cover at exactly 0500hrs and walked casually to the yacht. He was met at the entrance by 2 guards and escorted into a room inside the craft.

"You are welcome, your majesty maskman, they chided, "the chief is waiting for you."

"Thank you." He had replied.

As soon as they entered the room he was suddenly seized and violently brought down by 3 giant men who must have been specially selected for the job. They achieved their aim of removing the mask after some good struggle and all had happened in the presence of chief Aborungun who sat on a sofa, smoking his pipe gracefully as he enjoyed the entertainment.

"Well, at last, my dear maskman, this is your face," the chief said in his heavy Yoruba ascent, "It means you are not too tough *paapaa*. You impressed and surprised me the other time so I thought I'd better give you mine. No hard feelings. One for you and one for me. I love games and I never leave without giving back. So shall we say we are even? ha, ha, ha," he laughed contentedly. "Besides I need to know who I'm dealing with. I am chief Aboripe Aborungun, the Jim himself." He finished that with a little threat in his voice. "Now," becoming very serious, "to the real issue! And don't make mistake about it. You are going to tell me who exactly you are, who you work for and every single detail of your organization. The way you do it you will decide by yourself but the only sure thing is that you are going to tell me. Now shall we?"

"But, chief, do you have to do this?." The man on the ground asked.

The 2 hefty men just picked him up like a toy and gave him a slap that echoed over the water waves. "Spill!" they said but the man was just looking at them. Then they really descended on him and after some good beating they sat him on a chair.

"Tie him up!" ordered the chief, becoming enraged, "let's see how much torture you can take!" and they were surprised when the man asked them back, "let's see how much you've got." A second slap on the other cheek could have torn his tympanic membrane.

"Release him!" sounded a deep voice, quiet but terrible. Everyone looked around and standing there at the door was another masked man, pistol in hand, "you hears me!" he menaced and of course, they obeyed. After giving the chief's men a thorough look over he just put his pistol in his shoulder holster. As he did that the men rushed at him. The next 3 minutes gave the chief something really to watch. A fantastic show save for the fact that the end result was not at all in his favor. This second masked man just weaved and shuffled and weaved as he dodged kicks and blows, initially not making any attempt to fight back. Suddenly, as if when he decided to end the show, he was up in the air and in a flying simultaneous front and back kick and the right hand delivering a crushing blow, the 3 men were down immediately. Then he mimicked a ballet dancers bow before he said, "chief, your men are good but they need to be trained, most especially the ones out there."

The chief quickly raised the window curtains and looked outside, never bothering to relight his pipe that had smothered in his mouth. There he could see his men were being matched towards the yacht, hands tied behind their backs, looking roughened and dazed with their perturbed leader in their front. The chief let down the blinds and quietly relit his pipe, painstakingly, and took a satisfying puff before he said, "I have more men on the yacht."

"As I said earlier, they are good but they need to be trained."

"It's still a matter of calling them in and you'd be helpless."

"Chief, with due respect, you have a total number of 22 guards. You left 4 at home, 15 are out there and your best, your personal guards are here on the carpet. I have no doubt, however, that you could secure help any bloody time of need from any bloody where. I'm even surprised that I have not heard the noise of a helicopter overhead but won't you be wasting a fight, fighting the wrong people?"

"I simply underestimated you, or rather you took me by surprise. You won again, maskman. Two for you, zero, zero for me."

"Chief, right now I wouldn't know whether this is a game or it's for real. The sure thing is that I'm not taking chances. My men are out there and on this yacht of yours now and ready to blow it to pieces on a cue, if you know what I mean."

The chief puffed gracefully and smiled. "Quite clear. The fact that one of them is ready to endanger his life acting as a decoy for you tells a lot."

"Yeah, gives a good indication of their loyalty, not only to me but to each other. Once we have identified some course of action as a necessity danger itself becomes a welcome necessity. You see, chief, most of those men out there have one or more axe to grind with Bwallangwu. So they would do anything for our army which for now is the only platform known to them which allows them to contribute their meager, widow's might to the eventual annihilation of Bwallangwu."

"Yes, I'm beginning to understand now and I must tell you that we are on the same track."'

"Very well, chief. I'm glad to hear that."

"Then we can make a toast. A glass of wine for you? Please take a seat and pour yourself some. Honestly speaking, I don't waste compliments but I can't help but admit that I like the sight and company of invincible men like you."

"Thanks all the same."

"You're not drinking? St Remmy. ... Or would you rather prefer some other wines?"

"No thanks, chief, but I thought you know already that ghost have little appetite for mortal wines."

"Well, then, let my men get back on board and we would go on our pleasure cruise and discuss."

"And my men?"

"Well not enough seat."

"They will stand, if necessary but they would have to go with me." Saying that with a note of finality.

"The yacht is designed for a maximum payload."

"Simple arithmetic. Some of your men would drop to accommodate mine. With due respect."

"Still not taking chances, huh. Not good to trust even one's own mother in this game of ours, heh."

"I don't even know mine."

The chief took him to an inner chamber where beautiful girls served drinks. Later he dismissed the girls and they started talking. But then the chief was surprised when the maskman took a glass and poured himself some wine."

"Well, you mean this ghost is developing appetite for mortal wines...so fast?"

"If we have to work with mortals it might not be a bad idea. And believe me, chief, ghosts can be very fast, even in developing appetites for mortal wines."

"You refused to drink over there but here..."

"Well, chief, let's just put it as survival instinct that warns when all is not well..."

"Cheers, maskman," clinking classes, "you got me again. Three for maskman, zero for me." Then after some moments he said, "My dear ghost. I am very impressed. By your personality, your seriousness and all, I might consider your proposal."

"This might be a God given opportunity to mellow things with the Easterners and mend this long term broken relationship and by extension, goes a long way in enhancing your political position in the society.....hmmm...and muffle the grudge they have had with your predecessors."

"You seem so sure they are not involved in that ambush..."

"Because they are not fools. The Easterners don't have any reason to want you dead however much you constitute a threat to their chief Ogomigo's chances."

"But if I'm dead Ogomigo's chance is improved. Isn't it?"

"Yes, but they certainly would not go to that ridiculous extent of killing you in such a thoughtless manner. They are no fools not to realize once beaten twice shy. What the people want now is equal right and the opportunity to perpetrate their business. Well, they have their own problems but they wouldn't want a war with the Yorubas for no just cause. And it is crystal clear it is not the northerners. They just signed a pact with you last 2 weeks… Isn't it?"

"Then who?" *Howu, agbon nse, ikamudu nse, oju oloko ree to wu kandukandu*[31]," said the chief in his typical Yoruba proverb.

"Somebody or some group must have set the stage up to look as if it was the Easterners that ambushed and tried to kill you."

"You said that before but I have my source of information. At least 4 out of the dead men have been identified.: Chinedu Obinna from Umuahia, Ndoru Oboro Local Government; Alex Okoro from Mbaise; Chidinma Okadigbo from Nnewi and Isioma Okoroafor. How about Udo Ukere and Abang Ete both from Uyo in Akwamabo State?"

"Those wouldn't represent the whole East. It is my guess those few have been induced one way or the other to join for this particular purpose I am talking about. Don't forget Bwallangwu perpetrates everywhere."

"Are you suggesting those were the only Easterners among them?"

"Exactly, chief. We have bad eggs everywhere. Even we Westerners can't boast that we don't have our own share of vagabonds."

"Sounds ridiculous."

"You really believe the Easterners want a civil war with the Westerners? With the much investment that they have in Yoruba land?"

"Hmmm, not really."

"Then don't work yourself into a cross road. Lay the blame where it belongs…..this Bwallangwu. In fact chief, I like you to see the blessing in this incidence. Your predecessors were not in good terms with the Easterners. Isn't it? And that has always had a negative impact on your political career. This could be a golden opportunity to improve relationship with them. I am sure this ambush has constituted a major embarrassment to them and they would be coming to have a meeting to discuss the issue with you."

Chief Aborungun had quiet minutes of considering the matter.

---

[31] Literal: All insects are denying but the face of the farmer is covered with sting marks.

He looked at the maskman and asked, "what do you know about Bwallangwu?"

"Well, I think he is some goddamn son of a gun who acquired so much wealth, power and influence, arrogates as well so much to himself and convince some gullibles that he is invincible...errr...and uses such fools to perpetrate all sorts of evils. I think he is a mighty godfather and all these problems are connected to him one way or the other. I also think he might have his eyes on the presidency, and you having constituted a formidable barrier and that is probably, most probably why he wants to eliminate you and of course, clever, frame the East for it and thereby use 1 stone to kill 2 birds."

"Hmmmn, good reasoning that moves somehow close enough to some aspects of the truth but you, maskman, what you do not know surpasses what you know."

"Meaning what?"

"Then I'd better intimate you a bit about Bwallangwu."

They refilled their glasses and the chief refilled his pipe.

"Bwallangwu is a terrible name and even a terrible memory for some people, who are increasing in number."

"Very unfortunate in a country that has a government. What are our leaders doing?"

"Naïve, maskman, just listen. Bwallangwu is not a man."

"Then what is he, or a she?"

The chief laughed and almost choked on his pipe. He got up, paced up and down and came back. "I am going to tell you." Even his demeanor and solemnity warned the maskman to fasten his seat belt in preparation for something unexpected.

"Bwallangwu is god!"

"A god!? I see. Even you?'"

"What do you see?"

"How people are enslaved by the abstract. Not even the said ultimate God and they are this enslaved!"

"You are correct but people who live by fear tend to fear much what is present than the greater things in the abstract."

"This Bwallangwu stuff?"

"Bwallangwu lives among us physically and he is not human."

"Then what is he?"

"Irunm*ole*[32]. *Orisha ni.*"

"Irunmole!?"

"Yes, the biggest of the irunmoles. Agbaa irunmole and is worshiped so to say, directly by some, while some, still going to their modern religious houses, worship him secretly indirectly."

"Can I see him? You can make the arrangement with your powers."

Again the chief laughed, "Nobody sees Bwallangwu."

"Because he is god. Here we go again."

"One that lives among men."

"C'mon chief. If I am going to believe this stuff it is because of what is presently happening and of course, this wine."

"Then take some more because you would need it to believe a lot more strange and seemingly absurd truths. But by the time the whole thing dawns on you and pieces fit themselves together in your mind all wine you might have taken would be cleared."

The maskman actually reached for wine while the chief continued.

"I know Bwallangwu when I was a very small kid, about 5. My father then, was the highest in the services of Bwallangwu; the chief priest, most respected and feared, before Enlaye. Well, my father, Chief Areyingba Aborungun, may his soul rest in peace if it can. My father had his own ways of life and I had mine. I still have. All attempts to inculcate me in the ways and services of Bwallangwu proved abortive. For all I know, since I started reasoning, my father was a good man trapped in there but refused to think of it that way. To me his case was like that of a man who is famous by riding on the back of a tiger. He is trapped on that back, isn't he? With all his glory can he get down? Let him just ride forever and enjoy his fame for as long as it lasts. For the day he gets down…" the chief opened his eyes so wide, "*Olorun mi oooo!*[33]" and both laughed. One could see obviously the interest that this story has provoked on the maskman eyes.

"Among us kids at that time who were cup bearers of the shrine

---

[32] Demon

[33] Oh my God!

chief Enlaye was the most interested. He had always been very greedy anyway right from childhood. He covets everything but he can hardly do anything on his own. He just waits for others to accomplish and then he takes part of the glory or sometimes even take it all. So I was not surprised he quickly gave himself to the services and complete control of such a horrible creature. He wasted no time at all. It might interest you that I grew up with this Enlaye and 5 other kids, four of who died of one mysterious death or the other.. They were orphans and my father gave them home. My father, I must say, is a generous man. His only regret being that I refused to grow in the ways of Bwallangwu, much as he would have loved me to take his place…huh huh…on the back of the tiger," he paused with a little laughter even from the maskman.

"So it was Enlaye that took his place when he died. You know as you grow up there are some things that might dawn on you one way or the other. Some might even be triggered by some careless remarks, especially in a ceremony or a quarrel or some other hilarious situations. The other kids as I said, probably getting a hint of what death befell their parents, decided to take it upon Bwallangwu. Well, they died. It was quite clear to them that I was not with them in mind but I was left alone partly for the sake of my father. I wouldn't know a lot of stuff… errr…local insurance he had performed on me, again partly because they know that I knew that the only way to stay alive was to leave Bwallangwu in peace. You don't fight Bwallangwu. Nobody does. And most especially because they thought with time I would still come back for some much coveted things. It was too late before they realized that was not going to happen. I do not have a living god but I have the Living God and I have my own organization. They can't just touch me anyhow and I leave them alone. As I said, they know that I know that the only way to stay alive is not to fight Bwallangwu."

"But when now Bwallangwu threatens your life, chief?"

"Then that probably might change the situation. Everybody dies one day, one way or the other. I might just choose to die a hero."

"I suppose you know that he would not be put aback by your teleportation ability. Your enemies might make other attempts."

"I'm afraid I can't dispute that but all I have to do is strengthen my security because carrying a war to Bwallangwu is suicide. I am not a coward but the kamikazes ways are outmoded. My maskman, as long as that creature remains, no matter how many people you kill, you have not solved any problem. I mean what's a couple of termites killed in the anthill when the queen herself is down there laying 60 eggs per minute and her king relentlessly fertilizing her? Hah, hah, hah," he laughed.

"So all you're trying to do, I suppose, is protect yourself from Bwallangwu, you don't rock the boat until the Bwallangwu dies a natural death. Well he must be old by now, so his days are numbered." To this the chief llaugh aloud.

"He would not die."

"Ho, ho, I bet he's gotten you too with this god opinion."

"I told you he is not human. He is a monster!

"Monster!? C'mon chief!"

"He is not mortal. He hasn't died since the days of my forefathers! You don't get it!"

"Has anybody tried?"

"Those who tried are long dead. If anybody can kill him such person has to be guided by God when the God himself is ready to remove him from this world of ours."

"And you believe all this, chief?"

"Seeing is part of believing. Let me tell you a lot more, maskman. Fill your glass while I fill my pipe."

The maskman filled his glass and laughed while the chief prepared his pipe.

"I have two reasons to tell you today what I'm going to tell you now. The first being that the time has come and the second I would tell you perhaps after the story, but nevertheless, sometimes before you depart today." Then he lit the pipe and the aroma of captain black permeated the room gradually, offering a certain splendor and class to the atmosphere.

"It all dated back to so many hundreds of years. Orisha, the deity had two sons named Orishagbemi and Orishadami. They were twins."

The maskman rolled his eyes and took some wines, "here we go again," he must have said in his mind.

"Orishagbemi was the good one while Orishadami is bad, a traitor as the name suggests. You probably would have been told the story concerning the Rosary, so let me skip that and concentrate on the part that bears directly on Bwallangwu."

Well, at least he never heard that part before. So it wouldn't be a boring repetition on the long run.

"Orishadami in turn had twins. Hmmmmn. He attempted to apply the Rosary in a reversed engineering process to create a superhuman with the intent of generating a family of men above men. Men 16 times more endowed than other men who in turn would reproduce and populate his intention. With the right number in place and well distributed to other countries he can enslave the whole humanity. For this to be a complete success Orishagbemi would have to participate because he was the opposite side which we want to call 'good', and only he can decode that particular section and tell him what he must do if certain things were not going as planned." The big man paused to take a sip and puff his pipe, while the maskman adjusted himself in his seat.

"And that is when and where the horrible story began. Orishadami knew he could not rely on his twin brother. So he gathered his closest priests who advised him to entice one of the Orishagbemi's priests for the job. Well, by hook or by crook, that was successfully done and Orishadami went into his wife at the precise phase of the moon, the precise day, the precise time, the prescribed food and concoction in his stomach and under the supervision of priests. There we go and what was supposed to be a 9 months pregnancy went on for 12 years!"

"Twelve years!? Are you kidding me sir?"

"Well 16 multiplied by 9 should be equal to what?"

"144, chief. What is that?"

"The 9 is for the normal pregnancy period while the factor of 16 represents the scale factor of endowment."

"Wha!?!44 months!"

"And when you translate that into years?"

"Twelve!"

"Yes. 12 good years, I pity the poor woman."

"Holy Mary!"

"Now listen very carefully and refill, refill your glass, my man!" the chief kind of urged. "After the 12 years the twins were delivered. One of them, a female was completely normal, and a beauty to behold, so I was told, while the other one turned out to be a monster. A monster of the worst kind. Something smelling and chocking....indescribable! The story had it and it was confirmed; my father was that close, closer than Enlaye will ever be until his tenure expires. The story has it that the monster has no hands but a total number of 16 outgrows in place of the normal human genitals. Their mother died, of course, at that childbirth. And people on seeing the horrible creature took to their heels. By the time they returned, with the hope that the horrible thing would have died and they could carry the beautiful female away, my maskman, listen to what they saw and hold your guts."

The chief gave the man a steady look, shrugged then smiled and continued,

"They saw that the monster had inserted all its outgrows into the body of the beautiful baby girl and had sucked her dry. Moments later it dropped the mere bones and wrinkled skin and that was the end of the twin sister."

Both took wine but the maskman took two glasses.

"They looked for the traitor priest of Orishagbemi but alas! He had committed suicide. Well, bad experiment."

"Experiment gone rogue!" added the maskman.

"Well with Orishadami's go ahead attempts were made to exterminate the life of the horrible thing but all who so much as raised a finger against the monster were de-enervated, de-energized and chocked to death, especially when it made some horrible noise in the name of crying. Soon the words came from the priest and the father was acquainted with the fact that the monster must not be killed and it must be accorded all the rights of a new born baby. So preparations were made to conduct its naming ceremony. All the required rituals were made right from the first day, 16 rituals each day for seven days and on the seventh day the monster was given its name which is Agbalagba Irunmole shortened Agbaamole meaning the big old demon. It was christened Bwallangwu which means 'I am here to stay' in their ancient language. Bwallangwu lived and grew up. It rejuvenates every seven years in the same manner as he treated its twin sister and it has been like that for the past thousand years...and I can't see anything suddenly changing. It has no life span. Do you now understand? It rejuvenates on peoples' life! Preferably girls, virgins if available!"

"Then it can be killed!"

"How?" with that steady look again at the maskman, but shaking his head.

"Anything that feeds can be killed!"

"Its feeds are guaranteed!"

"Not by starvation! The monster could be pierced!"

"Nobody can move near except its high priests. Those are the only ones immune to its emanations and sound, but only within 2 meters!"

The maskman was silent for a while, then asked in a much lower tone,

"Even with the holy Rosary?"

"Haaah, I can see that you have done some research. The most Holy Rosary has solutions to all problems and I suppose it has antidotes to any problems the monster is capable of causing."

"This monster himself is a problem and so the Rosary, if it's real, should possess a solution to it."

"Haaah, I know what you mean now. Interesting! But where would you get it? It is lost and I doubt if anybody can recover it from that God forsaken valley of the crocodiles."

"Hasn't there been some attempts?"

"Well, I heard something once in a while but nothing has been certain. It's long forgotten now."

"Can you tell me more about it?"

"Well, perhaps something different from what you might have known about it?"

"Who knows?"

"You will decide that, so listen, but first, our glasses are empty. Let's refill."

"The Most Holy Rosary, others might call it the Most Blessed Rosary, legend has it that if you have it on your body you could go to hell itself and back unscratched, no matter the situation. Only you couldn't kill a soul. You would not be harmed but you shouldn't harm anything. So it's true if you have it on you Agbaamole couldn't harm you. You would be completely protected against its emanations but as I said, you too can't kill it. If you raise your hand against a soul you would be defiling the Rosary."

"But why?" The man dropped his glass furiously.

"I don't really understand. I tell you I don't really comprehend the complexities of nature's laws and principles. The 5th Commandment perhaps; thou shall not kill. I don't know. Much the same as I still can't comprehend why Jesus Christ wouldn't lay his hands on those who were killing him but instead he healed them....err....might not be exactly the same but for me, my dear masked ghost, if I know somebody is attempting my life, too bad for that son of a bitch!"

"Makes 2 of us, chief and that's why we are here."

"The chief looked pensive and at him, "so what the hell. Nobody has it, so why worry about It?"

"Nevertheless, this fight goes on. We are between the devil and the deep sea.....Now passivity would not help anybody."

"I will not wage war against Bwallangwu."

"He is the one waging the war against you!"

"Then I will defend myself!"

"Your God-given right and responsibility but attack is the best form of defense, so I heard."

"Just what exactly do you want from me, ghost? I have survived so far and if you think I would deviate from my survival principles just because a person I cannot identify tells me to do it then we need 2 separate doctors to get our heads examined. For you, no problems, 'adaba o naani a nkun'gbe, ina njo eiye nlo.'[34] When the shit hits the fan you would just vanish! Who can identify a maskman? A ghost! But I, Chief Aboripe Aborungun, heh, I have a lot at stake! I will not and I repeat, I will not carry a fight to Bwallangwu's door mouth."

"But you would defend yourself as you said, huh?"

---

[34] The dove does not get concerned if you burn the forest, once fire starts it flies away.

"Yes of course! It's my goddamn right!"

"So, please chief, just do that right!"

"Meaning?"

"Would you support those that are ready to carry the war forth? Right to the door mouth of Bwallangwu...errr... as you said, to the innermost chamber of the anthill where the queen and king reside?"

"Boko harams!"

"But I prefer Kamikazes, If we have to be. *Howu, sebi eyin agbalagba Yoruba naa le maa nso wipe iku ya j'esin. Toto o se bi owe o.*"[35]

After a brief silence, during which the big chief of Yorubaland puffed his pipe quietly, he asked most solemnly, "support in what form? What do you want from me?"

"We could do with your backings in several forms. Your advice, to a large extent your information network, of course money to expand what we have on ground now as an army and your identity would be secret."

"You have just said what I want to hear. If you have a reason to keep your identity secret then you should understand why whatever the support I might be able to give has to be underground."

"Perfectly well, sir. God bless you sir."

"Well then, I'm ready to form a defense alliance with you and I think we stand a better chance to survive that way. I will support you to the best of my ability. My entire intelligence network will be at your disposal. After all what goes round comes around, just as you have done for me. To this shall we drink a toast?"

They shook hand and drank a toast, and the maskman, looking at the glasses of wine, asked inspirationally, "but chief, doesn't it drink?"

"Hahaha, I can see that you have already started. But if that's what you have in mind, my ghost, poison does not affect Bwallangwu That is even if you are able to get the person to put it. Yes of course, the monster drinks. We used to put the bowls of water or whatever, about 2 meters away from the black curtain and then use wooden stick to push them a little closer."

---

[35] After all, you Yoruba elders believe that it is better to die than to live in shame.

"A wooden stick?"

"Dry wood to be precise. Dry wood is a bad conductor, isn't it?"

"Strange. To think that it is possible to conduct death from Bwallangwu. Electricity or what?"

"Electricity, magnetism, whatever, who has ever thought about it? A great subject of research. Isn't it?"

"More of electricity."

"Is it not your generation in your infinite wisdom that separates fundamental phenomena into different aspects? Confusion! What my generation was taught is that electricity derives from magnetism but.... We should not allow that to divert us. Should we?"

"Keep talking, chief. Any little thing you remember adds something to the clue."

"Well that's about all. If I remember anything else…"

"Magnetism…." The maskman repeated, interrupting the chief, "if it is magnetism… like poles attract…unlike poles repel…"

"What are you getting at?"

"Chief, did anybody ever go to the shrine…well, magnet in pocket…you know kids…"

"Haaah, maskman, if he can be demagnetized or something like that. *Howu, iwakuwa l'aa wa nkan to sonu.*[36] None that I can remember. But one thing I know is we never served Bwallangwu with silver bowls. He hates silver. I remember vividly an occurrence one fateful day. You see, we used to be very curious, well, kiddies. We used to go as close to the black curtain as possible just to wonder at the labored breathing coming from behind the black curtain. If not that the strong emanations was too much to bear we would have gone beyond that limit of 2 meters. One of those days, Enlaye had stolen a tee spoon from my father's room. He normally flings stuffs like that in the Olufi open market. This spoon was in his pocket when we entered the inner shrine that day. As soon as we entered there was a terrible noise from behind the curtain and all of us were instantaneously flung on the ground. I did not know what pushed us but whatever it was made a terrible

---

[36] We search for a missing item in all sorts of places and manners

impact. It was later, when the priests searched us, that they discovered the spoon in Enlaye's pocket. And we were warned never to approach that shrine with any silver object again. Look, boy, all of us were sick for 3 days and since then my father banned the use of silver objects in the yard. We use other materials including gold."

"But you were not a priest. How come you could get as close as 2 meters to the black curtain?"

"Well, kids were protected to that extent since we had not known a woman. But virgin or no virgin you lose the protection at the age of 13. Something about puberty, hey?"

"Shit!"

"Thinking of sending a kid?" the chief laughed, "always resourceful... Ghost."

"Not half as much as my chief. *Eyin l'omodie n to'ya e*[37]. Toto o se bi owe o."

"O kare laye Waa pa mii. By the way, I never thought ghosts had this capacity for wines," casting a glance at the empty bottles of wines."

"Well we could adapt, especially if we are urged, especially by my and my only chief who might want to get me drunk."

"Hmmmn and how did you escape that because 4 bottle of Remy Martins and 3 of champagnes seems beyond the capacity of 2 men one of whom concentrated more on his pipe."

"Sometimes it works, a little bit of salt in the socks, plenty of onions, moringa and *eyin olobe*[38] leaves in the stomach, patanmo leaves in the split of the buttocks and the leaves of ajeobale in the armpit."

"You came for war?"

"My chief is very resourceful and he never stops playing. He just changes tactics."

"Hmmmn. I told you I was going to tell you what I told you that time for 2 reasons. The first I have already told you."

"And the second?"

"Based on my research and what I have found out and continue to

---

[37] A chick follows closely behind its mother.
[38] Philantus amaritus

find out about you I have arrived at the conclusion that if anybody had the slightest chance of fighting Agbaamole it is you."

"You couldn't possibly have conducted a research on a ghost."

"Believe you me when I tell you I am a typical Yoruba chief. I have my soft wares."

"Interesting!"

"What I was made to understand, though still had to belief, is that when the time comes a strange man would emerge to take this war to Bwallangwu. That is why I took the risk to tell you what I had never told a soul. That is, the secrets of Bwallangwu, because having done that I have not more than 77 days to live."

"Whaaat!?"

"Yes I would die unless Bwallangwu is weakened. I still have my reservations about the whole thing…abstract..hmmm. I will give you my support and that will be all."

"Thank you chief. It's a blessing and a great honor meeting you sir."

"The blessing is mine I hope"

"But do you belief this 77 days thing?"

"My father made me to take the oath in front of the black curtain when it turned out I was not for them and, if care was not taken, the next thing might mean my death, especially after his tenure. He gave me something to swallow, told me the monsters secrets and took me to the shrine as somebody who promises to keep Bwallangwu's secret in return for being left alone. So if I leave Bwallangwu alone I would be safe. But I guess the situation has changed now. Hasn't it."

"Yes, of course, my chief. And nobody lives forever."

"Let's see what you can do and we might drink a toast to the second time of my life saving.….77 days, or get ready to have a chief ghost after the funeral of a high chief. Keep that in mind."

"All the more reason chief. I'll sure keep it in mind."

"So four for the mask man, zero for Jim."

Back in camp the masked man wrestled unsuccessfully with the crystallizing conclusions. Only a priest can get close enough to Bwallangwu, or a kid. Then only a priest has the chance of killing the monster. And it can only be done with a silver weapon. Well silver weapons are not the problem. It is getting the priest. He had to find a priest. How? He contacted Friar Maria who could not help in that respect. How could Maria of all people know a priest of Bwallangwu when he doesn't belong to the cult? "I will find out and tell you if I discover anything," was the best he could do. "Whatever you do just do not breadth a word of it to your cave men most especially your highly resourceful Cardinal Mansuri." He in turn had cautioned.

His dreams and inspirations constitute another enigma. He dreamed and saw a man who he remembered had thrown him into a den of lion coming back to pull him out. What a dream!?" In another he saw the same man holding a key that he had been looking desperately for. He wondered at the close relationship of the two dreams. But how possible is it that a man who had thrown him into a lions' den would come back to bring him out and then have a key that he has been so desperately searching for? "What a dream. What a joke." He said to himself.

CHAPTER 13

Jobilah pondered on the information the scouts have brought to him. His hope rose highly when they told him, "the men are all sleeping and their commander's tent is unguarded." He smiled to himself in anticipation of future benefits. If he could just catch this maskman perhaps things that are turning bad for him might just set on the highway back to normal and he, Jobilah, would regain and command the respect of being the best capable operational commander the Bwallangwu Strike Force (BSF) would ever have. More so, he could still have what had been promised to him but which he was yet to get due to the unfortunate failure of Operation PAKUFINRIN.

He considered 2 options: To go in quietly, steal into the camp and pick their masked commander; or go in in an all out assault, kill all the soldiers and capture the commander. He considered the second option the better. He might as well incapacitate the enemy now that he has the opportunity. Why waiting for the enemy to carry arms before you destroy him? Again the prospect of convincing him over to Bwallangwu would be easier if his army were ruined. Besides, destroying that army would give him, Jobilah, so much credit that might even endear him to Bwallangwu himself and who knows the next thing......

Just then to his amazement, he caught sight of a figure in black trousers, black sweaters and black mask strolling nonchalantly down the stream. What a lucky day! From his cover he watched the masked man as he bent over the water and washed his face, rinsed his mouth and then strolled along the stream, seemingly enjoying the cool breeze of the early morning. "Gooood, very good, keep moving, just keep moving away from your men, maskman. Just the right thing to do," he whispered and smiled to himself, and thinking perhaps this enigmatic man is not all that good after all; his myth is just his luck, "which sure has started changing now; of course, with me, Jobilah, son of Okworikwo involved in his matter." With the snap of his fingers he signaled 4 hefty men and they followed the masked man surreptitiously. The gap between them had just reduced to about 10 meters when the man looked back abruptly and broke into a run. Jobilah and his men pursued him. Soon the ageing BSF Commander couldn't keep up the pace and had to slow down. "Get him, boys! Make sure you get him alive!"

"Don't worry boss, he is ours."

Panting like a dog tired in a race, Jobilah finally slowed down and walked along in the direction of the pursuit, none of whom he could see again as they had given him such a wide gap. Occasionally he had to stop to determine which direction to follow judging by the disturbance of the shrubs. As he bent down to look closely at some shrubs he felt the coldness of a metal at the base of his skull. "I will split your medulla if you make a sound," said the voice holding the knife. "Stand straight, wisely, your hands up and keep walking....turn right...walk!. Never mind, let the boys play with each other. You and I need to have a talk in privacy."

The maskman led the tall saggy man to his tent in the camp.

"Now you can sit down and relax, Mr. Jobilah, commander of the formidable Bwallangwu Strike Force."

"Who are you and how do you know me?"

"You couldn't avoid being known in such a sensitive position, in such kind of job that you do."

"What do you want?"

"I said we need to talk. Sit down. Here we like to be a little more refined than the Bwallangwu society. Let's talk over wine. But I assure you all will be well."

"You are really an enigma. How did you do it?"

"Do what?"

"My boys were hot on your tail and almost on you and suddenly you appeared behind me!"

"I'm proud to inform you that I'm Yoruba to the core."

"Another case of Egbe teleportation, perhaps?"

"*Oodua ni mi tokan tokan*[39]." He served Campari which Jobilah did not refuse.

"You are still to answer my question."

"*Bi a se gbon ni'le ale bee naa l'a gbon n'ile oko.*"[40]

A report had come from the sentries at dawn that there were some noticed movement within the vicinity of the camp, "and I've dispatched a 3-man scout to go and find out who they are," the serge major had told the maskman. A couple of minutes later 2 of the scouts had returned to report that there were 12 men out there in the bush south west of the camp, all armed with Tovar and Kalashnikov. On impulse the maskman had asked, "anything peculiar? Any familiar figure?"

"Yes I think I have seen the figure of their leader before, somewhere…I am not certain."

"What does he look like?"

"He is tall, very tall, with a dome head and he is bent haggard."

Hearing this, the maskman's eyes narrowed, eyebrows forming a groove behind the mask as he thought rapidly.

"Any problem commander?" asked the serge major.

"Hmmmn, maybe yes, maybe no, it's time to find out. Please send for John and get a section ready. It's time to play some game. Just as the chief said, all is now a game."

He had played the game right and the hunter is now a captive in the tiger's cage; Jobilah is now in his tent.

Jobilah had seized the opportunity to gulp down greedily the glass of campary. He poured himself another before he got a replied to his question, "another case of Egbe teleportation, heh?"

"Yeah, not very different from the type chief Aborungun used."

---

[39] I am Oduduwa (descendant) to the heart.

[40] Just as the concubine is clever so is equally the husband

The mask man replied watching intently Jobilah who reacted instantaneously. "What do you want!?"

"No BSF commander, I'm the one to ask you what you want around my camp with your boys, 12 in number....am I correct?"

"I am impressed," replied Jobilah giving his interlocutor a thorough look. "I must confess you are really much better than what we imagined. No wonder ...errr...without mincing word, you are an asset and a man of your type and qualities has no limits. You can rise to the highest level and beyond if you serve in the right organization. The sky would be the beginning for you and that is why I am here. What is the name.. Mr...Mr....What is the name?"

"Go ahead Jobilah. Very good joke over wine. What a good treat."

"Look, you this masked man, good man! You are wasting! Bwallangwu is the place for you. Bwallangwu has a lot to offer. Anything you want! Money, women, beautiful ones, virgins, properties in choice places...just name it. What would it take to bring you on our side?"

"More, a lot more than what you can afford, commander."

"Really? Then name it. Just talk...C'mon, try us!"

"Justice, human right, freedom for all, love of good. Humanitarianism....Altruism... Your organization simply cannot afford those, can it? Of course they are not your specialties. Those attributes would destroy you."

"Oh my God you refuse to pull yourself out of this illusion! They are not real! Nothing but some rather simple man's unattainable ideal. Aphorisms employed to deceive naïve men to keep them in check. C'mon, I credit you with much more wisdom than this jabbering. Even in the jungle it is the survival of the fittest!"

"We are in a city, Mr. Jobilah."

"It is the law of nature!"

"Individual interpretations of natural laws depends on individual state of awareness and maturity. You fail to see the power of love and respect over shear fear, brutality and oppression which are your way. We live in cities but for you it's still an animal kingdom."

"Jesus Christ your greatest advocate of this so called virtues, love and respect, was not that loved and respected. He was repaid on a cross, with nails through hands and a crown of thorns. Beaten to pulp, denied and rejected! Wake up man, don't be a fool!"

"Well, Jesus realized he had come for a mission for which he was prepared to pay the price. And for people like you involved I can imagine how heavy the prize was. He fulfilled the mission before he died. You may call it a matter of opinion because the realization of such as a successful mission requires an evolved mind to comprehend. Much as I wouldn't expect a goat to understand algebra, Mr. Jobilah."

"Aren't you eerrr being insultive?"

"I'd rather fight Bwallangwu than join it."

"Joke! Nobody survives fighting against Bwallangwu. Take this chance! Don't die like a fool!"

"Everybody dies, sir. Let me choose the way I'm gonna do mine. I'd rather die a free man than in mental bondage. Tell me, Mr. Jobilah, do you have your own life? And you call yourself a free man? Do you take your own decisions? Do you plan your own life? No you'd rather be a puppet, controlled and used anyhow by some higher dudes in Bwallangwu. You are in a cult where you don't have your own will but to make manifest the selfish and abominable wishes of some dudes meaner than you in the chain."

"No! You've got it wrong!.....n no..."

While Jobilah continued stammering, the maskman's mind was on his past vision. Yes it has to be a vision if it is the same man he saw in his dream that is right here captive in his tent. A man holding the key he had been searching for. Keys in dreams, the elders say, means solution to a problem. Definitely a divine help is nearby but how does he use it? What would this dialogue, rather the whole occasion lead to? And if this Jobilah constitutes the solution to his problem how does he use the key? Nature may not present another opportunity. But how, how, how?

On Jobilah's side, he is still hopeful but a bit disappointed yet. But if he could just bring this man in then he is in business, he, Jobilah. For another side of the advantage has just occurred to his clever mind. This man would be a stalemate to that arrogant Zokalaus. Yes, if he plays his game right he could even turn them against each other…..Of course this is his opportunity. He has to bring this man in at all cost.

Both men seemed to be meditating fast and deep within so brief a time. The maskman knew this is the only chance he has to use the key of opportunity offered to him by divine forces. But how? He ran briefly in his mind the conclusions arrived at concerning Bwallangwu. "Only a priest and kids can….." Then like a flower bud gradually unfolding, he brightened. Why not convert this one trying to convert him. Then he might have gotten a priest! A priest of Bwallangwu. Only a priest can get close to 2 meters of the monster. Only a priest has the chance to kill the monster.

"You have been very lucky, that's all? How long do you hope to ride on this mantra of luck?" Jobilah was still talking, trying to find the best reasons to get his man. "Not for long and you know that," pointing a finger at him, "As I am seeing you now I know you know that. Nobody fights Bwallangwu. Nobody does and nobody ever will."

"Because there had never being an organization bold enough. Now there is an army. Bwallangwu had hitherto enjoyed hitting sitting ducks. Now its fortune has changed. Its fruits of past labors have ripened and so it's time for it to reap. Bwallangwu had destroyed so many souls, wrecked so many lives and had removed the hopes of so many good people. Its basket is full, its measure is overfilled. Has it not been said that the destiny of the wicked is destruction? And if for once nature has to take its ideal course then Bwallangwu would be destroyed. No doubt about it."

"I must admit you have courage. You have guts. But come to reality, you don't have anything except some green boys who just learned how to point a gun and pull trigger. Is this what you call an army? How can you fight if you are so poor? Talk less of waging a war against Bwallangwu. What a joke!" He poured himself another glass.

"Has it not been said that no man is poor who has himself to give? Those men you call few green men give themselves freely. It's all that matter to them to start with."

"You don't seem to understand but I don't blame you. Initial strength and momentary assembly of men out of the blues to jeopardize an ambush does not make an effective army. It is the maintenance and constant training among other essential things. Very soon your logistics would be depleted. Do you have the fund? What kind of weapons do you have? What training have you got? All you need is a massive attack and all is finished for you, my friend? Where will you get more? From that loonie that you helped?"

"Never mind, more will come where the present come from. But you seem to forget that the will to fight is the most important. Weapon is next and is a catalyst. The most important to us now is the readiness with which the boys sacrifice themselves, not for any individual reason but for our collective common cause. Interest and fear are two levers for moving men. We are moved by interest, with respect and responsibility to each other, but not by fear, your primitive and oppressive ways. Each of these men you call green, I can bet you on that, is worth more than ten of yours. With this category of men we will attain our objective."

"Which is?"

"To destroy Bwallangwu, and when that is done the question is, what would happen to you?"

"You will die!"

"Everybody dies. Mine will be a death without regret when we die for what we believe. But what do you believe, Mr Jobilah? You believe in fear and brutality, oppression and cheating, sadisms and all sorts of deprivations. You just take it and find opportunity to take it on others. Can you ever find happiness? Law of the jungle, you call it. You've been cheated but you are weak and so you take on the weaker ones. Can you ever find happiness? You may experience joy and elations out of your wicked acts but happiness is far from that, my dear old man."

"Now I can see how confused you are and that is your problem! I have all I want. Bwallangwu is where you get all the kicks and the joys. Then tell me how would you not be happy? If that is what you want we give that to you!"

"Haaah! I am afraid I am disappointed to hear that from you, sir. All you ever get from wickedness and all act of sadism is that kick you call it; that momentary elation called joy. But when the image produced in your mind of everything that matters is so warped, out of alignment with reality how could you ever attain happiness? The world is ever changing but you remain stubbornly rigid for material reasons. Imagine you roam about physically in mega cities but you still live mentally in the jungle. Eric Berne said happiness depends in large part on other people in this ever-changing world[41] and he is absolutely right. Meaning your happiness depends on the people you so much hate and maltreat. And if our world is ever-changing and you cannot change your mentality along with it how would you ever attain happiness, talk less of retaining it? For happiness rebounds from your dealings with your environment, especially how you treat people and lesser beings. Well, who feels it knows it. You don't even know the difference between joy and happiness. I expect a priest to know better!"

He thought it was high time he stated playing his cards and hoping Jobilah was a priest he would be able to convert. He had no doubt the job of winning him over was never going to be easy, if at all possible, and if not how could he at least arrange some understanding with him, leveraging on his greed. But Jobilah's reaction to the word 'priest' was unusual. He became suddenly red despite his color and his hard attempt to conceal his feelings. So he decided to linger more on that word to see what useful clues he might be able to gather.

"Are you a priest, Mr. Jobilah?" watching him with maximum concentration to pick the smallest cues from the latter's silent body signals.

"Let me tell you what you don't understand," letting loose his emotions now, "I am as important as any priest in the organization. I'm even more important than some of those so-called priests!"

"Then why are you not a priest?"

"The fact that I'm not a priest is not due to any shortcomings of mine. It is is...due to a reason you would never understand because you don't belong!"

The maskman opened a fresh bottle of campari while he raked his mind. A little disappointed at the discovery that this man is not a priest of Bwallangwu, How could he then be a solution to this problem?

---

[41] Eric Berne. A Layman's Guide to Psychiatry and Psychoanalysis.

Reacting to a flash of idea, he called 2 of his men and instructed them to "keep this man here for a few minutes. I have a pressing issue that cannot wait. He could be tricky, mind you, but give him as much wine as he wants. I think he would do same for me in his shoes...any time I return his visit...huh."

He went straight to consult Chief Aborungun by phone. He first dialed the security code the big chief had given him, then dialed the secret number only known to the topmost bosses of the Nigerian Telecommunication (NITEL), then the chief's voice came on line.. The line is scrambled. Even if anybody tapped it, it would be meaningless to them.

"Hey, you sound a lot human on phone. Took some human voices on loan? How'd you do? Surprised though that you call me. Something must be urgent. Anything the matter?"

"I'm fine chief but you're correct. Something came up. Is it possible you might know one Jobilah? Emm.. one tall..." the chief didn't need any description.

"Oh Jobilah. Eiye meji kii j'asa. Jobilah, Jobi trouble, Jobi case. That is what we called him Oh yes, I know him. He coordinates most of Bwallangwus dirty jobs and is under the direct control of Enlaye who he serves subserviently for little personal favors outside his entitlements. He is the BSF commander."

"Yes you got it, chief. That's him. Tall, bent and like a crab that he is he never walks straight."

"Then you must have come in close contact. Be careful, my man, he kills without feelings..."

"That is expected."

"His first victim was his school mate at the age of 7 for not giving him groundnut. He still does for flimsy reasons, especially material. He's worse than a rattle."

"I only wonder why the man, having served Bwallangwu organization for so many years is not yet a priest."

"You surprise me. What could have triggered this concern of yours? Planning to be his in-law?" the chief finished jokingly.

"Well, chief, I thought you might be able to tell me."

"Well...if you have a good reason to want to know, why not? Yes I can tell you something. You see, just as might obtain in many other organization, positions are not always definitely a function of time spent or duration of service in an organization. There are other factors, especially that of eligibility."

"Eligibility? Jobilah who put in so much as the Strike Force Commander? Who else could be more eligible?"

"Listen then. Part of Bwallangwu's organizational regulations as concerned priests is never to ordain a man who might have an axe to grind with Bwallangwu. Yes, Jobilah might have given himself completely to Bwallangwu and he does beyond his best to prove this daily but the fact irrefutably remains that Bwallangwu does not take chances. The organization would not take chances. Period!"

"But what chances, against Jobilah, for all he is giving for the organization? His pride! His entire life! His freedom! His happiness! He has been in the hot spots for most of his life, risking his miserable neck for Bwallangwu! What chances are you talking about?"

"You sound desperate. Curious. What are you up to? You care to share?"

"Well I thought that might lead me to something tangible in my line of thought."

"You see. Jobilah's father deserted the organization."

"Could that have been possible?"

"Well one man did it. Jobilah's father, Alfonsos, Oriagbalumo Okworikwo, popularly known as Orikanbody. He disappeared after arranging with his friend within the organization to have his wife and little Jobilah sent to him later. The unfortunate thing is that friend of his, his best friend, tried to have an affair with the woman but she did not cooperate. So what might be the best way to cover his ass and of course to punish her? He just reported the case. So you can imagine what they did to her. She was once Miss West Africa, you know, very beautiful. Bwallangwu had her. You know what I mean?"

"Yeah, I guess I know," the maskman said sadly.

"With the help of this best friend of his who knew where he was,

Okworikwo was caught up at Ajebandele village and was gunned down in the fiercest gun battle ever witness in the history of Gbongan.""

"Until recently." The maskman supplied as a joke.

"Oh yeah, until recently," laughed the chief, then continued. "So little Jobilah, barely one and half years, unaware of these, grew within the organization and he soon exhibited some qualities and abilities which Bwallangwu found irresistible."

"Does Jobilah have a hint about this?"

"No. He doesn't. And Bwallangwu knows that he doesn't know. All the priests swore the oath of secrecy. Ordaining Jobilah means empowering him. But Bwallangwu will never take chances. He would never empower such a man."

"All is clear now I suppose."

"Hmmmn. I suppose the ghost is not trying to solicit for Jobilah in his organization."

"Not really, chief. What are my chances?"

"Just wondering the interest of yours....errr...do not think Jobilah could be relied upon to strike the organization he enjoys.....or what?"

"Well, chief I just thought the more you know about the devil the better your chances of survival."

"Why don't you just tell me you'd tell me later?"

"You got it, chief."

"Any other thing you might need?"

"Not really but eeerrrr, would you be able to supply some dates and events for references?"

"Look, whatever I tell you is first hand information. But what the hell, if you want some dates I'll give you dates. But you have to hold a second while I consult my computer."

The 2 gentlemen who tendered Jobilah were not as friendly as their commander. In fact one of them made it quite clear to him, "if the boos had had nothing against killing in cold blood I would have strangled you right now, you bastard and that is to say you should not give the slightest reason to do so. I'll be just too glad to cut your throat." The second soldier just stared at Jobilah and the only word he said was, "his blood is ever hot. Not cold.. Just the slightest reason I will kill this dog without thinking. After all what are we supposed to do if he is running away?"

Throughout his whole life Jobilah had never been talked to in such manners before, especially by those he had referred to as green hands. But he had no doubt that green or yellow these ones would kill him if he gave them the reason to do so. He was only praying that they would not find a non-genuine reason to kill him before their boss arrives. For this reason he, just like the organization he serves, did not take chances. He just kept his mouth shut, his figure straight and he did not even take the risk of driving away the tsetse fly that was sucking away the blood on his nose. He was very much relieved when the maskman returned.

"So, how are we doing, Mr. Jobilah?"

"Well, the wine is good but your boys destroyed my appetite."

"They don't take chances, that's why."

"They are not refined."

"A matter of opinion."

"I hope you have reconsidered my wonderful proposal. It's a wise man that considers his afterthoughts first."

"Still bent on convincing me to join you. Isn't it?"

"Your best bet under the situation. What other offer can be better?"

The man looked steady at Jobilah who returned his gaze evenly, and then consider it was time to play his aces.

"I wonder, Mr. Jobilah, how many of your bosses you personally recruited…I mean if you don't mind?"

"What do you mean?" getting uneasy.

"Oh, c'mon. Sir, the implication is clear enough. You know if I join Bwallangwu I'm sure gonna become a priest. You know that, of course, don't you? Otherwise, no deal!"

Jobilah looked down, a cross between anger and self pity, and while he was groping for words the man continued, "You know what men do to donkeys? Use them until they are no more useful, then ditch them. They have been using you right from when you were a kid, they are still using you and they will continue to use you until you are no more useful and then what, they drop your carcass."

"You don't make sense!"

"You know I do but you are trying to solve the problem by pretending it doesn't exist. *Eni to r'oku aparo to ndiju. Se ko ti ri oun to ri?*[42] Ostritch."

"Look! If are talking about that bastard in custody…he is finished! Ok I recruited him, dusted him up and installed him in Bwallangwu. Yet he bites the hands that once fed him and he is made a priest. He is rising and he has forgotten that I…..heee, *b'omode ba l'aso bi agba, ko le l'akisa bi agba ke*[43]." He finished with a proverb, really becoming uncontrollable."

"Easy, Mr. Jobilah." He patted him on the shoulder, thinking about what he just heard him said and what to make of it

"That boy is just lucky, you know, and I'm not jealous."

"Do you know why all these years Bwallangwu has refused to ordain you?"

"I don't want to talk about it."

"Bwallangwu does not take chances."

"What chances? What do you mean?"

"Bwallangwu will not take chances to empower you."

"I am the Bwallangwu Strike Force Commander. I'm already empowered!"

"How close can you move to Bwallangwu?"

"What concerns you? Are you an insider?"

"You know, ordaining you means empowering you with the real power. Only a priest can get close to 2 meters of Bwallangwu. Bwallangwu will not take that chance with you. But you can do their dirty jobs around and they give some funny ranks and appointment to keep you there. Do you attend the priests' meeting where important decisions are made? And you call that empowerment. They will not take that risk!"

"What do you mean?"

"You close eyes to reality because you are afraid of death and you cling subsequently to false security. But death is unavoidable, even for

---

[42] Closing your eyes quickly after seeing a dead bush fowl would not help. You have seen it already..

[43] A kid might possess as much clothes as the elder but he couldn't have as many rags.

Bwallangwu. Bwallangwu will never spare you however subservient you make yourself to be. All they need is a credible replacement and your own is finished. I even wonder if they haven't got that already."

"Rubbish! Bullshit! I'm part and parcel of Bwallangwu! And Bwallangwu knows I can never turn against it!"

"But can the same be said in reverse?"

"Bwallangwu has no reason to deal with me! I do my job!"

"Yes, I don't doubt that," now picking his words carefully and laying the right emphasis, "but just as long as you are not aware of the truth."

"What truth?" Eyes beginning to dilate.

"The truth of what happened to you parents"

"What happened to my parents!?"

"How your parents died."

"You stupid man, mind what you say about what you don't know..."

"The horrible death that killed your parents."

Of course he was ready as Jobilah launched himself headlong like a missile from his seat towards him and he stepped aside just at the right moment, to hold him back from busting through the tent fabric and hit him so hard that his knees buckled. He then held him until he calmed down. Strange enough, the tall ageing man started sobbing. The maskman knew that victory was at hand. He allowed him to sob the more and later helped him back to his seat. He gave him more wine and later he was much sober.

"it's true I don't know my parents but all is in the past now, and you don't build a future from the past, do you? I think we should just forget that aspect and concentrate on the ...on....."

"And there would be no history, sir, no foundations, no experiences. So how does the present stand? Just as the building is placed on a foundation so is the present erected on the past and in turn the experiences of the past and the present serve to modify the future otherwise there wouldn't be development based on experiences and correction of past mistakes. To me, Mr. Jobilah, the past could constitute a foundation upon which we build the present and the future in turn. There is no doubt that our decisions are based on experiences.

And you don't talk of experiences from the future but from the past. Even Bwallangwu, and especially your Bwallangwu has made some regulations, especially the ones affecting you now, based on the past. The absolute truth is that the God almighty always chooses the right time for everybody to know the truth. He has chosen this time for you, for a specific reason. So make the best of it." He looked at the sober but confused man, refilled his wine glass which he never refused, and he continued.

"Your old man, Sir Orioye Oriagbalumo Okworikwo, popular among his friends and followers as Orikanbody, may his brave and gallant soul rest in peace, was in the service of Bwallangwu. Somehow he must have seen the light; rediscovered himself and decided to quit or something else must have happened to warrant his decision to quit. Whatever the case, he deserted and arranged for his best friend to send his wife and little Jobilah to him later. You were just barely one year old. Typical of Bwallangwu friends who wanted to have an affair with the most beautiful woman at that time but the decent woman refused him he decided to blow the whole thing open. To cut the long story short, it is in history that Sir Okworikwo created history in Gbongan. It was the fiercest battle in history before he was finally gunned down at Ajebandele. Well, little Jobilah grew up in the organization and they allowed you to grow since you did not know anything and very soon you started exhibiting some traits of character and qualities of your father. Qualities very much admired by the organization. You killed your first human being known at the age of 7 for refusing to give you groundnuts. Bwallangwu decided to take care of the mess because they have decided to use you instead of killing you. They came swiftly to your rescue and from then on you have held reference for Bwallangwu."

While the maskman paused to fill his own glass, and to study his captive, Jobilah just sat there, head in hands and probably slowly digesting his own bile.

"As a matter of fact, you have done more than your own fair share for the organization. I mean all the dangerous missions and operations. You are almost indispensable but the fact remains that you constitute a threat, a potential danger to them and that disqualifies you forever from being ordained as a priest of Bwallangwu. Again because once you are ordained you would have access to certain records and who knows, you might just be acquainted with something that might make you curious to start looking for certain things and so on and so forth. Now tell me, if this Bwallangwu of yours were the god it makes you people to believe he is why does he fear anybody? Bwallangwu fears you sir, but you are not aware of it. It fears you because of the qualities you possess and what you could do to it if you were ever aware of the truth and if you were empowered to be able to go near it."

The maskman paused to allow what he had been telling Jobilah to sink while he paced around, thinking, watching his captive's reactions and planning his own next line of actions. He even wondered if he was playing it right, honestly admitting to himself that he lacked experience in this sort of things. One thing he is sure about is that all the divine help he needed has been given to him, both spiritually and in the material. His next prayer now, so to say, is to be able to use it well. He noticed that Jobilah was yet calm, still stunned perhaps, expected, but nevertheless a hard nut to crack.

"Your noble father, may his noble, tough, fearless soul rest in perfect peace, would not be happy if you disappoint him. I mean how can anyone expect him to rest in any peace and be happy with the memory of all that happened, most especially what happened to the beauty queen, his wife? Your mother!"

Jobilah has started weeping again, though quietly, head in hands. The maskman continued, "The great Sir Orioye, a warrior of Ipetumodu lineage, whose forefathers migrated from Ile-Ife, will never want to rest in peace if his own son, the only son he had, kisses subserviently the feet of Bwallangwu and is a personal tool more or less of the son of his own best friend who betrayed him and even facilitated his capture and death? Would you blame him in heaven if he refuses to rest? It is not that easy sir. And if it might interest you, though I know you want to forget the past, that best friend of your father's was nobody else than Chief Eniorisha, yes, the father of your dear chief Enlaye!"

Jobilah stiffened, then relaxed and when he spoke it was a solemn and quiet question.

"What happened to my mother?"

"No, no, no. You wouldn't want to know sir. Let's not dwell on that aspect of the past now."

""Tell me!!!" Jobilah's voice was quiet but compelling."

"They gave her to Bwallangwu."

The spasm that seized the ageing man was convulsive. Jobilah locked his jaws, skin stretched tight over his knuckles as he closed his hands into tight fists, then without warning he vomited some of the wine he had gulped. The maskman did not even bother to get out of the way.. He just went to him and sent for water and towel to take care of the older man and calm his nerves. The embarrassed man first look at this man in mask and much as he tried to control himself he bust out weeping again.

"I'll k could kill them all…"

"So why don't you?"

All was silent again. It was another minute before Jobilah said pensively, "clever. The bastard is clever. He never made me a priest…I can't move close. I am a disgrace…Hmmmmn, *Iku ya j'esin.*[44] I could just kill myself…It's all over now."

The maskman was waiting for this. "Nothing is over sir! Over for who?"

"It's over for me. I'm no priest. A lineage of warriors that can't even avenge the death of his parents! I'd rather die now than …"

"If you're ready to die why not die fighting?"

"You don't understand."

"Educate me sir."

"I could kill those priests but with Bwallangwu still alive it's a waste of time. It's Bwallangwu I want,…but I'm no priest….yeepahhhh"

"The will to fight him is what matters sir. Can we be together on this?"

"Yeeeparipaaahhh!!!!"

"Sir!?"

"I heard you but for what useful purpose?"

---

[44] Better to die than to live in shame

"To fight!"

"I can't get close....I'm no priest."

"But we can get a priest. Can't we?"

Jobilah dropped his head down this time around in thinking, and after a long consideration he said, "Fadi Zokalaus," half to himself.

"Your wounded man in police custody?"

"Yes. Fadi Zokalaus."

"Can he do it?"

"He is the perfect man."

"Reasons?"

"Best known to me."

"Then we get him out!" He felt like break dancing. He could feel the key now in his hand.

"Hmmmmn. Bwallangwu will get him out as soon as he is well enough, and just as you said, he is my replacement...they have planned to kill me...It's all over...but before they kill me I will...will....."

"Not if we get him out first and.... but are you sure he can be convinced?"

"Yes. He would. I alone know something concerning him that the organization does not know."

"Then we are in business."

"Hmmmn. Clever bastards."

"What is that sir?"

"Getting Fadi out would only save my skin. No other purpose."

"But just now you said he could do it!"

"You don't understand....a lot you don't understand about the complexities of Bwallangwu..."

"So what again?"

"Zokalaus will not sell out; will not listen to anybody and neither will he talk in that custody no matter the method of interrogation."

"But you just told me you knew something that.."

"Not so much for his allegiance but because his faculties are blocked by Bwallangwu."

"What!? New things I'm hearing now...Oh c'mon, old man. Wines....."

"Listen. Bwallangwu has a stronger reaching hold on his priests. When ordinary soldiers are captured we get them eliminated before they have a chance to talk. But when a priest is captured we do not worry as such because they automatically go into amnesia. Such memory loss happens to them because they have shared Bwallangwu's blood and he can reach them from anywhere. And they can only regain their memories when they are brought back into the organization. It is a sort of programming and not even a fellow priest can deprogram him. Only Bwallangwu. The monster has reserved that exclusively to himself."

"Hmmmn, fitting into place now, like a jig saw puzzle. So that little girl you people kidnapped for ransom has been confused by Bwallangwu...?"

"Oh, not really. By some odd freak Bwallangwu cannot zoom in on ordinary subjects who have not taken their concoction. Otherwise I wouldn't be here talking to you now?"

"What concoction?"

"Some liquid they give them when they make them a priest. I told you it includes the blood sample of Bwallangwu. It tunes them in, making them receptive much to Bwallangwu's most delicate vibrations."

"I see. Very interesting, but what happened to the kid?"

"Haa, funny enough, his priests when within range can do that to some people. But again they cannot heal."

"Only destroy. Typical."

"Well, now you understand..." and brightening up somehow, "You are so enigmatic. I believe you can do anything. So get Fadi out before Bwallangwu lays his hands on him!"

"To save your ass. Right?"

"Well I am in no position to argue with you now." Jobilah resigned. "My main concern now is even about what happens after here. But I can't stay back here. God I am so confused but I will work out something."

He attempted to help himself to replace the much he had vomited but unfortunately the bottle was empty as he turned it upside down and nothing seemed able to come out again. The maskman had had time to think on the next step to take. Just this one meeting would not be enough. There was need for a lot more of it until the objective is achieved. He drew closer to him for a tete-a- tete and discussed quietly with him, then he got up and went out of the tent.

A few minutes later witnessed a hectic and courageous fight on record as Jobilah suddenly emerged in the clearing where his four hefty men were tied to trees and guarded by 3 men. Springing from behind cover he assaulted with a right hand karate chop on the neck of one and the guard was down without argument. One of the remaining two thrust out his rifle and Jobilah grabbed the muzzle, pulling and simultaneously dropping on his ass as the rifle fired over his head while at the same time pushing with his legs in a jiu jutsu throw that sent the opponent flying over his head to go and crash into a tree behind him, Seeing the BSF commander getting up unscratched, despite the rifle shot, the third man just turned and took to his heels. Jobilah made a show of running after him but stopped abruptly and wheeled about. The two men who were now on their feet just took dressing from their fellow man and fled. Then the gallant BSF commander drew his dagger and cut lose his boys,

The maskman watched from behind a tree. He had evolved a plan that would enable the continuation of this clandestine meetings with the BSF commander and this was what he discussed with him, to his relieve, in that tete-a-tete; in low tone he had said, "Well, Mr. Jobilah, I think our next step is to agree on how I will capture you again to enable us work out details and finalize our agreements. It is time to go back."

"What about my men?" Jobilah had asked.

"Your soldiers are still intact where you pinned them down."

"And my 4 boys pursuing you? What did you do to them?"

"Captured but don't worry. We have set the stage for their gallant BSF commander to rescue them. But first we have to rehearse."

From behind the tree where he was enjoying the show he commented silently, "not bad, not a bad performance at all. Now your boys will even give you more respect. More so, they will spread the story and there would be less suspicion for our next activities."

CHAPTER 14

"What do you know about brainwashing...mental programming or deprogramming or whatever the goddamn hell it's called?" the maskman had asked Friar Maria during his next nocturnal visit.

"Haaah. Psychiatrics stuff. Next to nothing. Why do you ask?"

"It's claimed that Bwallangwu has the power. That it can just blank out a person and the only thing such subject would be able to remember, if lucky, is his name."

"Oh yes. Quite a number of people have suffered that fate and are still suffering."

"No remedy?"

"All hope is lost when the Rosary was gone." The clergyman lamented, close to tears.

"The Holy Rosary? What concerns the Rosary again?"

"I told you it has all remedies. It indicates the part of the scroll to consult for the remedy."

"Scroll? That is a new one. What scroll?"

"The Holy Scroll."

"Jeesus! Holy this, holy that, everything is holy. What again is this holy scroll and where is it this time around? In cobras' pit?"

"You wouldn't expect every remedy procedures to be contained on the tiny beads of a rosary, would you? Even by the shortest shorthand writing, such rosary would be miles long with each bead resembling a tabloid."

"Yeah. I have been wondering as well...I get it now. Clever, isn't it? So you check the Rosary, the black side, for the manifested problem, disease or anomaly, and check the other side of it for the antidote...oh no, not the antidote per say but a reference code. You now use the code to locate the exact part of the Holy Scroll to go and read."

"Exactly!" replied the Friar lamentably.

"So this scroll, is it incantations or what?"

"Go ahead and make jokes. The only blessing is the fact that whoever would have the Rosary will not have the scroll and so we are still save....and I will do anything out of my way to protect it!"

"Do you have it?" The maskman asked rather desperately.

"Eeeer, I won't say I have it but the Covenant has it."

"And it's kept in your cave?"

"Yes. Why?"

"Would you do me a favor, father Maria? I don't beg for things but if I have to I would for this one."

"You know I would do anything for you if..."

"Thanks. Let me see the scroll. Let me just have a look at it. Find a way to bring it to me."

"What for? Don't waste your time. You won't even...Look, it is like looking for a grain of wheat in the beach, without directions from the Rosary you won't even understand it. It is all some strange words and signs and sacred vocals and tones etc and without the Rosary you won't even know which is for what!"

"All I'm asking you is to bring it to me. Would you oblige in the name of the God you serve and for the sake of Adams who you loved?"

"But why?"

"Shall we call it curiosity? Kills when not satisfied."

"Just for you to see?"

"Well I would like to see it."

"It's not going to be easy."

"You've got to try your best."

"Ok. Thursday is the feast of Bocapal when I usually have access to the Tabernacle. I have a big bible almost the same size of the Holy Scroll......," said this half to himself, "then come and disturb my sleep again Thursday evening or Friday morning, ghost, and I will show you. Then you would have made me to break the 7th commandment."

"It is loan, not steal. Besides, am I not worth it?"

"Yes, at least I could have my rest afterwards."

"Can you get him out, chief?

"Do you realize what you are asking of me?" Chief Aborungun had responded to a request made of him by the maskman. "You are asking me to get a criminal of the worst type out of police custody!"

"With your connections, chief. Unless you don't want to do it..."

"And what do we call that?"

"Obligation."

"And how about my reputation?"

"The end justifies the means, sir."

"It's hopeless! Can't you see? Even if I bring him out it's of what use? Don't you know what Bwallangwu does to his priests? That poor miserable bastard has a chance of being himself again when and only when he is back in the vicinity of Bwallangwu. So why the trouble?"

"I have a plan....good or bad whatever the case we don't want him back in Bwallangwu."

"Then you would only have a robot who would never think again talk less of talk or act. Of what use would that be? Even if he recovers by some odd miracles have you considered the risk in what he might become?"

"What chief?"

"A wolf among your flock of sheep....for don't you ever kid yourself that you could break the spell of Bwallangwu on his priest just like that, ghost or no ghost, he has taken his blood! So you see, getting him out is not just a waste of my time and resources but and worse still, a smear on my reputation and a great danger to your entire army. I am sure you know his capability by now."

"I said I have a plan. Just get him out for me chief, and leave the rest. That would be a formidable contribution to this war against Bwallangwu, chief."

"What plans, warrior?"

"Eeerrrrr, I know this professor of metaphysics who has the experience and might be able to do something."

"Hmmmn?"

"But for obvious reasons he would like to remain anonymous until the job is done. It is his own contribution to this war against Bwallangwu."

"You are kidding me?"

"He has done something close to that before and he is not likely to fail."

"Then I should have known about him."

"You should have known about me then, long before now."

"It cannot be done!"

"But the least we can do is try something! We are doomed anyway, come to think of the worse. The man on ground fears no fall."

"And wasting our time and worsening the danger is another issue!"

"Won't you like to find out? After all, no venture, no success. Think about what it means if we succeed, chief."

"So, what do you really want?"

"Get this man out for us. Get Fadi out. Fadimef Zokalaus."

"Okay but let me sound a note of warning to you and your professor off metaphysics. I'd rather have him eliminated than have him turned loose around my set up. I don't want you people to set loose within my environment a wild animal you couldn't control. Fadimefa Zokalaus is the meanest son of a gun on earth. He is your equal in all respect, the difference being that you are on the opposite side of the tug."

"Thanks for the compliment, chief."

"I am not kidding, ghost. I will get your man out but get it clear, the slightest reason I get I will kill him. Is that clear?"

"Crystal, chief."

"Deal!"

The black Benz with tainted windows rolled noiselessly through the gate of the gulf club. In a well rehearsed drill, the bodyguard was out in a jiffy to open the door for the commissioner of police, Mr. Henry Gbalus. The impressive old man, drooping moustache, sharp keen eyes set into a slightly oblong face, always conscious of peoples' awareness of him, stepped carefully out of the car in his white sportswear with practiced grace. A few seconds later a sleek green Rose Royce announced the arrival of chief Aborungun. They exchange pleasantries and without much waste of formalities they started a game.

Taking aim and before he raised his club the commissioner asked, "I was wondering, Jimmy, what you might be up to that you've decided to play golf on Sunday. Aiming for gold in the coming Black Games Festival?"

"The gold is in your custody," the chief replied cautiously.

"Oh really?"

"And I would be most appreciative."

"That is interesting. Jimmy, we've come a long way. Can there be anything I wouldn't be able to do for you?"

"His name is Fadi. Fadi Zokalaus."

"Fadiii, Zokalaus…"

"Recently taken to the police hospital."

"You are not one for sponsoring criminals and I never knew you to associate indiscriminately, Jim."

"As you know, there's always a reason."

"And what reason could that be?"

"Best known to me."

The commissioner hit the ball hard, suggesting he was still in good shape.

"Not bad, Henry. Not bad at all."

"Did you say the criminal is in police hospital?"

"Oh yes, Henry."

"His name again?"

"Fadi Zokalaus."

"Wait….!," the police chief straightened up. "Wait, Jimmy. Is that not the boy arrested in your…"

"Oh yes, Henry..Yes yes yes."

"Haaah! IFadimefa!?"

"Exactly."

"No wayyyy, Jimmy! That man remains until he is able to talk. We need a living witness and he is the only survivor so far. If anything happens to him....I fear a national disaster. The president is highly interested in this case, Jim."

"I want him, Henry."

"But for what? Look, you know what has happened, don't you? Do you think the Easterners really want you dead? We think that some people are inciting them against you. We also suspect that it is not the Easterners who are behind that ambush but work is going on on that. Furthermore we know that there is a dangerous racket, so to say, going on in this country and the headquarters is right here in this town. Could you believe that? And the only lead we have, the only one, Jimmy, is the one you want me to turn over to you!"

"Of course, yes, Henry."

"Look, you are probably not satisfied with the pace at which we are working but I assure you the police are careful and meticulous. Above all we are legal. Just relax, Jimmy, and allow us to wrap up this mess neat! One more thing I can assure you is that we are deeply concerned about your welfare, not only for the tremendous help you have been to the police but also because you are a good man of impeccable reputation. We don't ever want a reoccurrence of this thing that happened to you and that is why we are leaving no stone unturned. Are you still sure you don't need my police men to guard your estate?"

"Oh thank you. I can manage." Then looking directly in each other's eyes, "Henry, I want the boy."

"No, Jim, definitely no!"

"Don't say no, Henry."

"Why not? Any reason?"

"It is not the best to say no."

"How the hell would I explain my action? Not even to myself! The only lead, and I, the police commissioner turning him over to you...a friend....because you need him...C'mon, jimmy."

"You know what to do, Henry. It's your game. You've always known how to submerge inside a pit toilet and you would not smell the shit."

"Capital NO! And you know when I say no like this, there is no going back. You've known me for long, Jimmy."

"Ok, have it your way."

"Sorry, Jim, any other time, any other thing," the commissioner apologized as he took aim to put the ball in the hole about 9 inched away.

"Em, Henry," the chief called, interrupting his opponent from his easy potting.

"Yes Jim," he answered, raising his stick.

"There is a certain Miss Mary, a.k.a Magdalene, who somehow I know now lives in South of London...."

The police boss missed the hole by 10 inches. He looked furious but he calmed down just as instantly. Then he asked in the most solemn tone, "Chief, is this boy that important?"

"Oh yes, Henry. As important as to make us play gulf on Sunday."

"But you don't expect me to just turn over a criminal to you like that. Just because I am the police commissioner...? I am the law!"

"Well how do you suggest we go about it?" the chief asked calmly, sure he has his man.

"You gonna have to snatch him."

"Oh Henry, old fox," the chief laughed. "Breaking into your Apata barracks would be bloody and suicidal.. You know that, Henry, don't you?"

"Well, Jimmy," throwing his arms in a resigned gesture, "how else would I be able to help you? I've tried, you see? That's why I said this one is not possible. Any other criminal could easily be released without any eyebrows raised. This one is just too controversial. I told you the president is interested in this case, especially for your sake!"

"Henry!"

"Yes, Jim."

"Sign his movement warrant. Move him to Aiyepe barracks."

"What the hell!? Aiyepe barracks is my most secured barracks."

"But of course, yes, I am aware of that and that is why you are moving him."

"So why?"

"For best security. The president is highly interested in the case. Isn't it?"

"Yes. And?"

"So move him from Apata the less secure barrack to the more secure Aiyepe barracks where it would be hard, practically impossible for anybody to get to him."

"How does that make sense to your demand?"

"No, but you would be exonerated."

"I don't understand. Stop pulling my leg, you know my tight schedules on Sundays."

"There is rumor that some people are planning to break out Fadi from police custody. I would make sure their plans leak in the media. I own the Frake Radio and the Daily Request news paper. Of course, you know that."

"The hell I know that...." still not sure from where the sucker punch would come.

"So, my commissioner, I am sure you would not take chances on hearing some rumors like that. So move him to a more secure place. Move him to Aiyepe, your most secured."

"No problem if that is all you want. After all, what are friends for? A friend in need is a friend forever. Is that all?"

"Oh yes. Thank you."

"But why do you think your chance is better in Aiyepe? Not that it concerns me but just curious..."

"No, we will snatch him on the way."

The commissioner hit the ball so hard that he was panting after the shot.

"Take it easy, Henry," the chief patted his back, "you are not getting any younger."

Where he was didn't make any difference to him. Whether in the police hospital or in the mobile hospital tent in the camp, it seemed all the same to him. It wasn't really a tedious job to snatch Zokalaus after all the previous arrangement. But for Fadi, all is just the same or nothing at all. All he does is just stare at blank ceiling when on his back and at blank walls when he is seated.

"Forget it!" Jobilah said, "He is of no use to anybody now, Let us just kill him!"

"To think I went through all this commitment for more or less a moron! Oh my God! This boy would be lucky even to remember his own name, even after your professor might have finished with him. Or is he a magician? Because you're sure gonna need more than magic." Chief Aborungun had commented disdainfully when he visited.

"Yes, he could be a magician. He had done much more than magic before. He should be able to handle this hopefully."

"Haaah. You really need the hope."

"He is good enough to place my hope on. If he fails that's when I lose hope."

"Why don't we just kill him, he is of no use, and safe ourselves all the risk of dangers he might constitute later. I don't like sleeping with a snake under my bed!"

"We would do just that when the professor might have given up, sir."

"Does he also wear mask, this professor of yours?" The chief had asked mockingly as he got up and departed. Immediately the maskman sent for Jobilah to be brought in from where he had him waiting with wines. He has made sure the two never met and if they are going to meat at all by chance, not in his camp...at least not until the time is right.

"Yes, Mr Jobilah, I just want to make something very clear before you go."

"And what would that be, maskman?"

"If this man should die miraculously before I'm through with him you can rest assure of two things: I could kill you or this connivance of ours would be blown sky high to the notice of Bwallangwu. Because I know that all that concerns you is just to save your own hide. You don't really believe Bwallangwu could be destroyed. Do you? But you want to make sure at least that there is no replacement for you. For that you are in hurry to kill Zokalaus. I have warned you!"

Jobilah never heard that note in this man's voice before, despite the fact that he was getting used to him. He left without saying a word.

Despite the fact that Zokalaus was tied both hands and feet to the four corners of the bed, 4 guards were still provided, 2 inside with him, 2 to stay outside.

At 2 am in the morning, the maskman got up. He hadn't been sleeping, as a matter of fact, since 1800hrs anyway. He went into the tent designated 'hospital' where Fadi was kept. In addition to his voice, and the code word of that night, he has certain things which enable his men to know he is. They don't even know his name. He went inside and told the two guards with Zokalaus to go join their fellows outside.

⸻◆▸◈◂◆●⸻

"He just looks at us and you are claiming he can now talk! Is this what your professor told you? Metaphysics! Is he genuine? Have you paid him? I wonder if just making him recover the ability to just look is not what he had put in his term of contract. Clever! Where is he by the way? Or has he disappeared? Well....metaphysics, he should be able to do that one if only to save his ass. And where do we go from here? .....Another professor of...of...."

"He talked, Chief. He talked. He would talk again. He is just trying to orient himself. He will talk."

"Orient?"

"Yes. It is a gradual thing, stage to stage, step by step......"

The chief had come back the next day and had been informed by the mask man that the mystic man had performed on Zokalaus and had achieved result.

"Are you sure," the chief had asked in a mixture of excitement and disbelieve. "In fact, *a kii gb'odo jiyan b'ose ho tabi ko ho. Niso nibe!*"[45] He had broken into his usual adage. He had held him by the hand until they reached the tent where Zokalaus was kept. But in there, Zokalaus but merely looked at them for all sorts of things they asked and said to him and for the rest of the time he had looked as usual at the blank ceiling. Finally, the chief had come out in annoyance and started talking to the maskman.

"I have a busy schedule. You shouldn't be wasting my time. Of all the things you have been doing this one is gradually eroding my confidence in....."

"He talked, Chief. He talked. He would talk again. He is just trying to orient himself. He will talk." The maskman tried to assure the chief.

"Then he'd better start talking in a language not only you and your mystic man understand! If he is talking as you said. It is only you people that can hear him!"

"Relax, chief. He will soon talk again. Just a matter of time."

"I don't relax when a snake is under my ceiling! You know what I think? He cannot say a goddamn word but he knows where he should and should not be! He is just taking his time looking for the opportunity to break loose and when that happens, oh my God, you can kiss your army, your camp, equipment and tents good bye with all its implications!"

"Do not worry, chief."

"I warned you anyway. Just let me know on time if this thing is not working and I will kill that bastard."

"Chief, let's take some wine and after we go give another try."

They had entered the tent designated 'mess' and the maskman told the barman to bring palmmy[46] which he knows chief Aborungun loves. They chief drank but he did not stop complaining. The maskman just sipped his own quietly while he consulted his watch from time to time, an activity too obvious for the chief not to notice by his

---

[45] Whether a tablet of soap lathers or not is not by argument by a river where it can be demonstrated. Let's me follow you and you show me!

[46] Palm wine

question, "expecting someone? ....your professor...abi?" and to which the maskman just smiled for a reply. Then when it was exactly 5 minutes to 12 noon he said, "chief, let's go give another try."

"Just 2 more days! Two!" demonstrating with 2 fingers, "two more days if he is not talking to me I will kill him! Just keep him tied up like that. I don't care if he has been communicating to you and your professor of metaphysics in sign language. Just 2 more days and he is dead."

They then went into the 'hospital' tent and the maskman offered the chief a seat which he did not refuse but did not make use of. The maskman sat down, consulted his watch again which was about 45 seconds to noon. Then he dropped his head and closed his eyes, his right hand on the tied wrist of Zokalaus.

"El in harmonius aura biiliss," he whispered on the strike of noon.

"Resorting to prayer now?"

"Yes, sort of." He managed to answer, "the old way in latin."

"I did not...."

Chief Aborungun abruptly stopped mid-way in whatever he was about to say as he heard Zokalaus quietly asked them, "How were you able to bring me here?"

Hiding his surprise Chief Aborungun replied, "Bwallangwu is not the only magician around, Karl."

"Karl!? You call him Karl?"

"Yes he was Karl and he is still Karl. He became Fadi when the law went after Karl. Now both Karl and Fadi are in deep shit."

"Same Karl we heard off? Notorious, Karl the ball cutter?"

"Yes Karl the castrator."

"Why didn't you tell me this before?"

"I never thought it would make a difference to you."

"You don't really mean that, chief, do you?"

"Well, the hell! You wouldn't even remove your mask!"

"Okay, okay, back to the main business. You don't mind that, chief?"

They both automatically turned to the man in bed.

"You people are playing with the tiger. You are twisting the cobra's tail. My people will find you in no time at all."

"We are waiting for them.'

"You will get nothing but trouble from them. You don't understand."

"You don't suppose we are holding you to ransom, do you?"

"No. I suppose you are smarter than that." He replied, looking them over.

"Yeah, you are correct," replied the maskman, "ransom is not our way of fighting. Besides, it takes more than that to fight Bwallangwu. We don't need his dirty money. He should just roll it up, heat it up and shove it up his evil ass hole if he has any."

"Hoooh! Now you are proving me wrong. Now you sound more stupid than a stupid ass itself."

"Shall we get acquainted by insulting each other?"

"You're dead. You know you're gonna die."

"Yes but in honor!"

"I don't care how you die! Like a dog, monkey or like a cow! That's your fucking lookout. Big question is why, if not for ransom, are you holding me captive?"

"You remember where you were last?"

"Yes I remember every gaademn thing!"

"Then getting you here was really difficult and nobody takes all the risk and troubles if the objective is not worth it." The chief replied.

"Meaning?"

"We hope to convince you to join us, Karl."

Zokalaus laughed genuinely, but the chief continued.

"We want you because, at the stage we have reached now you are the only one that can strike Bwallangwu. As a priest you are empowered to move within range."

"Are you people normal?"

"We are perfectly sane, son, and so are you."

"What would you say when you wake up from this dream of yours?"

"If it is a dream, then we go back to sleep so the dream continues. This is real, boy."

"First you want to kill Bwallangwu and second, the most foolish of all reasoning, you want me to do it." Then he started laughing again. "Well, let me just chat away with you for entertainment. What makes you think Bwallangwu can be fought in the first place, not to talk of killing him?"

"If your tin god was really so powerful why are you here now and as his priest, able to chat away, as you put it, with us? Think, just think for a moment."

"Yeah…I wonder there must be some explanations.…but why the hell do you think I would strike him, if I could, for you?"

"Because you don't belong there. Karl, you don't belong to them. You have never belonged to anybody. Though they have made you his priest, he has chosen to ordain the wrong person for divine reasons. Just like clothing a shepherd in wolf's skin. You are certainly different from them all. Enilaye and all his cronies! You have honor. You have integrity and all those values Bwallangwu quickly noticed and ordained you before you were ever due. It is a sort of buy over! A bribe in disguise. The same values they exploited to get you trapped! But whatever you think you might be enjoying now you must realize that you cannot fulfill your life mission as long as you are with them. At long last you'll lose. You can't win!"

"You may wish to go tell them there that enough is enough. I am loyal. I have given Bwallangwu my word and Fadi does not betray short of death. So enough! I am tired of this game!"

"Haaaa ha hahah," it was the chief's turn to laugh. "Karl, listen to me. We are not Bwallangwu's men sent from the organization to test your loyalty after your ordeal. No! Far from it, son. He didn't give you back your mind. Think about that. We are the ones sent by God to crush Agbaamole because his days are numbered."

"And you are in the wrong profession, whatever it is. You should be a preacher or a lecturer in some bloody schools teaching jokes and dreams."

"Your loyalty is misplaced. You are a good runner but on a wrong track. How can you win? A good fighter, champion material but fighting on the side destined to lose. With all your qualities and hard work you end up losing."

"You go recite that poem to your wife and children who are probably in the wrong family. They would be fascinated."

"Shut up!" exploded the chief, "do you know who I am?""

"I don't know and I don't give a ggaademn fuck!" countered Fadi, making attempt to sit up but restricted by the ropes. Nevertheless he continued furiously, "and do you know who I am!? I am Fadi, IFadimefa Zokalaus! You think you can buy my allegiance with some funny poetic jabbers like you win over some father ass licking whores? I am Fadi! Fadi Zkalaus! I do not betray my people! Get that straight now whoever you are! You want to kill me? Fucking shit, why don't you just go the fucking ahead and don't waste my fucking time! And do that quick for your own sake if you're that clever! Because very soon you're gonna be wasting precious time trying to escape!"

They allowed him to exhaust his anger. It was necessary.

"If we ever thought you could sell out we wouldn't have wanted you so much, Karl."

"You are wasting your precious time. My people will be here any moment."

"They are not your people. I am convinced."

"Are you?"

"Of course! Yes! As you would soon find out. We could be a better people for you."

"Get fucked!"

"Sorry, chief," said the maskman. The chief made a wave of hand to indicate he was not bothered by the insult. And turning again to their captive he said, "Karl, Fadi. Karl, Fadi Zokalaus, whatever. The man with two names, two faces, two identities but ironically that does not make you a crook; at least for those who could see deeper...you are straight forward just like this man here with neither a face nor identity. It shows clearly in you. It can't be mistaken. I must tell you, you are not a man I would like to lose as a friend. But if that would not be possible I certainly will not want to have you as my enemy. I will be honest with you, Karl. You will not be chanced again to fight against me, if you know the implication of what I just said."

The man was not moved. He just replied casually and with no less equal honesty, "it's just the rational thing to do. No sentiments, no hard feelings. I wouldn't blame you if you kill me. I mean since I won't bulge and you can't keep me here forever."

"I am impressed. But your death now would be a great loss. Painful!"

"Always better than betraying my people. Honor! Have you forgotten what you said before?"

"Yes, honor. I have no doubt you will never betray. But Karl, we also know that added to all this noble value is rationality. You are a very rational person, you are not dogmatic and you could reason to genuine evidence. Perhaps if we could convince you that the Bwallangwists are not your people, they have never been but rather they are your enemies?"

Fadi chuckled, still furious, no doubt. "You go ahead I am listening, clowns. You go ahead and convince me why I should turn around and bite the fingers that feed me. Go ahead and teach me how to cut off the hands that removed my head from the hangman's noose. C'mon, you wanna try? I'll enjoy it. Politicians!"

"Ok, Karl, first you need to know that you're not the one but them who put your head in the noose. They put you in that trouble, Karl. They manipulated you. They set the stage and you just played the parts they wrote for you. They knew you don't belong to anybody and that was the only way to secure your allegiance. You were in the hands of long time manipulators. They set the trap and you just walked straight into it. They knew about your values and it was what they use against you as your weakness. Knowing full well you don't accept favors from nobody and you don't forget favors if you ever accepted any by some odd freak, they set you up for the trouble of the right gravity and set you up to accept the favors and you became their tools. They put your neck in that noose and they came to remove it. Again they have moved a step further to ordain you so as to use you forever."

"How does that sound in your own ears? You should have been

a fiction writer. I might have bought an edited copy but not this raw fashion coming from your gaaddemn shit hole now!" And turning to the maskman, he said, "by the way I had prayed to meet you again. You remember…"

"I too had prayed to meet you but save that for now. But perhaps it would start making meanings to you if somebody else can confirm this fiction of ours as facts…somebody who you know very well as much as he knows you."

At a movement of the chief's head the mask man spoke into the intercom and instructed that a man should be brought in.

"Whaaaat!? Zokalaus could not believe his eyes. "Jobilah! What da hell are you doing here!?"

"Fadimefa *omo* Zokalaus, [47] relax."

"Haaah! You sold out! No wonder! Doesn't take BSF that long to take action! Gaaddemn mother fucker! Mother fucking cheating cockroach! You're dead! Bwallangwu will get you! I'm sure you know that!"

"Yes, of course I know it and so are you. I was dead the very time I started operating for Bwallangwu. But now I will die with honor."

"Your honor my foot! Just look, look, look who is talking about honor! My bootlaces! You sold out! Because they wouldn't make you a priest!"

"No. I wouldn't say I sold out but I just discovered myself. I have seen the light and what were revealed under the light are not menu for weak hearts. Fadi, we have been cheated, manipulated and used! It's time to decamp and we should do that even if we don't want to join in the fight, with our honor intact."

"Still talking about honor!? Oh my God! Jobilah, you're the last person who would agree to die in honor. You bloody hypocrite… but what have this people promised you to make you turn against Bwallangwu? What have they done to you!? Hypnotism!?"

"On the contrary, they brought me out of hypnotism. They showed

---

47 Son of Zokalaus

me the light with which I was able to see the truth about Bwallangwu. His wickedness and true intentions and by the time........"

"How the hell do you think you can ever convince me? Do you think I am like you!?"

"You will be surprised. I promise you that."

"You're mad! You hypocrite of the worst gender! This is where you people are making a mistake. If you're gonna bring somebody to convince me and you think the right person is Jobilah ...you see, you've lost out!"

"The situation now is no more about who is talking but what he has to say."

"By the way, Jobilah, you and I have a serious discussion to make."

"What discussion?"

"I was shot on the right leg and then received later a second shot on the left and that was why I couldn't get away. The men we attacked were about 100 meters away and that second shot was from a pistol. What happened, Jobilah?"

"That I wouldn't know," taking a step back and instinctively raising his two hands in a convincing posture.

"And it was a shot from sig Sauer p226."

"Look em....I didn't shoot you."

"Jobilahhhhh!" the voice was something else.

"Look......I'm sorry...It was all under the influence of this Bwallangwu organization....all these wouldn't have happened. You ...emm...if I tell you I was just taking orders would you believe it? You know what happened between you and chief Enlaye just before we went on that operation...."

"Never!"

"Please Karl. I will confess everything but first listen to what I have to say. I am ready to die for all I have done but I want a chance to destroy Bwallangwu first for destroying my family...and yours."

"Nonsense! You really got me there by confessing outright," feeling his tied hands and shaking his head, "but that does not mean I will not kill you later! As for your family that's your fucking problem with Bwallangwu, not mine. Go and solve it your own way. I'm not involved!

And you can't recruit me for that. And that goes for every one of you here!"

"And what about your own family?"

"I am tired of all these bullshit stories!"

"You didn't drop with the rains, did you?"

"I wanna rest. You people should go or you wanna kill me now. Let's get it over with! Otherwise leave me alone!"

"Alright. But I still have another confession to make to you. Karl"

'What confession, you traitor? I wouldn't be surprised anyway."

"Thank you for listening, Well, chief Aboripe Aborungun might have told you that…"

"Who!?" Now Zokalaus eyes opened wide. "Who is chief Aborungun!?"

"That's him right here," replied the maskman, "the man you have insulted like shit since we arrived."

Karl was genuinely surprised. He looked at the chief for a long moment, then made a shrug of his shoulder and said, "might have told me what, Jobilah?"

"That we put you in that trouble right from the beginning magnified it and later came around to save you. For your information, that sentence was initially fifteen years imprisonment for a provoked action that it was."

Zokalaus just looked at him disdainfully. "Now you're beginning to sound really funny. What a cheap connivance. You think I am a dump headed monkey that would believe any shit? C'mon, give me a better story. The one that makes sense; one that I can believe!"

"A man is seldom cleverer than his manipulator. Now listen to this. We drained your motorbike fuel tank, yes, your Honda CD 175. We left enough to carry you up to somewhere out of town, out of reach of a fuel station and we had tampered with the fuel gauge. Later we sent the girl after you to render help. Look, the whole thing was a fix right from that time to the time you cut off that poor man's ball. Do you even think your idea to cut off the balls was purely your own. Just try and remember everything you could right from that very first day."

Zokalaus closed his eyes for some moments and Jobilah took a step further back and virtually jumped when Zokalaus shouted, "Fox! You clever fox. You collected information from Bimbi and manipulated it to suit you!"

"You've been blind for a long time. Now it's time to start seeing. Time to open your eyes!"

"How did you know me before, fox? What did I have to do with you? Answer that before you start manipulating gathered information and crediting them to your actions."

"We had watched you for months. All your activities and way of life, the way you survived, your hopeful but short-lived boxing carrier as a result of your episode with Little Tiger. But the final decision was made by chief Enlaye when you whipped that pastor or whatever he called himself, who was disturbing peoples' sleep in the early morning of 27 March, if you cared to remember the date."

For a second time Zokalaus closed his eyes and one could guess he was seeing the whole episode all over again.

"And Bimbi?" he asked quietly.

"Yes, Bimbiiiii. Bimbo was not an accident. She is a thorough bred Bwallangwist. A top Bwallangwist operative for that matter. Have you not been told that? Tough delicate assignment such as yours is normally given to her and her girls. The nurse that called you on that fateful day is one of her girls."

Once again Zokalaus closed his eyes and this time sort of let go as he lay limp on the bed. Jobilah continued. "You never accepted favors from anybody because you avoid indebtedness. So after making sure your head was well in the noose we stepped in to offer a favor you couldn't have rejected under the circumstances. Hence, a favor you couldn't forget in your life. Well, most of the rest of the story from thereon you know. Of course you wouldn't join us right away, still being who you are, and we allowed you to demonstrate for yourself that there was no safe place for you except in Bwallangwu organization. So eventually you ended up coming back to us. But I give it to you; you really tried, with a trail of dead bodies behind you. You actually could have made it but for the fact that we supplied the police with your day-to-day locations. Just think for a while, what you think and how you felt when you stood in front of your poster at Fatte, despite your disguise. We made things hotter and unbearable for you until you made up your mind to come back. Then we welcomed you back from the gate of hell, with open hands, gave you a safe home, a new identity. You know the rest of the story."

And how were you able to know all itineraries of my escapade?"

"If on your return to Chief Enlaye's study he ventured to place his hand on your shoulder in a fatherly way it was to remove the bug he placed on you."

"What da fuck!? Ok, ok. You people are so good; you've been able to manipulate Zokalaus. Where is Bimbi anyway?"

"Honestly I don't know. I told you before. There's a limit to what I know about movement of certain agents."

"Ok!" the terrible voice, "So I had been manipulated. I have been deceived and used. But that is my bloody fucking palaver and that I'll settle with them in my own term, at my own time! But if you people are trying to find some foolish priest to use, some dumb priest, who had been offended and has an axe to grind, to attempt your impossible suicidal ill-conceived, thought less plan, well, I tell you, you haven't found one yet. Keep searching, for I don't intend to be used again! Never! You haven't got your priest yet. Tell you what, why don't you wait, exercise a little patience until Jobilah becomes a priest, then see for yourself if he would agree to attempt this childish mission of yours!"

"We are all being used, Karl," said the chief very solemnly. "We can never avoid being used. Once you present yourself a good instrument a being would certainly be used either by the good which is God side or by the Lucifer which represents the bad. But we are part of the choice of which side uses us. Free Will they call it. A Good Material never lies fallow. It would inadvertently be used by one of the two seemingly opposing forces. For anybody, the best way to escape being used by the side he might perceive as bad is certainly to offer himself to the one he sees as the good side. Whether we know it or not and whether we like it or not we are being used. A good material never lies fallow."

"Agreed, chief but that is my personal look out. I will do what I deem fit for me. I don't need your preaching and enlightenment on it. Shit philosophy. So you people might as well stop jabbering!"

The chief and the maskman looked at each other, a bit disappointed and close to resignation. Jobilah who had started pacing up and down turned around abruptly, eyes glistening, highly determined.

"Alright, Karl, this will hurt you but you have certainly left me no other option. But a young man of your strength, mind and body will withstand it."

"You never stop trying, do you? What other cock and bull stories do you have again now? The way you were pacing up and down suggests you were up to something in your dome head."

"Nothing is cooked. They happened real and I will provide living evidences today!"

That got Zokalaus' attention. "What is it that happened?"

"Karl, please tell me, have ever seen a baby dropped from the sky or any one growing out of the ground like a tree?"

"What a question!? I said you're mad!"

"Therefore it wouldn't surprise you that you had parents."

The slight almost unnoticed corking of Zokalaus head indicated his attention. "Just mind what lies you tell about me that I don't already know." He boomed.

"If you listen I will tell you all you do not know and all you know already but which you can't link together for a comprehensible explanation of your life situation." Jobilah shook his head sadly before he continued.

"Way back close to three decades now there was great man called Emmanuel Ajahni. Oh! A man among men! A man Samson would like to befriend. A man the superman would envy, even the Spiderman would bow. A man of principle, a gentleman to the core, a very quiet but powerful man, a man the bionic woman would love to marry, Jezebel and Delilah would shiver, a man the queen of Sheba........."

"Shut up!" Fadi boomed. "Go straight to the point! Otherwise keep your trap shut!"

"Look here!" Jobilah retorted. "You will not talk to me like that! Don't ever forget you're still under me! I'm still your boss!"

"Don't get fucking carried away by certain organizational formalities. If I ever called you 'sir' it is because of your age! Nothing else! Boss my foot!"

"Jobilah!" intervened chief Aborungun, "I expect you to know better than to scoop up a quarrel at this particular occasion. You may not realize it yet but a turning point in life is as important as ones date of birth and date of death. This is a turning point for many of us here. I hope you agree."

"I am sorry sir, It's …err…" Jobilah apologized while Zokalaus continued to stare at the blank ceiling of the tent.

"Go ahead, we are all interested." The chief urged.

"Okay sir," Jobilah goes ahead, eyeing Zokalaus. "Emmanuel Ajahni founded the legendary school of martial arts that once existed in Modakeke. Emmajahny School of Martial Arts. ESMA for short. There were certain unequalled techniques and qualities of his instructions that soon became irresistible to Bwallangwu. This is especially so when Ajahni worn the world title for the 7th consecutive times and remained yet undefeated. He definitely was going to be an asset to Bwallangwu and he really proved his mettle. But to get him in was a drama of its own. He just wouldn't cooperate and was never ever ready to serve the organization. Ajahni was a man of himself, for himself; never works for anybody nor any group whatsoever. He makes his honest living without even demanding much from his students. He was loved but he never gave a damn how people felt about him." Then he released his typical cynical smile, "But when Bwallangwu wants anybody he always get him." Then he coughed and the maskman refilled the cup of wine he has been eyeing. He thanked him, took a good gulp and continued.

"First we ruined his school and it happened like this: we were able to sponsor a girl to work as a server with a local food seller close to the school, where most of the students of Ajhani's school eat. Her instruction was to put a special poison in one of the students' food. This poison starts reacting at a particular rate of heart beat, otherwise it can remain dormant for long in the carrier's body. But as soon as such person starts any vigorous exercise the cyanide effect is activated in the blood and the person dies within half an hour. That was how a student suddenly collapsed and died during training in ESMA. Post mortem result attributed the cause of death to internal hemorrhage caused by a crucial blow on a critical internal organ. Well I'm sure you know that we have not only doctors but we have also the law in our pocket"

"I might be able to contest that, Jobilah." Interjected the chief.

"Agree sir, but for the few like you sir. Very very, few sir. But we have a sizeable proportion. So it was immediately decided the school was going to be shut down pending investigation of a murder case allegation. But we knew that was not going to be enough to bend Ajahni. Not even the promise to save his school. So while the case was still on we sent some greedy fools, martial artists as well, from another school to go round him up in an alley with the instruction to kill him. No shootings! They had all other sorts of weapons, knives, chains, etc. Well, obviously we already knew the result before we sent them. Ajahni crippled one, another one died and a third one hospitalized for 2 years. The fourth one and perhaps the cleverest among them, was able to regain consciousness within three weeks. That was the one that was able to tell part of the story and of course, the key witness."

Everyone paused to drink something, water or wine, even beer except Zokalaus who stared at the ceiling. Jobilah emptied his glass for the umpteenth time and continued.

"Now the law in this state is very hard on martial artists. They are regarded as experts at managing terrible situations. It believes they have all the self controls and restraints and they don't have to kill unless they want to. So combined with his ongoing case it was proven that Ajahni enjoyed killing or in the least did not give any regards to human life. That the condition of his mind was questionable and such a person should not be allowed to roam freely in a decent society. His sentence for murder was death or as the defending council pleaded for mercy, he was to be locked away in an asylum prison until he could show improvement of a sane mind. Now Ajahni was in deep shit and he knew it. But fortunately Bwallangwu was there to offer its loving fatherly hands in dear need. And just like magic it made all the troubles to disappear. What was not immediately quenched was squelched and postponed etc, etc, and never again to be revisited as long as Ajahni remained in the organization. Gradually we won his heart over, telling him our divine mission in life and that the people we are up against were no other than the sort that ruined him and who would have terminated his life if not condemned in asylum prison if Bwallangwu did not intervene."

"Hmmmmnn!" came out of the listeners as some extended their glass for a refill. Jobilah downed his and asked for more before he continued.

"Thereafter we started sending him to eliminate those sort of people as we indicated to him and may I tell you, gentlemen, Ajahni moved about like a ghost. He could move inside a crowd, guards, soldiers, whatever to carry out his missions and could kill so silently that even the next man in line would not be aware of anything until he had gone away from the location. He was made to believe he was doing all this for humanity; to ensure that the fate that hitherto befell him would never happen again to defenseless people; that he was hence a messiah." A little pause.

"Everything went on and smooth until one particular period. You know in its modus operandi Bwallangwu never takes chances and that is why the organization has survived for ages till date and still is...errr.... You know when Bwallangwu condemns anybody to death it makes sure all those connected to such person who might later seek revenge are eliminated. Hence, certain persons who are too attached or sympathetic, especially children and wives, depending on the circumstance, and even certain friends and kins who might have enough reasons to avenge the death might be eliminated. That's what we mean when we say RRR or R Cube operation. Remove Roots and Remnants. When we send an operator on a RRR operation he would eliminate all those closely associated like such. So Ajahni was dispatched on an RRR mission on an enemy of Bwallangwu and these happened to be two children, one of 5 and the older a 7 years old boy, both in the orphanage. Ajhani did not only refuse he prevented the rest of his team from accomplishing the mission. "I won't kill children," he had declared, "and I would not stand by and see it done!" The four others either out of dullness or directly received orders, tried to handle

Ajahni but I should not unnecessarily elongate this story by telling you what happened to them."

They paused for a refill and perhaps an opportunity to digest all they had heard so far.

"Ajahni was counseled and he told the priests point blank that he would not be found where children are being killed. Now please listen to these tape recordings, gentlemen. Courtesy of ABOGINT.

> "You should have carried out that mission without letting me be aware of it. I can't take it! Sorry."
>
> "Ajahni, we don't have to remind you that it is in the survival interest of the organization that the roots and remnants of Ademulegun must be removed. And you not only refused but sabotaged the entire operation. It is rather disappointing if we have to start reminding a man of your status."
>
> "What possible harm could two innocent little children constitute to anybody at this moment?"
>
> "It's not the way of Bwallangwu to sleep with snakes under its pillow. You must solve little problems before they become enlarged and later unmanageable."
>
> "I will prefer to strike them when and if they take up arms against Bwallangwu."
>
> "Would you rather relax and sleep when you have fire on your roof? Won't you rather make haste to put it out?"
>
> "That should not mean we should fear matches until they are struck. We have to be fair to the future."
>
> "When Bwallangwu decides your own is to carry it out!"
>
> "I will not kill children!"

The tape was stopped and Jobilah continued. "The man was adamant and situation degenerated between him and the organization. It soon gravitated to that unavoidable situation where Ajahni ended up being condemned. After an abortive attempt to eliminate him he vanished seemingly into thin air. But as I said earlier on, the organization has weapons and men that are ready to use them. Above all, the thought that only one man could constitute such a problem was humiliating to a lot of us who I must confess were motivated by jealousy. We spurred on relentlessly in pursuit. The price Bwallangwu even placed on his head was enticing enough. Look Ajahni killed more than 200 men and in most cases only the leader of such raids returned alive. The thing is you don't really see him and how the hell do you shoot a man you don't see? I will never forget the day we cornered him in Agala forest in Ibadan. It was with the help of the local and federal police. Bwallangwu lost 45 men that very day. I, Jobilah alone returned alive with the leader and I know if I didn't disobey his orders to pursue him I wouldn't have survived. Well, nevertheless, a man who has a weakness for something is not difficult to catch, provided you have the guts to exploit that weakness. After suffering so much casualty we decided to exploit that very weakness of his that we know; the weakness that is the cause of his trouble with the organization." He paused to wet his throat.

"It happened in Iwo at River Oba. We released a kid, barely 7 years old, and gave Masa a knife to pursue him. You know Masa the pedicide? That mad boy who loves to kill children. Well we got him released to us the previous day as soon as we conceived of this plan. And if I knew Masa well on that day, he was going to carve that little boy. Masa caught up with the little boy in no time. The boy dived into the river and Masa dived after him. Masa grab him and raised his dagger and the next thing we saw was blood on the surface of the river. Not the boy's blood it turned out but Masa's. An arrow was stuck into his left side. The little boy's attempt to swim ashore was turned into a nightmare when a crocodile resurged from somewhere all of a sudden. Like a second arrow, Ajahni flew from nowhere apparent and dived in between the boy and the reptile. That was when our men in hiding opened fire from all direction, sprayed all the three, Ajahni, the little boy and the crocodile."

"Very good story Jobilah. Very good. What has all this to do with me?"

"Just hold on Karl, it has an extension." The maskman implored.

"Go ahead, we haven't got all day," urged the chief.

"Now it appeared all about Ajahni had been completed. He was not married, no known serious attachment to anybody and no known 'dangerous' emotionally attached persons....well only some few friends who already denounced him, some of who even participated in the hunt. But let me show you something." He removed from his bag some old newspaper clippings and spread them to show all,

"This birth was the top of all news all over the country when it happened. Siamese twins! The very first that survived at that particular time." He pointed to illustrate. The ragged paper revealed two newborn babies joined together at the hips, and the second picture showed when they were separated.

"Well, it wasn't a difficult operation and nothing so dramatic as to be worth remembering. A lot of things more strange happens daily than the case of ordinary twins joined but separated successfully..... until words came to the organization that the mother of the twins was impregnated by the then BSF commander Emmanuel Ajahni. Then it started all over again. The woman had disappeared with the children before we got to her dwelling place at Lagbaka village. By the time we tracked her down later it was her dead body we found, with a large wound in the belly. She was still clinging to the knife with which she killed herself."

He took some wine. "Well, about our Siamese? A dead woman couldn't tell us anything and there was nothing we didn't do to find them but all in vain, short of ordering the extermination of all newborn babies in the city at that period."

"A king once did that, so I heard in the bible." said the maskman.

"Herod!" supplied chief Aborungun, "Kings of those dark ages."

Everybody permitted themselves a sardonic smile with the exception of Zokalaus.

"So," continued Jobilah, "events soon overcame the concerns about the twins...well two suckling...which were not even certain would survive. Who would even tell them any stories in any case? Even the names of the children were not known. So it was more or less forgotten by and in the organization …again until recently, after twenty good years, when a doctor had to perform another surgery. This time around a plastic surgery on an adult and had to get some tissues and skin from some hidden part of the body of the patient and noticed a scar which he could recognize perfectly well by the shape mostly perhaps -the scar of separation."

One could notice Zokalaus turning his head in anticipation of what Jobilah was going to say next. Even the maskman was curiously anxious.

"Yes," continued the old man, slightly drunk now, "the doctor had to get some tissues and skin from a hidden part of the patient's body and so he noticed a peculiar scar on the hip of the patient," and turning towards Zokalaus emphatically, "gentlemen, it was this same doctor who separated the Siamese twenty years ago and is no other doctor than Doctor Oluseyi Payida, a Bwallangwist."

A kind of silence prevailed which was broken by Zokalaus.

"You're full of crabs! You fox! If this was the case you would have told the organization long before now to curry favor and especially to save your position! I know you, you greedy son of a bitch!"

"Sure but I didn't know until recently when Dr. Payida confided in me."

"And why didn't your good doctor Payida tell the organization the moment he saw the scar of separation….errr…which he recognized according to you, before he performed the second surgery?"

"I guess he did that to make up for his past mistakes; torn between loyalty to Bwallangwu and his love of children maybe. I'm sure he allowed your mother to get far out of reach before he, must have been him, slipped the word that time."

"Whose mother!? What are you insinuating? You're incoherent! Gaadmn mother fucker!"

'Well, well, well," interrupted chief Aborungun, "*a kii gb'odo jiyan b'ose ho tabi ko ho*[48], a scar on the hip is probably not that controversial unless your member surgeon had covered it up. We shouldn't beat about the bush. If there's anybody here who has the said scar on his hip the story is most likely his own." And turning to Zokalaus, "Fadi, son, do you have anything to say to this?"

"Yeah, yeah. I have a scar quiet right," shouting, "on my right hip but I don't know about any scar of separation! What da hell!?"

"Then you must have been on the left side of the twins!" said the chief, each word slowly and deliberately."

"But that doesn't prove all he has said to be true. This old crab can just cook anything around any available thing!"

"But do you know how yours got there, son?" asked the chief in very fatherly way and tone.

"No I don't. Could have been…."

"Then do not fight it yet. Let's rather proceed logically to the root of the matter."

All was quiet again for a long moment, everyone to his own thought. The maskman paced up and down the tent. Zokalaus on the bed turning his head right and left slowly.

"Well it's safe to assume for now that we have found one of Ajahni's boys," the chief broke the silence, "What about the second one?"

"No news sir. My guess is he…he must have died by now. It is really tough to survive, especially in this very case and the economic downturn. Again the Oyunlola river disaster happened when they were tots and so many children went with it. It was later followed by the lukuluku epidemic that wiped a total of 640 children at that time. That second one must have died. In fact, what this one went through before I found him……."

"Quiet!" Zokalaus voice threatened to tear the tent fabric. "Before you found who? Who was lost? Just thank your luck that I'm tied down to this gaaaddemn bed! Found who?"

The silence that ensued infected everybody. Jobilah seemed to be at a loss for what further to say. The chief's head was bent down

---

[48] It is not necessary to not argue on whether a tablet of soap lathers or not whe we are by a river.

in thought. The maskman continued to pace up and down the tent. Karl stared at the tent roof with the movement of his eyeballs trying to betray what was going on in his mind. Jobilah, physically shaken, reached for the wine this time without permission and the maskman did not bother to stop him. He drank the wine like fish in water.

"Well," the maskman said at last, "I suppose we leave matter as it is today. Everybody I believe will need time to sort himself out, if the chief agrees with me sir?"

"Good idea, ghost. I will be the first to leave. I need some updating to do and the earlier the better. I presume you would not hesitate to call me any moment anything crops up before tomorrow."

"I sure would sir."

"One more thing," the chief said at the entrance, "I don't know whether to hold on or to say this now. But it's what I have said before. It's a blessing meeting a ghost." Everybody laughed as the chief departed.

Everybody departed. The guards came in to take post beside Zokalaus, and their orders remains the same. Jobilah was drunk, completely drunk. He was more or less half carried half dragged into a tent where he slept on the bare ground.

At about an hour and a couple of minutes later the maskman reentered the Hospital tent with a bottle of wine and 2 glasses. The guards went out on his signal, with specific instructions that nobody must disturb. He set down the wine and the glasses on the bedside bamboo table and he sat himself unusually too close to Zokalaus. Both looked at each other, Zokalaus the more curious, and the mask man smiled, white teeth showing in the mask.

"Good wine," he said.

Zokalaus looked at the wine briefly, and then turned his face to stared back at the ceiling, with a comment, "Certain things you hear dismiss your appetite." He said.

"And certain things you discover in the revelation restore back your appetite." The maskman replied

"I guess I would continue to drink mine in sorrow. By the way, I have been longing to meet you but not in this circumstance."

"You mean the ropes?"

"Well part of it. And I must confess you are the toughest guy I ever struggled with in my entire life. You preempted my moves so accurately it seems you read my mind."

"Incidentally that feeling is mutual."

"You made me curious. First I was out and you had your chance but why didn't you shoot? Tell me why."

"I just couldn't and I didn't know why." He drew out his dagger and threw it up, letting it roll several times in the air before catching it in his palm. Zokalaus eyed the knife without showing any feelings.

"So you wanna do it now, with a knife?" He aked.

"Nope," replied the maskman, "thou shall not kill."

Then Zokalaus watched him in amazement as he cut the ropes that tied his hands and feet to the bamboo bed."

"You don't suppose you're taking a great risk, do you?" he asked, rubbing his aching wrist to restore blood circulation.

"Probably not."

"Because of all the shit stuff you people have made that old fox to tell me?"

"Not as such."

"Because of my legs that were shot?"

"Nope."

"The 4 guards within range?"

"Again, nope."

"Then while the hell you wanna cut me lose when nobody is around?"

"Because I know you will never kill me much as I will never kill you."

"You belief yourself. Why?"

"You know why but you're only looking for the explanation. We tried it before but we couldn't."

"Betting on that again?"

"Because I don't believe it's the right thing to do now that we have found each other.."

"Becoming sentimental. Aren't you? Killing is for survival."

"Not all the time Fadi. On the contrary, most of the time, saving is for survival."

"Some poem…but tell me first. Why do you wear that mask?"

"Almost the same reason why you got a new face, but slightly different. You hide from your enemies, Fadi, I hide from my friends. I wished I had seen your face for real before the exchange. You see how selfish you can be, Fadi."

"The hell are you talking about?

"You have two faces while I have none."

"What are you up to anyway," curiously looking at him.

"What do you think is the implication of this Jobilah's revelation?"

"Had to think of anything. Jobilah is a crook. He can just cook anything around any available facts."

"You really got that separation mark?"

"I know I have a scar but I wouldn't know about any separation shit."

"On your right hip?"

"Yes on my right hip. Hip is hip! What da hell? Look, what's this?" he was becoming irritated by the mask man cowling behavior.

"It must have a definite shape and size."

"What is this? Of course, all scars have shape…definite shape… what the hell?"

"Fadi, can you show me?"

"Hey look! What a shit!? I don't show hip to men!. Gay or something? In fact by the way you fret over me it shows you are. In that case you better watch it!"

The maskman laughed. "Now Fadi, listen. The feelings I have for you is real but not sensual. My touch on you should not convey a carnal message but rather in anticipation of what might be the obvious; what I hope we might be to each other. Fadi, I happen also to have a scar which I could not explain how it got there."

"Whaat?"

"Yes I also have a scar."

"On the hip?"

"Yes, on the hip! And if yours is truly on the right then it is most likely that we are brothers. Because I have mine on the left!"

"Now wait a minute."

"And the utmost test is if the scars fit."

Just like military men on parade ground, doing things automatically, or two synchronized robots, they both got up at the same time, tugging at each other's trousers. The maskman unbuckled his belt while Fadi was helping him to pull it down. Fortunately for Fadi, his own was easier because his belt had been removed as is usually done with captives; both in a hurry to discover what all revelations might be pointing to. What an irony of fate for two straight men to be helping each other to pull pants.

Both had scar on the hip! One has his on the left, the other his own on the right. The scars were two halves of an imperfect circle, but which fit exactly when the two grown up toughies stood side by side in a manner of this dance style called 'bump'. Instantly Zokalaus reached up and did what no man had ever done and no human born by woman can ever dare. He yanked the mask off the maskman's face.

"My God! You are wearing my face!"

"What a wonder of nature how pod explosions, in ballistichory following its genetic program, could scatter the seeds of the *caeba petanda*[49] in different directions, to different destinations, asunder, and the wind of fate can blow them around, wandering, only to, by chance or by providence, bring them once again together, in the most unexpected way but devine, purpose being the order of nature. Fadi you are my brother!"

They grasped each other and hugged. "You call me Karl...my brother...I am Karl."

"I am.....", the maskman whispered his name into Karl's ear. "But don't tell anybody yet."

They held each other tight like that for so long, trousers dropped down to the ankle and they didn't care! Bloody hell! If anybody had come into that tent at that moment it would have made the headline in the most scandalous story to be told in the country.

---

[49] The Kapok tree or cotton tree (South America)

The elder stateman of the Eastern Region, Dr Ignatus Ogomigo Nwaokoro had arrived with his entourage at about 10 0'clock in the morning and the meeting, so to say, had started immediately in the big conference hall in chief Aborungun's estate.

"…needless to say this unfortunate and rather absurd incidence has been a great source of embarrassment to me and the whole of my people. It was unimaginable and the implications in jeopardizing……"

"The implication is quite plain and obvious," cut in chief Aborungun, "and what beats my imagination flat is the manner and extent to which we are ready to go in expressing our feelings towards each other or do I rather say the way we go about in obtaining the object of our desire. The implication, of course, doctor, is grave and far reaching."

"May I say that the chief should not consider this unfortunate incidence as an organized act committed by the Easterners. This is not the way we express our feelings and we would not go to such a ridiculous extent of assassinating….emmmn….for no reason at all! It is absurd and ridiculous!"

"Hmmmmn."

"Look, Jimmy, although we find ourselves in different quadrants of area of activities, agitations and actions within our polity where everyone is struggling to lead for his own peoples' survival and betterment, we have been friends and we are still friends and more to it, enlightened. We both know that eliminating you does not improve my chances of becoming the president of this country in anyway. Does it?"

"I am afraid some people might think different. Isn't it, Ignat?"

"I assure you such people do not represent my community."

"Haaah, Anisiam Edtejere from Asslochukwu Local government, Titus Okikiiafule from from Mibase, Ondoru Osboro… the list is plenty."

"Jimmy, I have thoroughly investigated this case. All those involved are outcastes. People that are condemned and had been banned from ever setting their feet in Eastland again. It would surprise you that some of them are not even Ibo. Ebenezer Nwobodo is not Ibo! His mother, a Cameroonian, came to Nigeria 56 years ago while his father, from

Gold Coast came much earlier. They met and lived in Eastland land since them. They were not even married but they gave birth to that bastard. Another person on your list is Thomas Nwankwo who had been jailed for armed robbery after he ran away from home. He cannot come back again, and we are still investigating. Look, Jimmy, these are the sort of characters that have been used by the evil minded, negative and destructive elements in our society, who I believe are against you and want to cause confusion around it to prevent recognition. Jimmy, remember that we have been friends for long, long during our school days. Why would I for heaven's sake, I, Ignatus Nwaokoro the son of Ogomigo, ever want to kill you? Even then do you think I would have gone about it in such a foolish and absurd way?"

"Oh Ignats. Believe me I never for once thought you could and I never will think so because a man of your intelligence and foresight could not easily miss the grave implication of the incidence. Long before now you and I talked about the fact that our survival rests solely upon our unity. If we were and are still sincere, Ignats, you would agree that this situation now is extremely embarrassing not only to your side but equally to mine. You would agree that it threatens dangerously the foundation upon which we plan to place the outcome of our much coveted wish – Unity. Some people actually do not want this unity and if we allow this situation between us now to linger it would permanently destroy the relationship that is gradually establishing root between our two great cummunities." And looking directly into the eyes of the great Eastern chief, he said, "a tribal war is just not what we need now."

The effect of the last statement was not lost on the Eastern chief and the impact on his reply, "I want and will continue to implore you, Jimmy, to do your best to calm down your people. It is very essential for the existence and development of our nations. I assure you we do not want war. We never wanted it at all. What we want is peace. We saw it once and we know its implications in all ramifications. Once is enough. Once beaten twice shy. We might be found to fight but not a stupid war ever. I want you to believe me that my people are not responsible for what happened. It is just an attempt to frame us by some evil intentioned people whose activities require an atmosphere of disunity to thrive and survive. We should be careful so as not to play into their hands."

"Fortunately, Ignats, I believe you. The most fortunate thing is the fact that we are friends and we can easily understand each other. It wouldn't have been easier were the situation to be different."

"This is most pleasing news, Jimmy. And this friendship is a great blessing to our two peoples. We must exploit it to the fullest mutual advantage. We must prevent a looming national disaster. We know it is very rational for the Westerners to want to take up arms following what happened. We wouldn't blame them. In fact we are very graetful to God that you escaped. If not...hmmn...there would have been no remedy. Even now I must confess I was afraid to come to Yoruba land even after you had assured me that I am perfectly safe."

"You are perfectly safe in my land, Ignats."

"But our innocence could not be proved until we get to the very root of this matter. We must know, as a matter of urgency, those perpetrators of this evil agenda. Otherwise my people would continue to be under suspicion, making the situation between our two peoples a time bomb waiting to explode under the slightest provocation; a situation that could easily be exploited by the negative elements. Jimmy, my peoples' innocence in this matter has to be proved for both our sake."

"I understand. I quite understand."

"Thank you so much. We have to set the machinery in motion, Jimmy."

"Leave that to me, Ignats. I will find the root and," putting his fist inside his palm, "crush it!"

"I intend to send some of my experts to help out in the matter. We should work hands in hands right from now, Jimmy."

"Very well, Ignats, but are people not likely to misinterpret your good intention the more? I mean your operations in Yorubaland might produce a more implicating result which in turn might result in playing us into the hands of these perpetrators. So, do not worry. Just let me handle the situation, at least for our friendship sake and for the foundation of unity we are trying to build upon. I promise you I will find the root and destroy it."

"This will pass down in history as an act we could never forget. I thank you so much Jimmy."

"It is very essential, though, Ignats, to let your people know that I bear no grudge against them. I am theirs and they are mine. We are for each other now and for ever. In fact, Ignats, I have a great idea."

"Tell me."

"I think this idea would unite us the more. I like to come over to your community, tour your states and talk with your people. The more we know each other the more we learn to trust one another. Don't you think so?"

"Of course, yes," said the Eastern chieftain, "and when you finish your tour I would begin mine."

"Very well."

They had lunch afterwards, more entertainments and once in the light atmosphere chief Ignatus had asked curiously. "This Egbe teleportation technology of yours, why don't you at least tell me the secret, so that I can make mine, as a mark of our great friendship and to mark this visit of mine? You know, a great souvenir…"

"Haaah, Ignats," the chief replied with a smile," there are so many categories of it all over the country. All you need to do is get closer to the strong men of your society."

I mean this particular one which is, as we say in the market, tested. Give me the secret and I would use it to mark this great day of ours."

"Oh tested tokunbo. No problems except just one."

"What is that? Ego, money? Of course I know a genuine product costs money. Original! I will pay."

"Oh, Ignats, I would gladly have given it to you free but it is handed down the line of my forefathers and thus a family secret and as a matter of fact the power lies in the aecret."

"I guess as much."

"But small thing, after all we are more or less family now."

"So you will give it to me?" chief Iganatus brightened with anticipation.

"Incantations. It has to do with intonations, frequencies and powers in words."

"So?"

"You have to first learn Yoruba."

"Haa haaa, I understand now."

CHAPTER 15

WAR AGAINST BWALLANGWU

"We will strike at noon. Exactly." Adams commenced the ops briefing.

"Why broad daylight? Sacrificing the element of surprise in enemies territory?" asked Chief Bobade in enthusiasm but careul not to condemn the decision of the maskman because of past experiences.

"Bwallangwu is weak in daylight. Its sense perception grows weaker as the sun rises and is weakest when the sun gets over head." Karl replied.

"Confirmed." Augmented chief Aborungun's representative. "If Bwallangwu takes a rest, or any form of relaxation at all, it is in daylight, just the opposite of human systemic activities. Secondly, my chief Bobby, they probably would not expect an attack at noon, so the element of surprise is still intact unless, of course we have a mole among us."

"Nevertheless, movement and deployment of our troops are not expected to be easy in broad daylight." Added the maskman.

"Well, double edged sword. Isn't it," this time Jobilah.

"So what are the plans?" Asked chief Aborungun's representative.

"We will filter in." Karl has taken over. "You know what I mean? In small packages. We infiltrate in groups of 3. But we will assemble in Orijin Forest individually, unsuspectingly, dressed as farmers, hunters, palmwine tappers and all sorts of menial job's attire as suits individual tasks, especially those of us with special tasks. From morning till dusk we would have all assembled in Orijin forest, which is just about 600 meters to the abode of Bwallangwu.

This plan discussion had begun in Heaven's Camp among the maskman, Karl, Jobilah, chief Bobade who is found now more in the camp than anywhere else, and the technical and strategic representative of chief Aborungun. Funny enough, chief Bobade and chief Aborungun do not see eye to eye, so it's always either one or the other. On this occasion chief Aborungun has sent his representative. In front of them is spread a large sketch of Bwallangwu's environment drawn by Karl. All necessary intelligence about the Bwallangwists are being supplied by chief Aborungun's representative of the ABORGINT (Aborungun Intelligence) division, and the 2 men to reckon with in the Bwallangwu Srtike Force (BSF) in persons of Jobilah and Karl, who supplied vital information such as the current overall strength of BSF, techniques and capabilities, equipment in use, sentry deployments, key points and vulnerable points, habits, etc.

"We will divide our force into 3 main groups," Karl had commenced. "The first group will create diversion in the north while we penetrate from the south, while the the third group, the reserve, will rapidly deploy to support where help might be needed; in other words, take care of emergencies.. The diversion team's roll is crucial and is to serve two purposes. You see, here in the northeast is the fuel depot and here towards the northwest, down there, is the main armo depot. The diversion team will blow up the two places one after the other within a gap of 10 minutes. The first being the fuel dumps followed with some sporadic shootings to announce the attack. That creates the diversion needed for the attack group in the south to commence their own."

"Why the gap of 10 minutes? Why not simultaneously for surprise element?" inquisted chief Bobade.

"The blow up of the fuel dump is a diversion for the clandestine operation men whose job is to go for the key points and the vital points in Bwallangwu's camp, and Ismaila would rationally assemble men to issue them weapons at the armmo depot, right? And from experience and practiced drills it takes 10 minutes to assemble Bwallangwu's men at the armo depot. Then the explosives planted in that depot would be triggered. Hopefully we can trust Jobilah on that. Then Bwallangwu loses men and ammunitions."

Chief Bobade sat down quietly, seriously looking dazed and somehow afraid. Chief Aborungun's representative said something inaudible with something like a sign of the cross, surprising enough for a Moslem that he is.

"And all the above, if all goes well, constitutes all the diversion required for the strike team in the south, and if I knew Bello well enough he would deploy the guards away from the abode of Bwallangwu to the location of the problems bcause, as we all believe, nobody can kill Bwallangwu," releasing a wicked smile, "so the monster is perfectly safe. Now any questions, clarifications, additions or subtractions?" Karl paused to ask.

"Go ahead first," said the obviously impressed maskman, "though I have reservations which I would expressed later."

"I would have suggested that the maskman should take care of the diversion while Jobilah, who knows Bwallangwu security in and out, to take out the vital points and key points while I go in to give Bwallangwu his last sacrifice, but that is only if I could trust him."

"What do you mean by only if you could trust me?" Jobilah reacted, growing red.

"Because I have learnt, from past experiences, not to trust the cross-breeds of a fox and hyena like you, even when you are fighting for them their own battles."

"Insolent! You!"

"Not now please," implored chief's representative.

"Okay, we settle this later." Jobilah swallowed his pride, almost choked on his anger.

"Now about Bwallangwu. What intel do we have on him?" The maskman demanded pressingly. Then chief Aborungun's representative stood up. He opened his folder and commenced.

"From chief Aborungun's reports, Bwallangwu's skin is impenetrable by most metals. That is probably why so many attempts in the past had failed, even before he deploys the horrible choking emmanations, which eventually added up to his myth of invincibility, and as a result, nobody wants to even try again at the risk of their lifes.

"Guns!?" asked chief Bobade. "If we spray him with 5 machine guns deployed in automatic mode, pumping hot bullets, five of them simultaneously....boy oh boy, that son of a gun couldn't possibly withstand 6000 round per minutes from each gun and totaling 30000 from 5 of them if we use the Vulcan cannon or the M-134 minigun."

"Guns, of course have been known to have no effect on him."

"Exactly what I want to ask. But why?" asked Karl this time aound."

"The powder in the bullets kind of liquefies. The worst, records have it that its skin has been known to reflect bullets in a sort of back-to-sender phenomenon. The other cases are the issue of back firing, this thing akin to our traditional *tidijos*[50]."

"So if that is so with what are we going to work on this bastard monster?" Stammered chief Bobade, "certainly not wrestling or boxing," trying to introduce some jokes into the issue.

"The report is not yet finished sir." Cautioned the maskman. They kept quiet and listened while the chief's rep continued.

"However, we gathered that Bwallangwu as a kid sustained an injury at the age of 7 and the metal was silver, and from further observations we gathered that Bwallangwu is never served with silver bowls. All silver materials are kept away from the shrine. So putting two and two together, it's only silver that can hurt the monster and without beating about the bush, gentlemen, the weapon the strike team should be using should be made of silver."

"Exactly!" commented Jobilah. "I could remember one time Enlaye told me he had silver spoon in his pocket while in the abode of the em... Bwallangwu and they were kind of ....em..""

"Talk straight! Goddamn it!"

"Please Karl," the rep begged.

"And I heard when they serve they use dry wood to push the bowl further close to him," the maskman chipped in.

---

[50] A charm that makes an attackers firearms to backfire.

"Dry wood!?" asked chief Bobade.

"Yes, dry wood is a bad conductor, chief," explained the rep who seized the opportunity to talk to chief Bobade. "One could conductor even death with a good conductor in ones hands."

"In school we talked about good or bad conductor of heat or ectricity. Here, in this advanced school of war we talk of good conductor of death!" This time around chief Bobade eventually succeded to make them laugh..

"And what do we call this advanced school of ours?" asked Jobilah, laughing.

"War College!" supplied the maskman and they all roared in laughter.

"That is beautiful, and I will give my chief the reports." Said the rep jokingly and he added, "gentlemen all this add to the description of all weapons to be used by our srike team. They must be silver bladed with wooden handle."

"We have already taken care of that," informed the maskman. "In fact, the first sample of the special weapons has been delivered. I will have them brought here for you to see." He called one of the boys and gave instuctions. A minute later three knives, silver bladed, two with wooden handles while the third was fitted with plastic handle, were brought and placed on the table. Karl picked up and examined one mean looking glistening silver dagger, tested the sharpness by moving his thumb slightly over the blade, then getting a piece of paper and seeing how the blade just cut through without resistance, smiled, a kind of wicked one, and said, "yeah, to think Bwallangwu did this to us, changed the course of my life, in fact ruined me. I am a twin and I didn't know my own brother until 25 good years of separated, miserable lives, and then after we had nearly killed each other, not to even talk about the cases of our own parents who we had never known....." hmmmm" As he talked some eyes were moved to tears in the silence that accompanied it, then he broke that silence when he finished by saying, "Alright Agbaamole Bwallangwu, you might as well begin to say your last prayers to Lucifer because I'm coming to give your last sacrifice."

"Second time you said that, brother," noted the maskman somehow uneasy, "What do you mean by sacrifice?"

"I don't just kid myself brother, if it means dying in order to kill that bastard monter, then I would die there with him."

The maskman put a hand on his shoulder. "Nooo, you won't die, my brother. You couldn't possibly die now that we have just found each other. It's not right. You wouldn't have to die. You won't move close until that bastard is incapacitated. The boys have commenced work on the silver tip arrows. The spears and swords are almost done. All wooden except the blades and heads. They would be ready in 24 hours."

"So goes another saying, my brother," Karl injected heartily, "when you're fighting with the devil you've gotta get yourself a long wooden handled silver weapon." And everybody had laughed, genuinely partly but most of all to dispence the the looming sadness.

"When Bwallangwu is down sir," cut in the representative, "you need to cut the tail."

"Tail!?" More than a voice echoed that in surprise.

"Yes sirs. The bastard has a tail!" replied the rep. "As we can see in the ABOGINT intel on Bwallangwu, the creature has a tail which is invisible because he has buried it in a hole dug by itelf."

"Well, we shouldn't be supprised," interjected Jobilah, "the cobra also does that."

"This tail," continued the rep, "composes of millions of millions of nerve terminals and nerve centers and special glands. It is, technically speaking, the nerve center of its body and more to that, the meadium that connects its soul to the other spheres, whatever that means. But the import is that it is capable of regeneration in a matter of time, years, century, millennium, we don't know for certain. It depends on certain societal situation or fertility or conduciveness for it, I beg you sirs, this is not my specialty. It is beyond my comprehension, talk less of its explanation. But the implication is that if this tail is not cut we would not have destroyed Bwallangwu but only place it on hold temporarily, a sleep mode with only the loss of its present body."

"Very interesting!", exclaimed chief Bobade in a thoughtful and a little dramatic way that betrays his respect for this prudent, respectful, accurate and up to the point representative of his antagonist.

"Well then," said Jobilah somehow boisteriously, "that should be simple once the monster is down."

"Will you come along to push him down and cut it?" demanded Karl, turning to give him a disdainful look.

"No I couldn't possibly be there since I will be elsewhere taking care of explosives."

"Then shut up!" Karl's voice had that knee weakling effect and Jobilah needed no other persuasion.

"How soon can we get these gadgets…timed explosives and the like?" asked the maskman, diffusing the tension.

"You would have them within 24 hours." Replied the rep

"Then I guess we can move in on Friday and strike at noon. Any dissent?" asked Karl.

"That's just the day after tomorrow. Fine by me." Replied the maskman.

"Yeah, I guess that's about the earliest time we can do it, considering the availability of all we're gonna need and it affords the men enough time to practice and rehearse. Isn't it?" contributed Jobilah heartily.

"That is the only sensible thing you have said in this gathering."

Jobilah went real hot. "Karl! When this thing is over I promise you….."

"Promise what? Jobilah, I'm game, provided you don't shoot me in the back."

"Ooooh! Well, gentlemen, how about some wine?' demanded the maskman.

"You know something brother?"

"What?"

"Bwallangwu endorsed his own death warrant when he made me a priest."

"Hmmmn, very interesting. It's been a universal truth. Chief

Aborungun has a book on Suntzu. There is a passage there that says every idea contains the seed of its opposition. Nature has a way of feeding you back with your own output. Someone said it maintains stability."

"Some philosophy, my brother."

The two Siamese had decided to sneak into Akinfojatola Estate that evening for Karl to familiarize the maskman with the area. The latter was amazed at how cleverly concealed and camoufladged the nefarious activities that goes on in that estate. What was made out as a restarant bar was in reality an armoury underground. All sorts of human activities going on in there appears normal and nothing out of the ordinary to the uninformed but underground and behind all facets of professions is the real thing.

"Papa was great, you know…real great. I'm proud of him though I don't know him."

"Hmmm, so inhuman and debasing the way they eventually got him."

"Yeah, using a little kid as bait is the apex of ruthlessness."

"Inhumanity! That's the way of the devil.."

"And that's why I said we should be as ruthless as ruthlessness can possibly be in dealing with them! No half measures. No room for mistakes. Left to me alone, brother, we wipe them all out with cyanide gas."

"But how do you sort out the innocent?"

"Innocents?"

"Or rather the ignorants…em the wives and the kids."

"Why would you want to sort out the wives and kids in an all out war against snakes? Some of those wives are equally dangerous. With the children they are the roots and remnants."

"Here we go again. I hate killing…children!"

"There you are, brother, papa's mistake! History about to repeat itself!"

"Karl, papa's mistake was in serving the organization at all. His fight aginst them thereafter is an afterthought. It was a fight he should have taken right from the beginning instead of joining them. It was a prosponed fight. Why accepting in the morning what you would end up rejecting in the evening?"

"You might not want to agree that if not for that kid he wouldn't have been caught so easy. *Baba kii s'eran riro ke.*"[51]

"It appears apparently so but I maintain that his mistake was in serving Bwallangwu at all. His love for children is perfectly alright. I'm afraid I could have fallen for the same trick. A good lesson for us all."

"I don't want to quarrel now with my only brother."

"No, not quarrelling. We are only rendering accounts of life as essentially required at this critical stage of our life."

"Hmmmn. you're damn right. In every sense of the word. I mean to think I would turn out to fight Bwallangwu now....a fight I should have undertaken at the initial stage instead of joining them."

"Again a twist of fate. Like you had no choice. It's now you know better. I guess if papa had established a similar organization undergroung to fight evil all this things would have been more straightforward. Because every good material, as it has been put, would have drifted to the side where it wants to be used. Not now when you have to find out the hard way before you know where you belong and sometimes it is too late for some. Not entirely your fault, brother."

"I'm proud of you brother. You'ren't just telling, you have done exactly that. You have provided a platform to fight the devil. For me I'll make it up." Karl said soberly.

"God bless you brother."

"You know sometimes it seems there is no much difference between the two situations. Where every one is bad except you alone, you get punished; where all else is good except only you, you get punished. Either way you are finished. Once you dare to be different, you've bought it! Even Jesus of their bible got punished! So what da hell!"

"Now you are dabbling into the spiritual issue which we don't understand yet. I believe after all this we should devote time to this essential aspect of life and we would understand. That man you just

---

[51] Papa was not such a cheap kill.

mention represented so many aspects including the law, the universal law itself. He and his life are worth studying."

"Hmmmn," reflected Karl with a sarcastic smile, "the difference it seems is that one is punished here and in hell while the other is punished here and enjoys in heaven."

"Somehow, but I'd rather think of you as Moses."

"The one they said was leading his people to the promised land? No. You should be Moses because you're the one who will do just that."

"No. You don't know what I mean."

"That he never got there? He died? Yeah…if it has to be so…. but for me…"

"No! Stop that."

"What da hell? Ok, in what other aspect?"

"In the aspect that you had to be with Bwallangwu for a divine reason. So was Moses raised in Pharoh's palace. He learned all there was to learn about the kingdom and even lead their armies in their battles, all the time thinking he was Egytian.. But when God was ready to use him He showed him who he really was. A Jew! And since then Moses never looked back."

"Haaah. Is that what really happened?"

"Yes."

"In their bible like that?"

"Yes, of course."

"I never get to read one."

"You will. And you will see that all good men like children, just as papa did. So you see, to love kids is to be humane. It's perfectly alright to be humane. It's an advanced spiritual human virtue."

"Yeah, brother,…I think I can like children too…yes, in the right atmosphere, within the right group of people…in the right frame of mind…yes, yes, I think I too can like children. But when a man is denied the opportunity of appreciating himself how then can he ever get to appreciate his own product? Could he even think of producing?"

"The beginning might be to first settle down."

"Hmmmn. Tell me, brother, have you had any girl? I mean any serious girl in your life?"

"No Karl. Not really. How about you?"

"Yeah…Oh yes, yes, but..eeerrr."

"I know, I know all about that, but I mean a reasonable girl.. A good girl."

"Bimbi is reasonable!" Karl reacted.

"Take it easy brother, we're getting close."

"I am going to tell you this, brother. Bimbi still happens to be the only woman I've ever really known. She opened the door to those lockers that showed me those hidden aspects of me as a man that I had never known. My life had been on the go; as it comes. I never planned, I just existed and waited for life to act and I reacted and most of the time it's trouble and I seemed to enjoy it and welcome it. Bimbi came into my life and a lot started changing. Not much but I saw the way. Bimbi came into my life and despite all that happened she is still there…in my life. She gave me certain feelings I never got from any other woman, and being without her all these days has been hell. Brother, I have balled other girls but those were nothing but balling and discharges. Most often, perfunctory in line of duty. If you know what I mean. Not, never like Bimbi. None like Bimbi."

"Haaah. I see. That is what they call love."

"And you, what do you call it?"

"I should call it love…errr…but I think you are lucky."

"What do you mean?"

"You have at least experienced it, love or whatever the name, for a woman. I haven't."

"You never …emmm…have you done it before?"

"No."

"Not balled?"

"No."

"A woman?"

"No, Karl. What else do you ball? C'mon."

"Haaah."

"For me I just have a general likeness for them and sometimes I wonder why God created them so different.

"When you ball them you will know something. But I've balled several but I still don't have those feelings that I've had with Bimbi."

"That is why I said you are lucky. That love I know it exists but I don't know yet what it feels like. Words are not adequate to describe it to anybody that hasn't had similar experience."

"Mine is painful."

"Courtesy of Bwallangwu, brother."

"I'll carve that monster…"

"You know, Karl, once in a while I can't help feeling guilty for allowing you to go for Bwallangwu. I could go intead."

"But no, my brother. That part is not for you. It's mine. Even fate itself has designed it to be so Nature had arranged it that way. Remember I was on the left, the strong hand of our father, Ajahni, while you were on the right hand, the right hand made for man's decent jobs. Let me carry out the rough and dirty jobs assigned to me by default while you should not fail in those decent ones that are yours."

"Now the philosopher?"

"But It's a fact! When I shit I wipe my black nigger ass with my left and you as well you wipe your cute brotherly ass with your left. Then you do those things like eating etc with your right…"

They both laughed.

"So it's been nature's obvious allegory and it's been proven true. So let me perform my duty. It is naure's assighment for me. I have always known that. You're the decent right hand of Ajahni. You are different and it shows."

"That does not make me any better than you. I have caused death too."

"If that is so it's because you can't stand injustice! You can't just stand and look when innocent people are oppressed, raped and sacrificed! If you kill it is for self defense, a God's given right. Not even to defend yourself but for the defense of others! The defenseless and the weak. I know your type the first time I saw you, brother. I envy you. You even kill decently if you have to. You work for God while I had been working against Him."

"We have both inherited something uncommon from papa and which had to be used inadvertently."

"But I had been on the opposite side all along. On that side destroying God's work while your side was repairing. Thank God I found you for I never would've known the difference. That you can still express your powers without destroying, without hurting, without so much hatred! That selfless love manifesting in you is the greatest power. I have realized that when I found you. Mine had been the primitive way. I took what I want but people give you what you need out of love. I sure have a lot to catch up and make up for."

The maskman's mind went back to his experiences during the Ife-Modakeke conflict when young boys were being drafted into the armies. Though he had to fight on the side of Ife he wasn't really sure which side he should fight for. For besides not knowing which side he belonged to, he did not like killing and he did not see any sense in Ife and Modakeke fighting. His being drafted into Ife army was just for the fact that he was caught in Ife at that particular time. He might just as well have fought on the side of Modakeke, it wouldn't make any difference to him. But one thing was certain for him; he felt something the same when a soldier died no matter from which side. His utmost loath for killing made him to volunteer as a scout. A job in which various duties revealed his special gifts and assets.

"Besides," Karl continued, "I am the priest of Bwallangwu, empowered to get close. You can't resist the emmanations of Bwallangwu. See?"

"Perhaps I ccould if I had the Rosary..."

"Haaaah, the Most Blessed Holy Rosary...ha ha ha. You too believe the story about that thing? That thin is not what it's claimed to be, my brother or perhaps it has lost its powers. It is too old. All the inscriptions on it are unreadable. In addition to that, we don't have the book of interpretation. We even tested it. The poor subject that we made to wear it and we pushed close to Bwallangwu was, instead of Bwallangwu being affected, choked to death. Or was it Bwallangwu that destroyed its powers? Look, that thing is there now in Bwallangwu's shrine for exhibitions. No powers whatsoever in it, any longer. I wonder if it even ever had."

"The maskman kept quiet for some time. A silence a bit induced in Karl who asked in his carefree attitude, "what's the matter, brother?"

"Karl, my brother."

"Yap?"

"Now let me disclose something to you which up till now I have never divulged to anybody. Not even the only man I trusted......" But suddenly with natural agility and military precision the Siamese twins separated, one to the left, the other to the right of the bush path. The reason for this sudden movement soon became obvious when both reappeared from behind and caught the intruder.

"Jobilah! I never trusted you in the first place. You sneaky son of a thousand gun! We can manage without you anyway."

"No! Karl, don't kill me! I have come to tell you something!"

"Then spill quick! Otherwise you gonna be the first to feel the effect of the silver blade!"

"They are going to offer Bwallangwu a woman tonight!"

"So what!? Is the conference of the priests not going on now? Are you not supposed to be close by to gather useful info for us? Now you are here to tell me a woman would be offered to Bwallangwu. Is it the most important to you now? Is this the first time Bwallangwu would be taking an offering? Just tell me your real mission here or you die now!"

"The conference has ended. They've just finished the last agenda item ...so I took permission to go to toilet!"

"So you could come and tell us about the offering!?"

"Alright, Karl. I thought I owe you this favor, though you might not appreciate it. It's...it's....the woman is...Look it's Bimbo!"

Karl just held Jobilah, that strangling hold. "Whaaat!"

"The woman they're going to offer is Bimbo!"

With that strangling hold and that unmistakeable look in his eyes, you wouldn't blame Jobilah for shievering so violently.

"Which Bimbo, you old son of a bitch!?"

"Your Bimbi!...It's your woman! Bimbi"

Karl instantly released hold and down went Jobilah whose

shievering legs could not support his weght for that moment. Then like a lion Karl growled.

"Nooo! They will not offer Bimbi to monster!"

He drew his knife and with that warrior look on his face he said, "I'm going in!"

"The maskman cast a terrible glance at Jobilah, held his brother's hand and said, "no! We don't go in until noon tomorrow! Besides, you don't have the required weapons except the knife. No sword, no spear, the long spear! You don't have the bow and arrows! Your silver vest is not here! The knife is obviously too short. It will make you go too close to the monster!"

"My Bimbi would not be devoured by monster!" Was all Karl had to say and the maskman knew it was useless and a waste of time to try and change his mind.

"Wait Karl!" he said, and to Jobilah, "go back to camp and send the special weapon! Get the men assembled and mobilise. The mission is moved forward and has just commenced!"

They heard the sound of drums, singing and the usual familiar noises and Karl and Jobilah looked at each other briefly. Karl became desperate and restless and the maskman's heart sank. The ceremony is about to begin. He pulled out his walkie talkie and issued orders. Karl had moved.

"Angels Camp for Michael!"

"Archangel Go!" cracked the ever ready voice of the serge major.

"Holy Forces move in!"

"Archangel, say again?"

"Holy Angels move in! Commence Opreration TapRoot Immediately! I reapeat, Angels move in! Operation TapRoot Commence India Mike Mike!"

"Confirm St Michealngels speaking!"

"Afirmative! Goddamn it! Move in the Angels to join Michae! Position 500 meters west of Turkey den!. Dispatch holy weapons India Mike Mike!"

Cool fresh breez blowing, Jobilah was up on his feet and agile again. "That's good thinking, son. Now I'm gonna shoot all these bastards."

"Don't you call me no gaddamn son! You wait here for the troops! I've got to go see what my brother is up to." He left immediately and soon got to a place, stopped and strained his senses. This Siamese are so mutually tuned that if his brother is anywhere around there he would feel it.

"I'm here!" Karl whispered audibly from behind a cover about 50 meters from the shrine. He had created a hole through the barbed wire fence. Only the devil knows how he had managed to do that. The maskman crawled through and dropped beside him.

"Karl, I have sent for the forces. All your essential weapons would soon be brought; the sword, the spear, bow and arrows and your silver wear. Karl, are you listening!?"

"Yeah, brother, that's good. You see, my brother, let's while away the little time to talk about children."

"What we should do is to go over your new emergency attack plan."

"Naaa, it is more straightforward now. No fancy details. I know what to do.The situation would dictate the rest."

"But at least..."

"Good little children...playing and climbing on your back, pulling on your trousers...hmmm....playing with daddy.....hmmmm, you know....loving them but without spoiling them...even if you have to be a little hard....on them to guide them. Children...are the light in a home that turns the otherwise perpetual darkness into brightness. They are flowers, the blessing of the plant; otherwise the plant is just another green shrub, not attractable. Even the flowers reassure the existence of the next generations. So young and beautiful kids, so pure at heart, closest to God, they are the gateway to paradise."

"Never knew you could sound so poetic but brother, wrong place, wrong time, nevertheless I think you are absolutely right, the love of children is the love of nature and its creatures. But let me go now back to Jobilah's position and see if the boys have arrived with your gadgets. One has to be ccareful with that old cock."

"Ok brother, you hurry and go! But first give me a hug."

"What for?"

"Just give me what I need now, brother. It's all I ask for."

The maskman found Jobilah busy smoking and the smell of the stuff was unusual. "You this old man, what the hell is that?"

"Charrrge."

"Charge. What is charge?"

"Weed, igbo. Marijhuana. It encourages my failing heart... replenishes my weakening muscles and augments my dulling reflexes. Gives me the lifts required in times like this. You want some? Good for you. Try it."

"No, thanks, I'm still young, heart, muscle and reflexes, but thanks...em... the forces are yet to arrive?"

"It will take about 15 minutes to make that distance. Don't worry, they would soon be here." And while the maskman paced up and down somehow restlessly Jobilah asked, "tell me ghost, what do you use as a charge? I mean with what do you charge up for actions like this?"

"Nothing. I don't need anything. I just think about whatever I'm about to do and I'm naturally charged. You wouldn't expect ghosts to need such artificialities, would you?"

"Hard to belief! A lot of people in this job of ours use pills such as dexadrine, and drugs like LSD. Sometimes morphine, heroin, if you can afford those."

"That is your goddamn business!"

"Sorry! I don't mean to be hostile. I'm just em sort of curious and perhaps I might learn one or two things."

"Well, well, what the heck, you may call it inherited natural opiates. Encephaline."

"I heard some steps! I think the boys are approaching!"

"Yes. I think they are close by. You know what to do as soon as they arrive. Just take over command of your men immediately. The plan has not changed, only the timings."

Suddenly the noise coming from Bwallangwu's shrine grew louder, more drumming and singing, then silence. Super silence.

"They are about to offer her now," said Jobilah.

The maskman grew very restless. He looked here and there, alternating Karl's direction and that from which the forces were expected to appear." He decided to break radio silence. "Holy Angel for Michael!"

"St Michael Go!"

"Where the hell are you?"

"Traffic! In your loc now!"

Just then the serge major appeared with the boys. The maskman gave the signal which they recognized. Jobilah broke cover and both joined them.

"What took you so long?" The maskman asked aimlessly.

"What happened for this change of timing?" The serge major asked for a reply.

"Did you bring Karl's gadgets?"

"What the hell, I dispatched Cpl Solomom in advance. He is not here?"

"Holy shit!" Reacted the maskman.

"We have reserves! But the operation is scheduled for tomorrow!"

"The operation has just been moved 12hrs forward!" the maskman replied and gave orders rapidly. Jobilah took command of his troop and left immediately with them. The serge major was to operate with Jobilah and had been specially brieved by the maskman on what to do if the old man behaves funny. But the present situation warrants a little adjistment. The maskman moved with Karl's and his own boys, saying, "I'll take you to your commander, then we separate. Follow me!"

He got to the position but Karl was not there. "Damned! Serg major, take the men to loc A and start the diversion. I will go with these men lto locate Karl. He needs these gadgets."

As they proceeded in the dead dark silence they heard, "who goes there!?"

"Friend!" answered the serge major.

"Password!"

"Owo n' towo." He supplied the password Jobilah had given them.

"Approach to be recognized!"

The serge major approached the guards as two of his boys crept on them from behind and silenced them. They proceeded in search. Suddenly they heard the terrible voice. The maskman especially knew the unmistakeable voice of his brother.

"Baaaallaaaannnngwuuuu! Mo-n-s-terrrr! I'lllll kill youuuuuu!"

The whole area shook and simultaneously came the reports of fireworks here and there as Jobilah obviously got into action. The maskman threw caution away and commanded, "move!" and he rushed in with the boys.

It had happened that Karl, knowing what the grave silence, preceeded by the sudden accentuated tempo of drums and shouting indicated, had left. The offering was going to be made to Bwallangwu in perfect silence. He had moved closer and got behind a cover some 25 meters from the abode of Bwallangwu. From there he had seen Bimbo being prepared. He watched his life love being made up, decorated, oiled and perfumed. Her long hair braided into 201 strands, the way Bwallangwu likes it. Bwallangwu wants his offerings decorated georgeously and they must be beautiful. His heart ached with dejection and burning fury as the priests led her silently along the 30 meters length of way, carpeted red, towards the abode. Towards the black curtain! He had seen her face transfixed in the usual manner peculiar to the entranced offerings of Bwallangwu who are drawn to the monster by some kind of magnetic attracting force. The praying mantis walks into fire of its own accord. He had looked frantically back and forth and around, desperately thinking of his bow and arrows, the long spear with the wooden handle, the silver bladed sword. He thought if only he had, in addition to this goddamn short knife, his silver vest. He looked again at the knife in his hand and shook his head and murmured something. He continues to look desperately front and back, alternating the direction where he expected his boys and weapons to arrive and the scene right there unfolding in front of him.. He had changed position though but he had no doubt his brother could always find him. Back to the abode every slow step the escorting priests take with Bimbo towards the black curtain constitutes a stab in his heart. He looked back again desperately, straining his ears. He thought he heard something...yeah...faint but getting loud....yes some footsteps advancing. Yeah, for sure some people coming in his direction quite alright. He thought of breaking cover and collecting from them the most essential of the gadgets, perhaps the bow and arrows so he could take out the monster from that distance, or perhaps the long spear or even the silver wear..... Thinking of the silver vest, a grapple with the monster is an idea he would have so welcome. He looked again at the knife in his hand and shook his head and murmured something. But as the priests advanced within 3 meters to the black curtain the reality downed on him. He muttered half aloud to himself, "sorry, brother, I've got to do this." And with this he had covered the distance between himself and the offering party in no time at all, the way he likes to put it. And that was when he had shouted to break the silence. That unmistakeable voice heard by his brother and others.

Just before then, as the priests approached with the offering, the thick black curtain virtually vibrated with the heavy now accentuated labored breathing of Bwallangwu in excited expectation of his offering. It was a deep throated breadth, transforming the black curtain into some sort of acoustic membrane that actually vibrated the air and whole of the surrounding. In one single action, like a phantom appearing almost from nowhere apparent, just as the offering party was withing pushing range and the chief priest recited the vocals of presentation:

"Most divine Bwallangwu,
Agbabalagba Irunmole of ages
Honourable representative of Lucifer on earth
Our venerable Lord and Saviour
Please accept this offering from us
As a humble token for your rejuvenation."

Then as the rest took some steps back and the chief priest, chief Enlaye, placed the tip of the long wooden rod on her spine which in the next couple of seconds would just tip the offering within range where she would on her own rush into the waiting embrace of the monster, Karl was there amid the ensuing flabergastr, ripped off the black curtain to reveal the most horrible sight that words could never be adequate to describe. The priests and the offering all fell at the direct hit of the emmanations of the monster without the curtain that must have been serving as a filter or some sort of attenuator. Karl was seized by the monster with its numerous tentacles but not before he had dealth one mighty blow that pierced the toadlike smelling body, like hot needle into fats. The monster shouted and the whole environment shook. Blocks and fragments fell off some ageing buildings. It became a struggle between Karl who stubbornly kept the blade of the dagger and twisting it inside the monster's body and the monster, and with one organ wrapped around the latter's wrist, to exploit available chances of removing the silver blade from its body before it could wreck the irrecoverable havoc to its being. Karl kept his dagger in, cursing and abusing the monster. "You can't have Bimbi, she's mine! She is my woman! You horrible, smelling bastard! Bimbi is mine! You want a woman you go to hell where you can find your ugly smelling type and get yours!"

The creature that Karl has revealed, by tearing the curtain, was a being as enomous and shaped exactly like a termite hill. It has one dark red eyeball and a single orifice in what you can regard as flat face holding a mock smile. No neck at all, the anthill is just the perfect word. Jutting out of the toadlike skin are 16 outgrows, 15 of which are 2 meters long with sharp piped heads while the 16th one is located lower and about the centre of the body and about half as long as the rest but a little bit bigger. At the base of this 'anthill' are two very short legs with flat feet each having 6 toes with nails that look like they are meant for digging.

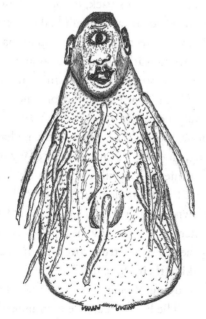

BWALLANGWU - AGBAAMOLE

The monster released another shout of horror and pain before it fell to the ground with Karl, revealing another outgrowth at its base, in between the short legs but which was hitherto dipped into a hole. A kind of greenish liquid issues out of the dagger wound as both continued struggling on the ground with Karl keeping the dagger inside the body seemingly with his last breadth. That was when the maskman arrived with the boys. By this same time some brave priests of Bwallangwu and some men had overcome their fear but still very confused and only appear to want to act when Bwallangwu called in a last desperate effort, "Heeeellllp meeee!" but at the sight of the maskman and the troops they came out of confusion and took to their heels, most especially the priests who bent down automatically to pull up the long robe that might have prevented them from deploying some god given talents in a life saving race.

The maskman drew the sword at once and cut off the monster's tail. Then once more, the monster shouted, and Bwallangwu gave up the ghost. Theoutgrows gradually withdrew out of Karl's body and shrank shorter. Karl was on his back, exhausted beside the monster; his body covered in blood, Bwallangwu's body covered insome kind of fluid a blend between green and red. The maskman, with the help of two other boys carried Karl to some place away from Bwallangwu's body. The maskman, exasperated and breathing unevenly. "Oh Karl, my brother, why didn't you just wait? Just one more second for us to arrive with your gadgets?"

"It's alright now, brother, nothing is lost…my half…nothing has been lost." smilling, "today is the greatest day of my life!...today is the happiest night of my life…I have killed the monster! We have destroyed Bwallangwu. I told you, remember brother? That Bwallangwu organized for his own doom by recruiting me....and later on, endorsed his own death sentence by ordaining me a priest. Now I can die with satisfaction…for the woman I truly love…for humanity that I had participated in making their lifes a hell."

"No! you'ren't dying! Don't talk like that, I've sent for the ambulance. They will be here in a couple of minutes."

"Brother, remember when we talked about children?..little…little children…Errr.. find yourself some peace loving beautiful woman …a wife and make children…nice little children…to run about and call you daddy…daddy….daddy…. Give them the parental care that we were denied by nature…so they grow with feelings peculiar to true human beings, like the ones you have…the one I lack."

"Oh yeah brother but save your breadth. We have a lot of time to go over these things."

"And Bimbi? My BImbi still alive?"

And Bimbi came over, weeping, knelt beside Karl, "Oh Karl, my love. I am sorryyyy!"

Karl made to stand up but could not. "Bimbi! My Bimbi!," he said excitedly and breathily, "No regrets now in my life that I've been able to save you!"

"Can you ever find the heart to forgive me? My whole life is a shame. A shame to myself! All my life has been a disappointment to those who cared for me. Disappointment to father, disappointment to mother, to relations and disappointment to love. I have been a disappointment to you, Karl, my love. All I did Karl I had no choice! Oh Karl, Karl, I betrayed you…You should have allowed me to die! Why? Why? Why did you risk your life to save me? Upon all I did to you! I am not worth it! You should have let me go and end this miserable life of mine once and for all. I am tired!"

"It's al right now, my love. No regrets! I understand all. I know all, my Bimbi. Come closer."

Instantly Bimbi was on his chest, sobbing hysterically. "When it all started…when they assigned you as a mission, I thought it was just one of those things…but it soon dawned on me that you are not just one of those assignments. Not an ordinary mission. Soon I discovered I loved you. Something that had never happened to me before. When they realized I was failing my subsequent missions they accosted me and I confessed that I loved you and I needed to be reassigned to some other missions that have nothing to do with closeness to men. Since then I have kept myself for you…in the hope that one day we shall meet again and I would take the risk to come and explain things to you and maybe you might just find the heart to understand. I was not going to hope for forgiveness….just to understand….”

“And we have met at last my love. We have met again. Stop crying, instead say some nice words. Well I have never known nice words except the ones you taught me. Say some more, it's what I need now. For me I would've said some but I've never known any to say to women.. err…you know…”

“Please Karl, there is only one thing I want from you now. Just say you forgive me even though you don't mean it. I would manage on by just hearing the word. Because after what has happened there is nothing left that is real in my life. All is pretence and, all has been acting a scene written by people that are supposed to be my enemies. Can you see my life? Say you forgive me even if you don't mean it, and I should be able to transform it into reality even if I have to pretent that its true. Just say the words, Karl, you don't need to mean it. It would at list lift some burden off my chest and perhaps I might have some peace.”

“Bimbi! I have forgiven you…with all my heart. You did all you had to do and later I had to do mine. It was beyond us. I quite understand. I want you to know that you are the only one that has and will ever fulfill my dreams and desires. You woke me up. You awoke the feelings hibernating in me. You are the one that God gave the key to the secret closets in my body, mind and soul. You are the only woman that means anything to me. I have never forgotten you and at times I thought I had lost you forever. Bimbi I love you.”

“I love you more, Karl. They kept me away. I didn't even know your whereabout. I thought you were dead.”

“No, no, my love. Not yet. Not until this….this great mission,” pointing at Bwallangwu's body.

“Karl, I had a baby for you!” she revealed with a mixture of hope and apprehension.

“A What!?”

“A baby, Karl.”

“For me?

“Yes Karl.”

“Are you serious?”

"Yes Karl."

"Child...little children?" He made to sit up again but couldn't move a limb.

"Yes Karl. I was pregnant when that...that...that.."

"Yes I understand. Don't talk about that..."

"I didn't want to but they used eerrr..my father."

"Nothing to worry about..and my baby...little children?"

"He will be one year next month."

"He? A boy?"

"Yes Karl...look at him, coming."

All turned to see a little boy in diapers staggering innocently towards them.

"Just started to walk...they took him from me and gave to that woman." Pointing.

"Bimbi! A little boy for me!?"

"Yes my Karl, for you...and me. Our baby...By God I was..."

"Yes, yes, I quite understand. Thank you...thank you..."

"And I couldn't tell you I was pregnant because you said you didn't want children. You probably would have forced me to terminate it."

The lttle boy finally made it to mummy, held on to mummy and made some noise. A sure carbon copy of the father. Karl looked at him adoringly and smiled into his face and into the heavens.

"Now I know I'm not dead. I can't be extinct. Impossible!"

"Manuel, say hello to your daddy."

"What name you gave him?" Karl asked eagerly, neglecting his pains..

"Emmanuel."

"Emmanuel? Looking surprised.

"Yes, Karl. I wanted to give him Karl but the name was forbidden in the camp, so I gave him Emmnauel."

"How come?"

"It's the name that crossed my mind. It means savior. Why? You don't like the name, we could..."

"For heaven's sake why wouldn't I like the name of my own tough noble father?

"Whaaooh! What a divine coincidence! I never knew but…you never…"

"I only got to know of recent. What other name did you give him?"

"None again. Just Emmanuel." She answered feeling somehow, not wanting to disappoint.

"Ok, I give him Ajahni. He is the incarnate of my noble father. As I can see he's sure gonna be tough."

"And he is Karl junior."

"Good! But tell me something. Why would they want to give you Bwallangwu?"

"Oh Karl. My fate in the organization changed when I confessed to them that I fell in love with you. As a Bwallangwu special operator I was not supposed to get emotionally attached, not to talk of falling in love. Then the pregnancy confirmed my gradual uselessness to him. I was counseled by the priests but I maintained that I loved you. That was probably why they kept me away from you. But now I can see another reason. Karl they have changed you! I couldn't have recognized you again. Nevertheless, when the news broke that a certain priest Zokalaus had escaped from police custody and after 3 days they did not see you they had me brought for interrogation. They asked me if you had cantacted me because they thought you would one way or the other if you were still alife. That was when I knew Fadi Zokalaus and My Karl was one and the same person. Sooner than later, news had it that you had regained your mind and probably had known the truth. Then there was confusion in the camp. They'd had several emergency meetings and in their very last meeting they decided to commence RRR on you with the hope that you must surely emerge to save me. Little Emmanuel is still too young to worry about."

"And I surely emerged but they got the surprise of their life. I emerged, didn't I? But at the expence of their monster. ….their dear monster. They lost their Bwallangwu….ha.ha.ha. Like the tiger that I am I surely emerged but they got the surprise of their life. I emerged, didn't I? They lost their Bwallangwu….ha.ha.ha in Operation TAPROOT. The monster is their tap root." Karl laughed and coughed. The maskman cautioned, "take it easy!" as he looked down at Bimbo, not really knowing whether to pity her of to despise her for, as he was feeling, if not for her Karl would have waited for the DDay of the operation before plunging in in that suicidal manner. Again part of his mind blamed Jobilah who brought that information. But at least there's still hope to save Karl with immediate medical attention and….. just then a siren announced the arrival of the ambulance, reinforcing the hope, however little.

The ambulance parked close by. The maskman issued rapid instructions. He knelt down to join Bimbo over Karl, preparing to make chance for him to be carried... "Easy, brother, you gotta save your breadth and rest. Very important now."

"My dear brother, …., Bimbi my love " the maskman had instinctively cast a glance aound, first at Bimbo and at others around and was satisfied Karl's words were not loud enough as to reveal anything. "At last I found my brother and I found my woman. My life is now complete. Together we have destroyed Bwallangwu. This is the happiest moment of my life. My life is no more meaningless. My l life has been attached to something great in the scheme of work of the almighty. I found my woman who has regenerated me. I'm so happy. No regrets! Mission accomplished. The mission of my life is accomplished!"

"Karl, take it easy now. Save your breadth till later." The maskman said as he pulled Bimbo up and bent down to carry little Emmanuel to give way to the stretcher men. Karl growled and coughed, a very weak cough. Then he smiled painfully but happily. He mustered the strength and calling him by his name again and to which the maskman was glad nobody heard, he said, "take care of my family, the family I have remaining, you, my wife and my child."

"Yes I will until you fully recover and strong, the heck I will! It's my sole responsibility."

"You are supposed to understand. You're no more a child. The speed of realization and understanding are faster for me now as it has always been at the border of life. I have taken the terrible blood and I have used my own mouth to swear in an oath. The day I turn against Bwallangwu I die. That I would never turn against Bwallangwu.. yes…

provided Bwallangwu made its own commitment with sincererity. Instead he destroyed my family and my life and hid it from me. They made me to take his oath, fine. I will abide by the conditions of my oath. And under the situation that revealed itself later it's no more possible for me not to turn against him. But it's when I refuse to die as the advance stipulation of the oath I willingly took that I might have betrayed him and especially myself myself and most especially humanity. That's what Karl will not do."

"My brother!" the mask man said flatly. We are talking about two different people now! Listen! The man that took the oath was Fadi Zokalaus the priet of Bwallangwu. But the one we are talking about now is Karl my brother that we just discovered each other. Karl who has just found his woman and who his woman has just found. The joy of all these accomplishments can never be fully realized if you are not with us. We have just found each other. You are worth more than a thousand Bwallangwu alive. Just imagine what the human race stands to gain with us joined together to champion their cause. Stay with us we need you now. How much can one hand carry without the second hand? Right or left, Karl, it takes the two to put a heavy load on ones head. *Ajeje owo kan ko gb'eru d'ori* [52]We shouldn't lose you and we are not prepared to lose you now."

"Good logic but I'm talking about Caesar."

"Caesar!?"

"You give to Caesar what is Caesar's. I have taken that blood. Nature has to take its cause, ironically in its own RRR. Removing Roots and Remnants. The blood in that horrible concoction, I might not be able to control it. Bwallangwu will never regenerate through me. We shouldn't take chance. You are no more a child. In my own case I have had the opportunity to grow rapidly within these last few hours."

"Bullshit!" the mask man said, not willing to go along with Karl's mystical philosophy. "You are gonna be alright. I will get you the best medical care available. And by the power of the holy Rosary we will reverse the curse of Bwallangwu and Lucifer."

---

[52] Only one hand cannot put a heavy load on ones head.

Bimbo was crying. The maskman's mask was wet.

"Tell Jobilah that I have forgiven him," Karl continued, his voice growing very weak, "but watch out, a snake is always a snake and I trust you would use your discretion to deal with him." Then taking a very deep seemingly satisfying breadth he said, "my brother, my wife, my little child,...Mission of my life accomplished."

"No, no, no not yet my brother. You shall be well."

"I told you the oath I made is binding on me."

"And I said the oath is..." Then he realized that Karl had lost consciousness. At that same time Jobilah rushed in, covered in blood, and shouting, "I've killed them all!! All the priests!"

"All the what?" The maskman asked.

"All the Bwallangwu priests!"

"Where is chief Enlaye?"

"Dead!"

"You old son of a bitch! My instruction about him is to take him alve!"

"I didn't kill him!"

"So what happened? You just said he's dead!"

"He commited suicide! Right now he is stii agonizing, calling on Bwallangwu to accept his soul."

"Yes, you killed the priests," said the maskman looking at him disdainfully. Then he looked at the burning shrine of Bwallangwu, at the ambulance men carrying his brother away, then at Bimbo practically tearing herself apart, he muttered, "oh brother, I just found you and why should I lose you again so soon? I thought fate has decided to recompense, this time around to perpetrate us in togetherness, if only nature, at least for once, could decide to disobey its creator, then in ballistichory, the kapok pod would not scatter to separate pod and seeds from mother, and the wind of fate in its own contribution would not blow, all which are beyond their powers! But alas! Once again the pod has exploded, the wind has blown, carrying the seeds each to its own destination, which for some if fertile germinates to reincarnate the parent...." He looked down at the boy who was also crying for a reason he could rarely associate with what is happening around there.

He picked him up and little Emmanuel Karl Ajahni hugged him very close. He found himself saying, "father died, father remains...so is my brother...all combined in one...All has always being the same. Whatever remains is nothing but vanity. All is nothing but vanity. All we have does not matter but what we do and the legacy we leave behind. All the same, thanks to God almighty"

Still hugging the boy, he turned around to his boys and issued instructions. "Take the woman along."

A lot was available to eat and drink at the party thrown for the 'boys' by chief Aborungun. Obviously the chief wouldn't show his face but his representative made all the arrangements and was there to represent him.

"Gentlemen, respected gentlemen of valor," the representative commenced to read his address, "due to prevailing and unavoidable circumstances my honourable chief, Sir Jimmy Aboripe Aborungun could not be present at this memorable occasion, despite how he so wished. However, he has tasked me to do all my possible best to let you know his feelings towards you and how happy and pleased he is towards this success of yours at destroying for this generation the worst enemy of mankind. He said that you have achieved the apparently unachievable which indicates the irrefutable fact that a country that possesses people of your kind might be rocked temporarily but can never be defeated by any situation whatsoever. Gentlemen, I would like you to know my shortcomings in the ability to find the right words to adequately convey the chief's feelings to you. Thus permit me to say that the deepest import of the message could only be completely realized through the employment of your imaginations." He paused to take in air amidst adulations. "Gentlemen, my chief in his philosophical mind, has asked me to remind you, however, that to build a house in not just enough, the maintenance of it is of parallel importance; the cleaning, the weeding, the fixings and the repairs as need be. The import of this is no doubt clear to you gentlemen of more than average intelligence. To this end my chief has promised to continue to give his relentless support to the maintenance of this army and the great works you might ever be called upon to perform for this great country of ours....and needless to mention, gentlemen, that your welfare is guaranteed. For the time being, my great chief has donated, in his appreciation and happiness, a gift, a sum of Two Hundred Million Naira..." He found it difficult to immediately continue because of the jubilations, shouting and clapping of the people who were so elated in addition to getting drunk.

"So, gentlemen, shall we rise for a toast to the health and well being of our dearest supporter and amiable chief and father, Sir Jimmy Aboripe Aborungun."

Later on, as the merriment went on, the representative had called the maskman aside.

"You don't seem to be too happy. The hard times are over, my main man."

"I am ok, buddy." The mask man had replied him.

"I suppose you should let go and treat yourself to some real nice food and drinks and let's party!"

"Thanks, Tom but I assure you I'm enjoying myself the best I could."

"Very well. Errr, the chief is eager to personally commend you. You need to see how elated he was on hearing the success of the operation. He took it personally and for some odd reason as if his life depended on it."

The maskman smiled in acknowledgement of what even this representative does not know. "Believe you me, Thomos, it a matter of life and death to so many people."

"Just wait and see what he has in stock for you. He has asked me to give you an invitation to dinne with him in his estate tomorrow evening 1930hrs. By the way he has asked me to intimate you before hand to draw out a reorganization plan of your army. In essence, what you have in mind for them. This I am to bring back to him for his perusal before your meeting at dinner. Of course he has his own suggestions; as in how the gentlemen could be fixed and resettled into various walks of life according to their interests and passions, into various suitable jobs but of course maintaining regular contacts and training, and how they can be assembled in a jiffy whenever there is need to perform their noble task for our much loved country."

The maskman thought briefly and replied, "okay, tell the chief I've accepted his invitation. I would come for dinner."

"And that which concerns the army?"

"That I intend to discuss with him personally when we meet."

But that very morning about half past the hour of two, the maskman had made his usual night call to the chief.

"Whaa!? I'm not expecting you till seven thirty in the evening. Not to even talk about this ungodly hour. Must be something urgent. I hope not too bad?"

"Errrr sorry chief. Nothing urgent or too bad that cannot be fixed. We fixed Bwallangwu, didn't we?"

"And when are we going to change this clandestine activities and nocturnal visits? We can afford to relax now…well at least we humans. I suppose ghosts too do relax, don't they?"

"I am relaxed but humans may not realize it."

"Anyway I hope you're not coming in mask in the evening."

"Well, it depends, chief."

"So to what do I owe this pleasure of nocturnal visit and disturbance of my sleep? I must confess I find it hard to and I will never be able to get annoyed with you."

"But you would agree with me that some discussions are suited for dinner while some are not."

"And I was going to ask you of what you plan to do with your army or do I allow you to first tell my the reason why you have come at this particular hour?"

"I don't mind discussing that, chief."

"Really!? Then what do you propose? Have you considered and integrated my suggestions into your plans?"

"I am disbanding the army."

"Disbanding what!?"

"I'm disbanding the army, chief."

"Are you crazy…eemmm…Are you serious!?"

"Chief, the army has served the purpose for which it was established. Further keeping it is a direct and unwarranted stemming of trouble."

"I have always thought and I have no doubt that I'm right that with a level headed and disciplined man like you in charge there can never be anything going out of hand. Talk about the men who love you with all their heart and who would never do a thing out of cue so as not to disappoint you."

"But how do you figure one is gonna be around all the time in this business of ours where anybody can just drop dead any time? Combined with the fact, chief, that humans are easily corrupted. I'm not one to have a private army at the disposal of some politicians to use for their selfish ends. Elections are just around the corner."

"Hmmmm. You have a valid point there and I must confess I appreciate and envy your foresight and above all, your sincere selfless concern for your dear country. But imagine what would eventually happen to humanity without this army of yours. The essentiality is clearly evident. That army would subsequently constitute the required check and balance in the system."

"Chief I need to say that once I have bent the law based on necessity, but to perpetually keep bending it leads to something else we might not be prepared for. I for one would not maintain a private army in a federal republic. Do you know what we do when we hear police siren? We scatter! That means we know we are illegal. Outlaws, rougues, to call a spade a spade."

"Exactly my point. I admire your reasonability and selflessness. You also rightly noted that elections are just round the corner. That election itself is a pot of trouble which may tend to jeopardize all we have worked for in destroying Bwallangwu and his devilish organization. While I agree with you on the reasons for disbanding, the question of when is something you should agree with me we have to talk about. So why don't you let us find time to deliberate on this issue. Let's talk at length about it…say tomorrow…after dinner. Then we would have plenty of time and in the correct atmosphere. But mind you, your decision would be final. But let us just talk about it."

"Very well, chief. Dinner then. I look forward."

"Good. That's my ghost. Now that you refused to give your bank account details to my rep, may I know why?"

"Well, you see, chief, I don't see reasons why I should collect any money from you. You contributed more than your own share to the destruction of Bwallangwu."

"Haaaah, that one? It is double blessing for me, my dear masked man, and look, what I'm giving you is minute to what I'm capable of giving you. Just a token of a token!"

"But the most important reason is for me. I gotta sort myself out in my own way in my own very world. Making things soft for me might just make the whole life meaningless, jeopardizing my aim, robbing me of the experiences and benefits of living. Thanks all the same chief."

"I hope you're nor making a mistake. Look here, tough one, where money talks brains and gallantry cannot even take a decent breadth."

"But I guess what conscience and self respect would achieve for the bearer money and wealth could only manage to purchase the fake product."

"Hmmm, very soon you would know the limit of philosophy and sagacity."

"Most especially the genuine and the fake ones? With due respect, chief."

"You would soon learn, young man and know better."

"You are right chief. Learning….is it not about all we are here for in this great school we call world?"

"Exellent philosophy but hardly does the stomach any good."

"Not only man, even ghost does not live by bread alone."

"Just in case, ghost, even the greatest men change their mind. I promise you I would still be very much around. You know what I mean. Well, I suppose we will meet in the evening. I value my sleep. I don't suppose you ghost sleep at all, do you?"

The maskman laughed, "once in a while I give it a try but haven't quite mastered it yet. I am still learning." And both had laughed again. "And chief just in case I drink too much in the evening and forget to tell you, I like to tell you, sir, that it's been a great honor and pleasure knowing you too."

"Haaah, my masked man, my own pleasure surpasses yours. You never realize what you have done for me. But I reserve the greatest till this evening. I cannot wait to know what you really look like. A man who has done for me what all gadgets, money and barriers of guards and dogs could not achieve all these years. Liberation! You have set me free. No more worries about my enemies. I'm totally liberated. You never know what freedom really feels like until you are enslaved just for a short time. Thanks a lot."

"It's you I have to thank and God."

"Again you would not consider allowing me to show my appreciation?"

"You've already made the boys happy. If they're happy I am also happy. But you can still give whatever you reserve for me to the boys. I wouldn't mind. And I like the resettlement idea of yours for the boys. It is fantastic."

"Just remember, ghost, I am always around."

"You bet, chief."

"So dinner then. 7:30."

Chief Bobade had come looking for the maskman, so excited and had informed him that his daughter had regained her mind.

"Now she knows me! She c c called me papa and hugged me. She completely recovered!"

"Oh yes, chief, that is very much expected. I was coming to ask you about her."

"What do you mean?"

"When Bwallangwu died all his captives were set free."

"Is that s so? And the first person she wants to see is you."

"That's good, Chief. I'll find some time and see her."

"And…errr…how about the mask? I mean must you really wear it again? Will you wear it for life? The chief asked and received a beautiful smile for an answer.

"Well, I would like to thank you personally for what you have done for me. Take this, you will need it."

"What is this, chief?" looking at the brown envelope in the chief's hand."

"Just take. It's yours. It's a check of 20 million."

"Now chief let me be level with you. I needed an army to fight Bwallangwu and you provided just that. Without that army I wouldn't have attempted to wage that war. We both, and the other contributors, including the boys and the smallest foot soldiers among them are but agents, tools that had been gathered to be used by higher forces above us to bring about the end of Bwallangwu when the time was come as judged by the ultimate, God. Various reasons brought us together but we've been nothing but chess seeds in the hands of the higher forces. Everybody has played his own role and has been played in his own role and capacity. Chief you have contributed your own share and I would neither be justified nor happy at all if I should take anything again from you."

"But why?"

"Because I have not done you any favor."

"Angela is safe and recovered, body and mind!"

"You gave the means to establish the army required!"

"But I am giving you of my own free will. From the bottom of my heart and you would be doing me the greatest honor by accepting it. There is nothing I could spend that could be compared to the health and the well being of my daughter and nothing would ever be."

"You have done enough already chief. More than enough."

"I would be really offended if you refuse to accept my gift. Am mmm am I tt too s small to give you a g gift?"

"Chief you have contributed more than your fair share or may I put it right by saying that I have made you to contribute more that your fair share?"

"You didn't make me. I chose to."

"So as to get your daughter back?"

"Yes to recover my daughter."

"And if you should know that I already had your daughter before I came to persuade you to raise the army?...Stampede, as pundits put it."

The chief kept quiet for a while looking at him or rather trying to imagine the sort of face behind the mask. Then he shrugged, "I guess that was the best way under that circumstance to make anybody give his level best to anything."

"This thing had weighed so heavily on my mind. I am relived now haven made a clean breast of it and you took it in good faith. And I admire your sense of reasoning, judgment and objectivity. So, as I was saying it was no favor as such, instead, I stampeded you..."

"So what!? What the hell? And what did those bastards do to me? They stampeded me into giving them a lot of my hard earned money! Why should I be annoyed if you stampeded me into building an army to finish them! Eventually a war that led to the death of Bwallangwu that led in turn to the recovery of my daughter's mind. In fact If I know how I could I would stampede you into taking this m money...little gift....Take take take it is yours."

The maskman was just laughing.

"Why, w why are you laughing? Funny huh? The bastards stampeded me the bad way but you stampeded me the right way to take my sss sweat revenge..and You don't want me to stampede you to accept a gift. I will stampee you!"

More laughter.

"I could even give you more...masked man...can't even see your face to know what you look like. But no problem. Just take. And you don't have to touch it for any surgery, just in case something has happened to your face. I h have the best plastic surgeon. ..."

"Dr Payida?"

"P PPayida! You have not heard?""

"What?"

"He has f fled the country!"

"Well, but I assure you I wouldn't need the services of a plastic surgeon for anything."

"Then what!? Look, I would really be very offended if you..."

"Al right I'll tell you what I want," and looking the chief straight into his eyes, "I want the opportunity to earn my own living. That's all. I wanna survive the way it is and die whenever and however it comes. That's what makes life worth living for me. I don't ever want anybody to make life too easy for me. I couldn't possibly survive that way. I couldn't possibly enjoy life that way. I wouldn't want anything to change the pattern of my life. I must live to settle my karma. So don't be offended chief. I can't take it."

"What do you mean by kkkk karma?"

"It's some term I heard day before yesterday and it makes a lot of sense to me. I belief it totally but I'm afraid I don't have the right words to start explaining it."

"Well how about the army? Use it to buy some weapon."

"I am disbanding the army, chief."

"Whaat!" Disband?"

"Yes. Everything is good only for its purpose."

"You really think that a wise thing to do?"

"Yes, chief. The best and only thing."

"We need to retain our power…otherwise we are crushed! Krraaah! Like this!" He squeezed his fist.

"I am still subject to the law of this country and so are you, chief. It was the nessecity and desperacy of the situation that made us raised that army, otherwise I am not one for raising a private regular army in a country that has its own legal army. Ours is illegal."

"Do you think the same situasion has changed for good? This is still the same country. The poor and innocent are still being oppressed. People are tormented for no apparent reasons…sadists of all definitions. Yes Bwallangwuu is dead but that was just the Bwallangwu we know. What about thousands yet to be identified? Don't forget the words of Chairman Mao when he said the enemy with arms are finished, it remains those without weapons. You see, and those ones could take up arms and that's when it would dawn on us that you are still very much needed."

"The enemies without arms will be dealth with in the same manner they may choose to come. And whenever they choose to pick up arms and only and only if they pick up arms, modern weapons wuld be used to defend against them. I've had time to read a little about some great people. Riveron said, "we must assail opinion with its own weapon. It's no use firing bullets at ideas. As for the army there are no more jobs for now and to keep it is a direct invitation for trouble, besides its illegality."

Chief Bobade shook his head. "I know your problem. You don't have ambitions."

"I may not have certain ambition but I know mine."

"You don't even have any…none at all."

"Look chief Bobade! If you want a personal regular army you go find your own commander, but that is after I must have disbanded this one. This particular army has served its purpose. It was raised for its sole purpose which was to war against Bwallangwu. Never for any other reason! As for the money, well I don't mind if you give it to the boys. Of course that would go a long way in resettling them. I could call a parade now so you give it to them personally."

The parade was called but the maskman did not attend. He instructed the serge major to form them up for chief Bobade's address. He had retired into his tent to be later lost in thought, fighting an internal conflict. He was not decided on what to do with Jobilah. His late brother said he had forgiven him. He too, the maskman does not keep malice. However there sill exists somewhere in him this certain feeling that all has not been completely accomplished. What then remains? He asked himself. The Roots and Remnants of Bwallangwu? But who else?…Children? If it is the children then to hell! For he is not going to have children killed…Just then Jobilah entered, breaking his train of thought. And he thought, "very good, this old man might be able to supply the missing link."

"I did not expect to still find a masked man. You still find it necessary to hide your face from us?"

Ignoring the question, "What do you want?" he asked keeping his eyes on him.

"I just like to say that was a hell of a good job we did in there despite the impromptness."

"Yeah, yeah, that's okay" he replied without hiding his boredom.

"Well, then, what about life now?"

"What do you mean?"

"I mean..eeerrrr..look, it's sad the way that young man died. He was very brave, the hell of a kind. A thoroughbred. Like father like son. But nothing compared with you…..May his soul rest in peace."

"We were all there when he died."

"I wasn't there as a matter of fact."

"Of course you were not. I forgot you were busy killing the priests of Bwallangwu. By the way Karl said he had forgiven you. He said I should tell you that. Now I need to rest."

"Ok. Back to the real business. I just like to let you know for the record that I am ready to support you with my wealth of experience in fighting, which, of course, you're very much aware of. You, of course, remain the overall commander of the Holy Forces and as I said, I'm at your service. I am all yours."

The maskman looked at him rather disdainfully, more so as he reached for the bottle of wine with his haggard hands uninvited.

"You are gonna need to find a job, old man. So you safe precious time and go start looking for one. Don't try to pin a future on this particular army and the way I figure I doubt if the regular Nigerian Army would still recruit you."

"Why! Young man, what is wrong with this?"

"I'm disbanding it."

"What!?" looking horror striken. "So it's true!"

"So you've heard? Who hinted you?"

"Never mind. But you don't mean it. You are just joking, masked man. Aren't you?"

"I might joke with trivial matters but not issues such as this."

"Have you thought of what we could achieve? Just think of only, only what we could achieve. You and I, I am ready to serve you. Of course, you can continue to wear your mask, don't mind my intrusion. I will always be loyal. We have nothing to loose …..practically nothing! All we need to do is a little re-organization…structure. You on top, I, your second in command while your serge major is placed under me but nevertheless in direct control of his men. But I would for now handle special operations and Special Forces training until I know him better.

We have it all set up. Oh I forgot the sketch of the organogram that I have drawn overnight. I didn't sleep a wink until I was satisfied you know. You might be thinking of finances, ha ha ha. Nothing to worry about, my man. The army is self sustaining, you will see. Besides, the chiefs are ready to maintain us. I personally convinced Chief Bobby and he thrilled at the idea! Besides, losing the army means loosing the power that God has placed in our hands now. Losing our powers! Who would want to lose his powers? *Bi enipe eeyan fe ja'ra re l'epon ni yen ke?*[53] And as I said this sort of outfit is self sustaining, man, very, very lucrative if you know what I mean. We can be of tremendous assistance to very rich people in this country and you know some other countries. I have all the contacts and chief Aborungun has all the connections. I mean a man who has been removing and installing presidents. *Afobaje fun'ra re.*[54] And trust people, they would always be in trouble and they have dough. I mean real bread which they are ready to dish out generously for a mere humble service we could render. You haven't look at it from that angle, no, have you? Huh huh. You are not very familiar with this kind of set up yet, are you? Huh huh huh."

Jobilah's short broken laughter irritated the maskman all the more and he replied as the latter was busy gulping, glass after glass, wines he was not invited to drink.

"Yeah, you are right. I'am not. And maybe when troubles become scarce we could cause the troubles for them by ourselves before we come around to solve them for them...thereby simulating the market." Saying this with a serious look on his face.

"Yeees! You got it. You're even faster than I thought. There's a difference between working hard and working smart. I will show you all the ropes. I am just beginning to like you. You know...errr..not that I hated you before but only indifferent...impersonal.... just a matter of lack of closeness to know and appreciate each other before. But now I tell you, I think....I'm sure I like you..So em..."

"Same old Jobilah," he said contemptuously. "It's true the saying that man seldom changes. He may paint but he seldom changes. If he

---

[53] It's tantamount to cutting off ones balls.
[54] The king maker himself.

changes at all it takes a long long time. And that might be why God has left Satan to test him to be certain if he has changed under trying conditions. Mr. Jobilah, we would then be going the Bwallangwu's way and before we know where we are we are back where we started. Where it all started and maybe further back when the whole affair began when Orishadami decided to go the negative way. Really stemming the need. Jobilah, you tell me who we are then to have destroyed Bwallangwu if we should reverse to the deeds of Bwallangwu. Bloody, bloody stinking inhuman hypocrite. You go find yourself a job old man. I guess you'd need one."

"You are making a mistake! Being fanatic! Try and understand the world. Don't look at it with a naïve eye. Look, man, the doctor makes his money when people are sick. The many the better. And the panel beater, he prays to God and He answers. How the hell does he become rich if he does not have many people' cars to panel beat? Ok how about the coffin maker? Tell me!"

"It's despicable people such as you that turned life to such a parasitic affair that we witness now our days. The doctor you are referring to made more money, in the good old days, when people are not sick. When you recreate a system where doctors are paid more when people don't fall sick they would concentrate more on preventive medicine. I bet you wouldn't understand that. Now you could introduce killers in people's bodies and produce the antidotes and hence make a lot of money.

"Haaah, yes in those days. Those days are long gone. Come back to reality. Such is nature now. *Bi ereke eranko o ba tuka t'omo eniyan ko le dun*[55]. We are not responsible for that. One man's blessing is another man's misfortune and qute unfortunately there's nothing anybody can do about it."

"Then all the more reason why you should allow nature herself to choose who gets the blessings and who gets the disappointments!"

"Who is the nature? We, you and I! It all depends on how smart you are. It has always been survival of the fittest but survival of the

---

[55] If the jaws of animals are not scattered those of humans could not enjoy.

smartest is becoming the key issue. I bet the beef you eat was not a gift from the cow itself. It was killed and the meet taken from it. Who judges the lions? The god of the antelopes? Let me tell you and don't kid yourself, we are the architects and operators of nature."

"I can see clearly how afraid you are to survive in a decent society apart from the animal kingdom you have refered to. If you want to operate by the law of the jungle you go back into the jungle. Instead you prefer the clique who are, by virtue of their mentality and morality, animals but garbed in the finest human skin and outermost attire, living among humans so as to prey on them. You cannot survive in a decent society. Only in a clique. You are insecure outside the clique. In the open world you are worth nothing. In a world of peace, justice and equal right you are a misfit, like a fish out of water. And you're reluctant to find a honest job because you know you lack any decent skill. Nobody would employ you. Not even an abattoir. But why worry, if not for greed and some psychotic reasons, you might not need to look for a job; for you could live comfortably well on the dirty money you have accumulated so far, until death comes around and take your hopeless soul to hell. Of course you could live on the uncountable stolen properties converted to yours after killing their owners. And you! You were proud and shameless to tell me you killed all the priests of Bwallangwu, thinking you the worst hypocrite of all deserve to live? I would've understood if after killing the priets you also committed suicide."

Jobillah has become red hot with a mixture of anger and some other things only he can reveal to us.

"You're naïve! This is a moving train, you can't stop it. The chiefs are with me. Even some of your boys are just waitng to hear from me that I have convinced you. But if you refused to be convinced .eem I have warned you and I am doing you a favor."

"You, doing me a favor? God would not forgive you for saying that. You stinking old fool. May God punish that dirty mouth with which you have said that. You hopeless old cargo. I am going to live you alive for just the only reason that God owns live and only Him decides whose to take and when to take it. You don't value live. You don't have the higher feelings and those sublime attributes to be qualified as human. Have you ever wondered what fate befell the second Siamese? Well, one is dead but where is the second?"

"What the hell is my business with that!? They have called you his brother to make him happy and do our job but do you believe I believe that nonsense?"

"So where then is the second twin?"

"How should that concern me now?"

"Perhaps to complete your job in the RRR operation, you devilish son of a thousand dog! And you were the operator of that winch and you enjoyed pushing a boy down the valley of crocodiles. Was it not God who let me live in that valley?"

Then for the first time the maskman removed his mask.

"Look at me! Take a very good look you hagarg old crab. This is the face you've been longing to see. Now you can have your fun all over. Look at the face of the man you threw down the valley of crocodiles. You really enjoyed it that night, didn't you? You haggard old scarecrow!"

Jobilah was horror striken. Adams looked at him and smiled, "You think you are seing a ghost and you will see ghosts for ever. The first one that of Karl my brother and the one you thought you have killed. I am the second twin, I'm sure it's apparent to you now, you fool."

Adams smiled again and turned around backing Jobilah. But in the same instant he turned around just in time to catch Jobilah who had leaped at him dagger in hand and he shot him in the mouth, saying, "I've always known, those who can lick can bite." And as Jobilah was struggling for last breadth he added, "I told you it's God himself who decides who dies and how. If I kill you, I have killed in self defense."

He immediately put on back his mask, put the remaining things of his inside his sack, picked the silver bladed sword, bow and arrows, and the silver spear head whose handle he had broken off, took a final look around and said, "once again God has saved my life...and come to think of it ...is the destruction of Bwallangwu really complete with the BSF commander, Jobilah alive? RRR."

He sneaked out of the tent never to be seen by any of the men again. Of course Jobilah now choking to death in his own blood might be asked but it was doubtful if he would ever have the mouth to reveal what he had seen till he follows his Bwallangwu predecessors to waiting hell.

CHAPTER 16

Ex clergy man Friar Biodun Maria had reason to enjoy his sekete like he never did before this afternoon in the famous New Weyos club. He had tugged at the long chain attached to the handle of the bell so hard and the bell had sounded so loud and different that morning that everyone had wondered what might have possessed the soul of this dismissed clergyman. Now he just couldn't wait for midnight to come when the maskman would sneak into his house. He smiled joyously. He wished he had been physically there to witness the destruction of Bwallangwu and the devilish organization. Though he was there afterwards to take some pictures.

"Oh God!," he had exclaimed, I knew it! I felt it the first time I set my eyes on the boy, though now dead, that the hour of deliverance had come."

The ex minister was really indulging himself today. He is taking a mug too many of sekete but he has every right to be tipsy, what the hell! He motioned to the barman and passed his mug one more time for a refill. The only sad thought that he knows would haunt him almost indefinitely is that of the Most Blessed Holy Rosary and that versatile young boy that got killed in the attempt to recover it. He had gone to the Bwallangwu shrine certainly because of the Rosary but there was no how he could have been able to lay his hand on it. The whole camp was on inferno. Gracious God, he wondered….but the Blssed Rosary cannot burn. Then where is it? He wondered if the maskman might have any idea as to what might have happened to it. And this maskman, who God had raised upon the death of Adams, "who can he be?" He ended up asking himself aloud.

Just then a young man, immaculately dressed in a three-piece suit came by his side and asked very politely in a somewhat aristocratic manner, "may I sit down here sir?"

"Why not, young man," replied Fra Maria, mug in hand on the way to the mouth and taking his time to pull a full mouth of the stuff and gulp it down and taking equal time as well to place the mug down before he turned to look at this young well behaved impressive figure. The next second caught him eyes wide open, mouth followed suit in a reaction you would expect from someone who had seen a ghost.

"Flies are plenty around here in sekete joint and they don't appear to be the disciplined types." The man cautioned, "they can enter the mouth of even that of a clergy." He finished up with a smile and trying to look serious at the same time.

The old clergy shrank back a little, closed his eyes and re opened them a number of times to still find the man still very much around, still sitting beside him.

"Adams!?"

"Yes, Friar Biodun Maria, old man."

"You! Are you real..are..are y you a ghost...no, are you real?"

Real enough to be able to drink mortal stuff. In the next couple of minutes I should be holding my own mug full of the good stuff."

"But...you...you were dead!"

"Why don't you touch me and find out. Doubting Maria. We used to know only of the doubting Thomas."

"But ...the valley...you are dead!"

"I'm alive!"

"I'm drunk!"

"Not too much not to be able to share a drink with me."

"And the maskman...Where is ...What is happening?"

"Adams and the maskman are one and the same person. I'm alife old man."

"So you didn't die!"

"Otherwise I could have reincarnated so fast as to have taken part in the war against Bwallangwu. So old man, which one is easier for you to believe? God, I heard give a definite time for reincarnation."

"B But we were told the nerve gas did not last in effect more more than thirty seconds, that before you could do anything at all the crocodiles jumped on you and ate....shared...oh no, killed you!"

Adams laughed heartily. "In fact, a very credible story which would have held for eternity if really I were dead. What spoiled that story is the fact that I didn't die."

"But what happened? How did you escape the crocs. What really happened?...Are you sure I'm not drunk?"

"Sure the gas malfunctioned but it was not much of the nerve gas but those Bwallangwu bastards who threw me down the valley of the crocodiles."

"*Sopangannatan oo! Jesu Krisiti, Olorun Olugbala!*"[56] the old man exclaimed with both hands on his head, "But how did you escape?"

"You know lent and rahmadan coincided that period."

"Yes but what..?"

"So it's either the crocodiles were fasting, both Moslems and Christians of them, or they just lost their appetite or maybe God locked their jaws; He could have even given them the direct orders not to kill and eat me..or share me as you have just put it." Adams replied, in his usual tone of toying with an old man.

"Oh Jesus! Oh God of Abraham! Oh god of Isaac! Oh god of Jacob! Oh God of Moses!"

"All the same God, right?"

"You have once again revealed your powers! You have saved your child from the jaws of death! You who saved Daniel in the lions' den... Shadrach Meshah and Abednego!"

Adams just looked at this old man who had closed his eyes in deep praise of the Lord. Just as the the barman approached with a mug of

---

[56] Oh Christ the savior!

sekete. Adams looked at the short man and asked, "how did you know it's sekete I wanted?"

"That was what you took the last time you came here with Friar Biodun," the barman had replied confidently, "but that time, man you had not made it. But sir, if you don't like it I can..."

"Oh no. It's ok. It's what I want. I'm just surprised at your good memory."

"Thank you sir. But where have you been these entire days sir?"

"Saudi Arabia," answered Adams enthusiastically, obviously bginining to like it all in that environment.

"No wonder," the little man said and went away.

Adams took a satisfying gulp, took a deep breadth and said, "well Friar Maria, God exists and is really God."

"Oh halleluia! Good gracious God! Your wonders have saved and convinced an innocent soul You have chosen your own time.....How did it happen?"

Adams was not sure if the question was meant for him or for God.

"Tell me! Adams, tell me!" the old man persisted.

"A long story," he replied, but we sure have the time, haven't we, Friar?"

As he said this all started coming back, unfolding like a long folded away scroll, unrolling like a recorded video tape.

"That nerve gas could really have been switched for it had effect for not more than one minute instead of the expected three minutes of action. Nevertheless I was able to accomplish my task down there. I had barely finished replacing the Rosary when one giant croc stirred."

"Oh Jesus Christ."

"Like hell I gave the signal rope the agreed 3 hard tugs to signify immediate pull up and I was just able to get my legs clear of their reach; just barely on time as the winch pulled me up."

"Oh glory be to God!"

"But my fortune was short-lived; obviously I never knew the ace up those pilots' sleeves. They winched me up to 3 feet of the helicopter and stopped the device."

"Holy Mary! Why!?"

"They demanded that I gave them the Rosary before the final pull up into the chopper, otherwise they wouldn't. They said they were following orders."

"Oh God of Israel! Wicked people!"

"After much futile attempt to make them see reason and the choper's endurance was running out I eventually handed it over to them, which apparently proved to be a fatal mistake. For no sooner than the rosary was secured in their hands they just cut the winch and I fell right from that height down to the bottom of the valley of crocodiles."

"Oooh.." The exclergy couldn't complete this one. He just reacted as if he was the one that was pushed down the bottom of the valley. He just closed his eyes and opened his mouth, both hands on his head in shock. He seemed to recover when Adams took a mouthful of his drink and continued.

"From the moment I started falling I was sure I was dead."

"Oh Jesus Christ of Nazareth!"

Really I must have died or some sort of death dream. For I immediately found myself in a hospital under the care of some doctors whose overalls were made of crocodile skin."

"Holy Mary of Asumpta! Hope they didn't give you injection!"

"If I tell you I knew what happened it would be a lie. I wondered if it was the effect of the nerve gas on the reptiles but all I know is that when I regained consciousness I was staring eyes to eyes with several crocodiles. And they seemed to be just watching me, one or two occasionally moving their tails. It took me some moments to assure myself that I was not in some kind of heaven or hell."

"Oh God of Daniel in heaven!"

"Gradually I knew I was alife especially with the confirmation of severe lower back pains, with real life crocodiles in attendant."

"Oh mighty Lord of host!"

"My initial immediate preoccupation was how I was going to outmaneuvre those reptiles but then I soon realized my folly and I laughed at myself as it dawned of me that it was not due to my guiles that they did not touch me all those whiles when I laid unconscious among them."

"Oh my savior!"

"Soon it occurred to me to try and find out if they would harm me if I ventured to move. No venture no success, I had to try something. Gingerly I raised a finger, then the wrist, the whole hand. Soon enough I was on my hands and knees. I still had my knife and my pistol but with only 8 rounds against well over a hundred of reptiles. No, fighting was not my best option. But what? Soon I realized my greatest problem. The fact is that the reptiles have not touched me and I could only assume dangerously that they might not, but my big problem was that they had occupied what appeared to be the only way up the goddamn valley. Obviously as I couldn't fly I would have to make them move one way or the other. In a flash I remembered James Bond but I was not brave enough to try to step along progressively on their backs. I would have to watch that film over and over again in case of next time. I couldn't have started tickling them even if we were on friendly terms and neither would it be possible for me to start picking them up and rearranging them to clear a path for me even if I had worn that beautiful metal cupboard of an attire of yours in the cave. So you could see that my options were so infintesinally few."

Both had chuckled and for some times now it seemed the clergyman had run out of qualifying adjective for God and his beloved son. Taking a sip, Adams continued.

"Firing a shot appeared to be one best out of so many foolish options in my head. It would have agitated them into movement but who would know the outcome of that agitation. For the first time in my life I prayed and I think I got that psalm right...emm...the one that talked about God being with me in the shadow of death I shall fear no evil..."

"Yees psalm 23....Oooh God of Moses!"

"Yes Psalm 23 but I must have mistaken that shadow for valley, but I guess God understood all the same."

"He is an understanding God! And did you fire?"

"I was on the brink of it when I was hit by a draft of fresh air in that valley. Then it dawned on me that there was a good circulation of air. It could only mean the availability of another opening allowing for that cross ventilation and as luck would have it, it was right there by my back. Hope rising gradually. Slowly I drew my knife and scratched the area until it revealed the opening of an underground tunnel. Hope flickered!."

"Oh gracious Lord of Hope!"

"But another problem. A dark tunnel. What if crocodiles were lined up in there? And Nothing to assure me that they would be interested in performing guard of honour for me, that is even if they recognize me as their newly posted-in commander or a visiting general of some sort. Then I needed some light and that was when I remenmbered my headlamp. I instinctively touched my head but of course it was not there. It must have fallen off when I hit the ground in that fall. I looked around and saw it some 2 meters away and fortunately not among the crocodiles."

"Slowly, gingerly, I inched my way towards it and I finally got hold of it and after fiddling with it for a couple of seconds I got it working."

"Oh God of lightening!"

"I then saw that a few meters of the tunnel inside were free of any living soul."

"Oh thank you Lord, you that made way for your people to cross the red sea!"

"Well, whatever is ready should never be delayed; I back tracked gently, gradually but to my surprise and horror, for every step I took backwards the crocodiles took theirs after me."

"Yeepah!"

"But supposing I had moved before I discovered the tunnel is this what they would be doing? If I had taken a step towards them would they have taken a step backwards? Either I was not daring enough or there was no time or no point in finding out; I couldn't perform that experiment. So gradually I entered the tunnel, man-size, no problem about that. The next situation was to decide whether to face the direction I was going and thus turn my back at my bodyguards or to keep my eyes on them which means walking backwards with the risk of a surprise attack at the back. I found myself doing both, oscillating my neck to the point of almost cutting off. At a point I hazard the risk of facing the tunnel for much longer time, trusting God completely, which worked. I made progress but anytime I turned I found that my bodyguards maintained exactly the same distance behind me."

"Oooh God of David!"

"Friar, a lot has been existing. I continued to made progress. At times it occurred to me to quicken my pace and they did likewise, maintaining the same gap. Later I was tempted to run but did I know where the tunnel was taking me to? So I condemned that idea. Then curious enough I had to slow to almost a final stop to clear some cobwebs and Friar, they stopped as well, within 3 meters which was the distance they had maintained. That was when I made up my mind there was no point being afraid of them any longer. I should only concern myself with what lay in front as I advanced away in the tunnel."

"Oh God of wonders, signs and miracles!" This one was uttered so loud that Adams wondered if the clergy man had not gone beyond his usual measure on sekete. But what the hell, He has the right to get drunk.

"To cut the long story short, just like a totally bewildered emperor with a number of volunteering weird escorts, guards and servants, I went through the tunnel till I bursted out in the open."

"Good gracious Lord who took his children through the wilderness, Jerico and…"

"You don't suppose I should tell you where the tunnel terminated, friar? Where I bursted out?"

"Hmmmm, to be very honest with you, young man, I won't want to add more to my responsibilities now. Unless you think that knowledge would be of an urgent need and of some immediate benefit to all."

"Very wise old man. Then we'd better leave that for now. Anyway as I have said I believe now and there's no turning back, God is real!"

"Praise the Lord! Halleluiya! Oh goodness! Good things are happening today, on my own birthday! How do I deserve all this, my God? First the night caller is right here with me by day and then giving me very good tidings!"

"Friar, people are looking at you now…"

"What have I done?"

"You're shouting. Keep your voice down."

"Ok, ok, ok. Are they still looking?"

"No. They are looking at someone else now. Anyway, my good old clergyman, Happy birth day and may you live o bel hundred."

"Oh, c'mon, stop that joke. Hundred ko, hundred ni."

"Why not? You have the chance. Your indulgences are minimal, if any other, apart from sekete on rare occasions such as this, your diet is mostly herbal, healthy. As a matter of fact, this Taoist way of life of you people promote longevity. Just look, you are 65 but you're looking 40. Now tell me, God willing, why you couldn't reach 100 in good health?"

"With all this environmental pollution of this our modern society?"

"True, but better here still in Gbongan than a place like Lagos." Both had chuckled.

"That's the price of modernity." Lamented the clergy.

"But would you call it modernity or stupidity?"

"What do you mean?"

"How can man decide to promote himself by killing himself? There are better ways of producing energy. Clean energy. The fossil products underground are meant for something else. Fracking for example is cleaner. Even that process should lead to something else but it's the kind of door we knock that would be opened for us. What are we looking for when we live, breathe and bath inside the greatest source of energy itself? The sun can give us all. All we need is to research enough to tap it. For example we have proceeded from electricity instead of from magnetism only to come back to it and award ourselves funny degrees for the ability to come out of the bush which we shouldn't have been in the first place. You would found out again that certain advancemwnt are deliberately delayed simply for pecuniary purposes."

"Hmmmm, the love of money is the root of all evil..."

"And so on and so forth. Happy birthday Friar."

"Thank you so much. But how did you know all this?"

"Now make up your mind. Are you ready to add to your responsibility?"

"No, I am getting old."

"Where I came out from that tunnel and what I discovered and what I was made to swear is a subject I would come back to tell you one day. But God is alive and watching."

"Wonderful!" and now the elderly man dropping his tone, "that was err…eerr..a really…"

"I know what you want to say. Look Friar, I'm dropping out of town."

"Leaving Gbongan?"

"Yeah."

"Where to, son?"

"Just anywhere for some time. A change of environment, a change of scene."

"I understand. You need to rest. Some sort of vacation. But I bet you don't know all I wanted to say."

"I shouldn't contest that. You might not let me win." And both had laughed. Then the old man took a gulp, looked down, somehow gloomy, and said sadly, "how things would have been more glorious if only the….."

"That Rosary is real! Sorry to cut you short. Friar, the Rosary is the most blessed holy Rosary. It is real and still possesses all the attributed endowments and powers. It is a spiritual archive of antidotes…"

"Reading my mind?"

"Now you are letting me win!"

"How could you have guessed that right? Were you reading my mind?"

"Maybe some of the ghost's attributes have rubbed off on me." Adams teased.

"May God be blessed all the same. We must pray that the Rosary does not fall into the hands of the unworthy. Otherwise we are back to square one! Back to the days of Orishadami! And you can well imagine the implications of that now-a-days when everyone seems to have lost his conscience."

"Especially, technologically?"

"Exactly! Terrible, isn't it. Technology without discipline is doom to human race eventually."

"As if you knew, Father, the few ones to the last bids are concerned with this nuclearstuffs, and some other stuffs yet to be discovered as the greatest sources of energy, exponential multiplications of energies and direct synthesis of matter in sun."

"Can that ever be achieved?"

"Well, taking a cue from photosynthesis in plants and what Jesus had already demonstrated, we lesser beings should not have much doubt but just increase our discipline."

"Now you are getting me lost. You mentioned plants and Jesus...?

"Jesus fed the multitude with 5 loaves of bread and some fishlings..."

"Of course. Oooh blessed son of God!"

"Those food samples were exponetialy replicated or multiplied. Whatever. And plants don't cook and heat up the environment. They photosynthesize. There's the possibility of the reawakening of an advanced technology that would develop photosynthesis to such an extent that all this industries around cooking gass etc would become a thing of the museums."

"Jesus Christ are we not in trouble if this Rosary should get into the....by the way how do you know all these are in the Rosary....errr... pulling my legs?"

"No Friar, it will not get into the hands of the evil one." Adams replied so confidently that the clergyman became curious.

"But you said they made you to hand it over to them and we don't know its whereabout now!"

"The God of host has always protected it and would continue to protect it."

"I was thinking then...shouldn't you let us try and find it before you drop out of Gbongan because it is still somewhere in Gbongan..."

"No, that won't be necessary." The young man smiled confidently.

"Did you take it from Bwallangwu's den?"

"No Friar, not from Bwallangwu's den...but..."

Now the old man earlobes were virtually enlarged, eyes wide open in anticipation of what next was going to come out of the mouth of this enigmatic man.

"But what!?"

"Friar I mean to say.... thinking about it, how could I possibly have survived in that valley of crocodiles? It's more than mere coincidence to me."

"Well the work of God is limitless and most times inexplicable."

"Expecially for those who do not want explanations and are satisfied at the level of ...eerrr...miracles...?"

"What do you mean?"

"Let me now tell you something that will thrill you for the rest of your successful life."

"What is that!" Now ears enlarged again and looking like an antelope in cassock

"Some other aspects of my story concerning the mission." He took a long pull of his drink and the old man did the same instinctively, eyes glued on him. They had a refill and he listened.

"It started like this. I smelled a rat that fateful day we went to recover the Rosary. You know this feelings that comes out of nowhere...a premonition of danger sort of...em...a feeling that makes you aware that something is out of order somehow, somewhere, Friar, you understand what I mean..?"

"Yes, of course, son. It's intuition. It has to do with a developed pineal common in spiritually evolved beings. All these combined to make you the chosen one!"

Adams laughed pleasantly, in reflection of that immediate past, and he continued.

"More so before that, I had an experience during that prayer in the cave. It was either a dream or a vision in which I saw myself in the hands of men whose heads were those of crocs."

"Yes, I was watching you but I didn't know what experiences you were having. You were transfixed....but what a horror! Heads of crocodiles!?

"And the behavior of those pilots that day, your sudden attack of diarrhearr, etc were just things out of order. All those combined to strengthen my premonitions. So down the valley I put the Real one, the Most Holy Rosary in my pocket and what they took from me was a replica...."

Father Maria looked so confused now that he didn't know what and how to believe.

"Okay I didn't tell you that I went to that valley with two replicas."

"Oooh gracious God! How come? You made…"

"No, you people made. You remember the first replica you people made disappeared and we had to make another one?"

"Yes, the devil…"

"Blame no devil for that, I took it or rather I was the one who stole it."

"You? How did you do it?"

"When you people would close your eyes so tight in prayers like.. like…..praying mantis."

The ex clergy didn't know what so say. He just looked at this enigmatic man who had commited a crime to cure a sin.

"Though shall not steal?"

"No, no, steal, steal..no no don't steal..No…Don't confuse me!"

"So let's just conclude, holy man. I had the Blessed Holy Rosary on me when I was with the crocodiles and was unconscious amidst them. And the way I feel now, Rosary on me anytime, I could dare even the lions.. And I wouldn't dare carry my sweet black ass to that valley without the Rosary even if there were only a few monitor lizards and geckos down there."

"Oooh gracious God of the Holy Rosary!"

"Remember that time I told you to let me have a look at the Holy Scroll, yeah, I had the Rosary by then. The scroll or the book of interpretation indicated where to check on issues of 'mind capture'. So I was able to set my brother's mind free from Bwallangwu's amnesic mind hold."

"Oh Jesus be praised!"

"Now I declare to you before God and man, that I have not defied the Holy Rosary. I never had it on me in battle. I never had it on me when I had to take life. And the few times it inadvertently had to be on me I never even raised a hand in my own defense. I just trusted it completely just like it happened in that valley among the crocodiles."

"Ooooh good Lord even though you tread upon the lions and the adder no harm shall befall thee. A thousand ...."

Adams tapped the old man. "Let's get on with this and get it over with."

"What?"

"The Holy Rosary remains the most blessed, undefied and still as powerful as it ever was. So Friar Maria, Much as I would have loved to hand it over to you in a church, under the right atmosphere, and with all the solemnity the occasion demands, but now with good intention I hand it over to you now in New Weyos."

"Why, why can't you just keep it? You are qualified by heaven to keep it. You saved it. You never used it selfishly even throughout those dangerous times you knew you could have been killed, you never defied it. It has still allowed you to keep it with you even now, you know what I mean. You deserve to keep it because I know you will always protect and preserve its integrity."

"No Father Maria. I couldn't possibly keep it. One way or the other I have taken life. You have not. I've read some other parts of the Holy Scroll and I know what it says. I can use it for any useful purpose for humanity within a time limit to be dictated by the nature of the issue at hand, ranging from 7 hours to 7 days and nothing more by virtue of my having taken life. But for you, you are the most qualified to provide permanent residence for it. It's now your responsibility. You have nothing to worry about because you will preserve it and it will protect you. Of all you people in the cave, you are the most qualified. Simple and artless, permit me, but those are the like of the kingdom of God. Besides, you people sent me on that holy mission, to the valley of the crocodilles to bring the Most Blessed Holy Rosary back to you. So, here it is. Mission accomplished Sir."

The old man was just confused. Adams sipped his sekete and smiled as he seemed to wait for the man to sort himself out. He thinks he still needs a hand, a little more assurance.

"I know your worries, old man. Just as somebody once told me, you have no ambition and neither any ulterior motive to want it in your care. All your main concern is its safety but you don't trust your own ability to ensure that. That alone, father, is all the more reason why you are the most qualified. The Lord of host that kept it all these ages is still alive and functioning. That Rosary is self protecting and you know that."

Then the old man brightened up as if suddenly inspired. "Okay, I will keep it in the sanctuary in the cave."

"Very well, and you can have these silver weapons also in the cave as monuments."

The man looked up and down, with a display of some restlessness. Then holding the young man's hands he said, "but Adans, son, I would always need help!"

"And I assure you, you would always get all the help you would ever need concerning the Rosary. Heaven above would provide."

"Adams, you will always be needed. You who have guarded this Rosary more than you cared for your own life. You who recovered it from the valley and yet never attempted to use it for a selfish end. The sort of people needed are those who understand it. You understand. You will never defy it. Therefore you will always be needed. You keep the weapons, holy warrior, more as a reminder of your task towards the Rosary and humanity."

Without warning the old man placed his right hand on Adams head. "In the name of the Most High, I appoint you the Guardian of the Mystical Rosary." And for a moment, as if the world stood still for them, both were transfixed and all was momentarily quiet."

"What was that?"

"A guardian Angel has just passed. You have been accepted..as the Guardian."

Adams considered and smiled. "Fine, but you keep one of these in the cave beside the Rosary as a symbol." He gave him an arrow with the silver head.

"In case of any perceived danger to the Rosary I will always call upon you."

"And I will always be ready to serve. I will let you know my locations from point to point im my sojourn and I will be here in jiffy at the first call."

Then some period of silence pervaded which seemed to affect even the whole area like some angel of the lord was passing again and all was inevitably quiet. The silence was broken by the old man.

"Did I tell you the old man father Gbasero just collapsed and died?"

"No, you didn't. But I know."

"How could you have known?"

Adams smiled sadly. "How about Cardinal Jillas Mansuri?" He asked instead.

"He hasn't returned since he left this morning."

"He will not return."

"Why?"

"Because he is dead."

"Dead? How? How do you know all..."

"Jobilar killed him with other priests of Bwallangwu."

"Priest of Bwallangwu!?"

"And as concerned your old Father Gbasero, his heart left with Bwallangwu because he was one of the highest priests of their master. He had the ranking of Enlaye."

"Oh my God!"

"So that leaves you in charge of the cave now. It's God's own reorganization. You are now in charge. Form your own circle of twelve, sanitize the cave and keep it most holy. You have all you need now to continue the good work of Orishagbemi. You must watch out for weeds and thorns."

"I...I ...am terribly sorry about your..er...brother, One way or the other I feel connected to his death. I mean if ..."

"There's no iota of justification in blaming yourself for his death. Death, has it not being said, is the reward of sin. And he didn't die in vain. He died the honourable death."

"Was he really your brother? There has been a lot of rumours circulating but I feel the right thing is to ask you person to person."

"Yes he is. We are the Emmanuel Ajahni's twins."

"What!? You mean the Siamese?"

"Exactly."

"Oooooh……" probably out of stock or tipsy now, "what an arrangement of fate!"

"So when I acknowledged that God is real now you know what I mean?"

"Oh yes! I know, I know! The Lord of host has chosen his own time and means and avenues to reveal himself to the worthy. Ooooh God of Revelations! Thank you!"

"Well, old papa…gotta be leaving now."

"Just one more thing, son, before you leave. Have you realized your utmost purpose in life? You know a lot just wander about in this life doing things just as they come to them and never really giving it any thought. They live by the instincts…sorry to say, the way of the lowest animals. Then a lot are glued to the wrong path until the tail end before they see the light. Some unfortunate ones don't even realize at all that they are wrong. Those are closely related to the first group and you find some of them who might have developed some ostrtich philosophy in the way of development, visiting voodoo priests and some pastors alike to perpetrate their ungodly ways. The most unfortunate ones are those who deliberately choose the wrong path as the right path because it is faster and richer in material prosperity. It is the good ones that eventually know the difference between being clever and being wise. But he who realizes his life purpose or mission can never waste his life. And he would be guided constantly by the inner light."

"As a matter of fact, Father, I really can't say I know for sure yet."

"Then that is it!"

"What is that?"

"You would soon discover your purpose. For a man who knows that he does not know when really he does not know and can always admit that he does not know can never get lost because he is humble. Those who exalt themselves shall be humbled and those who humble themselves shall be exalted. As you go from place to place, as directed by the forces above, I want you to permanently keep the word 'purpose' in your mind. The purpose of your life."

"Thank you, father, I have really gained from you. The words of the elders are words of wisdom …"

"Me too, son, I have gained immensely from you. I could never have imagined the way.….em…I mean I have learnt form you the proper role of aggression in life."

"Well, the world was not created passive. To be permanently passive is akin to being out of existence."

"I agree, but aggression has to be properly channeled."

"That's right."

"Tell me one other thing, son. How about settling down with a good homely girl and raising a family. I want you to give it a serious thought. A man is never complete without his other half. His own allegorical rib."

"Sure, father, I would give it a thought."

"And don't make the mistake I've made. There is blessing in mistakes and there is blessing in avoiding them. But the most blessing comes out of learning from mistakes. In choosing a wife, son, women come in different categories. There are ones for social occasions, very beautiful and glamorous; there are the ones homely and docile and perhaps not on the pretty side. They might not give you heart attack but they might not contribute meaningfully to your development apart from raising children. Then somewhere in between these two extremes are those ones that are presentable, homely and would give you some challenges you need for your continuous spiritual evolution. Choose wise, son. Don't go and put in your house the one that is meant for parties and social functions alone. Neither should you put a completely submissive buffoon. You remember the woman that went and kept her baby in a freezer to cool her down from fever and froze the unfortunate child to death? I still keep the newspaper. Find your own lost rib that would fit snugly in there. Compartibility!"

"The words of the elders are words of wisdom. I thank you Friar Maria."

"Ex Friar. I'm now a bell man."

"To me you are Friar, and with due respect sir, do not argue with me. When I come back we would have a hell of a shot."

"I look forward to that, son. Provided you come back on time before I loose my strength to bend a bow."

"Sure I would. One more thing."

"What is that?"

"Can I call you father? I never had the chance to call anybody father. Would you oblige me?"

"And I never had the opportunity to call a son my son. Thank you, son."

Adams watched as tears rolled down the chicks of the old man, but both knew that they were tears of joy.

Adams had sneaked back to the vicinity of the camp that night. He had no difficulties whatsoever in completing this personal mission unhindered. He just moved about like a ghost, with the wind. He fixed time explosives in the armoury and had gone to take position at a vantage point. He smiled in retrospection. He had instructed the serge major, earlier that day to make the men submit their rifles to the armory for inspection, cleaning exercises and stock taking that was scheduled to take place the following day and he had given his most trusted boys among them clear instructions as to what to do in regards to them.

He sat at the vantage point overlooking the camp about one hundred and fifty meters away. He had a bow and several arrows fitted with explosive heads. He looked at the surrounding of the armory with his binoculars and could still see the two man patrol team lingering around the location of the armory. He waited for almost 3 minutes till when he saw them strolled well away from that location. He murmured as he fixed an arrow to the bow, "I watched Silvester Stallone used this in Rambo, but here I am, going to use it for real." And he took pulled and took aim.

The armory blast was violent and all the soldiers were out of their sleeping tents in pandemonium. Then he bent the bow again and released an arrow to the temporary hospital tent which went up in flames. He watched with his binoculars how the soldiers rushed to take cover in the bush. Then he released another shot into the second tent, then the third, and so on until the seventh and the last one. Amid the cconfusion he could hear the shout of "commander! Commander! Maskman! Masked man!" He shook his head and murmured, "there is no more commander."

Soon the entire camp was no more; empty as everybody took to their heels, especially when they heard the siren of the police from a distance.

Adams was satisfied. "Thank you God. I didn't have to take blood in disbanding the army."

He picked his rucksack and backtracked into the jungle.

At about 0800hrs in the morning he took a number he had written down in his diary and entering a phone booth he dialed.

"Hello, 041422456," a female voice had come up on the line.

"Please can I speak to Miss Angela Bobade?"

"Yes, speaking. Is that you my masked man?"

"What! How d'you know?"

"I know…I know your voice. Why wouldn't I know?"

"Are you alone? Are you free to talk?"

"Yes. I have been sitting here by the phone all day. I know you would call. Look! I want to see you."

"So do I…So why don't you come to the airport? You must come alone and you must not tell anybody. Very important! If you must see me…otherwise…."

Fifteen minutes later, Angela alighted from a taxi, confused, eyes wide open emphazing her innocent look and beauty, in expectation and excitement, not knowing who she was looking for. She paused at the entrance of the departure hall and looked and as she was about to enter through the self opened glass doors a man tapped her gently from behind and asked, "Can I help you, miss?"

"Oh…em..not really," she replied almost absentmindedly before she turned to look at the tall, very good looking man who exuded a kind of very strange magnetism. Then she decided to volunteer an addition to her reply, "well I am looking for a..m masked man." Looking a bit awkward herself.

"Masquerades are not allowed in this airport..em..oh, I think I noticed a man in mask behind that kiosk," the man said pointing in the direction of the kiosk.

Angela was excited and she exclaimed, "and you are built just like him. Not exactly…and you talk like him!"

The man smiled and said, "Aaah, very good recollections. He is my brother. We are identical twins."

"Oh really? And you were pulling my legs!? You are the brother!? The one they say is dead but killed Bwallangwu?"

"No, I survived," and looking at the girl somehow closely he added, "what Bwallangwu drained from me was what I took from him. It was not my life. Come, my brother is waiting."

"And why does he wear a mask?" The girl seems to want to know before getting to him."

"When you meet him face to face you ask him, he will tell you."

"When I meet him face to mask," she said almost grudgingly.

"C'mon, let's go. He is in a hurry." And he led her to the back of the Arigbabuwo Bureau de Change kiosk.

"But where is the maskman?" She asked disappointedly and imploringly.

"I am the one you are longing to see. I hope you like what you've found."

Angela was on his neck before he knew what was happening. She just jumped on his neck and hung there so tight, and kissed him so hard on the lips. The man had never been that close to the female counterpart before in his life. Even the parental embrace has remained a story to be read in books and perhaps real for those who have parents. And this strange feelings… what the heck is it and where the hell is it coming from? He just allowed the girl to do whatever he was doing without knowing what the hell to do in response. But all felt good. So good and cool and he never wanted it to stop. What it does is to urshered in the words of his brother and those of Friar Maria…to find a good waman and …kids. A man is never complete until he is joined with his complement. He had a quick mental assessment. Was he feeling complete now with the feelings he's having with this girls closeness? Her closeness, her soft body claiming right now to accommodate his tough rugged aggressive body, as she glue into his chest, as he grinds into her, seeming to remind him of the allegorical left rib. Rib severed by evolution, the deep sleep not remembered, a rib whose absence forms a nagging gap so uncomfortable, especially in inclement weather. A rib that must fit snugly in place, when too long huts like hell but when too short is no less a problem. Can man really ever find peace until the correct rib is found, brought back into his life to be fused once again into its rightful place...just as he was feeling presently? Has he found his half? And talking about halves. Didn't he bring his own half from heaven through the womb? Only to be separated, first by the sharp scarpel of Doctor Payida, allowing the wind of fate to drift them apart until they met again under the most unbecoming circumstances, but separated again by the sharpest scarpel of death this time by a wide distance that could only be traversed in dreams, imaginations, real out of body experience or eventually in the younder where they might not separate any longer. Only the wind of fate would not stop blowing. Who then is this lovely piece of living earth? Who could be this sweet sensational spark of God, encapsulated in a body supervised by Venus herself less some workers should mar the beauty of the outside which is supposed to reflect the beauty, albeit naïve, of the inside. Should this then be a replacement of his actual half lost. Inwardly he is beginning to feel this might be the woman.

He allowed the girl to satisfy herself and gently carrying her backward just a bit like beholding a loving child, he released a satisfying smile. For then he had become sure this is the woman of his life. He took a good look at her as she in turn had her eyes roaming all over his body, hugging again, continually, he said as in a whisper to himself, "strange the way nature directs the wind of fate to carry across your path, in the most seemingly unnatural way, what belonged to you."

The girl caught only half of what he might have said but never bothered to ascertain. She just kissed him and said, "when you mentioned the airport I knew you are travelling. So I've brought my own luggage."

"Where are you going to?"

"Wherever you go I'm going with you, my love, my savior, my maskman. You're very handsome with or without the mask."

"Angela," holding her hands, "I like you sincerely, as my woman. And I'll be honest with you, you are the only girl I have ever known. All things being equal I would gladly have accepted you to go with me now but please, my dear, I couldn't."

As if thunder struck her, she grabbed him, "why!?"

"I shouldn't be the one to start the problem all over again."

"What problem!? There is no problem! What problem?"

"Is your father aware that you're here with me now?"

"No!" she replied, so naïve.

"Your father might again need the services of another maskman to come and rescue you for a second time, from me this time around. In which case I would be nothing different from those who kidnapped you the first tme. It means stealing you away from your father."

"Oh no, not like that. I will phone him later."

"If your mother should faint again she might not recover..." he said that jokingly.

"I don't want you to leave me. I I just feel empty without you. I feel so insecured!"

"No, far from it, I won't leave you. I don't think I could ever leave you now that I have found you. But if you really love me then you must learn to wait. If you really ever love your father you must learn to wait. We must prevent certain little problems in order not to cause bigger ones. You can imagine what sort of stories would start appearing in the media immediately I might have gone with you. Dear one, it's just a matter of time. Very little lapse of time. Besides, you should not denigrate yourself. Retain yourself within that self respect that I've seen that is making me to like you. I don't wanna see you as a woman somebody would just pick off like that. Think of the respect we have to give your father as an eventual inlaw. The respect he and your mother deserve as parent who cared for you, bringing you up till you've matured to this stage. Do not let us spoil things with haste and then come back in an attept to mend things. Again think of me. I also deserve some respect. Should I steal you away now I would have lost it all."

"So you are going to leave me?" Tears now in her eyes.

"No I am not gonna leave you. But I would go now, briefly, and come back and marry you respectfully, legally and befittingly off your dear loving parents's hands. Hemmn, what the Yorubas call 'nisuloka[57]'. Yes that's what befits you, me, and your parents."

"Promise me you will not go and love somebody else and marry her."

"I promise only on one condition, no, two."

"Tell me. I would do anything for you!"

"First provided you are not in love with anybody yet and you would not fall in love with anyother until I come back."

"Never! And the second? Tell me."

"Promise you would never let anybody know, especially your parents that I am the maskman."

⸺◆◆◆◆⸺

Simultaneously about 5 kilometers away down there in chief Aborungun's estate a sumptuous dinner was about to commence. But the latest news was rather surprising and disheartening.

"Sir, this man is eratic!" exclaimed the chief's representative. "He is crasy. Not normal!...In fact the very first day I saw him I got that feeling. Who else could have burnt the camp?"

"Yes...yes, I know," said the chief calmly, "it's him. I know he did it. And that is his style, no casualities."

"But then sir, do you think he might show up for this dinner?"

"Well, who knows, such an unpredictable creature? He does exactly what you don't expect him to do."

"So I should go ahead with ...eeerrrr..."

"Oh yes. Go ahead with the arrangement."

The chief was right. A report was brought to him about 15 minutes later.

---

[57] With all cultural norms and requirements

"Sir the mask man has arrived…"

"Very good. Very, very good." said the chief, excited, getting up from his seat, "show him in right away!"

The masked man was ushered in with the same respect normally accorded to the chief's highest caliber guests and the chief himself was more than warm and cordial."

"Sorry, a bit late. I had to sort out some urgent problem at the airport."

"At the camp you mean? Oh, your camp is located at the airport general area. I almost forget."

"I never mince word, chief. Actually I was busy at the airport."

"Ok, son, it's alright. It's perfectly alright. In fact I was beginning to wonder if you would make it at all."

"Who am I to stand off a father like you?"

"You are highly welcome, maskman, if you would like," placing a hand on his shoulder, "please follow me." The chief was smiling brilliantly as the masked man followed him.

Actually, earlier on the maskman's itineraries had been communicated to him in detail since the previous evening. That a masked man had been noticed around the airport but had just vanished as fast as he had appeared. But nothing to worry, he is right here with the chief now. The chief had shown him round his estate and later they had returned to the dining and the excellent dinner had commenced. Sitting side by side they had had a lot to talk about.

"I wonder if you have reconsidered. You still won't take my little gift?"

"Thank you chief, but as I said before, I wouldn't want to live with a silver spoon in my mouth. Ground's gonna be too soft and I ain't gonna get the fun of my life."

"Hmmm, talking about silver spoon, so it's not only Bwallangwu that does not want silver…" Both had laughed heartily.

"Excuse me please, would you?" The chief had gone out and was immediately met by six hefties, looking like price fighters.

"Chief, is it the bastard?"

"Yes, he is the one for sure. I confirmed with all our previous discussions which I asked him again and he didn't miss a word. Nevertheless there is till a lot to talk about. I would signal you when I'm ready. But are you boys ready?"

"Since yesterday chief. Nobody treats Jacus like he did the other day and gets away with it."

"I don't want him injured, he is my friend. I only want to see his face."

"He is a tough nut to crack, chief; we have to be a little hash."

"Use your judgement..errr..how do they put it? ....minimum required force."

"A pleasure sir," enthused Jacus with a mean smile at the corner of his mouth.

The chief reentered and the conversation recommenced.

"Sorry I hope I did not keep you waiting."

"Oh, I quite understand. A high chief like you rarely has a minute for himself without one or two things taking you away for arrangement or rearrangement." Both had glanced at each other in understanding.

"You can say that again," replied the chief. "And back to our other discussion, look, son, we really have to deliberate extensively on this... errrr...I hope you remember..."

"If it's about the army, chief, with due respect, my opinion and decision remain the same."

"Now let me tell you something to open your eyes. Ours would not be the first private army in the world and certainly would never be the last. Examples of where they have been effectively used abound all over the world: Iraq, Syria, Afghanistan even Sierra leone to name a few. The various jobs available to them include training, vital assets and oil field protection, providing logistics, protection of rich companies and individuals that can afford them and of course, assisting in conflicts. The list is inexhaustible. But you know mercenaries have existed for very long, centuries! Don't you?"

"You mean we should become mercenaries?"

"No, no, no, far from it!"

"Then what are we going to be?"

"PMC!"

"President Mess Committee? What da hell?"

"Haa, ha ha, hahaha, Naïve! They are known as Private Military Contractors, PMC. Basically, PMCs are companies that have military operators for hire!"

"Mercenaries! Let's call a spade a spade."

"No, again, young warrior. Mercenaries are uncontrolled individuals but PMC are under very effective control of their parent organization. And they are so useful in the society!"

"Useful!?"

"Yeeees, yes. Provision of jobs for laid out soldiers who would otherwise become criminals in town and you can only imagine, with their sophisticated training, what a menace they would really become. With our PMC that problem would be solved for the society. But PMCs are useful most especially for those avoiding recognition for some important reasons and those who do not want their hands dirty. *Howu, a kii saa l'oko ni'le ka f'owo ko'mi!*[58] "

"I can understand you better now. The way vultures are needed to clean our environment."

"Good analogy, my maskman. But people seldom realize the usefulness of vultures until the communities start stinking."

"But supposing we stop creating the jobs for the vultures, would we need the vultures so much as to breed nose to nose with us? We should attempt to create a more decent society, morally and spiritually clean. Not the one we would need so much service of vultures to clean up!"

"Hmmmn, now I can see. Recent events have proved to me how adamant you are on this issue. Especially that you have expressed yourself with explosive languages. But I was hoping still that nothing was lost yet if there could be a change of mind…."

"With due respect sir, If it's about the army, chief, my opinion and decision remain the same."

Ok. Never mind. But if you ever have a change of heart, son, I am always available."

"With honor and pleasure, chief."

---

[58] Afterall we have a hoe we don't have to pack shit with our bare hands..

"And just in case, I almost forgot. I need to give you my numbers. This is a …."

"Chief, I have your numbers or have you changed them?"

"Oh pardon me. I have been drinking since morning."

"Not too good for your liver…"

"Thanks, I will watch it, son."

"You're welcome sir. And by the way, I took something on loan from you which I should return." He brought out a copy of of Eric Bern's A Layman's Guide to Psychiatry and Psychoanalysis to the surprise of the chief.

"When did you take that on loan from me?"

"That night or was it morning when you felf slightly uncomfortable and I had to help you onto a sofa."

"Haaa! I remember! And you seized the opportunity to help yourself…."

"I must commend you, chief, you have a very rich library. I am full of envy. Since then I have been using your library."

"Really!?"

"But I have always returned what I took."

"That I can confirm but I never knew you were such a voracious reader."

"The occasion demanded for it, especially when I needed all the help I could get to handle interpersonal relationship in dealing with the recent situation at hand."

"You will always surprise me. You used my library any time you felt like without my consent…"

"With due respect, chief."

"I am only glad you are not the type to take my beautiful wife on loan."

"C'mon, chief….haba…"

"I was surprised that you still come for dinner in mask. Now tell me now with your own mouth when you are going to show me your face."

"When iit becomes no more necessary to wear a mask."

"And I was hoping it was going to be today. I intend to have photogtaghs with you but now the idea of standing side by side with a man whose face is covered in mask does not appeal to me."

"No, chief. I wouldn't advice that, especially for your political career."

Both had busted out laughing and that was when the 6 hefties moved in. After some commotions in the room, they eventually removed the mask.

"Well, well, well. So this is the face behind the mask," said the chief with a look of satisfaction in his face. "You remind me of one of those western film heroes I used to admire. So we say, masked man, one to one, we are even, before we get down to some real serious discussions."

The now unmasked man got up slowly from the tiled floor and smiled as he asked, "I wouldn't mind the photograph now sir, if you would oblige me. It's something I need to remember."

Photos were taken in different postures and with a lot of jokes.

"Oh you can put on back your mask, son and let's settled for some very serious discussions."

"Haah, chief, I'm sorry I am going to disappoint you. I must confess, chief, this is the best dinner I've ever taken in my whole miserable wondering life. The cooking is superb and memorable. Your wine is simply the best! The music increased my appetite and I had never been waited upon in my miserable life, especially by beautiful girls assorted. So far so good until this serious discussion you have just mentioned. I'm sorry I am going to disappoint you because I wouldn't be able to read the mind of my master. I was able to answer your questions just the way he had briefed me but now I have exhausted the content of that brief and I doubt if I would ever see him again. I am sorry sir I am just a representative of my commander, I have nothing to do with this. He just told me to come here from the airport to come and represent him and told me what to say in response to certain questions you might be asking me and to make sure I returned your book. I am sorry sir."

"And you agreed to fake him, just like that!?"

"Yes sir."

"No chief, he is the one. His responses were too accurate for a mere brief. By the time we torture him he would confess."

"You would just kill me for nothing. And should you do that I don't know what he would do to this estate. I hope you are aware of what he has done to the camp."

But if you are not him and you are not reading his mind how come you are able to speak out his mind with the exact words he would be using if he were here himself?"

"Very simple sir. You remember you were so much part of the party you threw for us and, most especially all the vital discussions your representative had with my boss and his responses."

"So?"

"With due respect sir, it's by power of gadgets."

"Interesting! So he wired you up!? You were on one-to-one communication with him since?"

"Yes sir."

"Serious! And where is the gadget? Search him!"

The man was searched and the miniature transceiver was retrieved.

"Exactly like the one I used over there!" Exclaimed the representative. "Where did you get this?"

"From you sir. My boss stole it from you after you finished with him during the party. The repeater is outside there in the flowers."

"So you could even have continued to fool me if you wanted!"

"No sir. That gadget stopped working when that man slapped me. You see, all initial twelve slaps I received were on my left cheek but when that lefthanded man started his own, very horrible slaps, he damaged the gadgets, which were on the right ear. So game over sir."

"Hmmmm. What is your name, son?" The chief asked admiringly.

"Anthony Adebayo, sir."

"Hmmmmmmn," said the chief smiling. "Zero for me, five for the mask man. Give this man more food and wine and arrange a brown envelope for him before he departs. And find some time to come and see me, would you? I have a meeting tomorrow morning. I have to go in now and rest.

——◆◆✕◆◆——

At that particular time, seated and fiddling with her seat belt in the Chinook helicopter that shuffles Gbongan and Lagos was Bimbo, arms folded across her chest, eyes shaded behind dark large glasses and little Karl in between her laps. Suddenly, the appearance of a man at the door made her to scream and almost jump through the ceiling of the chopper. The man appeared to have envisaged the reaction, approached her with a reassuring smile.

"Do not be afraid, Mrs Karl Ajahni. Relax, you'ren't seeing a ghost."

That seemed to calm her down a bit though eyes remained dilated, fists clenched tight. She was looking at the man as he took his seat beside her. Thousands of thought ran through her mind. This was her Karl before the transforming surgery. The Karl she had known and with who she had vibrated in unison in all definable aspects of life. Karl! Exactly. Possiblity of a reversal surgery?" Then it dawned on her.

That fateful night of the day that witnessed the destruction of Bwallangwu, the maskman had instructed that she be lodged in Popoula Guest House with he kid. He had later called her on phone to give her an instruction to purchase a one-way ticket to Lagos and to make sure she took the evening flight of this particular day – unfailingly, and that he would be waiting at Ikeja local air port to receive her. But now as he took his seat beside her it was evident that he changed his plan. And that was the first time Bimbo was seeing the maskman without his mask on.

Bimbo couldn't say a word. She kept on looking at him. She could have sworn she was seeing Karl and the feelings couldn't help keep coming back. Then unaware of how loud her voice was she said, "God! No difference at all! No single iota of difference," as Adams leaned over and picked little Emmanuel Karl Ajahni and placed him on his lap, rubbing the hair on his head, and even the way he spoke amazed her when he said to himself, "woman..kids...sure, I'm sure gonna come back for Angela.

———◆◆◆◆◆———

ZZzzzzzzzzzzzzzzzzZZZZZZZZZzzzzzzzzzzzzzzzzzz **THE END**
zzzzzzzzzzzzzzzzzzzzzzzzzzzzzzzzzzzzzzzzzzzzzzzzZZZZZ

GOD TAKES THE GLORY

Printed in the United States
By Bookmasters